SPARK OF THE REVOLUTION

HARBOR OF SPIES ~ BOOK 1

MEGAN SOJA

WILD HEART
BOOKS

Brimming with intrigue, danger and a dash of romance, *Spark of the Revolution* hits all the right notes in this lovely debut. Amid the tumultuous backdrop of the Revolutionary War, Josiah and Patience's tale swept me into the precarious world of pre-war Boston, and beautifully displayed what it means to fight for conviction as well as how to love and forgive. A stirring novel and an author to watch!

— TARA JOHNSON, CHRISTY AND CAROL AWARD NOMINEE OF *ENGRAVED ON THE HEART*

For Mom and Dad
Thank you for being my first readers from the very beginning and for walking every step of this journey with me. I love you.

"The people should never rise, without doing something to be remembered..."

— DIARY OF JOHN ADAMS, DECEMBER 17, 1773

Now therefore ye are no more strangers and foreigners, but fellow citizens with the saints, and of the household of God.

— EPHESIANS 2:19 KJV

PROLOGUE

Atlantic Ocean
November 28, 1773

*P*atience Abbott was certain her parents had erred in naming her.

Clasping the smooth wooden rail of the ship, in part to steady her wobbly legs and in part to tame her utterly impatient thoughts, she stared across the expanse of sea that stretched in all directions.

"Surely, it cannot be much farther." She muttered the complaint under her breath, but not quietly enough, as evidenced by her older brother's chuckle.

He stood beside her, brows raised with a mischievous light in his eyes. "Come now, do you mean to say you find nothing enjoyable about these endless waves?"

She shook her head at his teasing. "You should not say such things when you know what those waves have done to my stomach."

Though their father had spent most of his life at sea, Patience had not inherited his fortitude for sailing. At twenty years of age, this was her first voyage. Hopefully, her last as well.

Will offered her his arm. "Indeed. I will be glad to reach Boston for your sake."

She tucked her hand into the crook of his elbow. "I should not complain when you had no wish to make this journey in the first place."

While Patience had yearned to escape England and the painful memories there, anxious to reunite with Father, Will had left his business and the woman he hoped to court behind.

He led her slowly down the quarterdeck. "I am glad to accompany you. I will keep my promise to return to England, but only after you are settled."

Patience clung to his arm and to his words. He had cared for her and Mama—God rest her soul—so well these past years. She trusted he would continue to do so.

They strolled the length of the ship as sailors bustled around them, busy with riggings and topsails that tugged and billowed in the wind. The *Eleanor* was a merchant vessel, not purposed for transporting passengers, but Father had used his connections with the ship's captain to secure passage for them on its return trip to America.

They approached the bow, and Captain Bruce greeted them. "Miss Abbott, I've something you will be pleased to see." He extended the spyglass he held. "Look at the horizon there."

She lifted the instrument to her eye and peered through it to the place where the captain had pointed. Far in the distance, a gray silhouette, barely visible, rose above the sea

"Is that land?" She lowered the spyglass and blinked.

He nodded. "We are a bit farther north than necessary, so I do not believe that is the colony of Massachusetts that you see, but we are growing near."

"That is wonderful news." Patience couldn't contain her

grin. She handed the instrument to Will, who took his turn examining the horizon.

Captain Bruce smiled at her enthusiasm. "I estimate we will make port within the next four days, should conditions remain in our favor.

Her heart pounded in anticipation. Soon they would arrive in Boston, and she would finally see Father again after years apart. Soon the sorrow of the past months would be behind her.

A wave broke against the ship's hull, sending a misty spray skyward. She closed her eyes, breathing deeply of the salty air. The wind tugged at the wayward, dark curls escaping her cap, and she laughed at the wild freedom of it all. She opened her eyes and focused her gaze on what lay ahead—a place to call home.

CHAPTER 1

Boston
November 29, 1773

*J*osiah Wagner stared out the window of his blacksmith shop at the thick clouds hovering in the sky, edged in a pale glow from the low morning sun. Though he was too far away to see it, he could almost picture the *Dartmouth*'s tall rigging against the backdrop of clouds as she sat moored in Griffin's Wharf.

News of her arrival and the cargo of tea she carried had spread throughout Boston yesterday, with meetings held that afternoon, despite it being the Sabbath. Lately, the gatherings of the Sons of Liberty and others of like mind had been as heated as the coals of his forge, the emotions of the men like embers waiting to be breathed to life. The arrival of the *Dartmouth* only stoked the flames.

He turned his focus back to the task at hand. Who knew what today would bring? Best get some work done while he was able. He rested the bar of iron in the coals of the forge, steadying it with one hand while reaching above his head with the other. He tugged the rope connected to the large bellow. A rush of air burst forth, and the coals flared, heating the metal until it glowed bright orange. Swiftly, he transferred the piece to the anvil, hefting the sledge up to strike the iron. Sparks flew as he molded the pliable metal, the last of a set of hinges he'd been commissioned to make.

He would do this work with excellence, as he always strived for, even though the man who hired him was a staunch Loyalist. That hadn't taken Josiah long to discover, for the older man, a shopkeeper, made no attempt to hide his opinions. Instead, he had outright boasted about how his was one of the few shops that still carried British tea. Josiah had said little in return but stored the information to pass on through the secret channels of the Sons of Liberty. He'd have to make a visit to Mr. Ward soon to report what he'd learned.

The door flung open, interrupting his thoughts, and a gust of cold wind followed the familiar form of Nathaniel Hadley inside. At eight and ten, the young man was seven years Josiah's junior, but they'd become close friends in recent months thanks to their shared commitment to the Patriot cause.

"Have you seen this?" Nathaniel shoved the door closed with his shoulder as he waved a paper in his hand.

"Give me a moment. I've almost finished."

Grasping the hinge with a set of tongs, Josiah plunged it into the trough of water beside his anvil. Steam hissed from the surface. He pulled the cooled iron from the water and placed it on the table alongside the other completed pieces.

He wiped his hands on his apron, adding to the black smudges already covering the worn leather, and crossed to where his friend stood waiting.

"Read it." Nathaniel handed him the page. "Aloud, so I can hear it once more."

Josiah clasped the broadside. "'Friends!! Brethren! Countrymen! That worst of plagues, the detested tea, shipped for this

port by the East India Company, is now arrived in the harbor.'"
He paused and glanced at Nathaniel, whose eyes shone with
excitement. "'The hour of destruction, or manly opposition to
the machinations of tyranny, stares you in the face. Every friend
to his country, to himself and to posterity, is now called upon to
meet at Faneuil Hall, at nine o'clock this day (at which time the
bells will ring), to make united and successful resistance to the
last, worst, and most destructive measure of administration.'"

"It's being distributed throughout town. I wish I'd been the
one to print such words."

Josiah handed the announcement back to his friend, who
tucked it in his pocket. Nathaniel was an apprentice at the
Boston Gazette, where his enthusiasm for the cause of liberty
might be preserved through ink and paper.

"Shall we walk together?" Nathaniel nodded toward the
door. "It will be nearly nine by the time we arrive, and if the
crowds I saw on my way here are any indication, there will be
little space to spare."

Josiah hung his apron on a peg jutting out of the wall and
rolled down the sleeves of his linen shirt. He pulled on the
waistcoat and overcoat he'd removed earlier. The forge kept his
workshop warm, but outside, the air was chilling.

He tried to straighten his queue, but as was often the case,
the unruly strands of black hair that had escaped during his
work refused to be tamed. Thankfully, his cocked hat hid the
disarray. He closed the shop, and together they made for
Faneuil Hall.

It was not a long walk from the smithy on Oliver Street, and
soon Josiah and Nathaniel joined the throng heading toward
the imposing brick structure, its domed cupola and unique
grasshopper-shaped weathervane distinct even from a distance.
Market stalls occupied the lower level which opened to the
public square. The area was always bustling with activity as
fishermen, produce sellers, and merchants of all sorts peddled

their goods, but today the crowds pushed forward with a different purpose.

Together they wove through the mass of people until they reached the entrance and climbed the stairs to the upper level. The men inside were packed tightly, and a din of voices echoed off the high ceiling.

"Do you think Adams will speak?"

Josiah didn't miss the spark of anticipation in Nathaniel's eyes. Nor could he deny his own hope of hearing Samuel Adams address the gathering.

He had first heard Mr. Adams speak in this same building, nearly three years prior, on the morning of the sixth of March, following the violence outside the state house. Josiah had joined the Sons of Liberty that very day, inspired by Mr. Adams's speech and by his own desire to be part of something bigger than himself.

"I am certain he will." Josiah craned his neck to see around a particularly burly man who had wedged in front of them.

Last month, Samuel Adams had been appointed to handle the tea crisis. Josiah would never forget Mr. Adams's words that night, as he declared anyone who aided or abetted the unloading and vending of tea to be an enemy to America.

Those words took on even greater meaning now, with the arrival of the *Dartmouth* and her one hundred and fourteen chests of tea. The bells began to toll, echoing outside and settling the rumble of voices indoors. The meeting was about to begin. Whether destruction or opposition of some other kind lay ahead, he could not say, but of one thing Josiah was certain —he would be there to stand beside his fellow Patriots, whatever duty demanded.

CHAPTER 2

*P*atience silently offered a prayer of thanks as her feet touched firm ground. She had never fully gained her sea legs, despite her best efforts. Nor her sea stomach, if such a thing existed. Her gown fit looser than usual around her already petite frame, evidence of her inability to maintain much of an appetite aboard the ship.

But those days were behind her now. She was standing, for the first time, on the shores of America.

The *Eleanor* sat moored in the wharf, next to another ship that had anchored there before they arrived. She glanced over her shoulder at Captain Bruce, who had disembarked with them and was now engaged in intense conversation with a group of men who appeared to be standing guard on the dock. His furrowed brow suggested trouble.

Will grasped her elbow and led her away from the crowd. "Wait here. I'll see to our trunks."

Patience watched his retreating form, then turned to better

observe the gathered men. They didn't look like soldiers, their clothing the same as any common man might wear, yet they stood with a bearing like the military men she'd seen from time to time growing up in England. The way she remembered Father looking when he'd sailed for the British Navy.

One of the men gestured to their ship, his expression resolute as he spoke words she was too far away to hear. She edged closer.

"You can unload the other cargo, but the tea stays on board." She barely caught the statement of the stern-faced man addressing Captain Bruce. "We've spoken with John Rowe, and you will hear the same from him."

"I want no trouble," the captain replied. "Only ensure my men and my ship are unharmed."

What did they mean, refusing to unload the shipment of tea? What trouble could that cause?

A vague memory flitted at the corner of her mind. Hadn't Will spoken of conflict regarding the tea tax? If only she could better remember what he had said. But her thoughts had been occupied by other, more pressing, cares. Like their mother's illness and their father's absence.

Patience spotted Will's tall form pushing through the crowd, her trunk in his arms, and she scurried back to the place he'd left her. She clapped a hand over her bonnet as the wind whipping off the sea threatened to pull it loose.

He placed the trunk on the ground beside her with a low grunt. "What did you fill this with? I cannot imagine petticoats weigh so much."

Patience laughed and swatted his arm. He flashed a rare grin, warming her even as the chilly air nipped at her cheeks.

As Will hurried to retrieve his trunk, Patience turned away from the sea to scan her new surroundings. There was so much to take in, it was nearly overwhelming. The lapping of waves behind her, a now-familiar sound after their weeks on the

Atlantic, blended with the squawks of sea birds circling above. The scent of salt hung heavy in the air, tinged with fish and an earthiness she hadn't smelled for nearly two months. She breathed it in, a strangely welcome odor after being away from land so long.

Sailors and fishermen milled about near the docks, while streets lined with buildings stretched ahead of them in several directions. The roads were packed with horses, carts, and people going about their affairs. She blinked at the bustle of the streets and the seemingly endless rows of shops and houses.

How would they ever find Father in such a place?

As she turned to search the other direction, her breath caught in her throat. A man stood just down the road, his silhouette much like she remembered Father's to be. Powdered wig tied in a neat queue, hands clasped behind his back as he stared at their ship. Was it Father, searching for them?

She glanced over her shoulder but did not see Will. The man turned and began to walk away. If she hurried, she could catch him. Certainly, there was no harm in straying from her trunk for a moment, especially if it meant she found Father. She rushed after him, eyes fixed on his retreating back, and abruptly collided with a broad chest.

A large hand wrapped around her arm, steadying her a moment before quickly releasing her.

"I beg your pardon, miss." The low voice drew her gaze upward to a pair of eyes so dark brown they were nearly black. "I did not see you there."

She straightened the wool cloak around her shoulders. "I am equally at fault. I was not paying attention to where I was walking."

"You are unharmed?"

Patience nodded.

His intent gaze rested on her a moment. "Are you looking for someone?"

She ducked her head, surprised he had guessed her situation so easily. "I am. I thought I saw him just over there." She gestured in the direction of the man she'd been following, who stopped and turned so she could make out his face. Even from a distance, she knew she had been wrong. Her shoulders drooped. "But it isn't him."

His thick eyebrows pulled low in concern. "I am sorry."

"Thank you, sir." She offered a quick smile, which faded when she spotted Will striding toward her abandoned trunk.

"Can I help you in some way?"

She turned back to the man before her, tilting her face to meet his gaze. The wind tugged at his black hair, barely held in place by a haphazard queue. It lent a certain wildness to him, in contrast to the gentleness of his expression. It struck her that this man was the first person to speak with her upon her arrival in Boston, and while their brief conversation was not truly a greeting, it warmed her to meet such kindness from a stranger.

"No, I am certain he will be here soon. But I do thank you and bid you a good day."

He touched his fingers to the brim of his hat and dipped his head in farewell. "Good day, miss."

Patience hurried to where Will stood, craning his neck, looking for her, no doubt.

When he spotted her, he rushed to her side. "Where did you go?"

"I'm sorry. I should have stayed where you left me, but I thought I saw Father."

He sighed but said no more. Perhaps he was used to it by now—the way her impatience led her to act without thinking sometimes. No matter how often she resolved to do better, she still struggled.

They stood in silence, both searching the crowd, and she felt, as she often had in recent months, that the two of them were like a lonely island in a vast ocean, buffeted by life's storms but safe so long as they were together. What would she do without him? Yet she would have Father now, to protect and care for her, and a new place to belong. All would be well, would it not?

"I see him." William stiffened, two lines appearing between his brows. "There's Father."

Patience sucked in a breath and stared at the spot where William's gaze had focused. There he was, indeed.

Father was heavier than she remembered, with a distinct paunch at his waist. His face had aged from the image she held in her mind, deep wrinkles around his eyes and a slight droopiness along his jaw. But when he noticed them, a smile brightened his countenance and seemed to push away the years. He limped toward them, leaning heavily on a fashionable cane.

Patience couldn't hold back a matching smile, though her stomach dipped as it had each time their ship crested a wave. She smoothed her hands down the wrinkled fabric of her blue striped gown and released a shaky breath.

"William and Patience." Father stopped before them, his arms outstretched. "I cannot tell you how good it is to see your faces again."

"Hello, Father." William extended his hand, and their father shook it heartily, though Patience noticed the lack of enthusiasm behind her brother's greeting.

All else was forgotten, though, when her father turned toward her and enveloped her in an embrace. The show of affection startled her but warmed her all the way to her bones, taking her back to childhood and the way she had always felt safe within his arms.

"My dear girl." He stepped back, clasping her by the shoulders. "Thank the Lord you are here. Though perhaps I cannot call you a girl any longer, for look at you now, a grown woman."

Her cheeks warmed at his words. She had changed since he

had seen her last, but in her heart, she was content to simply be his dear girl.

He surveyed the two trunks on the ground beside them. "I've hired a carriage." He gestured toward a conveyance on the street to their left, where a young man held the team of two horses steady. "We can enlist the help of the driver to load your trunks."

"I can manage them," Will said. "If you remain with Patience, I will return shortly."

Will's coat stretched taut against the muscles of his lean frame as he lifted the first trunk and strode away, leaving her alone with Father.

"I see my son still has his independent spirit."

Patience nodded. Will was not one to ask for help, but she could not tell if Father's observation was laced with pride or frustration, so she said nothing. Will returned quickly and hefted the second trunk off the ground. Father offered his arm to Patience, and she settled her hand into the crook of his elbow, slowing her steps to match his uneven gait. His letters had described his injury, the one that almost took his life, but it was different to see its effects in person.

"I am sure you are both weary from the journey." Father paused beside the carriage. "But I do have some important news to share with you before we depart."

His gaze landed briefly on each of them before settling somewhere in the distance, as if he was trying to see all the way across the ocean to the home they'd once shared there.

With a heavy sigh, he began, the words halting and hesitant. "I am certain you both know—that is, I hope you know—how devastated I was to receive the news last year of your mother's illness. All the more so of her passing this February. I have yet to forgive myself for not being there in her time of need."

He turned his focus back to Patience, and she swallowed a

lump of emotion at the sorrow in his expression. But something else there, a look of trepidation, caused her to catch her breath.

"Six months ago, a friend of mine died quite suddenly. You may remember the name James Caldwell from my letters. He was the doctor who cared for me after my shipwreck. I credit him with saving my life." He shifted his weight, grimacing slightly. "It was James who passed, leaving behind his wife and daughter. After all he had done for me, I felt it my duty to care for them as best I could."

Patience's mouth went dry, and her fingers twisted the fabric of her dress as she willed her father not to say the words she dreaded. William stood stiff, as though carved of stone, as he, too, seemed to brace himself for their father's news.

"We were married last month. Her name is Mary Caldwell. Or rather, Mary Abbott now. Her daughter, Elizabeth, is eight and ten. They are waiting with great anticipation to meet you both." Father's words came out in a rush, and he busied himself with straightening his already pristine stock.

Patience couldn't draw a full breath. Her lungs squeezed, as though her stays were tied much too tight. She swallowed, trying to bring moisture to her parched mouth, trying to form something to say in response to Father's astonishing news. Thankfully, William came to her rescue.

With a solemn nod, he murmured, "We congratulate you, Father, and look forward to meeting them as well."

Father's shoulders relaxed, and he pressed his lips together in a brief smile. "Thank you. And now"—he offered his hand to help Patience into the carriage—"let us depart for home."

*J*osiah stepped into the livery and scanned the building for John Ward, the owner and fellow member of the Sons of Liberty he needed to speak with. Soft whinnies echoed through the stables, and the smell of horses and hay filled the air.

A shushing noise drew his attention toward the end of the livery where Ward tended to a beautiful chestnut bay. Josiah strode toward him.

"Wagner, what good timing." Ward greeted him with a hearty handshake, the buttons of his waistcoat straining against his stocky frame. "She threw a shoe this morning. Though I suspect you came for another reason."

"Aye, but I can take a look at her while we talk."

He eased into the stall and murmured a reassuring greeting to the mare. She dipped her head, nudging her nose against his shoulder and huffing a warm breath.

Josiah ran his hand down the length of the horse's slender foreleg until just below her knee, guiding her to bend it and allow him access to her hoof. "The shoe came off cleanly. 'Twill be no trouble to replace. I'll see to it this afternoon."

He lowered her foot back to the ground and patted the horse's neck, then circled around to stand beside Ward, keeping his voice low. "I've a business to report, a shopkeeper who continues to sell British tea."

Ward glanced around to ensure that no one else had entered, then nodded for Josiah to proceed.

"His name is George Abbott, owner of the shop on Kings Street. He came to see me about some new hinges and had no qualms talking about his stock of tea. Seemed rather proud of it."

"He's careless to speak so freely. We'll add him to the list. Hopefully, a boycott of his shop will convince him to change his ways."

Josiah nodded. He wished no harm upon Mr. Abbott, but it was his duty to report what he had discovered to the Sons of Liberty. An orderly boycott was far better than an unruly mob deciding to take matters into their own hands. It was Josiah's hope that by reporting such information, he could both further the cause of the Sons, while also preventing more trouble in the long run. There was no guarantee, but their cause was worth the risk.

"Any other news? I heard the second ship arrived today."

"Aye, the *Eleanor*. Our men continue to stand guard. They've held steady three days now, despite Governor Hutchinson's orders to disperse."

Days ago, after the *Dartmouth* moored in the harbor, the Sons had decided to keep twenty-five men on guard as a barricade to prevent the unloading of the tea.

"I'm glad to hear it." Ward kicked at a wad of straw on the ground. "Though I almost wish Young's proposal had come to pass and all that tea was floating in the ocean already."

Dr. Thomas Young's suggestion to throw the tea in the harbor had been declined in favor of Samuel Adams's plan to prevent its offloading. But Josiah was privy to the discussions that were in progress regarding further action if they could not manage to send the despised cargo back to England.

Josiah pulled off his hat and ran his fingers through his hair. "You know as well as I that may still happen, but I think it best to do all we can to handle the tea in another way."

"I suppose you're right." Ward reached out to rub the horse's nose. "You'll come again when you have more—"

The livery door creaked open. Josiah glanced over Ward's shoulder as a stranger entered. Their conversation was over, but he'd done his duty and reported the necessary information. Ward would ensure it got passed along as needed.

"I will."

They made arrangements for the mare's new shoe, then bid

each other farewell, and Josiah set off to return to the smithy. With his task accomplished, his mind wandered to the young woman he'd met at Griffin's Wharf. He had recognized the look in her eyes. The expression of someone lost and searching for the comfort of a familiar face. Something there reminded him of himself when he first arrived in Boston as a boy of eleven years old, utterly alone.

When she'd walked away, he regretted not helping her further, but she had seemed determined, and he'd not wanted to interfere. Still, he had watched from a distance until she grasped the arm of a young man who appeared relieved to find her.

Josiah was glad she was no longer alone, yet he envied her too. How long had it been since he had someone to wait for him, to search for him and be glad when he was found?

Loneliness threatened to darken his mind like soot from a fire. He shook off the melancholy thoughts, silently scolding himself for dwelling on them at all. He'd found camaraderie and purpose within the Sons of Liberty. That was enough. It was an honor to be counted among such men, and he would be content. At least for now.

CHAPTER 3

*T*he carriage stopped in front of a two-story house with riven siding, faded to shades of gray by the forces of nature and time. A small addition jutted out from the back of the house, but everything else about the dwelling was symmetrical, from the double-hung windows on either side of the front door to the matching brick chimney stacks rising from the roof. It was neat and tidy and simple. Nothing at all like the thoughts whirling in Patience's mind.

She accepted Father's hand to help her out of the carriage, hoping he would not notice the cold damp of her palms.

He waved off Will's attempt to gather their trunks. "Come inside to meet Mary and Elizabeth, and the driver will unload your trunks."

Patience tucked a few stray hairs behind her ears as he led them into the small entryway. The comforting smell of woodsmoke and a savory meal drifted from the kitchen on the left, but it was the soft voices coming from the parlor to the right that drew her attention. Father turned in that direction, and Patience's gaze immediately snagged on the pair of women rising from their chairs in front of the fire.

Father cleared his throat as he stepped forward, hovering between the ladies and Patience and Will as though offering a bridge between the two families. "Mary and Elizabeth, I am pleased to finally introduce my children, William and Patience."

The ladies curtsied, a gentle smile on the older woman's face, while the younger one beamed as though she could hardly contain her excitement.

Patience dipped a curtsy of her own, though her legs felt soft as pudding that hadn't set. She should offer some greeting, but the words stuck in her throat.

"We are glad to welcome you. Thank the Lord you have arrived safely." Father's new wife crossed the room to stand beside him.

Though she now bore the same title of Mrs. Abbott, this woman looked nothing like Patience's mother. Tall and slender where Mama had been short with soft, womanly curves. Pale blue eyes and fair hair a stark contrast to Mama's dark hair and eyes, which Patience had inherited. Quiet poise in place of the warm conversation and lyrical humming that seemed to follow Mama wherever she went.

"Thank you." Patience could not muster the energy to say more. The floor felt as though it were rocking beneath her feet, and she blinked to clear the spinning sensation. Will placed a hand on her back to steady her.

"I am so very happy to meet you." Elizabeth hurried to join them. The young woman matched her mother in coloring but infused it with the vibrancy of youth. If her mother was fair as a frozen winter morning, Elizabeth was a bright summer afternoon. Her hair shone like golden honey, her blue eyes clear as the sky. She was not quite as tall as her mother but possessed a similar willowy figure, and her face held a youthful softness. Her light-blue petticoat with chintz jacket enhanced the feeling of freshness that seemed to surround her. Patience felt worn and drab by comparison.

Her greeting encompassed both Will and Patience, but then she turned her attention to Patience alone. "I must confess, I always wished to have a sister."

Patience swallowed. A sister? They were mere strangers. And while Elizabeth had the advantage of a month to adjust to the idea of this new family, Patience had only the carriage ride from the harbor. The silence stretched awkwardly long between them, but what could she say in response?

Thankfully, Father spared her. "I am certain Patience and William are tired from their journey. I think it best we eat and allow them to settle in."

He led them all to the kitchen where Patience took a seat at the worn wooden table beside Will as Mary served plates of chicken hash. While they ate, Father asked them about their weeks at sea, but Patience was content to let Will carry the conversation. Her head felt fuzzy, as though she'd awakened in the night from a strange dream and could not discern what was real and what was imagined.

Was this truly to be her new home? Her new life? Her new family? This was nothing like she had expected when she left England, nothing like she hoped her reunion with Father would be. And while the women across the table had welcomed them with kindness and enthusiasm, her weary mind could not comprehend how these strangers fit into the picture she had long envisioned.

Patience stared down the table at the man she called Father as an aching realization squeezed the breath from her lungs—that he, too, was a stranger to her, and her to him. The childhood memories she had clung to were hazy at best, like a field of wildflowers viewed through the morning fog. Snippets of beauty amidst the dreary gray of fear and loneliness and grief. But it had been a decade since she'd spent more than a handful of months at a time in her father's company, and nearly three years since she had seen him at all. Not enough time to plant any new memories in the garden of her heart.

Mama used to say Father had a wanderer's soul. A wistful smile always tipped the corner of her lips when she said it. Will's descriptions of their father were less generous, only spoken when he thought Patience wasn't listening.

How Patience longed for the sight of Mama's smile right now to cheer her heart, or for Mama's laugh to break through the stilted conversation that occupied their meal. Of course, if Mama were still alive, everything would be different.

Patience blinked away the sting of tears and lifted another spoonful to her mouth. The food was the tastiest she'd had since boarding the ship, but she could barely manage more than a few bites. Her stomach churned, though she had no rough seas to blame, only the unease and uncertainty that buffeted her just as fiercely as an Atlantic gale.

She stifled a yawn. If only she could push the dish aside and lay her head on the table instead.

"I think my daughter may be ready to retire." Father's voice caused Patience to blink. "Elizabeth, would you show her to the room?"

Patience jerked her head up. She had not realized it had begun to droop so low. Her gaze landed on the girl seated across from her, who smiled brightly as she rose from the table.

"I am sorry to be such poor company this evening." Patience stifled a yawn.

"No need to apologize," Father said. "We will have ample time for conversation in the days to come."

His words should have cheered her. After all the months and years of waiting to see him, they were finally together again. They had tomorrow and all the days after to share. But the reunion she had hoped for was overshadowed by Father's unexpected marriage.

She bid goodnight to Father, then followed Elizabeth to the second floor. Elizabeth held a candle aloft, its light casting flickering shadows against the plaster walls.

"We will be sharing this bedchamber." Elizabeth paused before the door to the right, and for the first time, her bright smile faded. "I hope you do not mind."

A wave of compassion pushed through the weariness clouding Patience's mind. She felt like an intruder, taking a place in Elizabeth's room, coming into this house that was already filled with an entire other family. Perhaps this was more difficult for Elizabeth than it first appeared. Patience determined not to punish the young woman for things outside her control. "Not at all. Thank you for the kind welcome. I do look forward to getting to know each other better."

A wide smile bloomed on Elizabeth's face once more. "I imagine this has been a tiring day. I will bring some warm water for you to wash."

After Elizabeth left, Patience turned in a slow circle, taking in the unfamiliar surroundings. A fire glowed in the hearth, smaller than those in the kitchen and parlor downstairs, but large enough to bring some warmth to the chamber. Above the mantel hung a framed sampler. Patience stepped closer, examining the intricate needlework that depicted a pastoral scene on the bottom, with swirling vines and flowers along the sides and top. In the center was stitched the Lord's Prayer, followed by the name *Elizabeth Caldwell* and the year, 1767.

Patience had gifted a rudimentary sampler she'd completed when she was ten years old to her father when he left to sail with the British East India Company. What had happened to it since then? It was certainly unworthy of being put on display as this one was.

She sank to the edge of the bed and eased off her shoes as an unwelcome ache grew in her chest. She didn't want to miss her old room, or her old house. She had been desperate to leave ever since Mama died. But this wasn't the fresh start she'd been hoping for.

She didn't belong here, in this strange home with this unexpected family, any more than she had belonged in England, the grieving daughter who watched her mother die and wondered when her father would come to set everything right.

Footsteps on the stairs pulled her out of her dismal thoughts. Elizabeth entered the room with a pitcher and basin balanced in her arms, a cloth draped over her shoulder.

"I've brought warm water, soap, and a towel." Elizabeth set everything on the table next to the bed. "Is there anything else you need?"

"No, thank you."

"I'll give you some privacy, then. And do not worry if you fall asleep. I shall be as quiet as a mouse when I come up." Elizabeth offered a smile and departed, pulling the door closed behind her.

Exhaustion tugged at Patience, tempting her to climb into bed immediately, but the thought of warm water to wash overcame that desire. She untied her garters and tugged off her stockings, then set to work on the rest of her clothing until she had undressed to her shift.

Patience washed her face first, then scrubbed her hands, arms, and legs. The smell of salt clung to her, as though embedded in her skin after weeks of ocean air, and she welcomed the rosewater-scented soap. She dried quickly, shivering as she changed into a fresh shift and located a comb within her trunk. She hurried to the fireplace, letting the flames warm her as she removed the pins to release her hair. Dark, wavy tresses fell to her waist.

She ran the comb through her tangled locks, remembering the way Mama brushed her hair as a child, her strokes long and gentle, singing a hymn all the while. In the last days of Mama's life, when she'd been too weak to lift the comb herself, their roles had been reversed. Patience had been the one to gently ease the knots from Mama's hair and sing her words of comfort.

"Oh, Lord, I miss her so much." She whispered the prayer in the empty room.

Mama's faith had always been strong. She was steadfast in the face of trials, from the loss of four stillborn children to Father's consistent absence at sea that left the burden of caring for their home and raising William and Patience upon her shoulders. Even in the end, as illness slowly drained the strength from her limbs and the breath from her lungs, still Mama had clung to God, unfaltering in her trust and praise of Him.

Patience winced as the comb caught on a stubborn knot. Was her faith as strong as Mama's, able to face whatever trials might come? Or, like the virtue of her name, was it something that needed to be honed and strengthened in order to bear the burdens of this life?

She sighed and set the comb down on the mantel. It was a comfort to know Mama was with the Lord now, but it didn't take away the pain of her absence.

When her hair was finally tamed into a long braid, Patience crawled under the blankets and gave in to the comfort of bed. The weight of the quilt pressed down upon her, matching the heaviness inside. The hopeful anticipation she'd felt earlier at the wharf had been snuffed out, like a candle burned too long and low.

Tears stung the back of her eyes, but she willed them away. She refused to give in to such melancholy thoughts. She was not so foolishly naive as to think that Father's presence and an ocean worth of separation from their empty cottage would immediately dispel the sorrows of the past year. Today had not been what she had hoped or expected, but tomorrow was a fresh start.

"'His mercies are new every morning.'" She repeated the verse her mother had often said and tucked the quilt under her chin, imagining it was Mama's embrace around her shoulders instead.

~

*J*osiah trudged home, the words of tonight's meeting swirling in his head like eddies of water caught on a rocky shore. The Sons of Liberty and their fellow Patriots had met at Old South once more to continue the discussions about the tea. With the *Eleanor's* arrival and the tax deadline growing nearer every passing day, decisions would need to be made, and soon.

"You're quiet tonight." Nathaniel walked beside him, his voice breaking into the stillness of the dark streets. "Quieter than usual, that is."

Josiah huffed a laugh, his breath clouding in the cold air. True, he was a man of few words, though he hadn't always been. He remembered Mama teasing that he chirped more than a baby bird in a nest. Was it her death that brought about the change? No, he had still been a boisterous lad, even when he and Papa set sail for America. It was Papa's death, and the realization that Josiah was utterly alone, that spurred him to silence. In the years that followed, he'd not had anyone close enough to care whether he talked more than simple necessity.

"I hope we can hold the harbor without much interference or any violence." Nathaniel interrupted his thoughts.

Josiah glanced at his friend, his features hard to distinguish in the low evening light. "I was there today and all seemed well, even with the *Eleanor's* arrival."

Though it was not the stalwart men that came to mind when he thought of the wharf, but rather the face of the young woman he'd met there. Those wide, dark eyes framed with long black lashes searching the crowds, seeking, as he once had, someone familiar. But it appeared she had found the person she sought, while Josiah never had.

"So what is on your mind, then?" Nathaniel paused at the corner of the street.

Josiah sighed, hesitant to reveal what truly occupied his thoughts. "I nearly ran over a young woman when I was at the harbor today."

"I've never heard you speak of a woman before."

"It isn't what you think." Josiah tugged off his hat and smoothed a hand over his hair. "She reminded me of myself, when I first came to Boston as a boy. I've not thought of that day in some time...That is, I'd rather not dwell on it..."

Nathaniel pressed his lips together as if to hold back more questions, and Josiah was thankful his friend didn't push him further.

"Was she pretty, at least?" A mischievous grin spread across Nathaniel's face.

"Prettiest I've ever seen." With that, Josiah turned toward home, Nathaniel's laughter following him.

He had answered in jest, wanting to elicit such a reaction from his friend, but now that he was alone, Josiah thought on the question again. He had not taken much time to dwell on her appearance, given the nature of their meeting. Aside from those expressive eyes, which had captured his attention most of all, he remembered the rosy flush highlighting her high cheekbones, put there by the cold air—or their collision. He couldn't be sure. Maybe not the prettiest he'd ever seen, but lovely in her own way.

Not that it mattered. He'd not see her again.

Josiah stopped in front of the blacksmith shop. The stone building was more home to him than anywhere else had been these past fourteen years. He walked along the side until he reached the house just behind the smithy. No candlelight glowed from the windows to welcome him, no smoke curled from the chimney to warm him.

He pushed through the door into the empty place, hardly enough to warrant the name of house. A single room, with a fireplace centered on the back wall to divide the space into two sections. To the left, a table and two chairs—a crude excuse for a kitchen. To the right, his bed, with a chest at the foot board to store his limited belongings.

Robert Sperling, Josiah's master during his apprenticeship, had built the rudimentary living space as a young man himself when he first established his shop. He'd moved to a larger house down the street as soon as he was able and raised his family of four daughters there.

Too young to be on his own, Josiah had lived with the family when he first arrived. They'd given him a small bedroom, tucked behind the kitchen. But when he reached five and ten years of age, Mr. Sperling had moved him to the house behind the shop. As a master, he had never been cruel to Josiah, but he'd not been especially kind, either, and he hadn't wanted a young man sharing the house with his growing daughters.

Josiah lit the candle on the table and started the fire, chasing some of the darkness and chill from the room. He yawned as he undressed, then sank onto the lumpy mattress. The quiet emptiness of the space didn't usually feel as lonely as it did tonight.

He rubbed the back of his neck. It was that woman, or rather the memories she had invoked, that had him in such a melancholy mood.

He pushed off the bed and pried open the chest, digging beneath the clothing until his hands grasped the worn leather book. Papa's Bible. Lifting it from the chest, he stared at it in the flickering firelight.

When Papa died, Josiah had slept with the book tucked

beneath his pillow every night, comforted by the nearness of the one thing he possessed that had belonged to his father. He'd long since grown out of that habit. A prick of his conscience said he should open the book and read it, seek guidance and comfort from the words inside. But that was another habit long set aside.

God felt as far and fathomless as the sea. Someone who had once been very real and present but was now a memory, blurred at the edges and bittersweet. Much like Josiah's parents. Loneliness ached within him, sharp as a pang of hunger but deeper, as though it dwelt within his very soul. He sank to his bed, hesitating a moment. It was a foolish thing to do as he was a grown man now, and yet there was no one here to see him.

He tucked the Bible beneath his pillow and lay down to sleep.

CHAPTER 4

*P*atience ducked into the house, easing the door closed behind her. She leaned against the solid wood and released a sigh, scrubbing her hands together in attempt to bring warmth back to her fingertips. The house offered some respite from the dreary cold, yet it was not enough to warm her fully.

She'd woken early, and sleep would not come again, no matter how hard she tried. She had slipped from bed as quietly as possible so as not to wake Elizabeth, dressed by the pale light of dawn seeping through the window, and crept downstairs.

Feeling unsettled in the empty, unfamiliar rooms, she'd decided to venture outdoors. There was something about a brisk walk and fresh air that always helped clear her thoughts and settle her heart. Not wanting to stray far, Patience had traipsed to the back of the house where she found a small patch of land, enough for a bit of a garden but not nearly the space she needed to stretch her legs and refresh her spirit. That disappointment, along with the frigid morning air, had driven her back inside.

Patience straightened at the sound of slow, uneven footsteps on the stairs.

"Patience?" Her father's eyes widened as he stepped down. "Are you unwell?"

She shook her head. "I only stepped out for a breath of fresh air."

He observed the wool cloak about her shoulders. "You are cold. I will see to the fire."

She followed him to the kitchen, where he lifted the curfew, the cover that kept the embers warm through the night while protecting the house from the danger of errant sparks. Coals flickered orange along the edges of the charred logs, and he reached for the small bellow to fan them into new life.

"Do you always rise early?" Father peered over his shoulder at her as tendrils of fire rose to meet the wood.

"I am in the habit of doing so, though not quite so early as today."

"I hope you slept well." He straightened, dusting his hands on his gray breeches.

"Aye. I am sorry I was not very engaged in conversation last night."

"You need not apologize. After such a journey and all of the..." He paused, rubbing one hand over his forearm as he stared into the growing flames. "All of the changes here."

Patience ducked her head. A long silence stretched between them. The fire crackled, and she stepped closer, holding her hands near the warmth of the hearth.

Father cleared his throat. "You will soon find that Elizabeth does not particularly enjoy mornings."

A quiet laugh escaped her lips. His revelation did not come as a surprise. The younger woman had not stirred once as Patience rose and dressed for the day.

"She is a good girl, though. Well-mannered and capable in

the home. I am hopeful you two will get along once you've the time to get to know one another."

Patience nodded, unable to form a proper response. She, too, hoped they would get on well together, yet she couldn't quite tamp down the niggling jealousy that arose at his words. He called Elizabeth well-mannered and capable. How would Father describe her? Did he even know her well enough to do so?

She stepped back and let her gaze wander around the room that she'd been too tired to observe carefully last night. She had spent countless hours in the kitchen with Mama, learning to recreate the delicious foods her mother made. This space was larger than the one she'd grown up working in, but it felt familiar all the same. The pots stacked beside the hearth with its large iron bracket crane hinged to the left and a bread oven to the right. The rough-hewn mantel topping the fireplace, with pegs from which hung spoons and tools required to tend the fire. Dried herbs dangled from wooden beams spanning the ceiling, their aromatic scent mingling with the smoke of the fire.

A wistful smile tugged at the corners of her mouth as she untied her cape and draped it over the back of a sturdy wooden chair. Perhaps Father simply needed an opportunity to see that she, too, was capable in the home. The kitchen, of all places, was the perfect place to show him.

"May I prepare something for the morning meal?"

"You needn't trouble yourself." He rested a hand on her shoulder. "You've not had the time to become acquainted with how everything is arranged here. I'm certain Mary will be down shortly to take care of everything."

His words were true. It would be more difficult to cook when she was not yet familiar with the supplies, nor with their preferences or habits in eating. But she could find her way. Her hands twisted in the fabric of her petticoat. She must find something useful to do. Even if only to start a pot of water to boil.

"I will stoke the fire in the parlor so you may sit there and enjoy a bit of rest." Father bent to scoop up several logs, his words interrupting her thoughts and spoiling her plans.

What need of rest did she have? She had done nothing yet today aside from dressing and venturing out to the frozen garden. But she didn't want to argue, so she followed him past the staircase and through the open doorway.

The parlor was vastly different from the humble yet cheerful space of the kitchen. A wide decorative mantel framed the brick fireplace, and the room was well-appointed, filled with quality furnishings that spoke of good taste and money to spend. Wainscoting circled the entire room, and the walls above were papered in an intricate blue pattern. It was a room to showcase, to declare your success and standing.

A pair of elegant chairs sat before the fire, and Father patted the high back of one before tending the smoldering coals in the fireplace. "Please, sit. The room will be warm shortly."

Patience offered a small smile that faded as she settled into the seat. She much preferred the comfortable family space of the kitchen over the stuffiness of the parlor. This was a place to entertain guests. Was that what he perceived her to be?

She clasped and unclasped her hands. Footsteps and stirrings upstairs suggested the other members of the house were beginning to rise, and she felt a sudden desperation to grab hold of this time alone with her father.

"Do you always wake early too?"

He glanced over his shoulder at her, his eyes crinkling. "I will answer as you did—I often do, but not quite so early as today."

"Where do you work? Is it far from home?"

As soon as the words were out, Patience wished them back. His work had taken him far from home—their home and their family—for her entire life. But she had not meant to speak of such things, especially not on their first morning together.

Thankfully, the question didn't seem to impact her father. He settled into the chair beside her, stretching his feet toward the fire, grimacing as he rubbed his right leg.

"The shop is on Kings Street, at the edge of Long Wharf. A short walk from here."

Patience knew, from Father's letters, that he had taken a position as shopkeeper, though she could hardly picture him behind a counter all day. It seemed strange that he should finally settle into such a sedentary job that kept him established in one place after his years of sailing throughout the Atlantic. But his injury had forced him to leave his life at sea, and his years of experience with the East India Company likely prepared him for working with merchants and their goods.

He started to rise, and Patience grasped for one last thought —anything to keep him to herself for a moment longer.

"Might I walk with you this morning? I was too tired yesterday to take much notice of the town, and I would like to know more of where you spend your days."

"I would be glad of your company, but I won't have you returning home alone."

"Will could come with us. I imagine he would enjoy it as well, and he could escort me back."

Father rubbed his chin. "I am not certain your brother holds as much interest in this town or my position as you do, but if he agrees to come, then I would gladly have you along."

Patience grinned. "I will speak to him first thing."

Father departed with a nod, and Patience sank back into the chair. Soon he would know her better and see that she had a place in this new family.

~

A damp wind blustered through the street as if the clouds themselves had settled between the buildings. Patience tucked her hands deeper in the folds of her wool cape. Her walk with Father had not gone as planned. Will had agreed to come, for her sake, but Elizabeth had also volunteered to join them. She expressed such enthusiasm to assist with their first tour of Boston that Father readily agreed, and when they set out it was Elizabeth he offered his arm to, while Patience took Will's.

Father pointed out places of interest here and there, but Patience could hardly focus, her attention fixed instead on the spot where Elizabeth's hand rested on his arm. By the time they arrived at the shop on Kings Street, Patience was certain she had seen no more of Boston than the previous day, and she most definitely had not succeeded in spending any quality time with her father.

"Here we are." Father unlocked the shop and ushered them inside through the white painted door in the front of the brick building.

A single window on each side of the door let in the scant morning light, and Patience blinked as her eyes adjusted to the dim interior. On each side of the room stood a long wooden counter, behind which were rows of open shelves full of a variety of goods. Woven baskets hung from the ceiling, and barrels stood at the ends of each counter.

Patience breathed in the smell of spices and wood and smoke, a comforting, homey scent that made the place feel welcoming.

Father limped toward the fireplace at the back of the shop, but William held up a hand to stop him. "I'll take care of that."

"There is wood outside." Father gestured toward a small door at the back corner.

While William stoked the fire, Patience trailed her fingers

along one of the polished counters, inspecting the goods behind it. There were glass jars neatly labeled and filled with spices such as nutmegs and cinnamon alongside cones of sugar wrapped in blue paper. Chinaware, paper, cocoa, and snuff also occupied the shelves.

"You have such a wide array of choices." Patience turned to face Father. "Does it all come from overseas?"

"Most of it does." He stepped behind the counter and straightened the scale sitting atop it. "I've a good connection with several merchants. And Boston being such a busy port, we receive much of the best goods, just as you'd find in England."

He turned and reached for a tin of tea from an upper shelf. "Mine is one of the only shops to still supply imported tea at present." He lifted the lid and peeked inside. A frown marred his features as he closed the tin and returned it to its place. "Though my stock is dwindling, and if these rebels have their way, I'll not be able to purchase more for some time."

Patience furrowed her brow. "What about the tea aboard the *Eleanor*?"

"Aye, but..." He scowled and shook his head. "You needn't trouble yourself. I should not have spoken of it at all. Forgive me."

"I do not mind. In truth, I would like to understand."

"This is a lovely pattern. Is it new?" Elizabeth's voice drifted from across the room, where she stood on tiptoe behind another counter to examine a bolt of fabric tucked on a high shelf.

Father seemed thankful for the interruption as he pulled out a thick ledger and leafed through the pages. "Just arrived on Monday. I will set some aside for you, if you'd like."

Patience bit back her frustration at their unfinished conversation, as well as the jealousy that crept into her heart. It was good of Father to be kind to Elizabeth, who likely missed her own father.

"Come look at this, Patience." Elizabeth held up a skein of wool. "It would be perfect for a pair of mitts. You'll need them soon with the weather as it is here."

Father nodded. "Elizabeth is right. Take that home with you, Patience, and the two of you can work on a pair together."

"Thank you." Patience pressed her lips into a smile, even though the thought of knitting brought her no excitement. Needlework of any sort was her least favorite of tasks, but she'd not reject Father's offer or disappoint him by saying such.

Will straightened from his spot by the fire, dusting his hands on his breeches. "The hinge on the back door seems loose."

"Ah, I'd forgotten that." Father leaned heavily on the counter, shifting his weight off his bad leg. "I had a new set made at the blacksmith earlier this week and have yet to pick them up."

"Perhaps we can get them for you." Patience tucked a stray curl behind her ear. Father's leg obviously pained him, and she much preferred the thought of an additional walk outdoors to being confined in the house knitting the remainder of the day.

"It would be a help." Father glanced between the three of them. "William must accompany you of course." Father turned to Elizabeth. "It is the smithy on Olivers Street. You know the one?"

She nodded.

"Very good." He slid open a drawer beneath the counter and counted some coins into his palm. "Take this, our agreed upon payment. And come back straight away. I'll package the wool and fabric for you when you return."

Will slid the money into his pocket, and Patience tugged her hood back over her head, bracing for the cold that would greet them when they opened the door.

She glanced over her shoulder and raised a hand to wave to

Father, but his head was bent over the ledger, quill to the page, and he did not see.

∾

*J*osiah swiped the back of his hand across his forehead, then gripped his hammer and brought it down upon the ax head, reshaping the old tool to make it like new again. He relished the familiar rhythm of his work, the smell of smoke and hot iron, even the heat that had him pushing up his shirt sleeves despite the cold outside. All of it helped clear his mind of the melancholy he'd felt last night.

He pumped the bellow. The burst of air sent flames licking higher in the forge, the coals burning bright. Holding the ax over the glowing embers, he shook his head to rid a stubborn strand of hair from his face, then turned to the anvil again.

A cold breeze swept across his back, even as sparks flew from the piece in front of him, and Josiah glanced over his shoulder to see a tall man holding the door open as two women hurried inside, their faces hidden by the hoods of their cloaks.

"Excuse me, sir," the man called, pushing the door closed and shutting out the cold once more.

Josiah set down his tools and nodded a greeting. He wiped his hands on his leather apron, then ran his fingers through his hair. Women rarely visited his smithy, and he was oddly conscious of his appearance.

The women hung back at the entrance as the man crossed the room in several lengthy strides. "Good morning. I'm William Abbott, George Abbott's son."

The name reverberated in Josiah's head like a hammer stroke, but he schooled his expression into one of simple civility. "Josiah Wagner."

"I am here to pick up some hinges you made for my father."

"They are ready." Josiah moved to the work bench along the

side wall where he'd left the hinges he'd finished earlier in the week.

He handed the pair, along with a set of nails, to the man and accepted the coins in return.

"My father said this was your agreed upon payment."

"Thank you." He tucked the money in his pocket. "I don't believe we've met before."

"My sister and I just arrived from England yesterday." He gestured to the women at the doorway, who stepped forward to stand beside him. "May I present my sister, Patience Abbott. And perhaps you know Elizabeth Caldwell?"

"I do not believe so. Nice to meet you both." Josiah turned to the two young ladies he had yet to observe closely, and his eyes widened.

It was her, the girl from the harbor.

She met his gaze and blinked in surprise. "You are the man who helped me yesterday, are you not?"

He nodded, unable to form a response. He had been certain he'd not see her again, and yet here she was, in his smithy. The lost expression in her face from the day before was gone, replaced by a wide smile that set matching dimples in her cheeks and brightened her dark eyes.

"It is good to meet you in earnest, Mr. Wagner." She dipped her head slightly before tilting her face to look up at him again. "I am happy to tell you that I found the person I was looking for."

"I am glad of it." It was the truth, yet a strange sense of disappointment settled in his gut. This woman who had occupied far too many of his thoughts was the daughter of a Loyalist shopkeeper? The very one Josiah had reported to the Sons of Liberty?

She turned to her brother. "Remember when you were fetching our things and I thought I saw Father from a distance?

As I was searching, I met this man"—her eyes flicked back at Josiah—"who assisted me."

"Thank you for helping my sister," Mr. Abbott said. "We had just arrived, and she was anxious to be reunited with our father."

"We'd not seen him for almost three years." Miss Abbott fiddled with the ribbons of her cape. "Father sailed for the East India Company until he was injured in a shipwreck. Our mother recently—"

"Circumstances kept us apart for some time." Her brother interrupted.

She dipped her head, but not before Josiah spotted a flash of emotion in her eyes. What more had she been about to say? He had an unexplainable desire to know, despite her being a near stranger to him. There was something about her forthrightness that he found appealing. Perhaps because it was so different from his own tendency to keep his thoughts close. Yet what business did he have, showing interest of any sort in the daughter of a man so staunchly opposed to his beliefs?

"We sailed aboard the *Eleanor*." Mr. Abbott spoke again.

Josiah raised his brows. Did the man know anything of the cargo that ship carried or the trouble it brought to Boston with it? "I did not realize she bore passengers."

"We were the only ones. A favor to our father."

"And have you come to stay, then?"

"I am committed to return to England once Patience is settled." Mr. Abbott glanced back at his sister and the young woman beside her. "I suppose much remains to be seen."

What had kept the siblings separated from their father for so long? What of their mother? Why would Miss Abbott stay, but her brother leave?

And why did it matter so much to Josiah?

His focus unwittingly strayed to Miss Abbott, and he found her gaze fixed on him. He swallowed, his pulse stuttering, and turned back to her brother. "I hope your time here is pleasant, however long it might be."

"Thank you." His expression was more grimace than smile.

The man turned and led the two ladies toward the door, but Miss Abbott paused, spinning to face Josiah once more. "Thank you again for your kindness yesterday. It was good to meet you, Mr. Wagner."

His breath caught in his chest. He cleared his throat. "And I am glad to meet you as well, Miss Abbott."

She lifted her hood over her head as she stepped into the winter air. A chilly blast whipped into the shop, raising the hairs on his bare arms. But then Miss Abbott peeked back over her shoulder at him and any sense of cold disappeared in the warmth of her dimpled smile.

CHAPTER 5

*P*atience stared at the imposing stone church before them, tilting her head back to peer at the massive columns that stretched toward the high square bell tower. It was the third morning since her arrival in Boston, and she hoped the Sabbath would allow her more time with Father. He'd been busy at the shop all day yesterday, taking Will with him but leaving her at the house with the other ladies. Elizabeth and Mary, as her stepmother had given her leave to call her, had been nothing but kind in their attempts to help her settle in to her new home, but what she really desired was Father's company.

She smoothed her hands down the fabric of her gown as they climbed the steps of Kings Chapel. She'd picked her favorite, a red and cream floral print, to wear for the Sabbath, though it was likely to remain mostly hidden under her cape now. She wanted to make a good impression as she attended church alongside Father. It was, after all, the first opportunity for him to introduce his daughter to his neighbors and friends.

Will glanced down at her, his lips tipping up slightly at the corners. "You look lovely, Patience. Do not fret."

"I'm not fretting."

He raised his eyebrows.

"You are right, I am a bit nervous."

"I know, but you have—"

His words were cut off as Father ushered them inside. She pressed her lips together to hold back a sigh. She had not managed more than a.moment to speak with Will alone since their arrival. She longed to know his thoughts, but at the same time dreaded hearing his plans. Would he return to England as soon as he could? She was not ready to say goodbye.

Father led them along the aisle, pausing before one of the dark wooden box pews. "This is ours." He opened the hand-carved door. "Though perhaps I need to rearrange it now that you are here."

He smiled at Patience as she entered ahead of him, but it did nothing to calm her nerves. Was he truly pleased to have her and Will with him, or was it a nuisance to have two additional people to fit into their family pew?

Elizabeth leaned close to Patience and spoke in a hushed tone. "Every family who owns a box can arrange and decorate it as they choose. Come, sit with me. We shall take the bench facing the back of the chapel."

Patience offered Elizabeth a small smile as she settled on the cushioned bench beside her. Will sat on her other side, stiff and silent, as Father and Mary settled on the bench across from them.

Father scanned the crowd, a small furrow in his brow. "I had hoped to introduce you to Edward Cunningham, but I do not see him here this morning."

Patience followed his gaze to an empty box ahead of theirs. "Is he a good friend of yours?"

He nodded. "Quite an impressive and accomplished man. He owns a fleet of ships and is one of the primary suppliers of goods for my shop."

"I look forward to meeting him when I am able." Patience would be glad to make the acquaintance of any of her father's friends, especially if it gave her the opportunity to spend more time with Father in the process.

She scanned the sanctuary. How many more of these unfamiliar faces were friends or neighbors to her father? It was another reminder that Father had a life here, established and settled, while everything was new and different for her.

"Admiring the church?" Pride edged Father's voice as he leaned toward her. "It was founded in 1686. The altar pieces were a gift from King William in the following year." Father gestured toward the painted wooden panels displayed behind the hexagonal pulpit. One bore the Lord's Prayer, another the Ten Commandments, the last the Apostles' Creed.

Though he had been wrong in guessing her thoughts, Patience turned back to Father with a smile. "They are lovely."

Father nodded in agreement. "A clear sign of the Crown's support for this chapel from its earliest days. May we continue to show the same loyalty in return."

Patience blinked at Father's statement and the intense expression that accompanied it. She was aware of the tension between the colonies and England, though she had admittedly not devoted much time to understanding such things. Elizabeth shifted in her seat, ducking her head. Had Father's declaration made her uncomfortable? Was it possible that the younger woman, born and raised in America, held a different opinion on the matter?

Strains of organ music broke through Patience's wandering thoughts, and she turned her attention to the service. The congregation joined in singing, and the familiar words wrapped around her like an embrace. Mama's voice came to mind, clear and warm, the memory almost as real as if she were there, lifting her song to God right beside them. Patience swallowed, unable to finish the final lines of the hymn as hot tears gathered behind her eyes. She blinked them away.

Reverend Caner took his place at the pulpit. His sonorous voice filled the room, but Patience struggled to focus on his words, her mind straying to beloved Sabbath days of the past when she was a child and Father was home from sea. Such days were few, but cherished in her memory. They would walk home from church together, past the shipyard, as Father regaled them with stories of his childhood, how his father was a shipbuilder and that inspired him to join the Royal Navy when he was of age. On very special occasions, they'd climb the hill overlooking Gillingham Creek as Mama hummed a tune to match the songs of the birds. Father would reach into his pocket and pull out a crystallized candy or brittle. "How did that get in there?" he'd say with a wink, and she would relish the sweet on the walk home.

Patience peered across the box where Father sat straight and still, eyes fixed ahead, the picture of attentiveness. She tried to do the same, but her hands seemed to fidget in her lap of their own accord.

Had she thought that being together again would somehow transport them back to those simpler, happier days? She wasn't that naïve, certainly. It had been many years since they'd shared such a Sabbath. She didn't expect the same feeling today any more than she expected Father to pull a candied treat from his pocket. But still...

She'd been ten when the Seven Years' War ended and Father left the British Navy. She had known nothing other than a life where her father was away more often than he was at home, but had desperately hoped that would change.

She would never forget the conversation she'd eavesdropped upon, hiding behind the door when Mama and Father thought she was asleep.

"Why not accept the shopkeeper position?" Mama asked.

"It is an honorable business, and I've no doubt you'd learn quickly."

"But to sit confined in a shop all day? I couldn't bear it."

"I know it would be a change, but you've had your adventures, have you not?" Mama's voice quivered in a way that made Patience's heart race. "What of our family? Do you not desire to be here with us?"

"I miss you every time I leave, but I'll return as always. Joining the East India Company will be exceedingly profitable. I could provide our family with so much—"

"I'm content with what we have, George. You know that. And what about the baby?"

Patience clasped her hand over her mouth to smother a gasp. A baby? Their voices dropped lower until she could no longer make out their words. She tiptoed back to bed, confused and afraid of the things she had heard.

Father had set sail a fortnight later, and Mama lost the baby two months after that.

Patience blinked herself back to the present and swallowed an unwelcome lump of emotion.

Will shifted on the pew beside her, his shoulder bumping hers. She glanced at him, and he nodded subtly to her lap, where her hands had clasped and twisted the fabric of her gown. She released it quickly, smoothing the wrinkles as much as she was able, then drew a slow breath as she directed her full attention to the preaching.

She would not let her mind dwell on the past any longer.

CHAPTER 6

*W*ednesday dawned clear and fair. The first light of dawn seeped through the kitchen window as Patience hung the kettle full of water from the iron crane and swung it over the freshly stoked fire. With Mary's approval, Patience had taken over the duties of tending the kitchen fire and cooking the morning meal. She was always the first in the house to rise, and the familiar rhythm of the simple tasks provided a much-needed sense of purpose and a distraction from all that felt so new and strange.

Patience brushed her hands across her apron and peered out the window at the small patch of land behind the house. The plots there would be gardens in the spring, and her fingers itched to dig in the soft earth, press seeds beneath the dirt, and watch life sprout up. If the past few days were any indication, it would be several dreary months before she could do such a thing.

Mama's gardens had been her pride and joy, overflowing with an abundance of produce to eat, herbs to dry, and flowers to admire for their sheer beauty. Patience had inherited Mama's love for growing and nurturing living things. In England, their cottage on the outskirts of Chatham had been surrounded by green space, with plenty of land to wander and fresh air to fill your lungs. Here in Boston, it seemed the buildings nestled as close to one another as possible, allowing only small pockets of greenery to peek out, and the salt-tinged air felt heavy and damp, when it wasn't so cold as to be nearly unbearable.

Patience set a trivet beside the fire and raked some coals beneath it. She balanced a heavy skillet atop the iron stand and added a generous pat of lard. As it melted, she bustled about the kitchen, thankful that Mary had graciously welcomed her into the space. Despite the uncertainty that lingered as each of them sought to find their place in this new family, Patience had to admit that Mary and Elizabeth seemed genuine in their attempts to make her feel welcome.

"Smells good in here."

She jumped, nearly dropping the eggs cradled in her apron. "Will. I didn't hear you come in."

"I didn't want to wake anyone." He yawned as he joined her beside the fire. "We've had hardly a moment to speak alone since we arrived. When I woke early, I thought to take advantage of the opportunity."

"I'm glad of it."

His eyes searched hers. "How are you doing, truly?"

"I cannot say for certain. As soon as I feel I'm beginning to settle in here, memories of Mama and home flood my mind."

"There's no shame in missing home and our mother. I do, too, you know."

"I thought coming here, being with Father again, would somehow take away the ache of her being gone. Or at least lessen it." Patience cracked the eggs into the skillet and scrambled the whites and yolks together with a wooden spoon. "I feel foolish to miss England now, after I was so anxious to leave."

"You're not foolish. Boston has not been what you expected. Nor I." He dropped his voice lower. "Neither of us could have imagined Father would take a new wife, let alone one with a daughter."

"I cannot deny that it was—it is—a shock. They have both been kind and welcoming, though, so I am trying my best."

"I have noticed and I'm proud of you." He reached out and squeezed her hand. "You and Elizabeth seem to get along well. I had wondered..."

Patience peered up at him. "What did you wonder?"

"Only that it might be difficult. She seems a good enough girl, but you have waited so long to be reunited with Father, and now you've no choice but to share his attention with another."

She ducked her head. "I cannot deny feeling jealous at times. But I realized from the first evening we arrived that I could not blame Elizabeth for the situation. She has as little say in the matter as we do."

"A wise and generous decision." Will crossed his arms over his chest. "I cannot claim to be as generous as you."

"You dislike her?"

"Elizabeth? No, I do not dislike her, nor her mother."

"But you are angry over Father's remarriage."

"Father's choices have angered me for so long, this remarriage is merely an addition to the growing list."

Footsteps above their head brought a halt to their hushed conversation. Patience busied herself stirring the eggs.

Will glanced at the doorway, then turned back to her. "Let's take a walk today, you and I."

Patience couldn't hide an eager smile. "I would love to. Though I wish we could go someplace with a bit more"—she waved her hand in the air—"open space."

"I'm certain we can find a spot."

A low cough announced Father's arrival. He shuffled into the kitchen, wrapped in his banyan, his nightcap still atop his head. Patience smiled and pulled out a chair for him. He settled in with a grimace, rubbing his bad leg.

"Good morning to you both," he said. "Did I hear you were looking for some open space to explore?"

"Will thought to take a walk today." Patience scooped eggs onto a plate and set it at the table before him. "I had hoped to find somewhere less crowded to enjoy the fresh air."

Father chuckled. "You always did need space to roam. A girl after my own heart."

Patience's cheeks warmed as she retrieved the kettle to prepare Father's tea. He remembered her love of the outdoors. What's more, he thought she had inherited her sense of adventure from him. The warmth traveled to her chest and settled there.

"Elizabeth would love to show you the Common." Father spoke around a mouthful of eggs. "I will ask her to accompany you both there today."

Her heart sank. Why couldn't Father simply tell them where to go? She did like Elizabeth, for all she knew her thus far, but she desperately wanted to speak freely with Will.

She met Will's gaze behind their father's back. Their opportunity for uninterrupted time together was spoiled. Will would protest Father's suggestion if she asked him to, but she didn't wish to start an argument or appear ungrateful. She shook her head ever so slightly.

Pressing her lips together in a smile, she handed Father a cup of tea. "Thank you. We appreciate it."

She would do what was necessary to prove to Father that she belonged here, that she wasn't a mere visitor in this town and his life. If only she could convince her own heart of the same.

~

*J*osiah clapped a hand over his cocked hat and tilted his head back to admire the clear morning sky, a welcome respite after days of thick clouds and rain. He'd made a visit to the Woodhouse family residing along Boston Neck, and though the walk home would be more direct if he continued straight, he veered west toward the Common instead. It would be a shame to waste such a beautiful day, especially with the depths of winter soon to set in. The forge could wait as he indulged in a few extra moments of fresh air.

He tucked the canvas sack slung over his shoulder closer to his side, relishing the warmth that seeped through his coat from the fresh loaf of bread within it. A bundle of carrots, a hunk of cheese, and a slab of smoked ham further filled out the bag. He'd been more than happy to trade his services in repairing farming tools for some fresh food from the Woodhouses' kitchen. His stomach rumbled in anticipation.

"Mr. Wagner." A male voice drifted toward him.

Josiah glanced up and spotted William Abbott approaching with his sister and Miss Caldwell at his side. His breath hitched. His mind had strayed to Miss Abbott more than once since her visit to his shop, though he could not understand why he was so drawn to her. Mayhap it was merely the sympathy he'd felt upon their first meeting that kept her in his thoughts, though that did not explain the eager speed of his pulse at seeing her again now.

The trio came to a stop before him, and Josiah touched his hat. "Good morning."

His greeting encompassed all of them, though his gaze settled on Miss Abbott. A small smile lifted the corners of her lips. Several dark curls had escaped her cap and brushed against her cheeks. He gripped the strap of his bag.

"Are you enjoying the beautiful day?" Miss Caldwell asked. Her gaze flicked between himself and Miss Abbott, and he swallowed as he focused his attention on the younger woman instead.

"Indeed. And you?"

She nodded, but it was Miss Abbott who spoke. "I am grateful to be able to be outdoors at last. I cannot bear being stuck inside overly long."

He understood that feeling well. "I am much the same."

Her dimples appeared then, and her smile warmed him more than the sun streaming through the bare branches of the trees above them. Was it possible she felt the same inexplicable connection to him as he did to her?

"Elizabeth is kindly showing us around, as we've yet to see much of Boston."

"Well, I've no desire to interrupt your—"

"Nay." Miss Abbott's hand shot out from beneath her cloak, almost brushing his sleeve, before she quickly pulled it back. "I did not mean to suggest that you must leave."

The warmth brought on by her smile was nothing compared with the heat that filled his belly at her words and the near touch of her hand. Did she actually desire his company, or was she merely trying to be polite?

"That is, we don't wish to keep you." She ducked her head. "But if we're going in the same direction, we might all walk together."

He nodded his consent, and the group set off at a leisurely pace along the edge of the Common. The grassy open space was dotted with trees and grazing cattle, gentle hills rolling across the landscape, with Beacon Hill to the north, rising above the rest.

"Who lives there?" Mr. Abbott gestured toward the stately manor perched upon Beacon Hill overlooking the Common.

"That's Mr. Hancock's home." Josiah paused beside the others who had stopped to admire the house. "One of the largest in all Boston."

"Have you always lived here?" Miss Abbott tilted her face to look up at him.

"No, I was born in England, in Suffolk."

"What was it like there? I never ventured much beyond our home in Chatham, until we traveled to London to sail here." She fell into step beside him as they began to walk once more. Mr. Abbott and Miss Caldwell proceeded ahead of them.

"Good farm land, mostly. That's what my family did for generations."

"What brought you here, then?"

Josiah rubbed a hand across the back of his neck. He did not mind her curiosity, but the story behind the departure from his home in England and all that followed was not a happy one, and he hated to spoil the day.

"My mother died in childbirth, along with my newborn twin brothers." He shifted the bag on his shoulder. "Soon after, much of the land was parceled off due to the Enclosure Acts. My father decided it was best to leave and make a new start here."

Of course, Papa's idea of a fresh beginning had been farther west. They'd planned to sail to Boston, then travel inland, find a spot to farm once more. Sometimes Josiah still ached to do so. To leave the confines of the town, settle on a plot of land, build a little house, and work the way his ancestors had for years.

"I am very sorry about your mother." Miss Abbott's voice was so quiet, Josiah almost missed it.

He turned to look at her. Her eyes met his, and at the sheen of moisture there, he swallowed. He did not want pity, yet something about her expression spoke to a level of understanding, of shared sorrow.

"My mother died in February after being ill for nearly a year. We were so close, her and I. I did all I could to care for her, but..." She dropped her gaze and released a shaky breath. "It is very hard to lose your mother."

He clasped his hands behind his back, squeezing them tightly so as not to reach for her, as he had the sudden urge to do. "I am certain your love and care were a comfort to her."

Words were a paltry offering in the face of such things, but hopefully, she could somehow feel the depth of his understanding. He knew too well the helplessness of watching a parent fade away and being unable to do anything to stop their passing.

"Thank you. I do not doubt she knew how much I loved her, and I know how much she loved me."

They walked in silence for a moment, their pace unhurried, widening the gap between themselves and Mr. Abbott and Miss Caldwell. Miss Caldwell chattered brightly, her voice carrying on the breeze like birdsong in spring. Miss Abbott's brother glanced over his shoulder at them but seemed satisfied that all was well and did not slow to wait.

"So you were a boy then, when you came here." Miss Abbott resumed their conversation.

"I was eleven."

"And your father, is he still with you?"

"Sadly, my father died on the journey. Smallpox." The toe of his shoe caught on a stone and sent it skittering down the path.

Miss Abbott stopped and turned to face him fully, her eyes wide, her lips parted in a gasp. "I cannot imagine the sorrow you must have felt. Such loss, and you were so young. I am sorry to have asked and made you speak of it."

"I do not mind." He rarely spoke of his past, but something about Miss Abbott's gentle gaze eased the pain that usually accompanied such memories.

"How did you manage, when you arrived here?"

"I entered a compulsory apprenticeship. It is not uncommon for orphans. I trained under my master, Mr. Sperling, for nine years, until I reached my majority. Now I run the shop he once owned."

"Was he good to you?" She resumed walking.

He matched his pace to her leisurely one, contemplating the answer. "Sperling was a fair man and a good teacher. He never treated me poorly." Sperling never treated him especially warmly, either, but Josiah didn't speak that thought aloud.

"But it's not the same as family."

"It is not."

Silence lingered between them, but it wasn't uncomfortable. Instead, they seemed to share an unspoken understanding that grief did not need trite words, but rather the quiet camaraderie of someone who had experienced similar sorrow.

Still, Josiah longed to turn their conversation toward happier things, to draw that smile out upon her face again. He grasped for something to say, but what could he offer to brighten her spirits? His days were filled with work at the forge, his nights occupied by meetings with the Sons of Liberty. He could not divulge the secret plans being discussed over how to deal with the tea, especially to the daughter of a Loyalist, nor did he suspect she would have any interest in hearing of the latest tools he had repaired.

He glanced across the grassy expanse at the pond not far off, his thoughts snagging on an idea. "Have you ever been skating?"

The beginnings of a smile tugged at the corner of her lips. "Not since I was quite young."

"Me neither, but when I was a boy, I skated there whenever I had the chance." He gestured toward the water. It was not frozen yet, but no doubt, it would be soon enough. "Mayhap you should try it again."

"I think I shall, though I would issue the same challenge to you." Her smile bloomed fully, and his heart stuttered faster.

She meant nothing by it, certainly, yet he could not help but imagine sliding across the ice with her hand clasped in his own. To hear her laughter, watch the wind brush her dark hair across her cheeks, and relive the freedom of childhood by her side. He blinked.

He must set aside such thoughts. Her father stood against Josiah's own beliefs for this country, and she had come from England just a sennight ago—on one of the tea ships, no less. He had no reason to be interested. And yet, he was.

William Abbott peered over his shoulder again, his stern expression softening when he caught sight of her smile. He paused, and Miss Caldwell stopped beside him, turning to look back as well.

"Mr. Wagner said this is a popular place for skating in the winter," Miss Abbott said when they'd closed the distance between them. "We should go, when the weather allows." Her smile faded. "Though, I suppose you may be gone by then."

Her brother laid a hand upon her shoulder. "I will not leave so soon as that."

Her countenance relaxed, but a more solemn tone settled over the group. Josiah looked between the other three. What an interesting mix they were. A brother and sister who obviously loved each other dearly and a young woman who seemed to desire to fit in with them, but lacked the years of closeness to warrant such affection. And himself. An outsider to it all, as he often was, with no family of any sort to call his own.

Josiah squared his shoulders and cleared his throat. "I should be off. The forge won't light itself."

"Thank you for joining us," Miss Abbott said. "It was a pleasure to talk with you."

"And you." He dipped his head in a nod farewell and turned toward home.

Even as he left her behind, Miss Abbott's words stayed close in his mind. Despite the sad nature of the things they had spoken of together, he had to agree that it was a pleasure to share part of his story with her and to hear part of hers. It was a pleasure simply to walk by her side. But nothing could come of it. He must put her from his mind.

CHAPTER 7

*P*atience could not keep her thoughts from straying to Mr. Wagner, even as Elizabeth chattered the remainder of the walk home. She'd been surprised by the flutter of excitement she'd felt upon first seeing him along the road and had perhaps been over-eager in inviting him to join them on their walk. But she could not regret the invitation. She had enjoyed their conversation immensely, painful though it was to recount the loss of Mama and to hear of Mr. Wagner's tragic past. Despite the sorrow in their stories, their shared grief seemed to link them together somehow, as though they might understand one another better because of it.

Nor could she deny the way his nearness had caused her pulse to quicken. If Will had not been there, his stoic figure just a few yards ahead, might Mr. Wagner have offered her his arm? Heat rose in her cheeks at the thought, and she pulled her attention back to Elizabeth, who was talking about how much lovelier the Common was in the spring.

Upon returning home, Mary met them at the door. "Oh good, you've returned. William and Patience, your father has a guest in the parlor he would like you to meet."

Patience removed her hat and tugged off her cape, hung both on the peg in the entryway, and smoothed a hand over her petticoat. She raised her brows at Will in silent question, but he just shrugged in return and gestured for her to proceed him into the parlor.

"Here they are at last." Father stood from his chair beside the fire as they entered. Beside him, another man rose from his seat as well, stepping around it to greet them.

Patience tucked a stray hair behind her ear as she came to stand beside Father. She smiled politely at the stranger, whose tall stature drew her gaze upward to his bright blue eyes, made more vibrant by the hue of his well-tailored jacket.

"May I introduce you to Mr. Edward Cunningham," Father said. "These are my children, William and Patience."

Mr. Cunningham offered a small bow. "It is a pleasure to meet you."

His words encompassed them both, but his gaze remained fixed on Patience. He smiled at her warmly as she bobbed a curtsy. This was the man Father had wished her to meet on Sunday? He was younger than she had expected, not much older than herself.

"Welcome to Boston. How are you enjoying our town thus far, Miss Abbott?"

Patience hesitated a moment. It was a simple question, and yet the answer was complicated. "It is very different from where I grew up, but I am settling in."

"I hope it will soon feel like home to you," he said. "Your father seems very pleased to have you here. He has told me much about you."

"He has?" She glanced at Father. "I am glad to be reunited with him."

"He could talk of little else today." Mr. Cunningham leaned slightly closer as if sharing a secret with her alone. "I came by to discuss all this business with the tea, and I must admit that your father's enthusiasm over your arrival was a welcome distraction from such an unpleasant topic."

The intensity of his blue eyes and the brightness of his smile brought a rush of warmth to her cheeks.

"Your father says you sailed aboard the *Eleanor*. I hope you did not experience any difficulties with those rebels at the wharf when you disembarked, what with the cargo she bears."

Patience furrowed her brow, remembering that Father had expressed a similar complaint just five days prior in his shop. She'd not yet had the chance to ask him more, and her curiosity swayed her to risk the embarrassment of admitting her ignorance. "We had no trouble. In fact, I must admit, I do not fully understand the issue with the tea."

He waved his hand as if to dismiss her confession. "All that matters is that you arrived safely. I'll not bore you with such talk."

"Actually, I am quite curious—"

"Edward is right, we have better things to speak of now." Father cut in. "He has graciously extended an invitation for us to join him next Friday to share a meal."

"I am delighted you can come." Mr. Cunningham smiled at her father, then turned back to Patience. "I regret that I must be off, but I look forward to getting to know you better, Miss Abbott."

Mr. Cunningham bid them farewell, secured his hat upon his head, and followed Father to the door. Patience watched as he departed, a striking figure with his tall stature and neat blond queue.

Father returned to the parlor, his face brightened by a wide smile. "He seemed quite taken by you, my dear girl." He patted her shoulder as though to congratulate her on some accomplishment. "We are sure to be treated to a delicious meal, and you will be quite impressed by his home. One of the finest in Boston."

"I look forward to it." Patience pressed her lips together into a smile which seemed to please Father.

"We all do, I am certain." Father glanced at Will. "Mr. Cunningham would be a beneficial person for you to befriend as well."

A muscle ticked in Will's jaw, but he simply nodded as Father departed, calling to Mary to tell her of the invitation.

Patience pressed a hand to her stomach. The kind attentions of handsome Mr. Cunningham and her father's eagerness over their meeting should have elicited some enthusiasm in her, yet Patience found her thoughts drifting to Mr. Wagner and the pleasant flutter of excitement she'd felt when he stood by her side instead.

≈

Josiah leaned against the wall in the back corner of the Green Dragon Tavern late Wednesday evening. Men packed nearly every inch of space, the smell of unwashed bodies mingling with the scents of tobacco smoke and ale. The room buzzed with voices, talk of the tea ships at the center of everyone's conversation.

Yet even as Josiah tried to listen, his thoughts wandered from tea and taxes to dark eyes and dimples. He'd thought of Miss Abbott nearly all day and wrestled with himself over his conflicting emotions. The connection he'd felt with her had only grown after their conversation, but a host of doubts overshadowed it.

Nothing could change what he knew of her father's loyalties, so completely opposed to his own. And what would she think if she knew Josiah was responsible for reporting her father's stance to the Sons of Liberty? Mr. Abbott's shop was now on the list of businesses to boycott, all because of the information Josiah had shared.

He tugged off his hat and ran a hand over his unruly hair. His dedication to the Sons of Liberty could not be compromised, not now when so much was at stake. Nor would he wish to put someone else at risk because of his actions.

He had seen how loss and hardship tore at a family. The deaths of his mother and twin baby brothers had nearly killed his father. Then they'd been driven from the only land they ever called home, sending his father deeper into despair. If Papa had more to live for, would he have fought death harder when it sought him out aboard the ship to America?

Josiah clenched his jaw against the memories. He knew what his father would say to such a thought. *God knows the number of our days, son, and when He calls us home, we can offer no argument. Nor should we want to.*

Loss and hardship would always be part of life, but love and happiness were part of life, too, were they not? In his determination to avoid the one, would he rid himself of any chance at the other?

Josiah scrubbed a hand over the stubble on his chin. Nay, it was not the time, nor place, to consider such things. With so much uncertainty lurking over the ships full of tea in the harbor, he needed a clear mind to serve the cause of liberty.

A shouted question drew Josiah out of his wandering thoughts. "What news of the *Beaver*? Why is she still anchored at Rainsford?"

He turned in the direction of the speaker. Word had spread of another ship's arrival earlier that day, but she had yet to moor at Griffin's Wharf like the other two tea ships before her.

"Quarantined. Smallpox aboard, I heard tell," a voice from the other side of the room replied.

A dull ache settled into Josiah's chest, the word *smallpox* taunting him.

"Perhaps it will take them all and leave her stranded. One less ship for us to worry about." A man at a table in the middle of the tavern raised his mug as he slurred the words, sloshing amber liquid onto his hand.

A round of rowdy cheers erupted from those seated around him. Josiah gritted his teeth. Though he hated the heavy hand of British rule as much as any, the sailors were not to blame, and he wouldn't want harm to befall them simply for transporting the dreaded tea.

A man standing near Josiah lifted his hand above the crowd and shouted, "Let us not wish ill upon them, only upon the cargo they carry."

"Hear, hear." The voices of assent rose louder, and Josiah gave his own silent nod of agreement.

"Thirsty, my friend?"

Josiah turned as Alexander Stevens nudged him with his shoulder, joining him in the corner of the room. He offered a pint of ale, which Josiah accepted with a nod of thanks, grateful for both the drink and the distraction.

"How goes it at the wharf?" Josiah asked.

"Holding steady." Alexander swigged his drink, then adjusted the strap of the musket slung over his shoulder. "We don't expect much trouble for now, though I'm curious to see what happens when the *Beaver* does arrive."

"I heard talk of a fourth ship. Is that mere rumor, or is there truth behind it?"

"It's true, but we've not sighted her yet."

Josiah raised the cup to his lips. Alexander was a fellow member of the Sons of Liberty and one of the men tasked with guarding the wharf ever since the arrival of the *Dartmouth*. An artillerist in Paddocks Artillery Militia, the young man had spent most of the past days on patrol at Griffin's Wharf, ensuring no tea was unloaded from the arriving ships.

Alexander tilted his head closer and lowered his voice. "Do you have another delivery ready?"

Josiah nodded and flicked his gaze around to make sure no one was listening. "I can meet you at our usual spot."

"Good. Tomorrow evening?"

"I'll be there."

They stood in companionable silence, listening to the discussions of the men around them. The wind buffeted the windows, but the storm brewing within the walls was even stronger...and likely to break loose any day.

CHAPTER 8

*J*osiah's greatcoat did little to protect against the rain as he strode through the darkness, up the incline of Fort Hill. Cold droplets snuck beneath his collar and dripped from his cocked hat, but at least the weather kept the streets quiet. He clasped the strap of his knapsack, eyes and ears alert to any movement or sound. As he approached the top of the hill, he whistled, three short higher tones followed by one low longer one.

A matching whistle echoed in the night, and a shadow emerged from a pair of trees. Alexander. At least it should be, though Josiah could not make out his face through the darkness and rain. Tension tightened his muscles as it did every time he made a delivery. They'd not been discovered yet, but he could not let down his guard.

He drew closer, relieved when he finally recognized his friend. Alexander raised a hand in silent greeting, and Josiah ducked under the shelter of the trees.

"Beautiful night for a walk." A wry smile grazed Alexander's face.

"Indeed." Josiah chuckled as he swung the pack off his back

and lowered it to the damp ground. Crouching, he opened it and reached inside to pull out two heavy pouches. "Musket balls."

Alexander took the bags and weighed them in his hand. "More than usual?"

"Aye. Where are they headed?"

"Concord, most likely. We're building quite a stockpile there."

Josiah stood and hooked the now-empty knapsack over his shoulder. "I'm glad to contribute, but I still hope it won't come to real fighting."

He'd been secretly contributing to the growing stock of munitions for months now, melting the scraps of iron in his smithy to mold into musket balls. While he hoped for peace, he knew the importance of having provisions at the ready, should those hopes not prevail.

"As do I. At least there are no soldiers in Boston for now."

"Let's hope those stationed at Castle Island remain there." Josiah shifted and peered through the darkness toward the direction of the harbor. He could not see anything now, but in daylight, Griffin's Wharf would be in view. "I thought to take a shift at the harbor tomorrow, if you need more men."

"Good. Be sure to stop at Edes and Gill and give your name. They are keeping a log of all the men who dedicate time to guarding the ships."

"Might that be risky? Keeping written record of the names?"

"I don't believe so. You know how staunchly Benjamin Edes is committed to the Sons, and both will be discreet. Even if the list fell into the wrong hands, what recourse can be taken? No violence has been committed."

"Let us pray it stays that way." Josiah turned back to his friend. "I'd best get home, but I will see you on the morrow."

Alexander nodded. "Until then."

The two parted ways, and Josiah trudged home, thoughts on the ships in the harbor and the efforts of men like himself and Alexander. Would it be enough? Could they truly stand against the mighty force of England, if it came to that? Or would the British Empire be like this downpour, unrelenting and overpowering? And might their decision regarding the tea be the tipping point?

$\sim$

*P*atience grumbled as she yanked at the tangled ball of wool on her lap. Rain pounded against the roof, and gusts of wind rattled the windows. A dull gloom hung over the parlor, matching her mood.

Damp weather had settled over the town the past two days, confining her indoors. Elizabeth had insisted it was the perfect excuse to finish knitting Patience's new mitts, but Patience would rather be doing almost anything else.

"What has that wool done to make you so angry?" Elizabeth settled in the chair beside Patience's own with a chuckle. "Here, let me help."

Patience sighed and handed the troublesome skein over. "It is my fault. I did not put it away neatly yesterday."

Elizabeth's slim fingers deftly untangled the knots, and she passed it back to Patience.

"Thank you." Patience ran her hand over the tidy strands as she stared at the rain pelting the window. "I dislike being stuck inside for so long. I begin to—"

"Lose your patience?" Elizabeth interrupted with a teasing grin.

Patience's laugh mingled with a sigh.

"I've come to know that about you." Elizabeth picked up her own knitting, her gaze focused on her lap as she continued. "I rather like days like this. It makes me feel safe and cozy and reminds me of all the evenings spent sitting here with my father."

Patience's gaze snapped to the younger woman. Sitting here? But that meant... "Was this your home?"

Elizabeth looked up, brows raised in surprise. "I thought you knew."

Patience shook her head as embarrassment heated her cheeks. She had assumed this was Father's house. He had never given her reason to believe otherwise.

"I've lived here all my life. When your father was ill, he stayed with us for a time." She twisted a strand of wool around her finger.

"Father wrote of the wonderful care he received from your father in his letters."

"He was a splendid doctor." Elizabeth smiled, leaning close and dropping her voice in a conspiratorial whisper. "He tried to teach me about medicine sometimes, when Mama wasn't nearby to hear and scold him."

Patience smiled, even as a pang of longing filled her chest. So many times, she had wished for Father to share some of his work, his life, with her, yet he never did.

"Papa and I spent many hours here together, him with the newspaper, me with my piecework." Elizabeth's damp eyes shone in the flickering light. "I miss him so very much. All the conversations we shared, the encouragement and advice he readily gave." The tears spilled onto her cheeks, and Patience swallowed a lump of emotion rising in her own throat. "I would give anything to feel his embrace again. To hear his voice."

Patience reached over and grasped Elizabeth's hand as tears filled her eyes. There were no words to sooth this kind of grief. She knew far too well.

"I imagine you understand. Missing your mother."

Patience nodded, not trusting her voice. Why had she not considered Elizabeth's grief earlier? She could not allow her own disappointments to keep her from noticing the needs of those around her.

"Look at the two of us. Weepy as the rain outside." Elizabeth gave a watery smile and swiped at her cheeks with her free hand. "I am sorry to speak of such gloomy things."

"I do not mind." Patience gave her fingers one last squeeze, then leaned back in her chair with a sigh. "I am sorry that I did not ask about your father before. I hope you know you can speak of him with me any time."

"Thank you. And you as well, about your mother."

Patience smiled her thanks, warmth seeping into her chest that had nothing to do with the fire blazing in the hearth.

"Patience?" Elizabeth's voice was quiet, almost timid. "My parents have always called me Libby. I'd be glad to have you call me that as well."

"Libby. It suits you." She smiled as a spark of joy replaced the sadness on the young woman's face. "I am happy to."

They set to work on their knitting, and settled into a quiet, comfortable conversation. The sounds of the rain and wind faded in the background as they spent the afternoon sharing stories of their childhoods and memories of the parents they lost. For once, Patience didn't mind the being stuck indoors because she was certain she was right where she needed to be.

$\sim$

A burst of wind rushed through the door behind Father as he returned home that evening. Patience hurried from the kitchen to greet him. He shoved the door closed against the howling storm outside and stood in the entry, rain puddling on the floor as it slid from his long coat and dripped from the brim of his hat. A damp chill hung in the air around him and matched the grim expression on his face.

Patience offered a bright smile in hopes of cheering him.

"Let me help you." She reached for his coat and hung it from a peg on the wall.

"Thank you." He removed his hat and slapped it against his leg. "I'd best go upstairs and change. I'm soaked through."

"Mary has a stew ready. It will help warm you."

Patience watched his slow ascent up the stairs. She'd spent much of the quiet moments of the afternoon contemplating what Libby had shared regarding her own father and the connection they had with each other. It was what Patience always wanted with Father, but he had never been home long enough to foster such a relationship.

Now that she had the opportunity, Patience would do whatever she could to remedy that. She would not try to replicate what Libby and her father had done, out of respect for the younger woman and her memories, but she was inspired to find something she and Father could share with one another. Something that spurred on conversation and left time to listen to one another. Something that could finally bring them together.

She returned to the kitchen and helped Mary set the table with bowls full of stew and hot biscuits while Libby filled five mugs of cider. Will, who had spent much of his day holed up in his back room, reading newspapers and writing letters to send back to England, smiled at her as she placed his food in front of him. They'd still had little time to themselves, but Patience was glad for his presence, even when they couldn't speak as freely as she might wish.

Father returned, dry and wearing his nightcap in place of his wig, and settled at the head of the table. His face was still set in a severe expression that put Patience on edge. She found her place beside Will and bowed her head as Father offered a brief blessing on the food.

The savory scent wafting from the stew and the smell of the fire made for a cozy atmosphere, yet the five of them began their meal in silence. Beside her, Will sat rigid in his chair, and across the table, Patience caught sight of the tentative glance Mary and Libby exchanged. Perhaps everyone else sensed, as Patience did, the tension that hovered over Father's countenance.

"These rebels will bring trouble upon us all." Father's abrupt comment and angry tone broke through the quiet.

Patience's gaze flew to his face. "What has happened?"

"Do you remember the men stationed at Griffin's Wharf when you arrived last week?"

Patience nodded.

"They call themselves the Sons of Liberty. Part of a larger band of miscreants and troublemakers who have set themselves against the king and parliament. They are a plague upon this town and all these colonies."

Patience balanced her spoon on the edge of her bowl. She'd been anxious to understand the situation with the tea ever since Father mentioned it a week prior. But the opportunity to ask him more never seemed to present itself, and she hadn't wished to instigate a conversation that might upset him, given the way he had avoided the topic ever since. Now, perhaps, he would be more willing to speak, since he was the one who had started the discussion.

"And they are causing trouble?" She pressed forward cautiously.

"They have it in their minds to block the tea from being unloaded because of their protest against the tea tax." Father muttered around a mouthful of stew. He swallowed, then continued. "It is an act of defiance and should be punished as such."

"So the tea from the *Eleanor* is still aboard the ship?"

Father nodded. "And that of the *Dartmouth* as well. I spoke with Captain Bruce today. He does not know what will happen. The rebels think to send it all back to England. I dare them to attempt it and see if they can withstand the guns of Castle Island."

He laughed, but there was no mirth in the sound, only disdain.

Patience flinched, beginning to regret her curiosity. Father's anger and disgust made her stomach churn. She glanced at Will, who clenched his jaw but remained silent. Across the table, Libby kept her head down, though Patience noticed that she gripped her spoon a little too tightly.

"I should not have spoken of it." Father scrubbed a hand across his chin. "I forget that you do not know or understand such matters."

Patience's neck heated at his words. He was right, but how could she know or understand as he did? She had been here little more than a sennight, while he had lived in Boston over two years now.

"Patience's time and attention has been devoted to other things this past year." Will's voice held a hard edge. "I would not fault her lack of knowledge, given her dedication to caring for Mother."

Father's gaze flicked to William, his brows drawn low and his mouth a tight line. Will's accusation was clear. Father's negligence in returning home had placed the full burden of Mama's illness and death upon their shoulders, Patience's most of all.

Father opened his mouth to reply, but Patience cut in hastily, hoping to stave off an angry exchange. "I would like to understand more now, though. You said these men, the Sons of Liberty, are protesting the tax on tea. Do they act alone, or are there others here in Boston who feel the same?"

Father's attention turned back to her. He swigged his drink before replying. "There are others. Rabble rousers who have stirred up trouble ever since I've been here, and years before. They are known to set mobs upon those who hold different opinions than them, to tar and feather and use other manners of force to intimidate."

Patience's eyes widened. "Are they all so dangerous? The men at the wharf did not seem so. Intimidating, indeed, but organized and under control, not an unruly mob."

"They are all dangerous in their own way. Even those men who do not have a hand in violence are still a threat, for in their minds and hearts, they harbor rebellion while parading amongst their loyal neighbors as if we were all equal citizens."

Libby coughed, drawing Patience's attention across the table. Her stepsister held a hand to her chest, clearing her throat as though a piece of food were lodged there, but the spark of anger in her eyes told a different story. Beside her, Mary kept her face down, but crimson crept up the sides of her neck and into her cheeks.

Patience bit her lip. What if Libby and her mother held to such beliefs as those Father was disparaging? After all, both women had lived their entire lives in America. Was it not possible that their loyalty was rooted in this land they had always called home rather than devoted to a king and country they had never set foot upon?

Patience furrowed her brow and turned back to her father. "I know I have not been here long, but I would like to think that men can still be neighbors and friends, despite their differences of opinion."

"That would be a naïve thought, indeed." He reached over and patted her hand, but if he meant for the gesture to soften his condescending words, it did nothing of the sort.

Beneath the table, Patience grasped her apron and twisted it in her fingers. Could Father not see Libby's and Mary's discomfort? Beside her, a muscle twitched in Will's cheek.

"You need not concern yourself overly much in understanding these matters." Father offered her a placating smile as he shoveled stew onto his spoon. "I know you are loyal to our homeland, and I will ensure you are not wrongly influenced by those who oppose us."

Patience could not bring herself to smile in return. She lifted her spoon and held it, hovering above her stew, but her appetite had disappeared. Father was right—she had no reason to be disloyal to England, yet it hurt to have her thoughts and questions dismissed. How was she to find her place here if she was never given the chance to learn and think for herself?

"I have followed the news of these colonies for quite some time." Will's voice broke through the silence. He propped his elbows on the table, his gaze fixed on Father, a glint of challenge in his stormy eyes. "I must admit that I sympathize with some of the colonists' complaints."

"You sympathize with them?" Father's face grew scarlet as he spat the words. "And what business have you to speak on such things? You have walked these shores for mere days and plan to leave as soon as you are able."

"I might turn the question back at you." Will tipped his chin. "Why do you hold so tightly to your loyalty to England, yet you chose not to come home, even when your wife was dying and your children left to care for her alone?"

Father slammed his hands on the table. Patience cringed as stew splattered from the side of her bowl. "You will not speak to me that way. You may be a grown man, but you will not disrespect me."

"I merely stated the truth of the matter." Will's calm, quiet voice seemed to echo even louder than Father's angry tone. "You may perceive it in whatever way you wish."

Father shoved back his chair, glowering at Will. "You can claim what you'd like, as you always have, but you understand very little."

Patience hunched lower in her chair, wishing she could run from the room. If only she had not asked questions, this argument could have been avoided. Mary and Libby both kept quiet, their heads down, expressions hidden, as if they, too, wished to disappear.

"I will discuss this no further." Father squared his shoulders and turned his back to Will. "Mary, Elizabeth, please excuse my son. It has been a long day, and I shall retire early this evening."

With that, Father stormed from the room, leaving a heavy silence in his wake.

"I apologize for any discomfort my words caused you." Will peered across the table at Mary and Libby, then turned to Patience. "I am sorry."

She shook her head, but no words would come. He did not need to apologize. While she wished Will's reply had not caused such trouble, she knew it came from a place of hurt, much like her own.

They had both struggled to comprehend Father's absence in the midst of Mama's illness, despite the reasons he gave in his letters. Patience had long tried to make excuses for him, but she knew Will had no place in his heart for excuses. He had held a deep-seated anger for years, even if he tried to hide it from her.

There was no hiding it tonight.

As Will excused himself from the table and Patience joined Mary and Libby to clean up the kitchen in awkward silence, she wondered how she might repair the damage her simple questions had caused.

CHAPTER 9

*P*atience woke later than usual on Sunday morning after a night of restless sleep, her mind whirling with thoughts she could not tame. Friday's stormy weather had abated, but Will and Father's argument at dinner had brought a different kind of storm that hung about the house like a dark, heavy cloud.

Father had left early yesterday morning, without more than a few words to anyone, and had returned late, missing the evening meal to dine with a friend instead. Will, too, had disappeared for much of Saturday, and Patience had yet to be able to ask him where he had gone.

She climbed out of bed, sucking in a breath at the chill of the wide wooden floorboards against her bare feet. For years, she had heard talk of the growing unrest between England and the American colonies, but she had never paid those discussions much mind. Now she wished she had. If she could have spoken more intelligently with Father, Will would not have felt the need to speak up in her defense and the argument would have never happened.

Perhaps today would be better. It was the Sabbath, and they

would attend church together. Hopefully, that would lead to a more peaceful feeling amongst the family. Patience still wished to find a way to spend time with Father alone. Maybe she could be the one to help mend his relationship with Will.

Despite the later hour, Libby still slept soundly, so Patience dressed hurriedly and crept downstairs. She found Will in the kitchen standing before the freshly stoked fire. He stared into the flames, but when he did not even stir at her entrance, it was evident his thoughts were far away.

When she came to stand by his side, he turned. Weariness etched his forehead, and Patience's heart ached at the sight.

"What were you thinking of just now?" She peered up at him. "You seemed far from here."

He rubbed a hand over the light stubble on his jaw. "I cannot hide much from you, can I?"

She smiled briefly as she lifted the kettle from where it sat on the floor beside the hearth. She peeked under the lid to ensure it was full, then hung it on the hook of the crane and swung it over the fire. Will would speak when he was ready. She'd learned long ago that more words from her would not serve to hurry him in any way.

"I wonder if I should have refused Father's request. If I should have kept you in England, continued our life as it was there."

Patience stared at him, wide-eyed. "You regret coming that much?" Boston and the life they'd stepped into here was not what she'd expected, but still, she could not imagine defying Father's wishes.

"I cannot say I regret it when I know you desired to come." He turned to the large wooden table in the center of the room and sank into one of the chairs beside it. "I had hoped Father would be different, more to your expectations, and now I worry you will be disappointed."

Will had never spoken quite so plainly about their father.

He was always honest, but she knew he often tempered his words to shelter her.

Patience brushed her hands on her apron and joined him at the table. Scuffs and scrapes on the top bore witness to years of use. She ran her fingers over a deep gouge in the wood. What had caused such damage? Was her heart at risk of a similar wound?

Will pushed a hand through his sleep-mussed hair. "I'm sorry. I should have kept such thoughts to myself."

"Nay. I asked. I wished to know."

They sat in silence for a long moment, before Patience crossed the kitchen to the shelves spanning the wall between the windows. She reached for the tin of bohea tea perched upon one shelf. Lifting the lid, she tilted it toward her face, leaning closer to breathe in the smoky scent.

"What do you know about the problems regarding the tea?" She carried the tin to the table, settling into the chair beside Will. "I cannot help thinking that if only I understood more, everything on Friday could have been avoided."

"You are not to blame for that. I shouldn't have provoked him."

"I was glad you spoke up. I didn't know how to respond when he dismissed my curiosity, as though my thoughts did not matter."

"In truth, despite my own frustration with Father, I do not think he meant his words to you to be hurtful." Will placed a gentle hand atop her own, his eyes reflecting a deep sadness that, for once, he did not try to hide. "He was already upset about the tea, so what I said regarding Mama only served to fuel his anger."

What Will had said Friday night was true. Nearly all her energy, all her thoughts had been focused on Mama. And Father hadn't been there.

Patience swallowed, unable to speak past the lump in her

throat. Despite the disappointments of the past, Patience had always determined to see Father in the best light possible. Perhaps because she so dearly wanted her own vision of the man to be true.

She longed to move forward, put the past behind them, and make a fresh start. She could forgive Father's careless words, forget the years they were apart, and build something new. But could Will do the same? Did it even matter? He was going to leave, after all.

"Will? When you return to—"

He shook his head "I will not leave yet. I cannot. I have determined to stay through the winter, at least."

"But what of your press? And Charlotte?" Patience frowned. 'Twas a great sacrifice for him to stay, to leave his print shop and the woman he cared for behind even longer.

"The press is in good hands, and I've written to Charlotte. You have nothing to be sorry for. It is my choice. I want to be here with you."

They stared at the flames dancing in the hearth for a long moment, then he reached for the tin of tea. "In answer to your question, the colonists are displeased with the tax on tea."

"Is the tax so oppressive?"

"Nay, it is a mere three pennies to the pound." He lifted a pinch of dry black leaves from inside the tin. "The tax has been in place for six years. There were other taxes upon the colonies as well, on glass, paper, oil, and such."

"I remember you speaking of those in the past. The colonists boycotted, did they not?"

"Indeed, and all the others were repealed three years ago. Only the one on tea remained."

"Then the colonists were successful in their pursuit, for the most part. Why are they choosing to take such a stand against the tea tax now, after it has been in place so long?"

"Many have stood against it for years already, refusing to

drink tea imported from England. They buy smuggled goods instead, or abstain from tea altogether." He dropped the leaves back into the tin. "But it seems the Tea Act that Parliament passed in May was the final straw."

"Did the act add more taxes?"

"Nay, it was put in place for the benefit of the British East India Company. A way to bail them out of debt. No new taxes, but it undercuts American merchants and gives the Company a monopoly on tea. Not to mention, further feeds the unrest that already existed." He crossed his arms over the table and leaned closer. "It is not so much the tax itself that angers them but what it represents. They see it as England's way of demonstrating power over them. A tangible reminder that the king and parliament can make and enforce any laws they should wish, and the citizens living here have no say in the matter. No taxation without representation—that is their claim."

"And you think they are correct?"

He leaned back, quiet for a long moment, then nodded. "I believe so. They are British citizens and see themselves as such, no less than you or I. All they seek are the same rights that other British citizens hold. To be treated as equals."

Patience twisted a strand of hair that had escaped her cap. "How do you know all this? I am ashamed to be so ignorant."

"Uncle kept informed of as much news as he could, even if we did not print all of it in our paper for the town to read. It always interested me. I've kept abreast of the tensions between England and these colonies for years now." Will placed a hand on her shoulder. "You have no reason to feel ashamed. Your mind and your time were occupied with Mama's needs. You stepped in to run our household when she could not, and you cared for her well. I was, and am, very proud of you for that."

Patience ducked her head and swallowed. "I miss her."

"As do I." Will squeezed her shoulder before releasing it

and leaning back in his chair, long legs stretched beneath the table.

The stairs creaked as slow, uneven steps descended. Father's gait. Will must have noticed as well, for he straightened and seemed to brace himself for their coming encounter.

Patience brushed her hands on her apron and hurried to the fire. The water was boiling, but she'd not prepared anything else for breakfast, so caught up as she was in conversation. Wrapping her apron around her hand, she lifted the heavy kettle from the hook. Hopefully, Father would not mind waiting a bit longer for his food.

She turned as he shuffled into the kitchen. "Good morning, Father."

"Good morning." His greeting was markedly less enthusiastic. Dark shadows lingered under his eyes. He rubbed his forehead and grimaced. "I am rather unwell and regret that I will not be attending church today."

"Can I offer something to help you feel better?" Patience eyed the shelves. "I will prepare some tea and—"

"Do not trouble yourself. Too much rich food, too little sleep." He pressed a hand to his protruding stomach. "Perhaps coffee instead."

Likely, too much drink as well, given the smell that lingered about his person, though she dared not give voice to such a thought. "I will make some."

"Thank you." His face pinched in discomfort. "I shall be in the parlor."

"I will join you there shortly." Will stood, shoulders squared. "I've something I need to discuss."

Father eyed him a moment, then nodded. "If you wish."

As Father departed, Patience glanced at Will, her brows raised.

"I must speak with Father about my plans to stay until spring. When I'm done, I shall take you to church." He started to leave, then turned and added, "I will try to mend things with him from the other night as well."

He headed for the parlor, and soon the rumble of their voices carried into the kitchen, though she could not discern the words.

Somewhere, in the memories she tried to keep hidden, she heard the echoes of Will and Father's past quarrels. Perhaps time had softened the sharp edges of their confrontations in her mind, or maybe she had chosen to forget in an effort to preserve her hope for a happy reunion.

She pressed her palms to the worn table, closed her eyes, and silently prayed for restoration of peace between the two men.

CHAPTER 10

*J*osiah found a place on a hard wooden pew in the spacious interior of Old South Meeting House just before the service was to begin. Lately, these walls had seen men pressed into every available corner, talk of the tea echoing throughout. But today was the Sabbath, and people gathered to worship instead. Josiah shifted in his seat as men, women, and children filtered through the door, filling the box pews below and the open spaces in the gallery where he sat.

Ever since the night he had pulled Papa's Bible from his trunk, Josiah had felt a nagging in his soul, like a sliver burrowed just beneath the skin. A little painful and very hard to ignore.

Perhaps it was the reminder of his parents' strong faith that convicted Josiah of the weakness of his own. For the first time in a long time, that realization brought a sense of regret.

The congregation began to sing the familiar hymn, "O God Our Help in Ages Past." Josiah joined, listening more intently than he had before. He attended church regularly, out of habit, but the words of the hymns and sermons never lingered long in his mind or heart.

Now those words stirred something inside, as though his soul was like coals that had grown dim, waiting to blaze back to life. For years, God had seemed so out of reach. The Creator who watched His creation from afar. What interest would He have in a life so small as Josiah's?

The song ended, and the congregation took their seats as the reverend read the Scripture passage. Josiah clasped his hands in his lap, knuckles white, unexpected emotion clogging the back of his throat.

Had he been wrong all this time? Through the loss and loneliness of the past, he had stopped looking, stopped listening, stopped reaching out. But what if God was actually near him all along? The words of the hymn had declared God to be his help in ages past, his hope for years to come. Could that be true in his life? Could he feel God's nearness? Know His hope?

The reverend's voice rose louder, startling Josiah from his thoughts. The message had turned from one about the verses in the Bible to one that included the current struggles the citizens of Boston faced regarding the tea. He scanned the congregation, seeing many nods of agreement, quite a few stoic faces, and a handful of angry grimaces.

The words of the hymn came back to him once more—our guard while troubles last. Trouble seemed unavoidable now, with the tea ships docked in the harbor and the tax deadline looming mere days away. Would God be their guard in the midst of the uncertainty and trouble that might come?

Shifting in his seat, Josiah froze when a familiar profile caught his eye a couple rows down. Miss Abbott. She sat beside her brother, her slim fingers fiddling with the ribbon hanging from her cloak as she leaned forward. She seemed intently focused on what the reverend was saying, but Josiah could hardly process the man's words, for she had stolen every bit of his attention.

What was she doing here? Josiah was certain her father

never attended this place of worship. It appeared to be only her and her brother.

He should not stare, but he couldn't pull his gaze from her. She looked lovely with her delicate nose, full lips, and high cheekbones. She blinked and turned her face slightly, her gaze landing on him. Her eyes widened in recognition, and a small smile curved the edges of her lips. Josiah dipped his head, then yanked his attention back to the pulpit. He rubbed a hand over the back of his neck. He could only hope his admiration had not been evident in his expression.

When the service ended, Josiah stood slowly, contemplating whether to greet Miss Abbott and her brother or escape out the door and avoid any further interaction. Despite his efforts to convince himself that he could not pursue her in any way, the thought of another opportunity to spend time with her was appealing.

Before he could come to a decision, the pair headed his way, Miss Abbott gently tugging her brother's arm.

A broad smile lit her face. "Mr. Wagner. How good to see a familiar face here."

He nodded a greeting. "Good morning to you both."

"Father is unwell this morning, and William thought to bring me here thanks to my..."—she glanced up at her brother —"curiosity to know this town better."

"I hope you found what you were seeking, then."

Her gaze found his and held for a long moment. He swallowed, his words taking a different meaning in his mind than he had intended. She had come to Old South for answers of some sort, not to seek him out. Yet she had found him as well.

The faintest hint of color filled her softly curved cheeks, like the sun rising over the harbor, and she dropped her gaze.

A small furrow appeared between her brother's brows as he eyed them both. "I believe it was an enlightening trip. For both of us."

A passerby bumped Josiah from behind, pushing him closer to Miss Abbott's side. His arm brushed against hers, and heat spread through him like a bar of glowing iron just pulled from the forge. She smelled of rosewater and a hint of coffee, a pleasant combination, feminine and comforting.

"I beg your pardon." He stepped back, needing space between them.

"Perhaps we should move outside." Her brother gestured toward the stairs.

Josiah led their small party downstairs and out of the meeting house. A brief image flashed in his mind of escorting Miss Abbott home, strolling together at a leisurely pace, her hand tucked in the crook of his arm. He glanced at her brother, whose keen eyes fixed upon him.

"It is a fine day for a walk," Abbott said. "Would you like to join us?"

Josiah felt his brows rise but quickly schooled his expression to hide his surprise. "Indeed. I would like that."

Abbott led the way toward Beacon Street. Miss Abbott fell in step next to him, and Josiah came to walk along her other side.

"I wonder if you might be able to help me with something." Abbott glanced over his sister's head to meet Josiah's eyes. "Do you by chance know any printers?"

"Aye."

"Do you think any would be willing to take on another man? I have decided to stay longer in Boston and would like to have work while I am here."

"I am glad to ask my friend, Nathaniel Hadley, but he is just an apprentice, so I cannot promise..." Josiah hesitated, glancing at Miss Abbott, who watched him expectantly. He hated to disappoint her, but the decidedly Patriotic *Boston Gazette* was likely a poor match for her brother, so recently arrived from England, and with a devout Loyalist for a father.

"William ran his own print shop in England," Miss Abbott said. "He apprenticed with our uncle and took over publishing the paper when Uncle Silas died. He does very well and would be a great asset to your friend and the newspaper."

Josiah couldn't hold back a smile at her enthusiastic praise of her brother. She must have thought his hesitation reflected doubts as to her brother's abilities. Abbott might not desire to work for such a publication as the *Gazette,* but Josiah couldn't bear to douse Miss Abbott's hopes. He turned to her brother. "I cannot make any promises, Mr. Abbott, but I am happy to introduce you."

"Thank you. I appreciate your help. And please, you are free to call me William."

"Aye, William, then. If you are able, I can take you to the press tomorrow morning."

William nodded, but it was Miss Abbott's face that drew Josiah's attention. Her broad smile made the dimples he had come to admire appear on her cheeks. As she looked up at him, Josiah was certain he would do almost anything to receive such a smile again.

～

*P*atience tilted her head to stare at the bare branches of the tree she and Will passed beneath as they walked home. They stretched toward the clear sky like fingers reaching for the sun. Despite the barrenness of winter, the open space before them and the fresh air were invigorating.

Mr. Wagner had parted ways with them after arranging a time to meet with Will tomorrow. She had rather hoped he would walk with them longer. His nearness as they strolled past the Common had warmed her more than the sunshine. More than once, she'd wished for some excuse to take his arm, though such an action would have been awkward under Will's watchful gaze.

Something about Mr. Wagner's presence made her pulse flutter like the last leaves clinging to the trees. Her thoughts had wandered to him more than she'd like to admit since their walk in the Common last week. Their conversation had lingered with her ever since, making her feel connected with him despite their brief acquaintance.

She couldn't deny that she found him handsome as well. Broad in the shoulders, he carried himself with an obvious strength. His straight nose and square jaw gave him a serious expression, but today, when he had smiled at her, his whole countenance transformed. She wanted to see that smile again.

She glanced at Will and found him watching her.

"You like him." Will clasped his hands behind his back. It was a statement, not a question, yet he continued to look at Patience, awaiting her response.

She could feel her cheeks warming and looked away, feigning interest in the scenery. "I am not sure what you mean."

He chuckled. "I am quite certain you know exactly what I mean. But I'll not push you."

A sigh escaped her lips in a puff of heat that clouded the air. Will might not ask more, but her thoughts spilled out, anyway. "I hardly know him. He seems to be a good man, though. And don't you think it interesting that we have met several times now, though we've been in Boston little more than a week?"

"Interesting, indeed."

She shook her head at his teasing tone and changed the subject. "Are you really going to take work at the press?"

"I am, if they are agreeable to having me. I do not wish to feel beholden to Father while I'm here."

"Or is it because you are afraid Libby will force you to learn how to knit if you remain at home?" Patience shot a grin at him.

"She has managed to encourage you in it, at least."

"I suppose she has. Though I believe the weather may have been a more convincing factor. I doubt I shall ever match her enthusiasm or skill." She stepped around a muddy puddle. "Why did you choose to attend Old South today?"

"I thought, after our conversation this morning, it would be helpful for you to see another side of Boston."

"I was surprised when the reverend spoke of the tea crisis in the midst of the service. It seemed as if he almost meant to encourage rebellion, or at least not condemn the outcry against the tea."

"That is because many in the congregation at Old South are Patriots. Did you notice their response to the reverend's words?"

"I did." Many in the congregation had nodded their agreement to the words spoken from the pulpit. She had even heard a few exclamations from the gallery.

Was Mr. Wagner one of the Patriots? If so, her budding interest in him was misplaced. Father would certainly disapprove.

A dry leaf skittered across the ground in front of her and caught under the toe of her shoe as she walked. The pressure of her step cracked the brittle leaf into pieces.

She looked up at Will again. "How did you know that Old South would be so different from Kings Chapel?"

"I am curious, in my own right, to understand this town and its people. I've done a bit of exploring and have read the papers, of course." Will tugged at the sleeve of his coat. "I think it best not to mention this to Father, though."

Patience frowned. She had no desire to be deceitful, but she dreaded another confrontation. "Let us hope he does not ask." They turned onto Marlborough Street. They were nearly back to the house, and the opportunity to speak freely would soon be over. "I suppose I'll have to wait until another walk for you to tell me more."

Will chuckled. "And can you truly wait much longer for that, *Patience*?"

He emphasized her name in a teasing tone that brought a rueful smile to her face. She raised her brows and widened her eyes in an innocent expression.

This time his laughter burst forth from a broad smile that crinkled the corners of his eyes. It warmed her heart to hear him laugh so deeply again. It was the first time he'd done so since they arrived.

His smile faded, though, as they approached the house and spotted Father, just stepping out of the front door. Father looked up, and his eyes narrowed as he seemed to consider the direction from which they'd come, the opposite of Kings Chapel.

Father greeted them with a brief nod and pointed with his cane down the street. "I'm off to meet with Captain Bruce this afternoon. I trust you both enjoyed the service?"

Patience tightened her grip on Will's arm.

"We spent a lovely morning together and took advantage of the pleasant day to walk the Common once more." Will's words were truthful without revealing more details than necessary regarding their whereabouts.

"Good," Father said. "I will see you both this evening, then."

He turned and limped away, his slow gait an ever-present reminder of the injury he'd suffered. The injury that had kept him from his family for so long. Though, the more Patience thought on it, the more she wondered if she could blame the injury alone for his absence. He had some choice in the matter. He could have made a different decision.

She shook away the thought, determined not to judge too harshly. She'd not had the chance to talk to Father yet as she wished, to seek some answers to the questions that plagued her. She committed to do so as soon as possible.

CHAPTER 11

"I am a fool," Josiah muttered to himself as he strode down Marlborough Street on Monday morning. He should have told William to meet at the press, but the hope of seeing Miss Abbott again had caused him to volunteer to come to their home instead. Why could he not shake his thoughts of her? He had never been so distracted by a woman before.

There was a depth behind her dark eyes that he longed to explore. He'd gathered bits of information about her much as he saved scraps of iron at the end of the day in his smithy. But just as he melded those pieces of iron together to create something new, he longed to take the little snippets he knew of Miss Abbott and put them together to know her better. To understand her story, who she truly was inside.

For some inexplicable reason, he felt connected to her, as though the lives they'd both lead tied them together in some way. He could give no logical explanation to such feelings, but neither could he deny his desire to see her and speak with her again.

He peered at the thick clouds hanging heavy in the sky and steered his thoughts toward another matter of great importance

—the tea. The tax deadline for the *Dartmouth's* cargo loomed mere days ahead. If they were unsuccessful in convincing the tea consignees to allow the cargo to return to England...

His thoughts and his feet came to an abrupt halt at the sight of Miss Abbott hauling a bucket of water around the side of the house. Her attention was on the ground as she stepped carefully around a patch of mud, giving him a chance to observe her a moment.

He'd told Nathaniel she was the prettiest girl he'd ever seen. At the time, he'd said so simply to elicit a laugh from his friend. But now, with the breeze tugging at the dark hair that escaped her cap and brushing it across cheeks made rosy by the chill, he thought his previous words were quite true, indeed.

She rounded the corner and looked up, her gaze colliding with his and a smile brightening her face. "Good morning, Mr. Wagner."

"Good morning. May I help you?" He strode closer and extended a hand toward the full bucket.

"Thank you."

He clasped the handle, his fingers closing over hers for the briefest moment. Heat rose through his chilled fingertips and spread up his arm at the contact. She sucked in a quick breath. Had she felt what he did at their touch?

She stepped back but still stood close enough that he could reach out and touch her again if he wished. He grasped the handle tighter.

"You've come to see William?" Her breath clouded the cold morning air in the small space between them.

"Aye." And to see her as well, though he would not speak that thought aloud.

"I must thank you for what you are doing for him."

"I'm glad to make the introduction, but I cannot promise anything beyond that."

"I understand, and I thank you all the same for your willingness to try." She glanced at the house. "Will and Father do not always get along well. I believe it would make Will much happier to have work of his own again."

"I hope I'll not make things more difficult between them by helping your brother." George Abbott would not approve of his son working at the *Boston Gazette*. Perhaps offering to help was a bad idea.

"Do not worry yourself on that account. Will is grateful, and I am hopeful that Father will come around." She dipped her head for a moment, and when she looked up at him again, her eyes bore an expression he'd not seen before, a shyness of sorts mixed with a spark of admiration. "I must thank you as well for your kindness to me. Did you know that you were the first person to speak with me when we disembarked the ship?"

"Was I?" He found himself stepping closer. To block her from the wind, he told himself, though in truth, it was more than that. The glow in her eyes was like an ember, and he could not resist the pull of their warmth.

"Your presence was such a comfort to me. Your willingness to help a stranger made me feel less alone." Her voice was gentle, and she looked at him with a guileless expression that bolstered his courage to speak frankly.

"I recognized something in you that reminded me of myself when I first arrived in Boston." His words came out just above a whisper.

"Now that I know you a little more, I can understand, for if I felt lost in those short moments, I can only imagine how you must have felt as a boy."

Josiah dipped his head as her words burrowed deep into his heart. How long had it been since someone understood him in such a way?

"I am sorry to upset you. I did not mean—"

He reached out to touch her arm, his fingers brushing over the wool fabric of her cloak for the briefest of seconds before his hand dropped to his side again. "You did not upset me. Quite the opposite. I am glad I was there to help when you arrived, to be the person I did not have as a boy."

She smiled at him, and it was all he could do not to reach for her again. To clasp her hand in his own or brush her wind-blown hair off her cheek. How soft would it feel, beneath his callused fingers? What would she think of so bold an action? He swallowed. He could not, would not, take such liberties.

A rosy hue filled her cheeks, more than was already there from the cold. He'd been staring at her too intently, hadn't he? Yet she did not look away.

He shifted the bucket to his other hand. "Miss Abbott—"

Out of the corner of his eye, a movement in the second floor of the house drew his attention upward. A figure stood at the window, but the curtain shifted closed before he could recognize who had been watching their conversation. Hopefully, not George Abbott. The man was not likely to approve of his daughter lingering outside talking with Josiah.

It was enough to interrupt the moment. He huffed out a cloudy breath. "It is cold. I should not keep you here any longer."

She nodded and moved toward the house. He fell in step beside her but came to a halt when she paused just outside the front door.

"Mr. Wagner?" She turned to face him again. "What is it that you were going to say?"

"Only that..." He glanced at the solid wood door, then back at her. "I am glad I was there the day you arrived, and I am even more glad to have met you again since."

The smile that bloomed on her face stole away any sense of cold from the December air. "Me as well."

He held the door for her as she led the way inside. She peeked over her shoulder and gestured to the left. "The kitchen is this way. Will is waiting there."

Josiah followed her into the cozy room, so much more welcoming than his own meager kitchen. The smell of hotcakes lingered in the air.

William rose from his spot at the table when they walked in. "Josiah. Good to see you."

Mrs. Abbott stood beside the fire, shoveling glowing coals into the bread oven. She glanced up, offering a quiet greeting.

"Where would you like this?" Josiah held up the bucket of water and raised his brows at Miss Abbott.

"Just here on the table."

He did as she directed, then turned to her brother. "Should we be off?" As much as he wished to extend his time with Miss Abbott, he needed to make the trip to the press and back to his smithy again before the morning was through. And he was not certain he could hide his growing feelings for her from her too-observant brother for long.

William nodded, and within minutes they set off for Court Street. It was a short walk, and they kept a brisk pace, Josiah's thoughts racing even faster than their footsteps.

This was a terrible plan. Josiah had been so eager to see Miss Abbott's smile, so hopeful that a connection with William would allow him to see her again, that he'd thrown off common sense. He'd spoken to Nathaniel last night, and while his friend had agreed to facilitate an introduction at the press, Nathaniel voiced the same concerns Josiah held. Concerns that only grew stronger with each step. William was certain to take offense to the politics of the *Gazette*. Though Josiah firmly believed their cause was right, he could not expect a man so newly arrived from England to sympathize with them.

Which meant he could not expect Miss Abbott to either.

He brushed the unwelcome thought away and cleared his throat. Best address the issue before they arrived. "I did not mention this when we spoke yesterday, but the *Boston Gazette* is a rather radical paper. The publishers, Edes and Gill, hold a decidedly Patriotic position. With you just come from England and your father a Loyal—"

William cut him off with a wave of his hand. "That does not bother me. It may surprise you to hear, but I can understand the Patriots' cause."

"Indeed?" Josiah couldn't hide the shock in his voice.

"I've followed the news from America these past years, ever since I began as an apprentice in my uncle's shop. He always encouraged me to keep abreast of it as much as possible."

"But will it not upset your father, if you are working with men so opposed to his beliefs?"

"My father is angry enough that I seek work printing at all. When I told him of my plans to stay through the winter, he was intent on bringing me into his business." William scowled. "He has never accepted the fact that I did not wish to follow in his footsteps. He refuses to acknowledge that I have a profession of my own."

Josiah glanced at William, unsure how to respond. It was evident that much hurt existed between the man and his father already. Miss Abbott had told him not to worry over his involvement, but if this job exacerbated their disagreements, would George Abbott place some blame on Josiah's shoulders?

"I will understand, though, if Edes and Gill do not wish to take me on due to my father's political stance."

"I cannot say." Josiah stepped aside as a horse clopped past them.

It was a precarious position, not only for William but increasingly for himself. Benjamin Edes was among the small circle of men to whom Josiah had reported Mr. Abbott's Loyalist leanings. Edes had enough discernment not to mention it today, but would he be suspicious over this intro-duction?

"Mayhap it is stubborn of me to seek work when I'll not be staying in Boston long, but I was certain my father would continue to push me to join him in his shop, and I needed something of my own."

"How long do you plan to stay?"

"Through the winter, at least. I have yet to determine. I had never allowed myself to think about how hard it would be to leave Patience behind. To be honest, I had hoped she would change her mind and return with me. Perhaps I can still convince her to do so, but I know how much it means for her to be reunited with our father again. I cannot imagine saying goodbye, especially with things so different here than we expected." William glanced sidelong at Josiah. "I must make sure she is truly settled and cared for before I can consider leaving."

Josiah swallowed the surge of protectiveness that filled his chest. He had no claim over Miss Abbott, no part in her life that he should feel so strong a desire to protect her. Yet the feeling blazed within him.

He clenched his jaw. He could not continue to entertain those feelings. William had just admitted how important it was to Miss Abbott that she maintain a relationship with her father. If she knew that Josiah had reported her father for continuing to sell British tea...

It didn't matter what he had seen in her expression this morning—he had to put her from his mind somehow, for there could never be anything more between them.

～

*P*atience dusted her hands on the apron tied about her waist and glanced at the front door again. It was well past midday and Will had yet to return from his visit to the press with Mr. Wagner.

"You need not fret about him." Libby peeked over her shoulder at Patience as she pulled a loaf from the bread oven, its fresh, yeasty smell filling the air. "It is likely good news that he has been away so long."

"I'm sure you are right." Patience sighed and turned back to the kitchen table. She set the next ball of dough on the long-handled wooden slab and carried it to the fireplace, sliding it into the oven to replace the one Libby had just removed.

Patience was glad for the task of baking bread, both to occupy her hands and her mind while she awaited Will's return. And while she pondered her conversation with Mr. Wagner.

His words echoed in her mind. Simple words, really, but in them she had glimpsed something deeper, as though he desired to say more but hesitated to do so. Or perhaps she only imagined it. Still, the way he had looked at her...

"Mr. Wagner is a good man." Mary glanced up from where she stood kneading dough at the table, her voice cutting into Patience's thoughts. "I am sure he will do all he can to assist William."

"Do you know him?" Patience hung the wooden slab on its hook beside the fireplace and turned to her stepmother, unable to hide the surprise in her voice.

"My late husband did. All that I ever heard regarding his character and his work were good reports."

"He told me about the deaths of his parents when we spoke last week. I cannot imagine arriving in a new country alone at such a young age." Patience bent to add a log to the fire, hoping her voice and expression did not betray how curious she was to know more about the man.

"It must have been difficult." Mary wiped the flour from her hands as she turned to look at Patience. "Yet God provided for him, as He does for all of us."

Patience met her stepmother's eyes and saw there a passing flicker of the same pain that lingered in her own heart. The pain of losing someone you loved. She dipped her head as a wave of shame colored her cheeks. Why had she not been more sensitive in considering the loss that her stepmother had faced? She could easily sympathize with Libby over the death of a parent, but somehow she had overlooked the fact that Mary would be grieving the loss of her husband.

"God's provision does not always come in the way we wish it to, but we must trust His love, wisdom, and sufficiency above our own desires."

Mary's words settled in Patience's heart, conviction rising like the bread they were baking. Was Mary's marriage to Father God's provision for herself and her daughter? It was not what Patience would have desired, and perhaps it was not what Mary wished for, either, especially so soon after her husband's death. But was it what they needed?

Patience's own plans for reuniting with Father had not been what she hoped, but did God have something more for her, for all of them, than she had the ability to comprehend? Was she letting her own disappointments cloud her trust in His infinite wisdom?

"You might be able to understand Mr. Wagner's experience better than you think." Libby nudged Patience's shoulder. Her voice took on a teasing tone. "But of course, you'd need to speak with him more to find out. Perhaps we can arrange—"

"Libby." Mary cut her daughter off with a firm tone, but her lips tipped up in a barely concealed smile. "You'd best tend those biscuits if you don't wish us to break our teeth on them."

Libby nodded her consent but tossed a wink toward Patience. Patience stifled a laugh.

The creak of the front door captured their attention, bringing silence to the room. Will entered, his eyes widening at the three women who stared at him in anticipation.

He squared his shoulders as a satisfied smile spread across his face. "Edes and Gill are pleased for the help. I return first thing tomorrow."

"Oh, I'm so glad!" Patience hurried across the room, arms outstretched, and grasped Will's hands.

"I'm glad to hear it." Mary's soft voice was accompanied by a sincere smile, and Will dipped his head in thanks.

He dug into his coat pocket and pulled out a folded scrap of newspaper which he handed to Patience. She took it, furrowing her brows as she looked up at him.

He lowered his voice so only she could hear. "I told you I'd answer your questions. What better way for a printer to answer but in print?"

She started to unfold the page, but he rested his hand atop hers, halting her motion.

"Best wait until later." He lifted his gaze over her shoulder to the other women.

Patience nodded, tucking the paper into her own pocket. Will was right. She didn't know what opinions Mary and Libby held and didn't wish to stir up trouble, especially when they had just begun to establish a sense of camaraderie.

Her curiosity over what the page said, much like her curiosity to know Mr. Wagner better, would have to wait.

CHAPTER 12

*J*osiah crossed his arms and leaned back in his chair, his belly full of a hearty meal. Across the table, Alexander soaked up the last of the stew from his bowl with a crusty hunk of bread while John Ward swigged his cider. Nathaniel sat beside Josiah, unfolding the newspaper he'd brought with him to their meeting. The din of conversation and the smells of food, ale, and smoke lingered in the tavern. Candles and firelight filled the room with dim, flickering light.

"The *William* ran aground east of Provincetown in last weekend's storm." Nathaniel handed the paper to Josiah, pointing to the article. "She was full of tea. One less ship for us to worry about."

"I hope the sailors are unharmed, though I have no regrets about the ruined tea." Josiah scanned the page briefly. "The tax deadline is this Friday. Four days left."

"And the Committees of Correspondence are meeting again as we speak." John thumped his empty mug on the table.

For the second time in several days, the Committees of Boston and five neighboring townships were gathered within the confines of Faneuil to discuss the tea crisis. Men from Dorchester, Roxbury, Brookline, Cambridge, and Charleston joined those from Boston and met for hours on end, though rumor had it the record of their meeting minutes read, *no business transacted.*

"Did you hear that Governor Hutchinson instructed Admiral Montagu to prepare for pursuit should the *Dartmouth* try to leave the harbor?" Alexander leaned closer.

Josiah shook his head.

"The armies at Castle Island have loaded their muskets and charged their cannon, even the forty-two pounders. They've stationed a battalion there, and Montagu's squadron is in place."

"They mean to intimidate us." Josiah scrubbed at the scruff on his chin. "Why Hutchinson thinks the *Dartmouth* aims to leave, I cannot say."

"A rumor, I suppose. There's been nothing on our part to suggest we'd attempt such a thing," Nathaniel said.

"Not without clearance from the customs officers, certainly." John propped his elbows on the table. "By my estimation, we'll be dealing with the tea in another way."

They all nodded their agreement as silence fell over the table. While many citizens still hoped to send the cargo back to England, each day that passed made that resolution feel increasingly unlikely. More and more, it seemed that the secret plan forged by the Sons would be necessary to rid Boston of the despised tea.

"As to that..."—Alexander turned to Josiah—"might you have some spare mallets we could keep on hand, should the need arise?"

"I do, and an old axe I could mend, if it would be of use."

"It would. Can you have it ready tomorrow evening? I can come by the smithy after my watch at the wharf is complete."

"Aye."

"What more can we do to prepare?" Nathaniel pushed his dish out of the way.

"Have supplies ready—disguises, should you wish it—and continue to keep the details of our plan to yourselves." John kept his voice low. "We'll take each day as it comes."

Their conversation wound down, and the men bid each other good night. As Josiah made for home, the secrets he carried weighed heavier on him than usual. Waiting for the decision on the tea felt as if they were holding a flame over a stack of kindling. It was not a spark that could be easily extinguished, but at what cost would they reach their goal? Could they come to some peaceful understanding with England, or had the time for compromise passed? And if so, what did the future hold for these colonies, this town, and the people who dwelt within it?

What did the future hold for him?

Miss Abbott's smile flashed through his mind. Would that smile fade if she knew of his involvement with the Sons? Would the hint of admiration he thought he'd seen in her eyes turn to disappointment? Or was it possible she, like her brother, could have some understanding of their cause?

Reaching home, he pushed the door open and tugged off his overcoat. The words John had spoken swirled in his mind. *Take each day as it comes.* Perhaps he needed that same advice when it came to Miss Abbott.

Josiah stoked the fire, changed into his bedclothes, and climbed into bed. He tucked one hand behind his head, staring at the shadowy length of the ceiling beams barely visible in the darkness. The sturdy logs held the entire roof in place. If they were to crack, everything would collapse.

Would the decision they made regarding the tea be the crack that brought the battle for independence crashing down upon them? Only the coming days would tell.

~

*P*atience climbed into bed beside Libby and burrowed under the covers, pulling them close about her chin. The fireplace warmed the room well, but not enough to fully ward off the chill. The flickering flames cast dancing shadows, and Patience yawned, blinking slowly as the weariness of the day finally settled upon her.

Libby shifted on her pillow, turning to face Patience. "I saw you from the window this morning, speaking to Mr. Wagner when he came to meet with William." She kept her voice to a low whisper, but even in her hushed tones, Patience caught a hint of teasing. "What did he say? Do you have a fondness for him?"

Patience stifled a giggle at Libby's enthusiasm. "I do like him, but I think you imagine more than it is. Mr. Wagner is one of the few people we've met thus far, and he has befriended Will."

"And that is all?" Libby pursed her lips.

"I hardly know him."

"People can develop feelings for each other quickly—even upon first meeting, I believe."

"Do you speak from experience?"

"I thought myself in love once." Libby shrugged, her hair tumbling about her shoulders at the movement. "It wasn't real, of course. I was far too young, just four and ten, and he saw me as nothing more than a child."

Patience shifted in bed, tucking one hand under her pillow. "Now I'm curious."

"He was a British soldier. An officer my father befriended. But it was nothing, truly." She tucked a strand of hair behind her ear. "Don't try to turn the subject away from yourself."

Patience laughed at Libby's astuteness. "I cannot deter you, can I?"

Libby grinned.

"Fine. I will admit that I have..." Patience flipped to her back, staring at the flickering light upon the ceiling, searching for the right words to express her feelings. She didn't think herself in love, certainly, but she did have more interest in Mr. Wagner than she had for any other man she'd met before. "I am curious to know him better. Will that suffice?"

Libby sighed. "I suppose it must."

Silence settled between them, and Patience closed her eyes, waiting for the drowsiness she'd felt just minutes ago to overtake her again. But now her mind was alert, remembering the words Mr. Wagner had spoken and the tenderness she'd seen in his eyes. Was it possible, as Libby said, that a man and woman could develop feelings for one another of such a nature even after so short a time?

"What about Mr. Cunningham?" Libby's voice broke into her thoughts.

Patience turned over to face Libby again. "What do you mean?"

"Do you have any interest in him?"

"I know even less of him than of Mr. Wagner. I've only met him once, and briefly, at that." Patience propped her elbow on the mattress, resting her chin in her palm. "Though he did offer an invitation to dinner, which Father seemed quite pleased over."

"I am not surprised. After his father's death, Mr. Cunningham took over the family business...and fortune. Your father has worked closely with him this past year. Mayhap your father hopes to further their connection through something more personal."

Heat filled her cheeks. Father had seemed rather eager to introduce her to Edward Cunningham. Was Libby implying that he hoped for a match between them?

"I've only just arrived. Father and I have not been reunited long. I cannot imagine..."

"You cannot imagine that he would desire to see you married, and separated from him...again." All teasing disappeared from Libby's voice. "I am sorry. I should not have suggested as much."

"Nay, you needn't apologize." She sank back into her pillow, wrapping her arms around her chest.

"Well then, I suppose you would not mind if I mention that while Mr. Cunningham is quite handsome, Mr. Wagner is even more so."

Patience couldn't keep another hushed laugh from escaping. Nor could she contain the yawn that followed. Sleep blurred the edges of her thoughts, like fog shrouding a landscape at dawn. She tried to settle her mind on the hazy silhouette of Mr. Wagner's broad shoulders and gentle smile, but it was a vision of Father proudly introducing her to Mr. Cunningham that overtook her consciousness before sleep claimed her.

CHAPTER 13

*P*atience pushed through the door to Father's shop the next afternoon, balancing a basket on her elbow and praying he was not busy with customers. He looked up from where he sat bent over the ledger, penning something into the thick book. A smile grew on his face, drawing one of her own in reply.

"Patience. I did not expect to see you."

"Hello, Father." She crossed the room and placed the basket atop the counter. "I thought I might surprise you with a special delivery." She lifted the cloth draped over the food to hold in the warmth. Steam rose from the stack of fresh corn cakes inside, and a hint of sweetness filled the air, thanks to the honey Patience had added to the recipe.

He closed his eyes and breathed deeply, then reached for a corn cake and ate nearly half of it in a single bite. "This is quite a welcome surprise." He spoke around the mouthful of food.

When Father had set out earlier in the day, bemoaning the overcast sky and damp, cool air, Patience had determined to make a trip to his shop for the midday meal. Hopefully, this gesture would help him see how much she cared for him, how she desired to be part of his life. If the shop stayed quiet as it was now, they might finally have an opportunity to speak more together. There was so much she wished to understand about him and so much she wanted him to know about her.

She could not rid herself of the words Libby had spoken last night, revealing her suspicion that Father might hope for a match between Patience and Mr. Cunningham. The conversation swirled in her mind, like sand spilling down an hourglass, pushing Patience to move with more urgency in her quest to build a relationship with her father.

He crossed his arms and leaned heavily on the counter as he chewed. He finished the first cake and reached for another but paused before lifting it to his mouth and looked at her. "Thank you, my dear girl, for bringing this. It cheers me greatly, as does your company. Business has been regrettably slow these past weeks."

"I am sorry to hear that." She ducked her head and followed the path of her finger as she traced it along the edge of the countertop. "Though I am glad for the excuse to spend more time with you."

Father reached across the space between them, his large hand enveloping hers and stilling her movement. Patience looked up and found a tenderness in his eyes that made her heart swell.

"And I you." He patted her hand, then drew back. He turned to stare out the window, though it seemed his thoughts were somewhere much farther away than the street in front of his shop. "I am sorry that I was apart from you for so long. From all of you."

Her breath caught in her throat as all the questions she longed to ask flooded her mind at his words. Should she speak them aloud? Did she dare? While this time together might strengthen the tentative bond between them, she did not wish to hurt or anger Father by revealing the things she wondered about him. And yet, how could they truly move forward if the past was never addressed? It would hang over them forever, a storm cloud waiting to burst at any moment.

She clasped her hands at her waist and spoke so softly she was not sure Father would even hear the words. "We missed you very much."

He turned back to her, his brow furrowed and his mouth drawn down at the corners. "I missed you as well. I always did."

She nodded.

"Your mother and I..." He paused and swallowed. Cleared his throat. "We loved each other, but we were quite young when we wed, and we had very little. I was determined to give her a better life." He brushed a crumb off the sleeve of his coat, eyes downcast as he continued. "I'd always been enamored with the sea. I knew I would not be content as my father was, building ships but never feeling the power of the waves beneath my feet as I stood aboard those vessels. Ever since I was a boy, I longed to sail out into that seemingly endless water. My love of the sea eased the difficulty in parting with your mother, but it did not negate my love of her. I hope you know that."

Patience pressed her lips together and blinked at the sting of tears. She had always told herself that her parents loved one another. That her father felt some sorrow and loss each time he said goodbye. But over the years, she'd begun to doubt those things she tried so hard to convince herself of. Hearing Father's words was a soothing balm, touching those places of doubt and covering them with reassurance.

"Mama loved you." She smiled through the sheen of tears. "She always had a different smile, a different look in her eyes when she spoke of you."

Father's chin quivered, and he ran a thick hand over his jaw as he composed himself. "I will never forgive myself that I was not there for her in the end."

Patience could not hold back the words yearning to escape. "Why did you not come home?"

For a long moment, he was quiet. He didn't look up at her as he fiddled with the stock neatly tied about his neck. Finally, he stood, the legs of the stool scraping noisily against the floorboards, a sound that made Patience wince.

She had pressed too far. Now he would be angry with her, as he was with Will when her brother threw accusations his way.

But Father's voice was low and calm, edged in regret, as he began to speak. "After the shipwreck, I was very ill. Still today, there is a stretch of months following the wreck that I cannot remember, no matter how hard I try." He paced slowly behind the counter, stopping to straighten a bottle here or dust a shelf there, as if the memories themselves set him in motion, too much to contain were he standing still. "I was told later that I had been near death for weeks. The bone did not set right. The wound was so bad that Doctor Caldwell thought I might lose my leg, if not my life. It is a miracle I survived."

Patience shuddered, though not for a chill in the room. She had read his letters so many times, she knew every detail by heart. Father had written of his illness, but never before had he spoken so plainly. To hear the words, to hear the ache in his voice as he said them, brought her own memories freshly to the surface.

She crossed her arms against her chest, running her hands over her upper arms to dispel the chill bumps that had risen there. "I will never forget the day we received your letter."

The smallest hint of a smile lifted Father's lips. "A letter as if from beyond the grave, I reckon."

"Very much so. When I saw the script, my hands started shaking such that I could hardly break the seal."

In December of 1771, they'd received official word from the East India Company that Father's ship had sank. He was not counted among the survivors. They had grieved, certain he was dead. But then, six months later, a letter appeared at their door, written in his familiar handwriting.

"Mama was certain you had sent it before the shipwreck and it had been delayed in coming," Patience said. "When we read what you had written and realized the truth, we were nearly overcome. Will returned from Uncle's shop to find us laughing and crying all at once."

His letter had brought news they could hardly fathom. He had survived the shipwreck that had destroyed his vessel and left most of the crew dead. He had clung to a piece of the wreckage and drifted in the current where he'd been discovered by some fishermen. His leg had been shattered by the falling foremast, and by the time he was rescued, he was too weak to speak, delirious from pain, cold, exposure to the elements, and dehydration. He could not even give his own name, let alone explain what ship he had come from.

The men had taken him to the nearest port, Boston, where he was cared for by Doctor Caldwell. Father had written his family as soon as he was well enough to do so but had explained in his letter that he was far too weak to travel home at that time.

Of course, they had understood. Even Will, despite his tenuous relationship with their father, was relieved to learn that he was alive.

Father swiped at the moisture gathering at the corner of his eyes. "I would have returned home with that letter if I was able. But I doubt I could have survived the journey."

"If only it did not take so long for our letters to cross the sea to one another. Perhaps things could have been different."

"Aye." He smoothed a hand over his wig. "By the time your reply reached me, I was healing well and had made connections with enough men in town that I had begun this position here." He gestured around the shop. "I knew my days at sea were over, but this was an opportunity to provide for my family in a different way. That is why I wished for you all to join me."

Patience shifted. This was the part she had struggled most to understand. If he was well enough to begin working again, why couldn't he have traveled back to England, not as a sailor but as a passenger? Certainly, he could have returned to Chatham, to his family, and found work there easily enough. Instead, he'd asked them to uproot from the only home they'd ever known and make the voyage across the ocean to join him in America.

By the time his request reached them that autumn, Mama had begun to decline. Her health had been poor for some time but worsened significantly in December. Will wrote back immediately, begging Father to return instead, for her sake. Patience had waited anxiously for him to appear at their doorway. Day after day, week after week, month after month as she cared for Mama, her waiting was met with silence.

A surge of emotion, something she could not—or perhaps dared not—name welled up inside of her. "Why did you not come back when Will wrote to you of Mama's illness?"

"I nearly did. I should have." His shoulders drooped, and he stared at the floor, his voice so low, she had to strain to hear. "There was a ship leaving a fortnight after the letter arrived. I thought to seek passage aboard. But I convinced myself otherwise. To my shame and regret."

Patience frowned and silently waited for him to go on. To explain what reason could have caused him to make such a decision.

"It was cowardly of me, a man who'd spent his life at sea, to fear crossing the Atlantic, but after the wreck I'd experienced..." He sighed and pinched the bridge of his nose. "I told myself she would get well and that when she did, it would be better to start a new life here. And if she didn't..."

His voice trailed off, and Patience swallowed, glad for once that he had not finished his thought aloud.

He stepped around the counter and reached for her hands, but his fingers were cold and clammy and didn't offer the comfort she so desperately needed. She stared at her smaller hands wrapped inside his larger ones, unable to force her gaze upward.

"Two months later, I was full of regret over my decision." His quiet admission brought her attention back to his face. To his downturned mouth and watery eyes and the sorrow etched in every line. "I found another ship to join and made arrangements to return. But William's second letter arrived days before I was to set sail."

Will's second letter. The one that bore the news of Mama's death. She could not hold back the tears that leaked from the corners of her eyes. If Father had sailed on that ship, he would have arrived too late. Perhaps even the first ship would not have borne him to them on time.

But at least she would have known that he had tried. At least they wouldn't have had to grieve alone with the uncertainty of his silence and absence adding a heavy weight to an already unbearable burden.

Instead, she and Will had waited, pushing forward each day through the fog of grief and doubt. She had tried hard to battle the emptiness that was so deep, it seemed bent on consuming her. Each day she had pressed on, surrounded by reminders of Mama and taunted by doubts about Father. Even the very roof above her head seemed as though it might crush her with its weighty silence, never again to echo with Mama's songs.

She had become so desperate to leave it all that when Father's last letter finally arrived, a missive filled with sorrow, apologies, and instructions for them to leave their home and join him in Boston, she had grasped hold of that thread of hope like a tiny bud in spring, stretching toward the sunlight. If she could escape that place, escape the grief that shrouded every corner, she could begin anew. She could never see Mama again this side of heaven, but she could be reunited with Father. He would make things right. He would help her find a way forward when she had so little strength of her own to do so.

Little did she know how different things would be when they arrived.

"I am sorry." Father's quiet words broke through her thoughts.

She wanted those words to be enough. Wanted his apology to soothe the ache of disappointment that no amount of excuses or reasoning had yet been able to. But wanting something did not make it true. She could accept his words, she could even forgive him, but the hurt was still there.

At the creak of the front door, he released her hands and stepped back, straightening his shoulders and smoothing his expression into one of a pleasant shopkeeper. Patience ducked her head and swiped at the tears on her cheeks. A pair of ladies entered, and Father greeted them. They moved to examine some fabric along the wall as Patience gathered the basket and made ready to leave.

She peeked at Father once more. His focus was on his customers, but he must have felt her gaze because he turned back to look at her once more.

"I am going to return to the house." She tightened the ribbons on her cloak and pressed her lips into a smile. "I am glad we were able to talk."

He nodded. "I will see you at home."

Patience pushed through the door and set off down the street, his words staying with her long after his shop had disappeared from view. For years, she had longed for this. For the simple pleasure of being able to share a home with her father. And yet, now that she had just that, why did the ache still linger?

CHAPTER 14

*J*osiah cupped his hands around the mug of ale on the table in front of him on Tuesday evening. The Green Dragon was full tonight, men crowding every table and spilling in and out the door, bringing waves of damp, cool air with them as they went. The breeze was a welcome relief from the tobacco smoke hanging heavy in the room and the yeasty smell of alcohol mixed with the sweat and dirt of men, most of whom had spent much of the day packed into Old South as he had. The body of the people had met once more, but still no decision had been reached. A steady din of conversation filled the room as groups of men discussed the events of the day.

Across the table, Nathaniel sat beside William. Josiah had been surprised when William arrived at Old South alongside Nathaniel. He knew the man was understanding of the Patriot cause, but Josiah hadn't imagined he'd go so far as to take part in a meeting. But William had watched the speeches and debates with rapt attention and rousing shouts of agreement.

Was it possible that Miss Abbott might not be opposed to Josiah for his Patriotic views? Despite all attempts to convince himself that his focus must remain on the plans for the tea and his duty to the Sons, he had utterly failed to keep her from his thoughts. Whenever he remembered the way she smiled at him, hope sparked in his chest like flint struck in the dark, bringing light to a part of him long shadowed and hidden.

Still, it was a fragile hope, for her father's loyalty remained a major impediment, even if she should choose to take the same side as her brother. She was so glad to be reunited with her father again, would she risk associating with someone like Josiah, knowing it could cause a rift between them?

"'Tis strange to think you sailed upon the *Eleanor*." Nathaniel's voice cut into Josiah's thoughts. His friend propped one elbow on the table as he spoke to William. "What did you think of Captain Bruce's response today, when he was asked if he would leave Boston with the cargo of tea still aboard?"

"I cannot say I blame him. He's right to be concerned about getting by the cannons of Castle Island without a pass." William drummed his fingers on the edge of his mug. "He was good to us, my sister and I, on our voyage. I feel for him in a way, being put in such a difficult position."

"Though they should have known, to some extent, the trouble it could bring to transport the tea in the first place. Tensions have been mounting for a long time now." Nathaniel leaned back in his wooden chair, crossing his arms over his chest. "And what of Rotch? He said he would apply for clearance of the *Dartmouth* but never did. Not until today, at least."

Francis Rotch, who acted as representative on behalf of the *Dartmouth,* had been called before the body of the people earlier that day. He'd confessed that his previous promises to request clearance had been made under duress, and as such, he'd not followed through. The man had seemed sincere in such a claim, but he could not put off the demands of the people any longer. A delegation of ten men, led by Adams himself, had accompanied Rotch to seek clearance from the customs officers, but the officers had refused.

"I heard they plan to send him to the naval office tomorrow to request a pass." Josiah rubbed a hand over his stubbled jaw.

"A request likely to be denied," Nathaniel said.

Josiah nodded. "I suspect you are right."

"What then?" William leaned closer, arms crossed over the scraped surface of the table. "If the *Dartmouth* cannot obtain a pass before the tax deadline on Friday, what is next?"

Josiah glanced at Nathaniel, who pursed his lips. Much as Josiah liked William, he still hardly knew the man, and some secrets were better kept to a very small circle. He stared at the amber liquid in his mug, contemplating how to answer without revealing too much or offending the man. "Then other actions will need—"

Josiah stopped as a hand clapped him on the shoulder.

Looking up, he saw Alexander Stevens standing behind him.

"Mind if I join you?" Alexander said.

Josiah stood and shook hands with his friend. He'd not seen the man since last Friday when they stood guard over the ships together.

"Of course." Josiah gestured to his now-empty chair, the only one unclaimed in the whole tavern. "Have my seat."

"I'll not stay long." Alexander sank into the wooden chair, stretching his legs out beneath the table with a smile. "Feels good to sit somewhere dry and warm for a spell." He nodded a greeting to Nathaniel, then turned to William. "Don't believe we've met."

"William Abbott."

"Alexander Stevens."

Josiah leaned against the wall, crossing his arms over his chest. "Any word on the *Beaver*?"

"She's arrived at Griffin's Wharf." Alexander cupped his

hands in front of his mouth and blew into them, rubbing them briskly together as he continued. "Finished her quarantine at Rainsford and has joined the others. All significant cargo still aboard, of course."

"Three ships." Nathaniel swigged his ale. "Over three hundred chests in all."

Alexander raised his brows. "Quite a load, that."

The men recounted the details of the day's meeting, Alexander cutting in from time to time to add something he'd heard or seen at the wharf. Josiah let his gaze wander the room. If he listened carefully, he could catch snippets of other conversations swirling around them. Almost all centered on the tea and what the next days might bring.

His gaze traveled to one of the dark windows. Did he dare hope the obstacles between himself and Miss Abbott could be overcome? Perhaps he should broach the subject with her brother. There might be some benefit in ferreting out his opinion on the matter, especially if William happened to be in favor of Josiah's pursuit.

"Where have your thoughts wandered off to, Josiah?" Nathaniel grinned at him. "Are you mulling over all that might happen this week, or thinking about that girl again? The prettiest one you've ever seen, I believe you said."

Heat rose up the back of his neck. "We all have much on our minds, I'm sure."

From the corner of his eye, he could see William's intent stare focused on him. The man's expression gave away nothing of his thoughts, but Josiah couldn't help but wonder if William suspected that the woman Nathaniel teased about was his sister. Josiah swallowed. Nathaniel didn't know of the connection, so Josiah couldn't blame his friend, though he would have been tempted to jam an elbow in his side had they been in closer proximity.

Alexander chuckled. "Well, I for one would rather have my

mind on a pretty girl than on crates of tea." He pushed back from the table, his chair scraping against the scuffed plank floor as he stood. "I'd best be off."

Josiah reclaimed his chair as Alexander departed. Nathaniel finished his drink, but William fixed upon Josiah with a curious stare. He tried not to fidget under such scrutiny. He was tempted to look away, but didn't want to appear as though he had something to hide. Even if he did.

Finally, William shifted his attention, peering out the window into the dark, starless night. "It's late, I should be getting home. I'm sure Patience will be worrying over me." Perhaps Josiah was hearing things, but it seemed that William put a bit more emphasis than necessary on his sister's name.

"I'll see you at the shop tomorrow." Nathaniel directed his words at William. He buttoned his coat, shifting his focus to Josiah. "Shall we meet at the smithy on Thursday and walk to Old South together?"

Josiah nodded. "Fine with me."

"Good." William stood and fixed his hat upon his head. "Perhaps then I can hear more about this pretty girl you've had on your mind." One corner of his mouth tipped up in the barest hint of a smile before he turned and headed out the door.

Nathaniel furrowed his brow. "I feel as though I might have missed something."

Josiah shoved a hand through his hair and threw a glare in his friend's direction. "The woman I spoke of before...she's William's sister."

Nathaniel's guffaw drew the eyes of more than one fellow patron. "And you have been thinking of her again, haven't you?"

Josiah pushed away from the table and tugged the edge of his coat. "As William said, it's late. I should be leaving."

Still chuckling, Nathaniel stood and slapped him on the

back. "As if this business with the tea wasn't complicated enough, you had to go and find yourself in love."

Josiah shook his head and followed his friend out the door.

Love? Certainly not. He could not commit to such a deep feeling after so short a time. And yet, for the first time, the word stirred something hopeful inside him. He had wondered if he could truly open himself to love, knowing that doing so put him at risk of enduring the same pain that he had as a child. Always before, his answer to such a question was no—it was not worth the cost. But now, for the first time, a quiet *yes* sparked in his heart.

CHAPTER 15

*P*atience stuck a clove into the onion's soft skin, turned it, grasped another tiny clove between her fingers, and pressed it in beside the first. Next to her at the worn kitchen table, Libby tied a bundle of sweet herbs while Mary sliced carrots. The rich scent of beef wafted from the pot hanging over the fire, where the meat stewed in a mixture of water and small beer.

Satisfied that the onion was well covered, Patience crossed to the fire and added it to the pot. She wiped her hands on her apron as she glanced out the window. Outside the light was already fading, the pale blue-gray of evening hovering over the bare tree branches and rooftops beyond. Father would be home soon.

She had thought over their conversation from yesterday many times, wrestling with her feelings on the things he had said, and what remained unsaid. She did not doubt the genuineness of his remorse over what had happened with Mama, and yet she still could not reconcile his reasoning in her heart. If you loved someone as much as he claimed to love

Mama, would you not do everything possible to be with that person? No matter how difficult, no matter the cost to oneself?

Much as she hated to admit it, she kept returning to the same conclusion—true love and devotion required sacrifice, but Father had sacrificed very little for Mama. He'd pursued his desire for the sea, even when she wished him to be home. He'd stayed in Boston because, as he explained, he had a good position to provide for them. But he could have found a position in Chatham easily enough. Was he too prideful to return home? Did he think he would be seen as a failure when he could no longer sail and had to settle for the kind of work he had so long despised? Even when Mama was sick, he had waited too long, indecisive about returning to her, his own fears outweighing her needs.

Another question plagued her mind. What had Father sacrificed for her? The answer hurt too much to consider.

She blinked and dragged her gaze from the darkening horizon, focusing on the stew instead. Perhaps it would help if she could speak with Will about the conversation she and Father had shared. Talking over her thoughts and feelings made them clearer than if she kept them bottled up inside. Mama had always been the person she depended on for such conversations, but Will had done his best to stand in her place.

Hopefully, he would be home soon. Although yesterday, he had returned much later than expected. When Patience asked him why he'd been out so late, he merely replied that there was work to be done. But his eyes had said more than his words implied.

Thankfully, Father and Will had seemed to come to some unspoken truce. There had been no more arguments over meals, no more raised voices from the parlor. But Patience suspected the peace between them was tenuous, and largely dependent on Will holding his tongue. She suspected he did so for her sake, more than anything else.

The front door thudded open, followed by heavy, uneven footsteps that Patience immediately recognized as Father's. She knew his evening routine well by now. He would stand in the entryway a moment as he removed his greatcoat and hung it from the peg on the wall beside the door. Then he'd stop into the kitchen with a brief greeting for the women of the house before trudging upstairs to change into his banyan and cap.

But today, instead of the usual shuffling of feet and rustling of fabric, Patience heard voices streaming from the doorway. Father's and another man's that sounded somewhat familiar, but not enough that she could place it. She glanced at Libby, who shrugged as she dropped the sweet herbs into the pot.

Mary crossed the kitchen, both hands full of carrots, and added them to the simmering liquid.

"Were we expecting company?" Patience kept her voice low as she stirred the ragout.

Mary shook her head and straightened her kerchief. "I'll go see who it is."

Before she could do so, Father's large form filled the doorway. "We've a visit from Mr. Cunningham." He glanced around the room, his eyes landing on Patience. "Patience, will you join us in the parlor?"

He disappeared back around the corner, and Patience blinked. She peeked at Libby, whose eyes had gone wide. Her previous implications over Father's desire for a connection between Patience and Mr. Cunningham seemed to echo between them.

Patience swallowed as she tapped the spoon on the edge of the pot and hung it from the hook on the mantel. She wiped her hands with her apron, aware that they smelled strongly of onion and clove, a pleasant scent for the kitchen but not for entertaining a guest.

"I'm sure your father can wait long enough for you to

wash." Mary smiled gently. "You may leave your apron here. Elizabeth and I will see to the meal."

Patience scrubbed her hands in the basin of water perched on the counter along the back wall and dried them on the edge of her apron where the fabric was cleanest. She untied the apron and draped it over a chair, smoothing her hands down the front of her petticoat. She'd worn a rather plain one today, a solid golden color that reminded her of late-summer wheat, with her navy short gown on top. At least her kerchief was a bit pretty, with little blue flowers stitched into the fabric.

Not that she worried much over what Mr. Cunningham would think of her appearance. He had appeared rather dashing when she'd first met him, and Libby had commented on his family's wealth. But Patience did not seek his good opinion that much, did she? No, in truth, it was more her concern for what Father would think of her that mattered. She did not want to disappoint him.

With that thought simmering in her mind like the stew in the pot, she clasped her hands a bit too tightly in front of her waist and headed for the parlor.

Father and Mr. Cunningham were seated side by side in the tall chairs before the fire. Mr. Cunningham glanced over his shoulder as she entered and immediately stood, his face breaking into a congenial smile.

"Miss Abbott, it is good to see you again."

She dipped her head. "You as well."

Father stood and motioned her over, offering up his seat. She took it, and Mr. Cunningham sat back down beside her while Father moved to the side of the fireplace, propping one arm against the carved mantel.

"I am afraid I come with some disappointing news." Mr. Cunningham shifted in his seat to face her fully. "I do apologize, but I must postpone the dinner invitation I offered when last we spoke."

Patience glanced at Father, but he did not reply. She tucked her hands in her lap. "I am certain we will be happy to come at another time."

"I am glad and look forward to hosting once this tea business settles down."

"Are you..." Patience pressed her lips together, searching for the right words that would assuage her curiosity. "That is, I do not wish to speak out of turn, but are you involved with the cargo aboard the tea ships?"

"I am a consignee." Mr. Cunningham rested an elbow on the arm of the chair. "But you, having so lately arrived, may not be familiar with what that entails."

Patience shook her head and swallowed against the rising sense that once more, she was an outsider, looking in on this world where she did not belong.

Thankfully, Mr. Cunningham's voice was free of condescension. "It simply means that it is my duty, alongside the other consignees, to receive the shipment of tea and arrange for its resale here in Boston."

Father shifted from his place beside the fire, the flames casting shadows against the wrinkled planes of his face and causing his stern brow to appear even more fierce. "The consignees have faced much harassment these past months from rebels and mischief-makers like Adams and Warren."

"Harassment? Truly?" Patience swung her gaze to Mr. Cunningham.

His blue eyes were serious, but his expression seemed more grave than angry. "In November, I was awoken in the middle of the night by a pounding on my door. All of the consignees were summoned to appear at the Liberty Tree, as they call it, to resign our commissions the next day."

Patience blinked, clasping her hands tighter in her lap.

"We did not go, of course. Instead, we gathered at Clarke's warehouse to discuss the matter."

"A violent mob stormed the building." Father's voice echoed in the room. Patience flinched at the sudden interruption. "They threw stones and mud and wrenched the door from its hinges."

"Were you injured?" Patience twisted the fabric of her petticoat in her fist.

"Thankfully, I was not." He stared into the fire, and his jaw tightened. "We managed to barricade ourselves in the second floor counting room until the crowd dispersed."

"I am sorry." Patience's whisper hung in the room as silence settled over them.

From her conversations with Will and the scraps of newspaper he continued to secret home from the press, Patience had learned more about the reasons for the Patriots' protests. She had started to feel as though there was some merit in their beliefs.

But this was something new. Something she had not heard before. A rioting mob threatening men who simply sought to do their duty? Could she truly align herself with people who behaved in such a way?

Unbidden, her thoughts strayed to Mr. Wagner. Despite his stature and the strength she'd seen in him as he worked at his smithy, he seemed to be one of the gentlest of men. Kind, too, in what he had done for Will. And sometimes, when he looked at her, it was as though, for the briefest moment, there was something in his eyes that she had never seen in another man's gaze. Interest that went deeper than friendship and warmed her from the inside out.

But he attended Old South, where the reverend spoke of independence, even rebellion, from the pulpit. And the press where he had helped Will secure a position was a patriotic newspaper. Mr. Wagner had never admitted it directly, but more and more, she suspected him to be on the side of the

Patriots. Would he approve of such behavior as that which Mr. Cunningham described? Worse, might he have been involved?

Mr. Cunningham rested his elbows on his knees, hands clasped in front of him as he leaned closer to the fire. Despite the events he described, he maintained a measured calm. Was he not upset by what had happened? Father certainly made no attempt to hide his feelings on the matter. Perhaps Mr. Cunningham was more practiced, more polished in his behavior. Or did he possess a similarly gentle nature to that of Mr. Wagner?

No, the two men were not alike in any way. Not in appearance, or mannerisms, or, if her suspicions were correct, in political beliefs.

Mr. Cunningham turned his head to look at her, as though he had felt her assessing gaze. She dropped her attention to her lap, but from the corner of her eye, she could still see him as he straightened in his seat, shoulders back, chin raised just a bit. That subtle movement revealed that his attitude was less that of a gentle spirit and more that of a man who was confident in his status and felt a certain measure of safety and protection as a result of it.

"We submitted a proposal to the governor's council regarding the myriad of insults and violence we suffered. We expressed our sincere concerns that the tea might even be destroyed upon its arrival." Mr. Cunningham shook his head. "To no avail, unfortunately."

"They had to flee town." Disgust tugged the corners of Father's mouth downward. "They relocated to Castle Island at the end of November for their own safety."

"But you since returned?" Patience furrowed her brow. She'd seen Castle Island, the small mass of land off the coast that bore a large military fortress. According to Will, the king's army was stationed there and heavily armed. It seemed strange to think of living there, hiding away within the safety of its stone walls.

"I did, but only briefly. When we met last week, I had come back to see to my mother and sisters. They remain here in town, and I worry over their comfort." He sighed. "I hoped to be able to stay with them, but this business over the tea has only escalated, and I am needed with the other consignees. I sail back first thing tomorrow morning."

Father crossed his arms over his chest. "Let us hope this matter will be dealt with soon, and with a finality that quashes any further protests of the sort that have overrun our town these past months."

"Indeed. We have our duty to perform. Our colleagues in London expect us to complete our half of the arrangement. We cannot comply with the requests of these committees." He sneered on the last word but then composed himself once more and stood with a tight smile for Father. "The deadline for the *Dartmouth* is Friday, just two days hence. I am hopeful for a favorable conclusion." He turned to Patience, who rose from her chair as well. "I apologize again for postponing our dinner, but I look forward to the opportunity of seeing you once more."

He bowed his head slightly, and Patience dipped her chin in return. Her cheeks heated from his words and from Father's steady gaze as he watched them.

Mr. Cunningham tapped his hat against his thigh before settling it deftly upon his head. "I'll bid you good evening. I shall send word when I am in Boston."

Father nodded. "We wish you a safe and swift return."

Patience murmured her own farewell as Father walked Mr. Cunningham to the door. She pressed her hands to her cheeks, dismayed by how hot her face felt. Should she be flattered by Mr. Cunningham's attention? Should she be convicted by the events he described? Perhaps so.

Instead, Mr. Cunningham's words and the ever-present uncertainties over the tea left her stomach churning and her heart aching for some semblance of peace that seemed as far away as a spring morning.

CHAPTER 16

*P*atience poked at the charred logs in the fireplace. She arranged fresh wood on top, then grabbed the hand-held bellow from its hook on the wall and pumped air onto the blackened coals. They flickered, dark edges turning orange for a moment, then faded again. Another burst of air, another attempt to flare to life.

The struggling coals seemed to reflect her own mood this morning. The conversation with Mr. Cunningham yesterday had left her confused, doubting herself and the things she thought she'd come to understand. Then Will was late, not returning home until after they'd finished the evening meal. Father had glared at him but said nothing, and while it was better than an all-out argument, the tense silence did nothing to ease her anxious thoughts.

At last, the coals glowed with new life, weak flames reaching tentative fingers toward the wood. Patience hugged her arms around her waist as she waited for the warmth and light to grow and fill the room. Outside, though dawn was nearly breaking, heavy gray clouds hung so low that it was unlikely she would see the sun all day.

She reached into her pocket, drawing out the most recent slip of paper Will had given her. It was a section of newspaper torn from the *Boston Gazette*. She'd read the words several times already, though she'd not yet been able to ask Will about them. The piece spoke of muskets and cannon, of battalions and squadrons, of armies stationed at Castle Island intent to *alarm and terrify all America*. Settling down in a chair, she spread the page on the table, flattening the creases where she had unfolded and folded it several times over. She traced a finger over the words *alarm and terrify*.

Last night, Mr. Cunningham spoke of mobs and threats against the consignees, but here the paper talked of soldiers and weapons prepared against the citizens of Boston. Was it possible that both sides could be wrong in some ways and right in others? And how could such violence and shows of strength somehow result in peaceful resolution?

"You're deep in thought."

Patience jumped at the low voice from behind her, a rush of heat filling her chest. She slammed her palm over the paper to cover the words.

But then Will's quiet chuckle helped her mind catch up with her reflexes.

She exhaled in a rush, pressing a hand to her chest as he sank into the chair beside her. "You should not sneak up on me. I did not even hear you come in."

"I did not intend to sneak." He grinned his crooked half smile and nodded toward the table where her hand still lay pressed against the scrap of newspaper. "What do you think of that article I gave you?"

"I hardly know. I thought one thing, and then last night when Mr. Cunningham came—"

"Cunningham was here?"

"Aye, before the evening meal. He arrived with Father when he returned from the shop. He is postponing our invitation because of all this trouble with the tea. It turns out, Mr. Cunningham is a consignee."

Will's eyebrows shot up. "Truly? That is interesting news, indeed."

"Is it?" Patience stared into the fire a moment, then turned back to her brother, her voice low but sparking with heat like the flames in the hearth. "I am not sure *interesting* is the word I would use, because I found what he revealed yesterday evening to be quite concerning. Did you know that the consignees were harassed in the middle of the night in their own homes? That they had to hide away from an angry mob that threatened them and attacked their property? That even now, they are staying at Castle Island out of fear for their safety. That is why he canceled the dinner. He had hoped to remain here and care for his family, but now—"

"Patience." Will stilled her tirade with a gentle hand atop her own. "I did know. It is unfortunate that some men allowed themselves to be so driven by their emotions as to form a mob and act in such a way. And yet, there have been wrongful actions on both sides. You cannot judge the entire cause by the actions of a small minority."

She sighed and dropped her voice to the barest whisper possible. "The trouble is, I thought I had begun to understand the side of the Patriots. From all that you have told me, all I have read in these papers you bring home, and what we heard on Sunday at Old South." She lifted her hand from the page and held it up between them. "And then this, with the actions on the part of the king's army when there has not been a single act to warrant it, as far as I can see."

"But now you doubt your previous thoughts?"

"I have no wish to align myself with people who threaten others with violence."

Will's brows drew low, but it was not anger that etched a frown on his face, but rather a certain sadness, almost resignation. "There has been violence already on both sides, and I fear there will be more before the end."

"You think there will be fighting? Over the tea?"

"I think there is a real possibility of war."

Patience sucked in a breath.

"Not because of the tea. The tea is merely a symbol, a tangible representation of so many grievances built up over time. If there is a war, it will be for something much greater and longer lasting than dried leaves swirling in a pot." He braced his arms on the table. "If it comes to war, I think it will be a war for separation from England."

"You truly believe that is what the Patriots want?"

"Some of them. I am certain many still hope for reconciliation, but if it does not come, they will not back down easily. Not after what I've seen and heard."

"That's what you've been doing, isn't it? When you come home late. You've been meeting with them."

"Aye."

"So you are fully in favor of their cause, then?"

"I support what they are doing, what they are standing up for. I believe they are in the right." He leaned closer, a brightness in his eyes. "I wish you could be there with me, could hear them speak. Their meetings are full of rousing debate, inspiring speeches, and such a firm conviction flowing through every man. I think, if you saw it, if you heard them, you would be impressed."

"But Father is so staunchly against them." She stood, shaking her head. "Either side I choose, I'll be at odds with one of you."

She paced to the fireplace and grabbed the metal rod, poking at the logs again, though they needed no help now with the flames licking high. Sparks shot into the chimney, and a plume of smoke billowed back at her. She blinked, her eyes stinging from the smoke and from tears that threatened to spill over.

All she had wanted, all she had hoped for in coming here to Boston, was to have a home, a place and family where she belonged again. Not an empty shell of a house that ached for Mama's presence to fill it. Not a gaping hole in her own heart that yearned for her father's love to soothe the grief and loneliness. But here there was only more division.

She loved Will and had always admired his wisdom. He had cared for her for years, providing all that he could in Father's absence. She trusted his judgment and had little reason to doubt his conviction over the cause of the Patriots.

Father had been gone off and on for years, even before he settled in Boston. In truth, he had never been a steady figure in her life, and yet she always longed for that. She'd always prayed that someday, he would be the kind of father she hoped for, that she would be the kind of daughter he found worth taking the time to know. How could she follow Will in support of the Patriots if doing so would sever any chance at building a relationship with Father?

Will came to stand beside her, wrapping one arm around her shoulders. She leaned into him. For a long moment, they stood in silence, his presence a steady anchor against the whirling storm of her thoughts.

"You don't have to choose." Will's voice was gentle.

She turned and looked up at him, waiting for him to explain.

"Your worth as a person does not depend on whether you call yourself a Patriot or a Loyalist." He clasped both of her shoulders with his hands. "You cannot make a decision out of fear that you will lose someone's love, for if that were truly the case, then such love is not worth having in the first place."

Patience swiped at her cheeks.

"You have always been curious and thoughtful, from the

time you were a wee little girl helping Mama in the garden." A tiny smile lifted Will's cheeks. "Do you remember how you talked incessantly? Question after question after question. And Mama would answer them all, patient as can be."

"She always did deserve my name more than I do myself." A watery laugh escaped.

He chuckled softly. "It is not something to be ashamed of. I've always admired your tenacity in seeking to understand the world around you, even if I've often feared you would be hurt by what you came to know." He dropped his hands from her shoulders and stared at his feet a moment before meeting her gaze again. "I know you are worried about choosing the right side, fearful that you'll let someone down no matter what decision you make. If you would like my advice, I say, don't make a decision. Not yet. Continue to be your curious, wondering self. Continue to listen, to read, to watch, to learn. And know that I love you and will do my best to protect and care for you, no matter what conclusion you come to in the end."

Patience sniffled and lifted the hem of her apron to dry her cheeks as his words sank deep into her heart, a soothing balm. "Thank you, Will."

He nodded.

With her tears quelled and her spirit lighter, Patience could not resist a teasing comment to lighten the serious mood. "You can be rather eloquent, you know."

Will smiled then, his rare full smile that made her feel as though the sun had finally broken through the clouds. "I should hope so. I wouldn't make a very good publisher if I weren't."

Footsteps and voices on the stairs told them the others would soon be down. Patience pressed her hands to her cheeks, hoping her tears were no longer evident.

Will lowered his voice. "The body of the people are meeting

this morning at Old South. I suspect this business with the tea will be dealt with today. I plan to attend."

"I understand." Patience tipped her head to meet his serious gaze. "You will tell me what happens, won't you?"

"I promise."

Would today's decision regarding the tea help clarify her own choice of which side to stand upon, or would it further muddle her already confused thoughts?

CHAPTER 17

Old South Meeting House was full to bursting on Thursday morning. Josiah braced himself against the jostling men and peered down from his place in the packed gallery to the pews and aisles below, which were equally, if not more, full. He dared not move so much as a single step.

Outside, even more flocked to the building, the streets overflowing with noise and movement and palpable anticipation.

"There must be five thousand men or more." Nathaniel peered out the window behind them. His voice reflected the awe that shone in his eyes.

"I heard one man say he had traveled a distance of twenty miles to attend." William raised his voice to be heard over the ruckus, even though he stood right beside Josiah.

Thankfully, William had made no mention of their conversation at the Green Dragon, sparing Josiah the awkwardness of explaining the feelings he was developing toward the man's sister. Perhaps the excitement of the day would be enough to make William forget altogether.

It was not only within the walls and surroundings of Old South that the people gathered this morning. Crowds filled the

Green Dragon, mingled in the streets, and congregated about Griffin's Wharf. Josiah had seen some of it with his own eyes. The rest he'd learned from the conversations swirling about the room. The whole of Boston seemed poised and tense, like a barn cat crouching low and steady, barely twitching her tail before she pounced on her prey

The deadline for the tea tax was at midnight, fourteen hours hence. The outcome of this day could impact the future of Boston, and perhaps the whole of the American colonies, forever.

The buzz of conversation dwindled to a murmur as a voice from the pulpit rang out above the din, calling the meeting to order. Adams, Warren, and Hancock were all present, along with many other familiar faces that Josiah recognized both as fellow Sons of Liberty and staunch Patriots who had regularly attended each of the past meetings. Samuel Savage was selected as moderator, and as the decisions of the customs house were read, silence fell over the crowd.

"Customs officers Richard Harrison and Robert Hallowell have determined that they cannot grant clearance for the *Dartmouth*."

Josiah strained to catch every word that rose from the front of the building, though he could not see who spoke them.

"Cargo has entered the harbor but not been unloaded, and duties have not been paid as the law demands. Thus, they refuse to grant clearance for the vessel."

A rumble rolled through the crowd, but another voice broke in, calling for order. Josiah stood as still as an iron bar, attention fixed on every detail. To his left, William, with the advantage of a bit more height, tipped his head and whispered, "I see Rotch. I believe they're calling him up."

"The refusal of the tea must be done in a legitimate and, if at all possible, legal manner." Savage reminded those gathered of what had been said many times before. "Mr. Rotch, you must use all possible dispatch to procure a pass for the *Dartmouth* to sail this day."

Shouts of agreement almost drowned out Rotch's argument against such action. More debate ensued, and finally, a decision was announced that Rotch would go to Governor Hutchinson himself to obtain a pass.

"It is impractical to do so." Rotch's words rose above the din. "Governor Hutchinson is not even in Boston at this time. He is currently at his home in Milton."

"Then to Milton you shall go." A shout from the floor stirred up more noise from the crowd.

Josiah peered between the shoulders of the men in front of him to where the leaders gathered close together at the front of Old South. Rotch shook his head and gestured in protest, though no one could hear what was said. Finally, he gave a nod of resignation.

"Rotch will go to Milton and speak with Hutchinson," Savage declared. The room erupted in huzzahs and cheers. "We adjourn this meeting until three in the afternoon."

"Do you think the governor will grant his request?" Nathaniel craned his neck toward the door where Rotch had departed.

"I doubt it." Josiah tugged at the sleeves of his coat. He felt nearly certain they would be boarding one of the ships tonight.

Old South buzzed with restless anticipation, men filing out the doors or gathering in small groups to discuss what had just transpired.

Josiah rolled his shoulders to release the tension that had begun to build there. "I am going to step out for some air."

"No reason to wait here." Nathaniel nodded toward the exit.

"We've enough time for some food, I reckon," William said. "I think I'll stop home. You're welcome to join me." His offer clearly encompassed both men, but his eyes fixed on Josiah's.

The expression on William's face seemed to hint that Josiah

would be especially interested in a visit to the Abbott house. Perhaps he'd been wrong to assume the business of the tea would be enough to distract William from any suspicions he might harbor regarding the "pretty girl" Nathaniel had teased Josiah about.

Still, he could not resist the chance of seeing Miss Abbott, even if it did further increase her brother's suspicions.

Josiah swallowed, considering how to answer without sounding overly eager, despite the way his heart galloped. Thankfully, he was spared by Nathaniel's enthusiastic reply.

"I'll take you up on that offer." He slapped Josiah on the back. "Let's all go, then we can return here together."

Josiah nodded his consent and led the way out the door, hoping no one else had caught sight of the smile he couldn't manage to hide.

CHAPTER 18

*P*atience dipped a rag in the bowl of vinegar, then the bowl of ashes, and set to scrubbing another pot. She hummed softly to herself, the crackling fire in the kitchen hearth her only accompaniment. Her singing would never rival Mama's, but she could hold a tune well enough, and the gentle lull of humming brought back memories of days spent in the kitchen with her.

Patience rubbed the cloth in circles against the blackened pot, the shiny copper beginning to show through beneath her ministrations. Libby and Mary were visiting a friend, Father was at the shop, and Will had gone to the meeting about the tea, so the house was empty. The ladies had invited Patience to join them, but she'd declined, desiring this bit of solitude. The steady rhythm of scrubbing and the empty quiet of the house left much time for thought, something she desperately needed.

Will's reassuring words repeated in her mind, that she need not choose a side, but she could not ignore the nagging voice that said she must make up her mind. Waiting in this strange in-between left her feeling like a leaf, caught in an eddy of a stream, swirling in circles and never moving forward. It was time to move forward.

She dipped her cloth again, turned the pot in her hand, and rubbed at a particularly stubborn spot. A few minutes later, she paused her work, her hand still against the pot, cloth resting at the smudged edge between what was black with grime and that which was already clean. Her thoughts and emotions felt very much the same. Muddled and messy and frozen between two worlds.

When Will explained the colonists' complaints, she could see truth in their reasoning. But then Father and Mr. Cunningham shared their side, and things seemed less clear. Worse still, though Will promised his love for her would not be influenced by her choice, could she believe the same would be true of Father? She had seen his steadfast devotion to the Crown, witnessed his anger toward Will when he voiced dissent, and heard the near-hatred that laced his words as he condemned the mob and all who protested against the tea.

She sighed and brushed a stray hair from her cheek. If only she could brush her confusion and worries away just as easily.

Mary and Libby never spoke of politics. They likely knew Father well enough to avoid discussions that would upset him, but did that mean they also believed as he did? Was it possible they harbored a different opinion, one kept silent in order to maintain peace? Could she do the same, should her heart and mind settle on the side of the Patriots?

At the creak of the door opening, Patience shot to her feet. Mary and Libby had stated they would not be home until midafternoon. Had Father returned early from the shop?

Will stepped into the kitchen, his gaze scanning the room before settling on her. "Are you here alone?"

"Mary and Libby went to visit a friend. What are you doing? I thought you were at Old South."

"I was, but the meeting is adjourned until later this afternoon. I thought we might stop here for some food."

"We?" She furrowed her brow.

"Nathaniel and Josiah are with me." He crossed the kitchen and stopped just in front of her, lowering his voice. "You do not mind, do you?"

She darted a glance at the entryway. Mr. Wagner was here? Her heart sped more than it should at the thought.

"What if Father comes back?"

"I doubt he will, and if so, I'll manage. They are my friends, and this is my home for the time being. I see nothing wrong."

Patience worried her lip, not fully convinced that Father would see it the same way. Still, the thought of some time with Mr. Wagner was more appealing than she dared admit.

Male voices drifted from the entryway, and her gaze strayed over Will's shoulder. She pulled it back to focus on him, hoping he had not noticed her eagerness, but the slight upward tilt of his lips suggested otherwise.

She turned her back on his too-intent study of her expression and placed the half-cleaned pot on the counter, speaking over her shoulder. "I've nothing much prepared as I had thought to eat alone, but I am sure I can find something for all of you." She wiped her hands on her apron, dismayed at how many black streaks covered the fabric. There wasn't another readily available in the kitchen, so it would have to do. If she turned up one corner and tucked it into the tie at her waist, it could hide the worst of the stains.

"Would you prefer that I have them wait in the parlor for now?"

"I haven't kept up the fire there this morning. You might all be more comfortable in here." Patience adjusted her fichu and looked back at Will.

"Curious to hear our conversation, are you?" He couldn't

hide a grin as he leaned closer, his voice a mere whisper. "Or is there someone you'd enjoy visiting with yourself?"

Heat crept up her cheeks, and she shooed him away with a wave of her hand. "Sit wherever you'd like. I'll have something ready to eat shortly."

He chuckled as he walked away.

Patience huffed and brushed her hands down her petticoat, wishing she'd chosen something prettier than her plain blue striped day gown. But she'd not expected company—most certainly not Mr. Wagner.

She tried to focus on what food she should prepare, but her thoughts settled on Mr. Wagner instead. He was here with Will, which meant he had been at the meeting. She was not surprised, and yet it added another layer to the complicated issue she had been considering before they arrived.

Mr. Wagner's gaze seemed to find hers immediately, an action that caused the breath to catch in her throat.

Let Will think what he wished, for she couldn't hide the smile that bloomed on her face, even should she want to. "Mr. Wagner, it is good to see you again."

"And you, Miss Abbott." His dark eyes crinkled as a small smile lifted the corners of his mouth.

Without his hat, his black hair was on full display, wavy and mussed, hardly cooperating with the cord meant to contain his short queue. His coat and waistcoat, while nowhere near as fine as those Mr. Cunningham had worn the day prior, fit his broad chest and shoulders well, displaying a strength she could not help but admire.

She pulled her attention away, focusing on the other man who stood beside Will.

"This is Nathaniel Hadley," Will said. "Nathaniel, my sister, Patience Abbott."

"Pleased to meet you, miss."

"You as well."

The men settled around the table as Patience looked over the food readily available. Salted pork would do well. There was bread for toast and peach preserves. Some sliced cheese would finish things off. It would not be anything particularly special, but hopefully, enough to satisfy their hunger before they ventured back to the meetinghouse.

"How far is it to Milton?" Will's voice drifted over from the table.

"Nearly ten miles," Mr. Hadley replied. "Quite a ride with little to be gained, I suspect."

Patience pulled a frying pan from its hook above the counter, spooned a large pat of lard inside, then carried it to the hearth, listening to the men's conversation as she worked.

"You think Governor Hutchinson will refuse?" Will asked.

"Aye." She recognized Mr. Wagner's voice easily. "I do not see how he could do otherwise."

Patience peeked over her shoulder at the trio around the table. Mr. Wagner leaned back in his chair, arms folded over his chest. From her angle, she could observe his profile, jaw set in a resolute expression. Strength and conviction radiated from his posture and grounded his words.

She pulled her attention back to the task at hand, crouching to place a trivet at the edge of the fire. She scraped some coals underneath, then balanced the frying pan atop it to heat, all the while trying to follow what the men said.

"We must show that we have done everything in our power to peacefully protest the landing of the tea." Mr. Hadley braced his elbows on the table. "Thus, this final request to petition the governor himself."

Patience carved thick slabs from the side of salted pork, careful to keep her attention on the knife in her hands so as not to nick a finger in her eagerness to listen.

"And when he refuses?" Will's voice drew a quick glance

over her shoulder. His brows were raised as he awaited the answer.

There was silence at the table for a long moment. Patience held her breath as she carried the slices to the hearth and laid them in the pan. Did they hesitate to say more because of her presence? Did they fear she might reveal some secretive plan? Or did they know of some violence that might occur this very day and thought to spare her hearing of such things?

She dared another peek at the trio. Mr. Wagner's dark eyes found hers. There was something in his expression she could not read, though she desperately wished she could. What would it be like to have the privilege to understand this man's thoughts with a mere glance? To be able to communicate with one another without the use of words. Her cheeks heated at the intimacy of such an idea.

He held her gaze a second longer, then shifted his attention to Will. "The tea cannot be landed, but neither do we wish for violence." His low voice held an intriguing mix of gentleness and strength that matched what she had come to know of the man himself. "We will know what must be done before long."

His answer was measured and purposefully vague, though Patience could not blame him. Perhaps he did not know what would happen next, or, if he did, he did not wish to reveal too much too soon.

She set to work on the toast, placing four pieces of bread in the toasting iron, which she rested near the edge of the flames so it might brown and crisp. As she returned to the counter to slice the cheese, Mr. Hadley and Will moved on to discuss printing business.

She crossed back to the fire just in time to see Mr. Wagner rise from his seat and crouch by the hearth to rotate the toasting iron, ensuring the other side of the bread would heat evenly. It was a simple gesture, but the fact that he had noticed the need and stepped in to help her made Patience's heart stutter.

She came up beside him, his shoulder brushing her arm as he stood. The top of her head came just to his chin, and she had to tilt her face to look up at him when he stood so close.

"Thank you."

He smiled back, a lopsided grin that warmed her inside like the first sip of hot chocolate on a cold winter morning.

For a moment, she forgot anyone else was in the room and would have relished his nearness beside her as long as he would grant it, but Mr. Wagner seemed more conscious of their audience and quickly returned to his seat. Was he as affected by her as she was by him? It felt silly to be so preoccupied by the man. They hardly knew one another. And yet she could not seem to convince her heart to maintain a steady rhythm.

When the plates were full and mugs of cider poured, Patience served the men, then took a seat at the table, directly across from Mr. Wagner. He ducked his head as Will offered a prayer, and Patience added a silent petition of her own to the mealtime blessing.

Lord, my heart and thoughts are drawn to this man seated before me. But there is so much uncertainty. Please show me what to do. Make it clear what path I should take.

They enjoyed the meal in amiable conversation, much led by Mr. Hadley, whose inquisitive and talkative personality seemed well-suited for his position at the press. Patience did not mind his curiosity regarding her impressions on Boston or his questions about their journey from England, but it was Mr. Wagner's quiet smile that truly drew her attention.

When there was a lull in Mr. Hadley's conversation, Will spoke up. "Do either of you know much of Edward Cunningham?"

"He's a consignee—I know that much." Mr. Hadley spoke

around a mouthful of pork. "Very wealthy. I've never met him and cannot say more than that. Why do you ask?"

"He is connected with my father through business, I believe," Will said. "He had invited our family to dinner but postponed the plans due to this business with the tea."

"He was here yesterday afternoon." Patience spooned peach preserves on her toast.

Mr. Wagner drew his head up swiftly. "He came to your house?"

She nodded. "But he said he was returning to Castle Island."

"I would have thought him already there." Mr. Hadley tore off a hunk of bread. "All the rest of the consignees are."

"He was staying there previously"—Patience fiddled with the handle of her spoon—"but returned for the sake of his mother and sisters. At least, that is what he told me."

She dared a glance back at Mr. Wagner. His brows were drawn together, and a muscle ticked in his strong jaw. Did he harbor some personal dislike of Mr. Cunningham? Or had they had some bad experience together? She swallowed as a terrible thought invaded her mind. Had Mr. Wagner been part of the mob that attacked the consignees? The food churned in her stomach. No, it could not be. He did not seem that sort of man at all.

"I was curious since our father seemed particularly enthusiastic about the invitation." Will seemed to sense the tension hovering over them and offered a wry smile. "Likely, he is hoping for an especially good meal."

The conversation moved to more comfortable topics, but Patience couldn't help noticing the change in Mr. Wagner's demeanor. He seemed distracted, his face drawn in a serious expression and his comments less frequent.

When all the plates were cleared and bellies full, the men thanked her for the meal and made ready to leave. Patience followed them to the doorway to bid them good day, but Will hung back a moment as the other two set off down the street.

"I am not certain what the rest of this day will bring." Will's stormy eyes matched the seriousness of his tone. "But I do not want you to worry for me."

Patience nodded, pressing her lips together to hold back the words she wanted to say. That she wished she could come with him, to be there to see and hear what he could. That she *would* worry, no matter how much she tried not to. And that it was not just him she would worry over, but the dark-eyed blacksmith as well.

He clasped a hand over her shoulder, and his expression shifted to something lighter as a teasing smile tipped the corner of his mouth. "I think I may need to speak with Josiah. It seems his thoughts are not so much on the tea this afternoon."

Patience's eyes went wide. She shrugged off his hand and shooed him from the house. "I have no idea what you are talking about."

Will's laughter was the last thing she heard as she shut the door.

CHAPTER 19

*J*osiah and his friends took their places in the gallery of Old South once more as the meeting reconvened at three in the afternoon as promised. Samuel Adams, Doctor Thomas Young, and Josiah Quincy Junior all gave speeches to those assembled, but as the minutes passed with no sign of Rotch, restlessness stirred throughout the room.

Josiah tried to focus on everything being said. Usually, he had no trouble attending to their inspiring words, but his thoughts drifted to Miss Abbott and the way her dark lashes framed her eyes as she looked up at him. When he had entered the kitchen, the bright smile that had filled her face and set those lovely dimples in her cheeks had further fueled his hope that she might care for him. And he could not ignore the burst of heat that had spread through his arm at the mere brush of her shoulder against him as they stood side by side at the fire. He would have liked to linger there with her, to converse with her alone, to reach for her hand and weave his fingers with hers...but he had felt her brother's watchful gaze, and that was enough to hurry him back to his seat.

Then she had sat across from him at the table, and he'd been granted the luxury of watching her smile as she answered Nathaniel's incessant questions. He'd hardly been able to focus on his food, distracted by the way those tendrils of hair escaped her cap and brushed the sides of her cheeks.

But the mention of Edward Cunningham's visit, and his upcoming dinner invitation, had been a splash of cold water on the spark of happiness in Josiah's heart. He was aware of the man's status and wealth, as well as his loyalty to the Crown. A loyalty that matched that of Miss Abbott's father. Certainly, George Abbott would be more inclined to see his daughter with someone like Cunningham over Josiah. While William had not said as much, his mention of the man in connection with his father seemed to imply he suspected more to his father's enthusiasm over the invitation than the enjoyment of a good meal.

Josiah clenched his jaw and pulled his attention back to the discussion at hand. An hour and a half had passed with no sign of Rotch's return. Darkness had fallen, the interior of Old South dimly lit by candles. Their flickering light matched the anxious pulse that throbbed throughout the gathered multitude.

William nudged Josiah with his elbow. "This might not be the best time, but I cannot help but ask..." He lowered his voice and dipped his head so Josiah could hear him over the steady din of conversation. "What are your intentions toward my sister?"

Josiah's eyebrows shot up. He swallowed. "My intentions? I am...that is, I thought..."

William chuckled and shook his head. "I had my suspicions, but our visit today confirmed it."

Josiah scrubbed a hand over his jaw. "I did not think it was so obvious." He glanced at Nathaniel, who had shifted away from them and was engrossed in conversation with another cluster of men nearby. "I do care for your sister, but with all that is going on right now, with what I am committed to, and knowing your father's loyalty..."

"I cannot say it will be an easy road with my father, but for what it is worth, you have my blessing."

"That is worth a great deal. Though I do not wish to cause strife for her. You said how much she desires your father's approval. And I don't even know what she would think—"

William's burst of laughter cut off Josiah's words and drew the attention of several men nearby. He held up a hand in apology and lowered his voice once more. "It is up to her, of course, but I suspect Patience would be pleased with an offer of courtship." His face took on a stern expression. "Assuming that is your intention."

Heat rose along the back of Josiah's neck. He'd not allowed his thoughts to travel that far...until now. Today's visit had proved that his feelings were still there, and growing stronger, despite his attempts to put her from his mind and convince himself that the hindrances to their relationship were too big to overcome. Was it possible? Did he dare pursue her in such a way?

William was awaiting his reply, but instead, another question spilled out. "But what of Cunningham?"

"Cunningham?" William scowled. "I believe my father would like to see a match there, though I have not seen any affection for him on my sister's behalf."

It was a paltry comfort, for while Josiah was glad she harbored no strong interest in the man, her father's opinions and wishes would certainly impact her, whether by influencing her own decisions or by more direct action. Would she defy her father for Josiah's sake, if it came to that? Did Josiah dare put her in such a position?

He tugged at his stock, which suddenly felt too tight. "I would very much like—"

His reply was cut off by a commotion at the doorway. Rotch had returned.

The man trudged to the front of the room, looking rumpled from his journey, his shoulders slumped. There was a flurry of discussion amongst the leaders who surrounded Rotch, then a loud call to order.

"Governor Hutchinson is willing to grant anything consistent with the laws and his duty to the king." Rotch spoke for all gathered to hear. "But he has confirmed to me that he cannot give a pass for the *Dartmouth* unless she was properly qualified by the Custom House."

A murmur of responses passed through the crowd like a wave crashing on the harbor shore. The Custom House had already refused. Now the governor had confirmed what Josiah had long suspected. There was no viable option to return the tea from whence it came.

"Will you send the ship back?" A voice rang out.

Rotch shook his head. "I cannot. It would be my ruin."

"Will you unload the tea?" Another gruff shout.

"I have no intention to do so, but if the proper authorities commanded it, I must comply for my own security."

Josiah had thought the meeting house loud before, but it was nothing compared to the roar of voices that filled Old South now. He could hardly hear the debate that continued on the floor below them.

"Who knows how tea will mingle with salt water tonight?" The words echoed from the gallery, not far behind Josiah. He turned and craned his neck to see the speaker, but whoever the man was, he had faded back into the crowd following his inciting declaration.

Huzzahs and shouts for a mob filled the room but were quickly brought to a stop by an order for quiet from the front.

"Mr. Rotch is a good man," Dr. Young said. "He has done all

in his power to gratify the people. Let no harm come to his person or his property."

Another man stood. Josiah leaned to the side to see who but could not make out his face. "Mr. Rotch, we must ask one final time. Will you send the vessel back with the tea aboard?"

Rotch squared his shoulders. "I cannot. I must repeat—to comply would prove my ruin."

Adams rose from his seat, a commanding presence despite his modest dark wool suit. His thick brows drew low over his eyes, and a hush fell over the crowd. "This meeting can do nothing more to save the country."

Immediately, the room erupted in a cacophony of sound. Shouts of "huzzah" and war whoops echoed from every corner of Old South. The mass of people began to move, some pressing for the doors, others pushing closer to the front.

Nathaniel's eyes glowed with excitement as he looked at Josiah. "That's the signal."

Josiah nodded, his heart racing. "That it is."

On the other side of the gallery, a voice called out, "Boston Harbor a teapot tonight. Hurrah for Griffin's Wharf!"

William adjusted his hat on his head. "Whatever is about to happen, count me in."

"Follow us." Josiah spoke as he began to weave through the men, aiming for an exit. "We're bound for Griffin's Wharf to fill the harbor with tea."

CHAPTER 20

*J*osiah, Nathaniel, and William wound their way through the crowd that swarmed outside Old South like bees around a hive. To the uninformed observer it might look like chaos, and in some ways, it was, with men shouting, huddling in groups, and fanning out in every direction. But Josiah knew there was order, hidden though it might be, in the plans that the Sons of Liberty had put in place and that order must prevail for their protest to be a success.

"This way." Josiah pushed through the thick of the crowd. "We'll stop at the smithy first."

William turned to Josiah. "What is it we are going to do?"

"Just what someone shouted before we left." Josiah tugged his hat lower over his head. "Boston Harbor is to be a teapot tonight, and those three ships will provide the tea."

"We're throwing it all overboard," Nathaniel said as they veered toward Milk Street.

"Do you think we'll meet with resistance?" William glanced at a pair of men scurrying through the shadows.

"We may, though I hope not." Josiah slowed as they approached the smithy. He tugged the door open and ushered them inside. "It is imperative that we do everything in an orderly manner, as peacefully as possible."

"Nothing is to be destroyed or damaged," Nathaniel said. "Aside from the tea, of course."

Josiah crossed the room to his forge and shoveled some of the cooled ashes into a pile on the edge of the bricks, then scooped water from the barrel and poured it on top. "We planned to disguise ourselves to varying degrees." He stirred the mixture into a thick black paste and rubbed some on his face. It wasn't much, but it would give some semblance of anonymity. "When this is over, we must not speak of it again. All those involved are sworn to secrecy."

William nodded his understanding and dug his fingers into the black soot, smearing it over his cheeks, nose, and forehead. Nathaniel did the same. The whites of his eyes, wide and bright with anticipation, stood out in the shadows of the smithy.

"Are we ready, then?" Nathaniel brushed his hands together to remove the excess ash.

"I am." William's voice echoed with the same enthusiasm that was clear in Nathaniel's expression.

"To Griffin's Wharf." Josiah tucked his hammer into the waist of his trousers and tugged his coat tightly around himself. He pushed his hat lower on his head and followed his friends out into the street.

Darkness engulfed them. They kept a brisk pace, no longer speaking, silent resolve pressing them forward. Josiah glanced over at Fort Hill, where men emerged from the shadows, all bound for the same destination. As they approached Griffin's Wharf, a din of voices and growing light greeted them. Torches lit the docks as a crowd gathered to watch what had begun to unfold. Already men were boarding the first of the vessels, while others paddled out in rowboats, and younger fellows scampered down toward the shore, taking advantage of the low tide to get closer. A few sentries stood guard, alert to anyone who might interfere, but as Josiah scanned the mass of people, he saw no resistance.

Their trio worked their way to the edge of the dock, joining the men waiting there. Some were dressed as Mohawks, their cheeks smudged with paint, while others had blankets thrown around their shoulders or soot-smeared faces like his own. Still others came in old frocks and woolen caps, while some came as they were, hats pulled low, heads down, the shadows of the night their only disguise. They moved in quiet procession, every face one of determination. The air seemed to buzz around Josiah, as though every fiber of space felt the gravity of their actions.

Josiah peered past the three ships moored in the harbor to where the British squadron waited, less than a quarter mile away. The moonlight highlighted the barest silhouette of the war ships, but their presence loomed large, nonetheless. Would they raise anchor and draw closer? Would they dare fire upon the men as they worked?

A burly man disguised as a Mohawk with a blanket wrapped about his back and feathers stuck in his hair waved Josiah and his friends forward, directing them toward the closest ship. The *Eleanor*. Josiah glanced back at William with a silent question in his eyes. Could William truly board the ship he had traveled upon for over a month across the sea and destroy its cargo? Josiah would not blame him nor think less of him if he would rather move on to another one of the vessels.

William paused, his mouth turned down in a solemn expression as he stared for a long moment at the ship. Then he squared his shoulders and, with a single nod, stepped forward to lead the way.

The first mate and other sailors still aboard made themselves scarce at the promise that no harm would befall anything else on the ship, and soon the *Eleanor* was teeming with men. Waves slapped the hull as they hung lanterns and rigged a pulley system to lift the heavier crates out of the hold. They quickly established a methodical process to handle the tea, with several men below to raise the cargo to the deck where others waited with axes and hammers in hand to break open the wooden crates. Josiah tugged his sledge free from his waistband and joined the crew that surrounded the hold.

A middle-aged man, sweat already beading his brow, hefted one of the chests up to Josiah. Josiah set it upon the wooden planks of the deck, his hand skimming over the East India Trading Company mark stamped on the side of the box. He swallowed and raised his hammer in the air, just as he did every day at his forge, then brought it down upon the top. No sparks greeted his strike, no ding of heated metal. Instead, his blow was met with the crack of splintering wood and the scent of Bohea that wafted from the gaping hole left behind.

He stared at the pile of black dried leaves filling the crate, each one so small and seemingly insignificant on its own. Much like the Americans who longed for freedom and independence. The men and women spread throughout the thirteen colonies who, on their own, might feel small and insignificant against the might of England. But together? Together they were so much more.

A rush of purpose stirred deep in his bones and coursed through his body. This act of rebellion was the start of something, and he was part of it.

Josiah hefted the box, and in three long strides, he was at the rail. He flipped the crate upside down. The tea fluttered in the air, almost peaceful in its descent, as though a tree had dropped its leaves under the weight of an autumn breeze. He shook the box once, ensuring it was empty, then heaved it into the dark water below. Nathaniel joined him, his arms full with another broken chest, and did the same.

Josiah returned to the hold as the man below raised the next crate above his head. Josiah took it, and in the dim light, when their eyes met, Josiah could tell he felt it too. This stranger, another small piece of the larger whole. A quick smile graced the man's face, not a frivolous or carefree grin, but the kind of smile a soldier might give his comrade before they stepped onto the battlefield. Josiah returned the expression with a single nod, then perched the crate on the deck and swung his hammer once more.

They continued, working as a unified group, diligent and efficient. Few words were spoken, but few words were necessary. Each man knew his part. Even the crowd gathered to watch had grown quiet, an almost reverent hush. In place of talk, the air rent with cracks of shattering wood and splashes as the empty crates landed in the harbor waves. Salt water and tea mingled in a strange scent that hung heavy around them.

The ruined cargo began to pile so high in the shallow water of low tide that it reached up the sides of the ship. Young men and boys in row boats beat their oars upon the floating leaves and drifting crates, pushing the tea beneath the surface and further breaking up the damaged wood. The light of the moon and torches from shore reflected off the dark water, barely illuminating the men who moved like shadows in the night, the same motions repeated on the *Dartmouth* and *Beaver* as upon the *Eleanor*.

When the last chest had been destroyed, the men below deck climbed the ladder that jutted up from the hold. Josiah offered a hand to the one who had worked with him the past hours. The older man joined him on the deck and clapped a meaty palm on Josiah's shoulder.

"You're a smithy?" He tipped his head toward the hammer Josiah held.

"Aye."

"I am as well, in Watertown, near ten miles away. I've a shop and small farm there." The man tugged his hat from his head and slapped it on his leg. Fragments of wood and tea leaves fell to the deck. "You live here, in Boston?"

Josiah nodded.

"Name's Phineas Stearns." He swiped a thickly muscled arm over his forehead and fitted his hat back atop his head. "If you've need to get out of town after all this and don't have another place to go, come find me. I could use a man like you."

Stearns's offer was a kind and generous one, especially to a stranger. Though, after the past hour, Josiah felt they were not so much strangers anymore.

"Josiah Wagner, and I thank you. I hope to stay in Boston, but I'll not forget, should the need arise."

Stearns smiled. "Good to work with you this evening, Mr. Wagner."

"You as well."

Several men set about sweeping the decks, ensuring not a single scrap of wood or leaf of tea was left behind. They put everything else to rights, so that, with the exception of the missing one hundred and fourteen crates of tea, it appeared as if no one had even set foot on the ship. Several rowboats continued to ride the slow swells beside the three vessels, and young men scrambled along the shoreline, ensuring nothing washed ashore to be salvaged.

As Josiah climbed off the *Eleanor* with William and Nathaniel, a shout rent the air. Josiah craned his neck to see a man leaning out of the upstairs window of a house at the head of the wharf. Josiah squinted as the man called out in a bitter tone, "Well, boys, you have had a fine, pleasant evening for your Indian caper, haven't you? But mind, you have got to pay the fiddler yet."

"Oh, never mind, squire," a man cried back from the crowd. "Just come out here, if you please, and we'll settle the bill in two minutes."

The man pulled his head back inside and slammed the window shut.

"I believe that was Admiral Montagu, himself." Nathaniel nudged Josiah. "I'm glad it was only a few shouted threats we had to face tonight, not the force of his fleet's cannon."

Josiah nodded. "I'm thankful it was peaceful."

No real resistance had arisen from the British squadron, nor had anyone assembled on land sought to halt their actions.

They passed by the sentries who had acted as guards while they worked. Now those same men watched as the party disembarked, checking for anyone who might attempt to ferret away some of the tea for himself.

Josiah spotted Alexander Stevens a little way off, near the bobbing hull of the *Beaver*. Alexander raised a hand in greeting and started toward them.

"How did you fare?" Alexander greeted the three of them. "Quite the tea party, aye?"

Nathaniel chuckled at the phrase, and William nodded, though his gaze remained fixed on the tethered sails of the tea ships and the dark night above them.

Alexander reached into his pocket and withdrew a padlock, holding it out to Josiah. "This was damaged amidst the work on the *Dartmouth* tonight. We promised no harm to anything on the vessel aside from the tea. Might you be able to fix it and return it tomorrow morning?"

Josiah took the pieces and examined them in the low light. The shackle was broken, but all else seemed intact. "I can. I'll bring it back first thing."

Alexander clapped him on the back in thanks, then bid them goodnight as he turned to other duties.

Josiah tucked the padlock into his pocket. "Best get home." The crowd was beginning to scatter as the men dispersed, each returning quietly to his own home, carrying his secret with him. A secret many would likely take to their grave.

The three of them departed in silence. No words seemed necessary, nor sufficient, to capture the significance of what had happened this night. As they turned toward Fort Hill, Josiah glanced back over his shoulder one last time. Less than three hours had passed since they arrived at Griffin's Wharf, and all the tea was gone, three hundred and forty chests completely emptied into the salty waves.

It was over, and yet in his heart, Josiah knew this was just the beginning.

CHAPTER 21

"*W*hat are you doing?" Libby's voice, a whisper edged in sleep, drifted across the room to where Patience stood at the window, peering outside.

"I heard something." Patience squinted into the blackness. A pair of dark shapes hurried down the road, but neither turned toward their house. "I am worried for Will."

"He still has not returned?"

"Not since this afternoon when he stopped in for a meal with Mr. Wagner and Mr. Hadley." Patience spared a glance over her shoulder.

"You failed to mention their visit before." Libby propped herself up on one elbow in bed, grasping the covers to her chin with her other hand.

"I did not want to say anything with Father there." Patience turned back to the window, and her fingers brushed the windowpane, sending a shiver through her whole arm.

Maybe she should not say anything more now, either, but she needed a confidante. Thus far, Libby and Mary had remained silent whenever the topic of tea came about, but every now and then, Patience caught a passing expression on Libby's face that made her wonder how her stepsister felt on the matter. Perhaps now was the time to seek an answer.

"They were at the meeting today, regarding the tea." Patience whispered the words, fogging the glass as she kept her eyes fixed on the street.

A sharp intake of breath was followed by the rustling of blankets and shuffling of feet. Libby hurried to stand beside Patience. Her blond braid hung over one shoulder, and she clasped her arms about her chest. "Did they speak about what was happening? What did you hear?"

"I heard a little." Patience peeked at the young woman beside her. "I do not wish to cause trouble for Will. I know how my father feels, but..." Her unspoken words hung in the air between them.

"You do not know which side I take in this." Libby placed a gentle hand on Patience's shoulder. "I suppose I am glad it has not been obvious. For the sake of your father, I hold my tongue, though I worry that I am not always successful in disguising my feelings."

"You sympathize with the Patriots?"

A single nod. "As did my papa before me, though he was very careful in his associations, and few knew the truth of where his loyalty lay."

Patience widened her eyes. "Did my father know?"

"Nay, nor would he ever suspect it, I think." Libby squinted out the window. "Look, here come more."

A cluster of men rushed down the street. Their features were indistinguishable in the darkness, and the pace of their steps spoke to a sense of urgency and purpose.

"Earlier, when the men were here, Mr. Wagner said the tea could not be landed and that they would know soon enough what must be done." Cold from the wooden floorboards seeped through Patience's wool stockings, and she couldn't suppress a shiver.

"What other choice can there be?" Libby twisted the end of her long braid. "The ships cannot be held in the harbor forever. There is a deadline by which the tax must be paid."

"It seemed as though they wanted to send it back." Patience stared into the darkness a moment longer but saw no more shadowed men moving along the road. She dropped the curtain back into place as another bout of shivering sent her scurrying back to bed.

Libby followed close behind. "I do not think that many men from the town would be needed to send the ships back. Most definitely not at this time of night. But what, then, would they be doing?"

Patience's voice dropped to the barest whisper. "I cannot imagine." She leaned against the headboard and tugged the covers close around her chilled body. "I pray there will be no violence."

"I hope not. I remember the massacre in 1770, though I was not yet five and ten." Libby tucked her pillow behind her back as she sat beside Patience. "Father spoke of it when he did not think I was listening, but it was not long after that he realized he could not hide what was happening from me any longer."

"How did your father manage to keep his loyalties quiet? I remember you talking about a British soldier he befriended, and he took my father in to his own home, though Father makes no effort to hide his loyalty to the king."

"Papa always held strongly to his conviction that providing medical care to people in need was his highest priority, no matter whether their beliefs aligned with his or not. He was very good at what he did, so his skills were in high demand from both Patriots and Tories alike." Libby fiddled with the edge of the counterpane. "And he was a kind man who was truly interested in the lives of others. It was not as though he kept silent all the time, but on the whole, he made a purposeful effort not to let his opinions be widely known."

"What of your mother? If she holds to the same views, it must be incredibly difficult for her to hear my father espouse as he does on England's virtues and the Patriots' faults."

"Mama was of like mind with Papa, both in her opinions on politics and her desire to keep those opinions closely held. I know it bothers her at times, but she has always been a more" —Libby paused and pursed her lips as though searching for the right word—"reserved sort of person. She cares well for those she loves and is content in her life, accepting it for what it is and not seeking much beyond it. I don't say this as though it were a fault, mind you. Sometimes I wish I could be more like her."

"I understand." Patience tipped her head to face Libby. "My mama was much the same. I often wondered how she could be so content, so joyful, even though Father was always gone. It seemed unfair to me, that he had his adventures while she was left behind, living almost as a widow even though he was alive. But I don't think she ever saw it that way. She deserved my name much more so than I do."

Libby giggled.

As Libby's laughter faded, Patience sobered. "I am sorry if my father has made life more difficult for you both."

"Do not worry yourself over that." Libby shook her head. "Your father has provided for us and allowed us to keep this home, which we could not have on our own. And now I have you." Libby smiled, and in that moment, Patience saw more of a little girl in her than the young woman she was. "I always wished for a sister and am grateful to have that hope realized."

Patience couldn't hold back a smile in return and her heart swelled with unexpected joy. Had it been but a fortnight since she'd first arrived and wrestled with the jealousy she felt over her new stepsister? Now they sat side by side, confiding in one another and trusting each other with memories and thoughts that were not lightly given. A friendship had blossomed, still new and perhaps a bit fragile, but with roots that would only grow deeper with time.

"I am thankful to have you as well." Patience bumped Libby's shoulder with her own. She and Will had always been close, so she hadn't much worried over the lack of a sister in her life, but now it was as though she'd been granted a gift she never knew she wanted.

"William would likely use the side door when he returns." Libby's voice broke into Patience's thoughts. "Even if you watched by the window, you'd not be able to see him."

"I did not think of that."

"I'll pray he returns safely." Libby yawned and snuggled down into the bed. "But I must get some sleep. You should, too, if you're able."

Patience lay down as well and tucked one arm under her pillow. "I will try."

Libby's even breathing soon proved her to be asleep, but Patience's mind refused to settle. Her thoughts wandered to her brother once more, and to Mr. Wagner. What had happened after they returned to Old South? She prayed they were in no danger. Father had said very little over supper, and while Patience suspected he might know something of what was going on, she dared not ask. He had already been visibly angry at Will's absence. Patience did not want to risk upsetting him more, or revealing too much of her own knowledge on the matter.

She closed her eyes, but sleep would not come, not until she knew Will was safe. She slipped from the bed and pulled on her dressing gown, then eased out of the room as quietly as possible and snuck downstairs. Will's room was in the small addition that jutted from the back of the house. It had been Dr. Caldwell's office, and as such was accessible by the door in the parlor as well as from the outside. Mayhap he had returned without her knowing.

She padded through the parlor and cracked the door open to peek inside.

"Oh, thank goodness." Patience breathed out the words when she spotted Will's tall frame. He stood by the washbasin next to his bed, his back to her, but turned swiftly when he heard her voice. She stifled a gasp. "What happened to your face?"

Will's eyes widened, looking especially bright against his skin which was covered with black smudges, as though he'd rubbed his face with soot from the fire.

"Patience, what are you doing?"

"Worrying over you." She ducked into the room and pushed the door closed with a quiet click. "Where have you been?"

"At Griffin's Wharf, though you cannot say a word of it." He squeezed the wet cloth in his hands over the basin, then rubbed it across his forehead. "The tea is gone."

"They agreed to send it back after all?

He shook his head. "No. We emptied it into the harbor."

Patience exhaled as a chill ran down her spine. The question regarding what to do with the tea had been decisively answered, but what consequences were to come of such actions remained to be seen.

~

*P*ale light slipped through the shutters as Josiah awoke Friday morning and climbed out of bed. The dirty rag he'd used to wipe his face clean last night sat crumpled beside his washbasin on the table. He huffed out a breath at the cold of the floorboards against his bare feet as he crossed the room and snatched it up.

For a long moment, he stared at the streaks that stained the cloth, nearly the only evidence of his involvement in the destruction of the tea. That and the padlock tucked in the pocket of his coat. He'd repair it first thing and return it to the *Dartmouth* today.

Josiah balled his fist around the scrap of fabric and tossed it into the low flames that flickered in the hearth. For one weighty moment, it lay there, untouched, then the edges caught fire, which quickly spread, engulfing the cloth and leaving only ashes behind.

Though his eyes fixed upon the smoldering coals, it was tea he saw in his mind. News would travel. Word of what had happened here in Boston would spread to other colonies. There were plans to send Paul Revere this very day with a report of the events, first to New York and then Philadelphia. It would take longer for the story to reach London, but no doubt, parliament would have something to say in response. What that might be, he could only guess.

He blinked and turned away from the fire, dressed quickly, then grabbed the padlock and headed for the smithy. While he waited for the forge to heat, Josiah examined the broken lock. It would not be difficult to repair. The mechanism was intact. He only needed to mend the shackle where the u-shaped bar had snapped in two.

He pumped the bellow, tied his leather apron around his waist, and grasped the small piece of metal with his tongs. As he held it over the flames, he could not help but marvel again at how efficiently and peacefully their plans had unfolded last night. They'd been met with no protest, and all had carried out their duties with quiet precision. Aside from the tea, and this one padlock, no other property had suffered damage of any kind.

Josiah bent the thin, glowing bar of metal over the narrow

end of his anvil, using his smallest hammer to mold it back into shape.

The one name Josiah had garnered last night, Phineas Stearns, echoed in his mind alongside the ring of his hammer against the iron lock.

A smithy and a farm, Stearns had said. Josiah rarely allowed himself to dwell on such an idea, but was that not what he hoped for someday? A piece of land away from the city, with room to wander and a house worth making a home out of.

And a family to fill that home.

That thought was new. Or at least the unexpected rush of hope that filled his heart at the idea.

A pair of dark eyes and a dimpled smile flashed in his mind. How had Miss Abbott managed to weave herself so deeply into his thoughts and emotions in so short a time? It was only a fortnight ago that he had run into her at the wharf, and now it was her face that appeared in his mind at the idea of a family of his own.

He shook his head as he sprinkled a pinch of borax on the glowing end of the padlock before holding the two pieces together with a steady hand. The white powder would help the metal mold into a single strong hook once more.

Would William tell his sister about what happened at Griffin's Wharf last night? If so, she would certainly suspect that Josiah had also been involved. What would she think of him? Of what they had done?

Josiah huffed, blowing an errant strand of hair from his forehead, and lay the finished padlock on the work table. He examined it from every angle. The shackle moved easily and fit snug into the lock. Good. It should meet with the captain's approval.

Approval. The word settled in Josiah's heart like a heavy weight. He'd never fully answered William's question regarding his intentions toward Miss Abbott. And though William had offered his blessing, approval from her father would be much harder, if not impossible, to gain.

Still, Josiah could not deny his draw toward Miss Abbott. His role in the happenings of December sixteenth and his work with the Sons of Liberty must remain a secret, for more reasons than one.

CHAPTER 22

$\mathcal{T}$ension hovered over the kitchen, thicker than the porridge in Patience's bowl. After Will had returned last night, she'd stayed up late with him while he recounted the destruction of the tea. His hushed whispers had stirred a mix of pride and fear within her. Even now, her pulse raced at the word he'd used to describe what he'd done —treason. An act that carried the sentence of death by hanging.

She swallowed and flicked her gaze across the table to Libby, whose eyes met hers for the briefest of moments. They'd had no opportunity to speak privately this morning, but Patience knew her stepsister was anxious to discover what had happened. Beside her, Mary kept her head down as she ate, her face a mask that revealed none of her thoughts or emotions.

Father brooded at the head of the table, hardly touching his food. He'd said nothing in regards to the tea, but his silence spoke louder than words. He could not yet know what had transpired last night, and Patience dreaded his reaction when he found out.

She dipped her spoon in her bowl, then nearly dropped it

when Father stood abruptly, his chair scraping against the wide-planked floor.

"I must go to Griffin's Wharf and discover what came of the meetings yesterday."

Patience dared not turn to look at Will, who sat beside her, but she sensed him straighten his shoulders at Father's words.

"Unless my son is privy to some information I am not." Father pressed his palms to the table, an imposing presence as he loomed above the rest of them.

Will raised his chin. "I did attend the meetings at Old South and can tell you the men were intent that no tea be unloaded."

Patience ducked her head. She did not wish for another argument between them, but it seemed unavoidable. How much worse would it be once Father knew the full extent of what happened? Would he suspect Will's involvement? Certainly, he would not inform upon his own son. She clasped her hands in her lap, her knuckles matching the white of her apron.

"Fools and troublemakers." Father scowled. "And yet you insist upon associating with them."

"I should not think my curiosity would be such a problem to you." Will stood and crossed his arms over his chest.

She looked up, glancing between both men. They were so different in nearly every way, save for their eyes, a matching stormy blue. If only she could soothe the hostility between them.

"You know where my loyalties lie, but still you do this, to your shame and mine." Father curled his hands into fists. "Are you so determined to always be against me?"

"That is not my intention, nor my desire." Will's voice held an edge of sorrow, so slight that Patience doubted anyone but she would recognize it as such.

Mary quietly pushed away from the table, gathering empty dishes and carrying them to the counter at the back of the kitchen. Libby cast a furtive glance at Patience, then joined her mother, intent upon escaping the hostility that hung like a thundercloud. Patience abandoned her own half-eaten bowl and stood, twisting her hands in her apron. Perhaps she could stave off the storm.

"Will has always kept abreast of local happenings." She smiled gently at Father. "'Tis part of his work as a printer. He does not mean it as a personal affront."

Father's gaze shifted to her and softened slightly. She prayed he would take hold of her attempt at making peace.

He was quiet for a long moment, then he bobbed his chin in a single nod. "Would you like to accompany me, Patience?"

Her eyes went wide. "To the wharf?"

Father nodded and tugged at the lapels of his coat. "I would appreciate the company."

She blinked, surprised at the unexpected offer. If she went to the harbor, she would need to temper her reaction so as not to reveal what she already knew, but she could not suppress her curiosity to see it for herself. "I would be glad to."

Father smiled briefly at her response, cast a final glance at Will, then headed for the door.

Their walk to the harbor was a quiet one, and slow to accommodate Father's pace. Though she was thankful for his invitation, she could not help but wonder at his reason. Did he truly wish for her company? Hope sprouted in her heart at the thought.

As they neared Griffin's Wharf, a strange scent of mingled tea and salt water wafted toward them, pulling them closer. Gray mist hovered over the harbor, shrouding everything in a dull, heavy damp that clung to Patience's cloak and matched Father's dark mood.

He drew to a halt at the water's edge, his face contorted in anger. "It is worse than I imagined."

Patience followed his gaze.

Remnants of tea drifted on the water like fallen leaves in autumn, pushed and pulled by the constant ebb of the current. Broken bits of the crates, splintered and sharp at the edges, bobbed at the surface. Several row boats floated in the swells, with boys perched inside, using their paddles to push the remaining tea deeper below the surface. How much of it already lay at the bottom of the sea, she could only imagine.

Waves slapped at the sides of the three tea ships, each looking strangely serene despite last night's destruction. The *Eleanor* was familiar from her weeks of travel across the Atlantic. Sailors moved aboard ship, like shadows through the fog, but in her mind, she could see Will in their place, heaving crates of tea into the sea below.

She blinked back the vision. Father could never know of Will's part in the destruction.

"Utterly ruined. All of it." Father's words were laced with disgust. "Do you know what that cargo was worth?"

Patience shook her head.

"Nearly ten thousand pounds, I'd wager." He slammed his cane against the ground, and Patience flinched. "They must pay for this. The perpetrators must be found. I hope parliament spares nothing in their punishment of this act of rebellion."

He started walking again, and Patience followed silently at his side, the wind tugging at her cape. Small gatherings of people lingered nearby, most faces lit with curiosity and excitement, some darkened by anger.

"I am sorry you had to see this, and yet, perhaps it is to your benefit." Father looked down at her, his brows drawn low. "You always look for the best in people, as your mother did. I admire that about you, but I worry that in doing so, you could be too easily led astray."

The hope that had begun to bloom in her heart wilted like a spring bud under a late frost. How could he compliment her nature, while also disparaging her judgment?

"I know how much you respect your brother, but if William is getting ideas from these rebels, I do not want you to be misled as well." He turned to face her fully. "I have given up trying to influence my son, but at least I can ensure you are not swayed by his misguided choices. I only wish to protect you. I hope you know that."

Patience tucked her cloak tighter around herself but could not ward off the chill brought on by Father's words. He'd not sought her company, after all. He only wanted to teach her a lesson, and to do so without Will present. For so long, she had wished for the comfort of Father's care, but this protection he spoke of felt anything but caring. His attitude toward Will and his low opinion of her discernment made her stomach churn.

She swallowed, trying to muster an appropriate response, but was spared the trouble when Captain Bruce strode toward them with a solemn wave.

"Miss Abbott." Captain Bruce bowed slightly.

"Captain." Father shook the man's hand. "What a grave day."

"I regret that you must witness such destruction." The captain directed his words toward Patience, then turned his focus to her father. "I know you planned to purchase some of the tea for your shop, but the entire shipment is gone."

Father grumbled low in his chest. "This after business has already been poor this past month. Can you relay all that transpired?"

"I have a few moments to spare, though I do not wish to burden your daughter with such talk. Mayhap another time would be better?"

Father hesitated a moment, then placed a hand on her shoulder. "Forgive me, my dear girl, but this is of utmost importance. I would rather not delay. You may wait for me if you'd like, though I must make for the shop once I am done here. I think it best you return home."

She blinked but quickly schooled her features. "I am certain I can find my way."

"Very good. I will see you this evening."

She nodded and dropped a brief curtsy to Captain Bruce when he tipped his hat to bid her farewell. For a long moment, she stood frozen in place, watching their retreating backs as they strode away.

Father had left her behind. Again. Just as he had every time he boarded a ship and sailed from their home in Chatham. Just as he had when he chose to stay in Boston instead of coming back to England. Just as he had when she needed him most, as Mama lay dying and their plea for his return went unanswered.

Her dark thoughts pressed down upon her, heavy and cold as the fog that engulfed the harbor. Patience clasped her hands over her arms, tucking herself within the shelter of her cloak. She should find her way home, but her feet seemed to be of a different mind. Her petticoats swept against her legs as she wandered closer to the sea.

She stared out, away from the shore and the remains of the ruined tea, past the ships with their sails tied and their holds emptied of cargo, to where the water held a grayish hue. The ocean stretched beyond what her eyes could see, melding with the dark clouds on the horizon, as though unending.

Not long ago, she had peered across the Atlantic from the other direction, full of hope and promise for the life she was sailing toward in America. Had she truly thought that reuniting with Father would be simple, erasing the years they'd been apart? That all the disappointments and hurts of the past would be instantly forgotten?

Patience lifted a hand to her hood as a strong gust of wind threatened to whip it from her head, but the chill that ran down her spine could not be blamed on the elements. She had carried the persistent weight of trying to earn her father's love for years, only to be let down time and again. She had come to

Boston, left the only home she'd ever known at his request, but little had changed. He was content to keep her at arm's length, never seeking to truly understand her. Happier, it seemed, to simply ensure she did not stray from the path he deemed right.

Perhaps those men that threw the tea in the harbor felt something akin to her own emotions. Was England like the father who had too often abandoned and disappointed his child? Or worse yet, sought to bend his child to his own will?

The realization rushed over her like a cold wave. These colonists only wished to be treated as equals, with the rights of British citizens, not as subjects to be pushed around. But they had been denied, over and over. Would last night's act of rebellion be just one of many to come? Would they strive to fully throw off the weight of England's rule?

She didn't wish to rebel against her father. She would always love him, even if he never was the man she hoped him to be. But she did long to be free of the weight of striving.

Tears escaped the corners of her eyes and slid down her cheeks, leaving behind trails of moisture that turned her wind-bitten face even colder. She swiped them away. She needed to go home.

If only there were a place that truly felt like such.

CHAPTER 23

*J*osiah kept his head down as he strode briskly toward the *Dartmouth*, the newly repaired padlock in his pocket. Best get this business done quickly. Crowds milled about, and he tugged his hat low. He did not want anyone to recognize him during this errand and guess at his involvement in the destruction of the tea. They'd not met with resistance last night, but that did not mean they had escaped all risk of consequences.

He approached the *Dartmouth* and flagged down a sailor who was descending the gangway. "Is the captain aboard?"

"Aye." The sailor pointed to the forecastle.

Josiah climbed onto the deck and made straight for Captain Hall. The man eyed him warily.

"I believe this was promised to you." Josiah reached into his pocket and held out the padlock.

Captain Hall took it, turning it over in his hand and inspecting it a long moment. Then he nodded. "Thank you."

Josiah touched his fingers to his hat and departed, glad the captain didn't detain him further or press him for any information. The last piece of evidence linking Josiah to the destruction of the tea was out of his hands. Now all that remained was the secret he and his fellow participants vowed to keep.

As he descended to the dock, a flash of red caught his eye. His pulse quickened. A British soldier, his crimson coat brighter than glowing iron fresh from the forge, was disembarking a small sloop that had anchored near the *Dartmouth*. A tall figure strode beside him, clad in an elegant greatcoat that billowed in the wind. The man turned to survey the harbor, and Josiah immediately recognized his profile and neat blond queue. Edward Cunningham.

So Cunningham had returned from his hideaway on Castle Island. Likely, to inspect the damage of last night's escapade. Would he stay in town or flee back to the safety of the fortress? If he remained, he was likely to renew his attempt to dine with the Abbotts. Josiah clenched his jaw.

The men stopped in the middle of the dock, blocking Josiah's path. He could not make out their conversation, but the matching scowls upon their faces spoke volumes. He kept his head low and didn't break his stride. He knew Cunningham by sight, but they had never actually met, and there was no reason Cunningham should recognize him. All the better.

Josiah moved to walk around the pair, but a commanding voice stopped him in his tracks.

"You there." The soldier nodded in Josiah's direction. "What damage to your ship?"

Josiah glanced up at the man, not failing to notice the gleaming bayonet scabbard at his waist. "Beg your pardon?"

"I saw you coming off the *Dartmouth*. Are you not part of her crew?"

"Nay."

The soldier stared at him as though challenging him to say more. The man had a prominent cleft in his chin, made all the more noticeable by the familiar high stock collar of the British uniform that kept his neck stiff and his head raised. He seemed to peer down his nose at Josiah, even though they stood nearly the same height, and his mouth turned in a scornful frown.

Josiah matched his stony gaze and held his tongue, praying his own expression did not reveal his racing heart.

"Come, let's be off. This fellow will be of no help to us." Cunningham waved a dismissive hand in the air. "We will speak with Hall ourselves."

The soldier grunted but stepped aside to let Josiah pass.

Josiah could feel the soldier's eyes upon him as he strode away, but he didn't look back. He clenched his hands at his side and ducked around a passel of young men gathered at the edge of the harbor. Maybe he should take a different route back to the smithy, on the chance the soldier was still watching. He angled south, picking up his pace, but paused when a familiar profile caught his eye.

Miss Abbott? The wind tugged at her cape, and she clasped it tightly around her petite frame. She seemed so small against the backdrop of the sea. A lone figure, bracing herself in the face of the salty wind. Her shoulders stooped, and he found himself walking toward her, the soldier and Cunningham forgotten.

Was she upset over what happened last night? If the destruction of the tea caused her grief, she'd want little to do with him now, for surely, she suspected his position on the matter.

Or was she missing England as she stared over the vast expanse of water? Did she wish to return to her old home? The thought made his gut clench.

He was nearly at her side when she turned and noticed him, her eyes widening. She swiped a hand across her cheek, but not before he spotted the tears there. His heart ached, and he shoved his hands into the pockets of his greatcoat to keep from reaching for her.

"Miss Abbott, are you unwell?"

"Mr. Wagner." Her voice wobbled, and she drew a shaky breath before continuing. "I am well. Better now that you are here."

She ducked her head, as though embarrassed by her forthrightness, but he could not quell the rush of heat that filled his chest at her words.

"Are you here alone?"

"I was with my father, but he met with Captain Bruce and told me to return home. I got lost in my thoughts and have yet to set out."

Josiah clenched his teeth to keep from voicing the words he wished to say. What business could be so urgent as to compel a father to leave his daughter behind in an unfamiliar place? Had he no concern for her safety and wellbeing?

"I'll walk you home. If you do not mind, that is." He silently prayed she would agree, for her sake and his own desire to share her company.

"I don't wish to trouble you."

"It's no trouble. I would like to accompany you." He offered his arm, brows raised in question.

The corners of her mouth tipped up, and she placed her hand in the crook of his elbow. Her touch seemed to seep through the layers of his clothing and sent a thrill up his arm. He tucked her a bit closer to his side than necessary as he steered them down Belchers Lane. Propriety might demand more space, but the wounded expression on her face spoke to a need for comfort, and he would lend her his strength if he could.

"This is the second time you've come to my rescue at Griffin's Wharf." The smile she offered made his heart stutter.

"You make it sound more valiant than it is."

"What some might see as a simple act, others would call heroic." She glanced over her shoulder at the ships and then looked back at him, as though to convey an unspoken message.

Is that how she saw the actions of last night? She must suspect his involvement to some extent, as she was too inquisitive and intelligent not to. She was also wise enough not to speak of it. But he could not resist prying further, curiosity to know her thoughts driving him.

He lowered his voice so only she might hear. "And what some call heroic, others call treason."

She held his gaze. "I am coming to believe the former and would not be ashamed to know such a man as those who took a stand last night."

Relief washed over him and his heart swelled. "I'm glad of it."

He could say nothing else. Not here, on the open streets. It was too dangerous a secret to reveal, one he had sworn to keep. But the smile that blossomed on her face and the matching one he felt tugging at his own mouth spoke more than all the unsaid words between them.

They turned down Summer Street, their pace unhurried. He relished the feel of her hand wrapped around his arm, the brush of her skirts against his leg when the wind blew. She was soft and feminine, so different from his world of hot iron and heavy sledges. What would it be like to have her part of his life every day? He glanced down, his gaze tracing the gentle curve of her cheek behind the edge of her hood. His fingers itched to do the same.

Dragging his focus back to the road ahead, he reined in his thoughts. After all that had happened less than twenty-four hours prior and all that remained uncertain for the days to come, the obstacles to a relationship between them seemed even greater than before. And yet, he'd never felt like this. Could he set aside the doubts and find the courage to try?

There were no guarantees for safety and certainty in life. He knew that well enough. The loss of his mother, his newborn brothers, and his father at such a young age had shown him the fragility of life and the risk of love. The hurts of his childhood had shaped the thoughts of his adulthood, like iron bent under a forge of fear.

But Patience—for that was how he truly thought of her—had lit a new fire within him. One that called him to melt away the protective barrier he'd placed around his heart and be shaped into something new. Something hopeful and willing to love.

The possibility of hurt and the uncertainty of the future dimmed beside the opportunity for joy and belonging that he had not experienced since he was a boy. How much deeper would it be now, as a man, to have someone to love fully and be fully loved by in return? To have someone to call his own. A family again.

He must speak to her now, while he had the opportunity. As he mulled over how to begin, Patience's voice broke into his thoughts.

"What will happen next? Surely, news of the destruction of the tea will travel to England. What then?"

"Then parliament will decide Boston's fate, I suspect." How severe a fate that would be, he could not guess.

"So, until then, we wait."

He heard in her voice the same trepidation he had felt at times. But he refused to let those uncertainties deter him from pursuing this woman he had come to admire.

He slowed to a stop beneath a tree, the limbs reaching over them like sheltering arms, and turned to face her. Her hand slipped from its place on his arm, but he caught her fingers in his own, weaving them together.

Her eyes widened. Did she feel, as he did, the spark that spread from where their fingers met? The touch anchored him, as though their hands were made to fit together, as if their lives might be meant to interlock as well. How could such a simple gesture create such a complex feeling?

He squeezed her fingers gently. "I cannot say what the coming weeks and months will bring for this town, but in the meantime, we must continue to live."

"Each day is one the Lord has made, a gift from Him that we give back by living in obedience and trust. To know tomorrow is His place, not ours." Patience looked down at their clasped hands. "Mama used to say that often. I suppose I still need the reminder now."

"As do I."

Her words burrowed deep into his soul with both comfort and conviction. For too long, he had felt as though God were far away, but instead of seeking Him, Josiah had let his faith grow cold. How different would the past years have been if he had lived with the obedience and trust Patience spoke of? Maybe the fear that had lingered in his heart would have been banished long before.

"Patience..." He could not hide the note of hesitation in his voice. "May I have leave to call you that?"

She looked up at him with shy smile. "You may."

He stepped closer, confidence bolstered by her expression. "I must confess that you captured my attention from the very first time we met."

Her cheeks, already rosy from the chill breeze, took on an even pinker hue.

"I should very much like to continue to know you better."

Her smile widened, her dimples appearing. "I would like that as well, Josiah."

His heart jumped at the sound of his name from her lips. Joy swelled in his chest, but it could not fully overcome the doubt that gnawed at the corner of his mind. The divide between Patriots like himself and Loyalists like her father would only grow wider with each passing day. He cared for her too much to put her at odds with her father unless she truly considered what was at stake.

"You know that your father and I hold different views about this country and her future. I don't wish to be the cause of strife between you and him."

She was quiet for a long moment, and his pulse pounded in his ears as he waited for her reply.

Finally, she tilted her chin up and squared her shoulders. "I am willing to take that risk, though I will pray that Father can come to accept what, and who, is important to me."

'Twas doubtful it would be that easy, but her words of optimism encouraged him. "Then I will pray for that too." He brushed his thumb over her knuckles, wishing he could press a kiss there instead.

The wind rattled the branches above them, and he tucked her hand into the bend of his arm as he led them back down the road. Though out of practice, Josiah breathed a silent prayer that God would make a way forward for them.

CHAPTER 24

*P*atience stared out the parlor window as sleet hit the windowpanes, tracing icy trails down the glass. A book lay open on her lap, but her mind refused to focus on the words on the page, instead repeating the words she had shared with Josiah over and over. Words that had said so little and so much at the same time.

She'd not told anyone of her walk home from the harbor with him yesterday morning, though she had scarcely been able to think of anything else since. Even now, she could almost feel the comforting warmth of his strong arm, the thrill of his fingers clasping hers, and the intensity of his gaze that had set her heart galloping like a runaway horse.

"You've not turned a page these last ten minutes." William nudged her arm from his seat beside her, newspaper in hand. "Is it that dull, or are your thoughts elsewhere?"

"My mind is wandering, I'm afraid." Patience closed the book with a sigh.

"Dare I ask what, or whom, occupies your thoughts?"

Patience hesitated. Her time with Josiah seemed something precious, to be held close and treasured, yet she longed to confide in someone. For once, she and Will were alone, with Father at the shop and Mary and Libby at the market.

"It's Josiah—I mean, Mr. Wagner." Patience stared into the fire, unable to bring herself to meet Will's probing gaze. "He did not ask to court me, not in so many words, and yet..." She left her words hanging at the sound of Will's gentle chuckle.

"Josiah, is it? I am glad for you. He is a good man, and I already gave him my approval."

"What?" Her eyes widened, and she swatted at him with her book. "You've spoken with him about me?"

"Of course. I suspected a mutual interest between you from that first morning we met on the Common. Why do you think I sought his help finding a position at the press?"

"Surely, not because of me."

Will shrugged. "Not entirely. But I could have looked for work on my own if I chose. I thought to get to know him better, find out what kind of man he was. If he was worthy of your favor."

"And you think he is?"

"I do." Will reached out and clasped her hand where it rested upon the book as his expression grew serious. "But I cannot say it will be easy for you."

"Because of Father."

"And because I do not know what the coming months will bring, after what happened with the tea. There could be trouble, both for those who participated if they are apprehended and for the whole of Boston, if not America."

"You think Josiah is in danger?" Patience's breath caught in her chest. "Are you in danger?"

"I'm not afraid for myself. Father's loyalty is a shield for me, whether I wish it or not. It is likely he already suspects I was involved in some way, or at least that I was present and giving approval to their actions, but it would bring him too much shame were I to be accused. I have heard of a man, though,

Francis Akeley, who was informed upon for his participation and has been committed to prison."

Patience worried her lip. She'd been so focused on Father's likely disapproval, she hadn't thought as much about the larger ramifications of Josiah's actions.

"I do not say this to frighten or discourage you. I promised you I would look out for you, and I will."

"You always have, but some things are outside your control."

Will nodded, his face solemn. Then a mischievous glint sparked in his eyes. "But mayhap I can arrange a clandestine meeting between the two of you. With me as a chaperone, of course."

Patience couldn't help chuckling, even as she rolled her eyes at his teasing. She'd missed that boyish grin and much preferred it to the serious expression he usually wore of late.

He returned to the paper on his lap, and Patience opened her book once more, but still could not fix her attention to the page, her thoughts wandering to the next time she might see Josiah. She was so caught up in her musings that she didn't hear the front door open or the footsteps that followed.

When Father's voice broke into the room, she startled. "Patience, you'll be glad to see who has returned." He ushered Mr. Cunningham through the door.

Patience jumped to her feet, the book tumbling to the floor with a thud.

Mr. Cunningham bowed. "It is good to be back in Boston, even more so now that I can see you again, Miss Abbott."

She clasped her hands in front of her and bobbed her head, unable to offer a proper reply. His greeting was nothing but kind, yet his eagerness set her on edge.

"Back from Castle Island?" Will asked as he rose to stand beside her, a polite smile on his lips but a wariness in his eyes that matched her own growing trepidation.

"Some of the consignees remain there, and some plan to retreat out of the city for a time, but I resolved to return home for the sake of my mother and sisters." Mr. Cunningham crossed the room to join them before the fire.

Father followed slowly behind and settled into one of the empty chairs with a grimace. "My apologies. This frigid weather makes my leg ache more than usual."

"I'll not interrupt your evening for long." Mr. Cunningham turned his attention to Patience. "I was sorry to put off my dinner invitation before but hope to offer something even better. My father had a long-standing tradition of welcoming the new year with a dinner and dancing. I aim to carry on that tradition and would very much like you to join me, Miss Abbott, on the first of the new year."

Patience glanced at Father, whose pleased smile only added to the tangle of nerves twisting in her belly. She had no wish to encourage Mr. Cunningham, but what reason could she give to refuse?

Father stood, aching leg apparently forgotten. "I think you've left my daughter quite speechless with your generous invitation."

Mr. Cunningham chuckled but kept his eyes on her. "What say you, Miss Abbott? Your father is invited as well, of course, and I would like to offer my carriage as transport, to spare you from the weather. I would be very honored if you would accept."

Out of the corner of her eye, Patience could see the rigid set of Will's jaw, such a contrast to the delighted expression on Father's face. In everything, it seemed, she was caught between two worlds.

She forced a smile. There was no way to refuse Mr. Cunningham, and he was Father's friend. She would agree to dinner, but must make her feelings known to Father soon.

She dipped her head in a polite nod. "Thank you. We are grateful to accept."

"Excellent." Mr. Cunningham's blue eyes shone with genuine pleasure. "I look forward to it with great anticipation."

After Mr. Cunningham departed, Father turned to Patience with a broad smile. "Well, my dear girl, this is quite a treat, indeed. Dinner and dancing. You shall have a new gown for the occasion. I'll tell Mary right away."

His cane drummed an uneven beat as he left the parlor. Patience released a sigh.

Will leaned close, his voice low. "Should I warn Josiah about his competition?"

His remark sounded like another jest, but the expression on his face bore a seriousness that mirrored her own foreboding.

~

*J*osiah rested the trammel hook on the coals and swiped his arm across his forehead. Four days had passed since his walk home from the harbor with Patience. He longed to see her again, but even apart, she occupied much of his waking thoughts.

What would her father say if Josiah knocked on their door unannounced and requested to spend time with her? Did he stand any chance of earning Mr. Abbott's approval? That question settled in his gut, uncertain and uncomfortable.

He picked up the hook again with his tongs and balanced it on the anvil, hammering the edge to shape it, allowing the familiar rhythm to push away his worries over Mr. Abbott.

The door swung open, a burst of winter wind sweeping into the smithy. William shoved the door closed, and Josiah raised a hand in greeting. Perhaps William might offer some advice where his father was concerned.

William crossed the room with a determined stride. "Do you have a moment?"

He nodded, concern worming its way through his chest.

"The local tea dealers met yesterday." William tugged off his cocked hat and tucked it under his arm. "They voted not to sell any more tea after the twentieth of January, nor to purchase any."

"So I heard." Josiah lay his sledge on the anvil. "And your father? Will he agree?"

"Nay. He said as much at dinner last night."

"I fear such a refusal could bring him trouble." Josiah's information had already put Mr. Abbott on the list of businesses to avoid. What if this repeated refusal put the shop, and even the man himself, in danger?

"As do I." William's mouth was a grim line. "I told him so, but he is determined in his decision."

"How has it been these past days between you and him? Has he spoken much of the destruction of the tea?"

"He ranted for quite some time on Friday, but since, has said very little to me. He knows that I went to the meeting, but beyond that, I have revealed nothing, nor has he asked."

Josiah frowned. "You think he suspects your involvement?"

"He must believe I was there at least, even if just as a bystander. I think he chooses not to ask because he doesn't wish to know. What would he do with the truth? He'd not turn me in, for the embarrassment to himself would be too much. It is enough for him that I'll be returning to England. Until then, it seems he has set his focus elsewhere. Which is the real reason I've come."

Josiah wiped his hands on his leather apron and waited for William to continue.

"Cunningham came by on Saturday. He's returned from Castle Island."

"I knew he was in Boston. I saw him Friday at the wharf but

hoped he would go back to the fortress once more. The rest of the consignees remained there."

"He seems intent on staying. He plans to hold a dinner on the first of the new year and came to issue a special invitation for Patience."

Josiah clenched his jaw as William continued.

"It has become increasingly apparent that my father wishes for a match between Patience and Cunningham, and it seems Cunningham is in favor, given the way he regarded my sister last night.

Heat flared in Josiah's chest. "I spoke with your sister last week. I knew then it would be difficult, given your father's loyalty, but this complicates things further." He shoved a hand through his hair. "I have nothing to offer compared to a man such as Cunningham."

"Nothing?" William furrowed his brow and crossed his arms over his chest. "You care for my sister, do you not?"

Josiah nodded.

"And she cares for you. That is worth more than any mansion in Boston, I'd say."

Josiah scrubbed a hand over his jaw, his doubts like a stopper over the flame of hope. "Do you truly think your father's mind could be swayed?"

"I cannot say, but are you willing to try?" William stared at him, and there seemed an unspoken challenge behind his words.

Josiah squared his shoulders and nodded. He was willing, more than willing. Not just to try, but to fight for her. He'd not be worthy of her if he wasn't.

CHAPTER 25

*A*s Patience followed Mary to the mantua maker's shop on Thursday, her mind wandered far from the task of choosing fabric. A sennight had passed since the incident with the tea, Christmas was just two days away, and life at home had settled into a precarious peace.

Father rarely spoke of what had happened, especially when William was around. It seemed they'd formed an unspoken agreement to keep their beliefs to themselves, and while Patience was thankful for the reprieve from arguments, the knowledge of her own feelings for Josiah was like a current, hidden beneath a calm surface but always churning. She had not dared to say anything to her father yet, nor had she seen Josiah since their walk home from the harbor.

She missed him. Despite her brave words about taking a risk and praying for her father to be accepting, worry had taken root in her heart and continued to grow, like a pernicious weed. She'd had doubts before, and Father's enthusiasm over Mr. Cunningham's invitation only added to them.

"Here we are." Mary ushered her into the shelter of the small building.

The room was tidy, the wide-plank floors neatly swept. Its cheery fire was a welcome respite from the damp and cold. A woman who looked to be Mary's age raised her head from the wide table in front of the fire where she sat, stitching a hemline.

"Mrs. Caldwell, so good to see you." She set down her needle and rose with a smile, then paused, eyes widening slightly. "Forgive me. I had forgotten...Mrs. Abbott."

"No matter." Mary waved her hand, dismissing the woman's mistake. "How are you, Mrs. Barker?"

As the two women greeted one another, Patience rubbed her hands briskly together and spun in a slow circle to take in her surroundings. One wall bore rows of pegs with colorful dyed wool and thread hanging from each, all the popular colors of the season on full display. Open shelves covered another wall, loaded with fabrics in every color and pattern Patience could imagine. A full-length mirror stood in the corner next to the window where the light was best, and on that very windowpane hung a printed sign which declared that Mrs. Barker possessed the latest fashions from London.

"Patience, come and I'll introduce you." Mary beckoned her over. "This is my husband's daughter, Patience Abbott. We're here so that she might be fitted for a new *robe a l'anglaise*. Mr. Abbot wants her to have something special for a dinner invitation Saturday next."

"How lovely." Mrs. Barker clasped her hands in front of her ample bosom. "Let me look at you a moment, Miss Abbott. You may hang your cloak by the door and then take a turn for me, please."

Patience did as she was told, feeling awkwardly on display. Mama had been so talented with her needlework that she had made most of Patience's clothes at home. Their visits to the mantua maker in Chatham had been few and far between, and the elderly woman there was nothing like Mrs. Barker, whose assessing gaze skimmed over Patience's frame from head to toe.

"I think something with blue tones would suit you well." Mrs. Barker gave a brisk nod. "Let me show you some of our newest arrivals."

The woman crossed the room to the wall of fabrics, standing on tiptoes to reach several on the higher shelves. She returned to the wooden table with an armful of options to choose from.

"This is quite a rich silk, and the deep color would pair well with your dark hair." Mrs. Barker lay the first option on the table.

Patience ran her hands over the smooth fabric. It was beautiful but seemed far more expensive than anything else she'd ever owned.

"I am partial to this pattern myself." Mrs. Barker placed the next bundle beside the first. "Quite intricate, isn't it?"

Patience leaned close to examine the tight swirls of white flowers over top a blue fabric that remind her of a jay's wing. She liked it better than the first, though it might be dizzying if used for an entire gown.

"And this combination would be very elegant." Mrs. Barker set the final two fabrics down together. "I would suggest the pattern for the main gown, with the solid blue for the under petticoat."

"It is beautiful." Patience was immediately drawn to the creamy white fabric with deep green vines gently swooping throughout. She traced a finger along one, following the design with her eyes. Narrow leaves branched from the edges, with large blue blooms at the ends of each vine reminiscent of the cornflowers that grew around their cottage in England. Wisps of star-shaped flowers in a deep maroon accented other vines. It was like a garden come to life.

"You like this one best?" Mrs. Barker held the fabric up against Patience's waist. "It does suit you quite perfectly, I say."

"I like it very much." Patience glanced at Mary, whose gentle smile and small nod was the final confirmation that she had made the right choice.

"Very good. Let us get you measured and fitted."

Patience spent the next half hour with fabric draped this way and that, measured and pinned and cut until the mantua maker was satisfied.

Finally, Mrs. Barker stepped back, hands on her hips and a pleased smile on her face. "If you will return on Tuesday, I shall do the final fitting and make any adjustments you require."

Mary made arrangements regarding payment as Patience pulled her cloak over her shoulders in preparation to leave. The dress would be beautiful, and it was generous of Father to invest in a new gown for her, but the knowledge of his motivation for the gift pricked her conscience like a thistle.

She glanced back at Mary, who was offering her final farewell to Mrs. Barker. It was bittersweet, too, to share this experience with her stepmother. Mary had been nothing but welcoming, yet it felt so strange to select this dress with her instead of Mama. Never before had anyone but Mama helped with her clothing—be it sewing, selecting fabrics, or simply mending a tear from one of Patience's childhood adventures. Patience's heart ached at yet another reminder of something she would never share with Mama again.

What would Mama think of Mr. Cunningham's invitation and Father's obvious delight over it? If Mama were here, Patience would be able to talk to her about her growing feelings for Josiah in a way she could not with Father. But Mama wasn't here, and Patience had to find the strength and courage to tell Father the truth on her own.

〜

*J*osiah tugged his chair closer to the fire and settled down with his Bible upon his lap. He had begun the habit of reading it every evening since Patience shared her mother's words about living each day in obedience and trust. Her conviction had stirred up old familiar truths in him. Truths that flickered at the edges of his soul like a fire too long banked, struggling to flare to life again. For years, he'd let his faith grow cold, the grief and loneliness of a young orphan transforming into neglect as a grown man. But no more. His time in God's Word had lit a spark within him, as warm and real as the flames that danced in the brick hearth.

Tonight, of all nights, he found special comfort in the Scriptures. It was Christmas, a day that often felt especially lonesome. As he traced his callused fingers over the familiar words of Luke chapter two, he wondered anew at the gift of God made flesh. Of the joyful news declared to poor shepherds. Surely, the God who was willing to humble Himself in such a way was near to Josiah, even now. If lowly shepherds were chosen to meet the newborn savior, then mayhap that same Savior did care about a simple blacksmith.

Josiah bowed his head and swallowed, his throat thick. "God, please forgive me for straying from You. For thinking myself alone when You were here with me all this time. I see now that You have been my help through the years, even when I did not acknowledge You. Thank You for Your steadfast love."

A knock at the door startled him from his prayer. He rested the Bible upon his chair and crossed to open it.

"Patience?" He blinked in surprise. He'd wished to see her every day since their walk from the harbor, but doubts as to her father's reception kept him from visiting.

William stood beside her, his tin lantern casting a flickering glow that highlighted the smile on her face.

"Happy Christmas, Josiah." She held out a basket, and he caught the scent of mince pie.

"Please, come in." He gestured for them both to enter, then closed the door behind them, shutting out the cold.

Patience tugged off her hood and set the basket on the table. Her gaze wandered the room, and he could not help but do the same, seeing his humble home differently, as if through her eyes.

Crumbs dotted his plate from the evening meal, still sitting where he'd left it on the scuffed table. A shirt in need of mending draped over a chair. His sheets and quilt were a twisted pile on the unmade bed, and wax drippings clung to the bedside table where he'd let the candle burn too low.

He ran a hand over his hair as his focus drifted back to her, but there was no judgment or disappointment in her eyes. Instead, her smile seemed even brighter than before.

William glanced between them with a barely disguised grin. "You're sure to enjoy what Patience brought. She made the mince pie herself from our mother's recipe."

The siblings exchanged a tender look as Patience unpacked the basket.

Josiah's mouth watered. "It smells delicious. Thank you for thinking of me."

"Of course." Patience glanced at her brother, who conveniently looked away and crossed to stand before the fire, affording them a bit of privacy. Her cheeks were rosy in the flickering light as she peered up at Josiah, her smile turning shy.

His heart pounded in his chest like a sledge on the anvil. "I am glad you came. I wanted to visit, but after William told me about Cunningham's dinner, I doubted the wisdom of—"

She shook her head. "I must speak with my father, and I will, but you are right. It would not have done any good for you to come now. Better to let things settle after the incident with the tea and allow me to say something to him first."

Josiah stepped closer and clasped a hand around the back of the chair to keep from reaching for her. He ached to take her slim fingers in his or to brush that dark curl of hair from where it rested against her rosy cheek. His fingers pressed harder into the wood. "Did you have a nice Christmas?"

"Aye." She smiled, but there was a hint of sadness in her eyes. "We sang 'Hark the Herald Angels Sing' at church, and I thought of Mama. It was one of her favorites."

"I'm sure you missed her even more today."

"I did, but I am at peace knowing she is with Jesus now. I hold tight to the precious memories I have of her."

"I wish I remembered my mother better. My father too. Their memories have faded over the years."

"You were so young." She rested her hand atop his for the briefest moment. "That is another reason I wanted to come. We both understand that a day such as this can be bittersweet."

"How did you manage to leave the house without arousing suspicion?" Much as he was thankful for the visit, he had no desire to make her feel as though she needed to go behind her father's back to see him.

"William asked Mary for a basket to deliver to a friend, then invited me to join him and bring the leftover pie." She glanced over Josiah's shoulder at her brother, who rejoined them by the table.

"A special Christmas gift to both of you." William grinned. "Though we cannot stay much longer."

Josiah nodded. "I understand. And thank you. This was a welcome surprise, indeed."

William cleared his throat. "Our father's leg troubles him in this cold weather. If he does not plan to attend church as often, mayhap I can escort Patience to Old South instead."

"I will watch for you, then, in case."

Josiah looked back at Patience, hoping his eyes portrayed what his words could not. How much joy it brought him to see her, and how it stirred in him a desire to share this day with her many times over, for every Christmas yet to come. If he were at liberty to speak so openly, would she be delighted or shocked by such an admission?

CHAPTER 26

*P*atience sat, straight and still as she could, in the wooden chair in front of the hearth as Libby fussed with her hair. She'd insisted on styling Patience's long locks before Mr. Cunningham's dinner tonight. Patience's stomach was as tangled as the knots in her hair, but she could not refuse Libby's kindness.

She stared at the dancing flames as Libby wound her thick tresses into a complicated style. She'd never been to a private ball before. In fact, she could hardly remember the last time she had danced. While she knew some steps, she feared she might make a fool of herself. When she'd expressed her trepidation to Father, he'd reassured her that Mr. Cunningham would not mind and was more than capable, that she need only follow his lead.

Patience ran her hands down the smooth fabric of her new gown. The dress was stunning, the most beautiful one she had ever owned. Father had also insisted she purchase any other bits and pieces she might need, so in addition to the gown, Patience wore a delicate new fichu and a fresh pair of shoes with intricate silver buckles.

She reached up and fiddled with the necklace about her throat, a final, unexpected gift from Father. It was a double strand of pearls, tied in the back with a blue silk ribbon that matched the color of her petticoat.

"It's very pretty." Libby wove a strand of hair into a tight twist. "The necklace."

Patience began to nod, but Libby stilled her movement with a gentle hand on her head. "Don't move. I've not pinned it all yet."

"It is pretty." Her voice didn't hold the enthusiasm it should. Patience let her hand fall back to her lap.

"But?"

"But..." Patience sighed. How could she put into words what she felt without sounding ungrateful or, worse, as though she did not love and respect her father?

"I know you're nervous about tonight, but I cannot help thinking there is more on your mind." Libby squeezed Patience's shoulder. "You do not have to say if you'd rather not, but I am a good listener."

Patience wove her fingers together on her lap and squeezed them tight. "I know Father has high hopes for tonight. He has never said it outright, but in so many ways"—she gestured to her new gown—"it is increasingly obvious to me that he would be glad for a match between myself and Mr. Cunningham."

"But you do not wish for that."

"Nay." She paused, searching for the right words. "Mr. Cunningham seems to be a good man, and I don't doubt Father means well, but it is difficult for me to muster enthusiasm for this evening when my affections already lie elsewhere."

Libby abandoned her work and scooted around the front of the chair to face her. Her eyes seemed to sparkle as she grinned at Patience. "I knew it. I suspected as much, but I did not want to press you. You must tell me, how have you even managed to see Mr. Wagner?"

Patience chuckled. "You knew it was him, without me saying?"

"Of course." Libby crouched before her and grabbed Patience's hands in her own. "Oh, it was him you went to see on Christmas night, wasn't it?"

"Aye, though it was before then, the day after the incident with the tea, that we truly had a chance to talk."

"And you kept it from me that long?" Libby clucked her tongue like a scolding mother. "Now you must tell me everything."

Patience ducked her chin and laughed, feeling a pin come loose as a result. Libby emitted a tiny gasp and hurried back to her place behind the chair to tame the wayward locks back into submission. Her fingers deftly twisted and pinned as Patience recounted all that had happened the past fortnight. She'd not kept it a secret from Libby because of lack of trust, but rather a hesitation to speak too freely about what was still so fresh and uncertain. Now, though, it felt good to have a confidante.

"Have you told your father any of this?"

"Nay. It has never seemed the right moment." She shifted in her chair, turning her head to look back at Libby, and was rewarded with an accidental jab in the head by a misguided pin. "He has spoken so enthusiastically of Mr. Cunningham, and we both know where his loyalties lie. I fear his reaction if I admit that my affections belong to a Patriot blacksmith."

"I understand." Libby paused and pushed another pin through Patience's thick tresses. "But you cannot know for certain unless you speak with him."

"I know. You have seen how he and Will are. I dread the thought of having the same strife exist between Father and I."

"But are you willing to sacrifice your future happiness simply to keep the peace?"

Patience drew a shuddering breath as Libby's hands fell away from her hair.

"I'm sorry. I spoke out of turn."

Patience twisted to look up at her stepsister, whose bright, youthful face was drawn in a worried expression.

"Nay, you did not." Patience stood and reached for Libby's hands, clasping them within her own. "You only said what was already on my own mind."

Libby squeezed Patience's fingers. "Your father may be understanding when he sees the depth of your feeling."

"I can only hope you are right."

∼

*P*atience had never seen so much food laid out upon a table in her entire life. A platter of mutton chops sat at one end, a goose at the other, with a myriad of dishes spread between. Candlelight from a trio of candelabras glinted against the glasses of wine and port and the silver-edged china at each place. The feast, and the elegant dining room within which it was served, left no doubt as to Mr. Cunningham's standing in society.

They had arrived at the stately mansion on Hanover Street not long before, in Mr. Cunningham's coach, and been immediately greeted by their host, who offered her his arm and escorted her into the dining room himself. Now Mr. Cunningham sat at the head of the table, with Patience and her father just to his left. His special attention had not gone amiss by the other guests, and as dinner commenced, she tried not to fidget under their scrutiny.

"It is a pleasure to have you here to dine with me this evening." Mr. Cunningham tilted his head ever so slightly in her direction as he served crab imperial onto his plate. He dipped the spoon back into the dish. "May I offer you some?"

"Thank you."

Her plate was soon filled until she was certain she would be unable to eat everything. Conversation filtered about the large dining room table, and Patience caught snippets of different topics. Across the table, one of Mr. Cunningham's sisters flirted with the young gentleman beside her, while Father and the red-coated soldier to his left muttered about the rebellious colonists who would soon pay for their actions.

Patience's forkful of potatoes stuck in her throat at the soldier's vehemence, her thoughts immediately upon Josiah and Will. She swallowed hard.

"I am glad to finally have the opportunity to get to know you better." Mr. Cunningham's voice drew her attention back to him. "All this trouble with the tea has kept me from your company that I anxiously awaited. I hope you are settling in well, despite arriving at a tumultuous time."

"It has been..." Patience paused, her fork hovering over her plate. What could she say to encompass the past month with all the unexpected change it had brought? And how much of her thoughts did she truly wish to reveal to this man? "I will admit that it has been different than I imagined."

"I understand. I pray the new year brings better things."

The intensity of his blue eyes and the brightness of his smile brought a rush of warmth to her cheeks. As the meal progressed, Mr. Cunningham engaged her in near-constant conversation. Patience tried to respond in a kind and polite manner, but his marked attention and Father's approving glances set her stomach churning.

The first course was cleared and followed by a selection of mince pies, sugar cakes, apricot fool, and syllabub, but Patience picked at her food, her appetite dwindling, despite the deli-ciousness of the fare. How could she discourage Mr. Cunning-ham's obvious interest without embarrassing herself or Father? If she could simply get through this evening, then she would discuss her feelings with Father. She silently prayed he would be understanding, but one peek at his pleased expression as

Mr. Cunningham called an end to the meal and ushered her into the large parlor told her otherwise.

Patience took in the room from her place at Mr. Cunningham's side. The high ceilings were edged in elaborate crown molding, and above the white wainscoting, intricate red floral stenciling covered the walls. Above the fireplace mantel, a scenic landscape was painted directly on the plaster. The parlor had been cleared of most furniture to make room for dancing, a pair of fiddlers waiting at one end, and soon the men and women were lined up across from one another, ready to begin.

Patience pressed her lips into a smile as she found herself the center of attention once more, paired with Mr. Cunningham at the head of the line. The music began, and he held out his hand, palm up. She rested her fingers lightly upon his, feeling none of the thrill that always ran through her at even the slightest brush of Josiah's hand.

Mr. Cunningham led them skillfully through the first dance, making up for her own lack of practice. He spoke with her when the steps brought them close enough, and she felt his gaze upon her every time the dance drew them apart. She caught Father's eye from his spot along the wall, and he smiled his approval. Her chest tightened, and her pulse thrummed in her temples. It took every ounce of concentration to mind the steps and keep a pleasant expression on her face.

She would trade all of this—the lavish feast, beautiful gown, and elaborate house—for a simple meal beside Josiah at the old table in his little home. To feel his work-worn fingers wrapped around her own. To talk together about what was truly on their hearts without reservation.

Somehow, she had to make Father see.

The musicians ended the first piece with a flourish, and Mr. Cunningham stepped closer with a slight bow. "I'd ask you for another, but I fear it would draw even more attention than we have already garnered, nor should I neglect my duties as host."

Patience dipped her head. "Thank you for bearing with my dancing. I fear I am rather out of practice."

"It was a pleasure, truly. One I hope to have again many times."

Patience tried to swallow, her mouth suddenly dry. She was spared a response as the guests moved to form new pairings. The soldier who had been seated beside Father at dinner stepped in to join them.

"Miss Abbott," Mr. Cunningham said, "may I present Lieutenant Croome?"

"I have heard much about you." The lieutenant bowed politely.

"Nice to meet you." She returned his smile with some effort.

"I became acquainted with Lieutenant Croome while I was at the fort on Castle Island." Mr. Cunningham clapped his friend on the shoulder. "This is a much better place to spend an evening, wouldn't you say?"

The soldier chuckled and nodded his agreement as the music began, and Patience took her place across from him. Lieutenant Croome looked older than Mr. Cunningham, though not by much. He wore a powdered wig and had a prominent cleft in his chin that gave his face unique character. He spoke little, which Patience was thankful for, but there was something in his assessing gaze that discomforted her, and she was glad when the dance was over.

The line shifted again, and the fiddlers started the next piece, a lively reel this time. As the night wore on, Patience's feet and head began to ache. She finally excused herself and set off in search of the punch, the press of bodies having warmed the room to an uncomfortable level. Ducking through the doorway, she paused a moment to catch her breath, then froze in place at the sound of Father and Mr. Cunningham in conversation not far away. Hidden in the shadows behind the door, she could not be seen, but she could clearly hear them.

"I advise you to use caution if you continue to sell your supply of tea," Mr. Cunningham said.

"I'll not be bullied." Father's voice held an edge of defiance. "The other tea dealers and merchants can do what they wish. I've stood my ground thus far and will continue to."

"You know I respect you for it, but given the struggles your business has met with these past weeks, I am already concerned that someone amongst the Sons has their eye on you. Use caution, for these rebels have proven themselves capable of violence and destruction before."

"All the more reason to hold to our convictions. We must show them we will not be intimidated."

"Let us hope parliament is as steadfast as you when word of what happened here reaches London. Their response must be swift and firm to quash any further rebellion." Mr. Cunningham cleared his throat and lowered his voice. Patience strained to catch his next words. "In the meantime, mayhap we can discuss happier matters. Your daughter is every bit as lovely as you described, and I hope you will grant me leave to further our acquaintance."

"Indeed, I would like nothing more."

Patience spun away, back to the crush of dancers in the parlor. Her breath caught in her lungs, and the room spun before her. She closed her eyes and exhaled slowly until the rushing in her ears had subsided. The evening could not end soon enough.

CHAPTER 27

*F*ather pulled the carriage door shut and leaned back against the velvet cushioned seat with a satisfied sigh. He turned his head to look at Patience, and in the darkness, she could just make out the whites of his eyes and his teeth as he smiled broadly at her.

"That was a splendid evening, don't you agree?" He patted her hand where it lay atop the lap blanket.

Patience could not deny that it was a pleasure to ride in the carriage, sheltered from the weather and warmed by the heated bricks at their feet and the heavy quilt over her lap. With the way her feet ached, the thought of walking back along the frozen cobblestones held no appeal, and yet she felt uncomfortable under such distinct attentions.

"It was an impressive party." She fiddled with the ribbon on her cloak with her free hand, knowing her response did not match Father's enthusiasm but unable to muster the same level of excitement.

"I cannot remember ever dining so well." Father crossed his arms over his stomach as if to emphasize his point. "I know you were anxious about tonight, but you carried yourself very well and made quite an impression on Cunningham."

Patience swallowed. The carriage hit a rut in the street, and she steadied herself with a hand to the door. If only she could steady her jolting stomach and whirling thoughts as easily.

"He asked my permission to court you, which I heartily granted. I suspect you will see him again very soon."

Patience ducked her head. Thank goodness, the darkness shadowed her face, for she certainly failed to keep her emotions hidden. She had hoped Father would be astute enough to recognize her feelings without her stating them outright, but now, as he spoke so effusively, it was clear the opposite was true. Difficult as it might be, she needed to put an end to his expectations before they grew even more.

"Father, the truth is..." Patience clasped her hands in her lap and swallowed, trying to bring some moisture to her dry mouth. "I was honored by Mr. Cunningham's invitation and am glad you think I handled myself well, but I do not wish to enter a courtship with him."

Father shifted so abruptly that Patience had to grab the edge of the seat to keep from tipping toward him. "What do you mean? How can you be certain when you hardly know the man?"

Patience's heart pounded in her chest so that it seemed to match the horses' hoof beats. Could she truly confess to Father that her affections were already engaged elsewhere? Tonight, of all nights, he was almost certain to disapprove. Before she could piece together a response, Father spoke again.

"I do not wish to rush you, my dear girl, but can you not see the opportunity you have been granted? You may not know him well, but you cannot deny that Mr. Cunningham has proven himself a generous and thoughtful gentleman." He gestured around the interior of the carriage. "Why even this, to offer his own carriage for our comfort, is a testament to his character."

"It was very kind, indeed, but—"

"I have known him for nearly two years now. Would you not trust my judgment of the man?"

Patience pressed her lips together. Everything Father said made it more difficult to speak her mind, for she would either seem to question Mr. Cunningham's character or Father's own.

"Even before your arrival here in Boston, I had spoken with Cunningham about you. His interest was piqued and has only grown more since meeting you." Father straightened his stock. "I know you have not had as much time to consider the idea, but won't you think on it now?"

Father had talked about her to Mr. Cunningham before she even set foot in Boston? What could he have said to draw Mr. Cunningham's interest? What did Father even know about her beyond what he read in their letters or what memories he held to from her younger years?

Patience struggled to draw a full breath. While she had been looking forward to her reunion with Father with great anticipation, he had already been laying the foundation for a possible marriage match.

"You will be one and twenty next month," Father continued, oblivious to her swirling thoughts. "I only want to see you settled and well cared for. Just imagine what a life you could have with a man like Cunningham. The connection would serve our entire family well, though that is of lesser importance than your welfare."

His words piled up like stones, hard and cold and heavy. He spoke of her wellbeing but did not deny the benefits he would reap. He pointed to her age and his wishes that she be cared for, but why could he not be the one to provide that care? For once, couldn't her father desire to be part of her life as much as she had always wished to be part of his?

The carriage rounded a bend in the narrow and twisting roads. An uncomfortable silence settled over them. Father was expecting some response, but what could she say? She would not agree to a courtship with Mr. Cunningham just to satisfy Father's hopes, yet she did not wish to cause strife between them. She must find the balance in her reply and pray for the opportunity to help Father understand better in the days to come.

Patience squared her shoulders. "I appreciate your concern for me, and I do believe you mean well, but I have hardly been here a month. I would like to settle in and—"

"I understand, but surely there is no harm in getting to know Cunningham better as you do." He looked over her head, his gaze fixed out the window, though only passing silhouettes of buildings could be seen. "Your mother and I, we knew each other from childhood. We grew up together, and when we were of age, our attachment to each other formed quite quickly. But not all relationships begin the same way. You must know that, given my marriage to Mary. There is something to be said for mutual respect, kindness, generosity, and provision, even without deeper affections at the start."

Patience dug her fingers into the blanket on her lap. Perhaps she should be grateful that Father spoke so openly with her about matters like this, but her discomfort only deepened. Not because of the way he spoke of Mama or Mary, but because of the conviction that only grew stronger in her own heart with each of his words.

She could not settle for respect and kindness, not when she had already begun to experience a taste of something deeper.

"I cannot deny Mr. Cunningham's good qualities, which you have espoused and I have witnessed of my own accord. But those deeper affections of which you spoke..." She drew in a slow breath for courage, staring at her hands as she spoke, unable to meet his eyes. "They do exist in my heart already, only not for Mr. Cunningham."

For a long moment, there was such profound silence that

Patience was not sure Father had even heard what she said. She dared to peek up at him.

He stared at her, his mouth a firm line and his brows knotted above eyes that searched every inch of her face. "How can that be? You never mentioned leaving a beau behind in England, and you hardly know anyone here."

Patience exhaled a trembly breath. "His name is Josiah Wagner. The blacksmith who made the hinges for your shop door. We met the day I arrived, and—"

"The blacksmith? The one who helped William find a position at that traitorous newspaper?" Father's voice rose, echoing in the confines of the carriage. "You can hardly know him any better than you know Cunningham—despite what William might have told you to cast him in such a favorable light in your eyes."

What would Father think if he knew how much time she had spent in Josiah's company? The depth of their conversations was far greater than anything Mr. Cunningham had spoken over the table in his elegant dining room, or across the polished wood floor of the ballroom. But she would not allow Will to take the blame in Father's eyes.

"It is not because Will—"

"I know my son values that man's assistance and considers him a friends of sorts, but do you not trust my thoughts on this matter?"

"That is not the reason for my feelings being as they are." Patience clasped her fingers together tightly. "The decision is my own, not based on the opinions of others. I don't wish to pit you and Will against each other in this."

Father waved his hand, swatting away her words as one might a fly. "You have not been here long enough to understand all that has transpired these past months, but I have my suspicions about Wagner and where his loyalties lie. You must not linger any more on thoughts of him. I am certain the affections you think you feel are not so secure as to be unchangeable."

Heat crept up Patience's neck. His words battered her heart like hailstones tearing the petals of newly opened flowers in spring.

She drew a fortifying breath. "I have had the opportunity to speak with Mr. Wagner on multiple occasions. In fact, he was kind enough to escort me home from the harbor the day you met with Captain Bruce. I had hoped to speak with you about my feelings, but I knew how important this dinner was to you and thought it better to wait. Now I realize I should have spoken sooner. I respect your judgment, Father, but I'm asking you to respect mine as well."

"Enough," Father shouted. He thumped his cane against the carriage floor.

Patience clamped her mouth shut and sank back against the cushions. He'd never used such a tone with her before.

He stared out the window for a long moment, then sighed and turned back to her, voice gentler. "I am sorry. I do not say any of this to accuse you of something untoward or to belittle you, but rather to guide and protect you. I am looking out for your best interest, and I can assure you, it is not with that man."

Patience sat straight and silent beside him. What more could she say? What could convince him?

The carriage began to slow, so they must be nearing home. Thank the Lord, for she needed to escape from her father's words that echoed within the confinement of this tiny space. Did Father think so poorly of her, that she was that easily swayed or naive, unable to comprehend enough to make her own decisions? Or that her affections were so fickle? She had no desire to go against him, but neither would she give up on Josiah after a single conversation.

The horses drew to a halt, and the driver opened the door of the carriage to let them off. Father exited first, then turned to extend his hand to Patience. She took it but could not meet his eyes as she descended. He thanked the driver and, as the carriage pulled away, shifted to stand before her.

"My dear girl, I do not wish you to end such a splendid evening in low spirits. We can speak of this matter another time. For tonight, I am thankful I had the opportunity to escort you. It was an honor to see you at your first ball."

Patience dipped her head and blinked back the sudden sting of tears. How could he manage to upset her so in one moment, then show such sentiment the next? A quiet *thank you* was all she could manage before he ushered her inside, but she vowed to find some way to make him understand.

CHAPTER 28

hree weeks had passed since Mr. Cunningham's dinner, and winter held Boston in its icy grip. Patience shivered beneath her quilted petticoat and heavy cloak as she and Will traipsed to Old South. Father had excused himself from church again, as he had every week of January thus far, for sake of the near-constant pain he suffered in his leg due to the bitter cold. Mary and Libby had also chosen to remain at home this morning, leaving Patience and Will free to attend Old South with Josiah.

Will glanced at her. "Regretting our decision to venture out today?"

She shook her head. Despite the frigid weather, she relished the opportunity to spend more time with Josiah. They'd managed to see each other once each week, thanks to Will's help in accompanying her on Sunday afternoon walks to the Common where Josiah met them. Together they'd stroll along the open space, her hand tucked in the crook of his arm. No winter wind could banish the warmth she felt when she was at his side.

Of course, Will was always there, too, his presence

preventing them from speaking as freely as she would have wished. But her visits would not have been possible without her brother's assistance, so she made the best of it. Patience cherished the conversation she and Josiah did share and parted each week feeling she knew him a little better, cared for him a little more deeply, and anticipated their next meeting even more.

"You've a rather thoughtful look upon your face." Will nudged her with his elbow.

"I am thankful for these visits with Josiah, but I cannot rid myself of the guilt of keeping this secret from Father."

"We've never lied to him outright."

"Only because he has never asked. You know he assumes our Sunday walks are just the two of us, and he would be furious to know we are not on our way to Kings Chapel this morning. Our actions are deceptive."

"I cannot fault your strength of conscience. I'm happy to take the blame and tell Father myself if you'd like."

"Nay, it should come from me. I must speak with him, especially if Mr. Cunningham continues to visit."

Mr. Cunningham had taken to visiting once a week, sometimes more. He and Father sat in the parlor together, sharing warm drinks and discussion, often about any new developments regarding the tea. After a time, he always asked Patience to join them, shifting the conversation to lighter, more personal matters. He was kind and engaging and seemed genuinely interested in her, but Patience could not bear knowing that he hoped for more from their relationship than she desired to give. She could not allow it to carry on, for Mr. Cunningham's sake and her own.

Will's disgruntled huff spoke his feelings for the man clearly. "Just know that I am here for you and will help in any way I can."

"I know." She sighed, her breath clouding the air. "I also

cannot help worrying over Father ever since they burned the tea."

On Thursday, the Committee of Correspondence had taken seven hundred pounds of tea out of storage and set it on fire in the middle of Kings Street, not far from her father's shop. He had come home Thursday evening nearly as angry as he'd been after the tea was thrown in the harbor.

"Your worries are not unfounded. I fear some harm could befall him if he continues to sell tea." Will rubbed a hand over his brow. "I have tried to warn him, but he refuses to listen to me."

"Even Mr. Cunningham advised him to proceed with caution, the night of the dinner."

"He is stubborn, on this and on many other matters." Will paused and turned to her, his brow furrowed. "For your sake, I hope he is more open to reason with regards to Josiah than he is about the tea."

Patience worried her lip as they ascended the steps of the church. Will was right, and the same concern dwelt in her heart, but neither could she put off the conversation with Father any longer. She set those thoughts aside as they made their way to the gallery, her gaze roaming the parishioners until she spotted Josiah's familiar broad shoulders and dark hair. His face broke into a wide smile when he saw her, and her heart took flight like a bird soaring at the top of the sky.

"I didn't think to see you here." Josiah stood to greet them, his gaze fixed on her.

"Everyone else chose to remain indoors for sake of the cold," she said as they took their seats.

"I am very glad you came." He leaned closer, his shoulder brushing hers and sending a rush of warmth through her that banished the lingering chill. "Though I may find it harder to concentrate on the reverend's words with you at my side."

She suppressed a giggle at the teasing glint in his dark eyes, but as the service started, she silently wondered if she might have the same struggle.

The reverend began reading aloud from Ephesians chapter two. "'But God, who is rich in mercy, for his great love wherewith he loved us, even when we were dead in sins, hath quickened us together with Christ, (by grace ye are saved;) and hath raised us up together, and made us sit together in heavenly places in Christ Jesus: that in the ages to come he might shew the exceeding riches of his grace in his kindness toward us through Christ Jesus, for by grace are ye saved through faith; and that not of yourselves: it is the gift of God: not of works, lest any man should boast.'"

The words resounded in her heart, like an echo of thunder, powerful and beautiful all at once. The truth seeped into her soul, like the first spring rain that soaked the soil and woke the bulbs from their winter slumber. She'd been slumbering too long, buried beneath the weight of grief when Mama died, hidden in the darkness of uncertainty as they awaited Father's instructions. Then she had come to America, so desperate for her reunion with Father to provide the fresh start she'd been longing for, only to be disappointed again.

She had become so focused on winning Father's affection and approval that she had forgotten about the gift of her Heavenly Father's love. When had she lost sight of the truth?

God's love, grace, and mercy were not something she had to strive to earn, but were freely given. God was her Father, the one who would never abandon her, never disappoint her. He had been there with her in her grief and uncertainty. He had never once forsaken her.

She exhaled as that priceless gift took root in her soul.

Josiah glanced at her, brows raised in question, and she realized her eyes were damp with unshed tears. She blinked them away and smiled to reassure him that all was well. He leaned ever so slightly closer, his strong arm pressing against her smaller one. How she wished she could lay her head upon his shoulder or feel those arms wrapped around her.

She cared for him as she had never cared for another man before. Today, when she returned home, she would tell Father that her choice was made. She prayed he would understand, but even if he did not, she would stand firm. She must, for she could not bear the thought of losing Josiah.

~

*J*osiah stepped out of church and squinted at the sunlight reflecting off the snow. The clear blue sky and bright sun were deceiving, as the temperature was colder than he could remember in recent years. In front of him, Patience wrapped her cloak tighter around herself. He would have pulled her into his arms if he could. Would she wish to forgo their walk home together given the cold?

"I saw Nathaniel on his way out, and I've a bit of printing business to discuss with him." William stopped at the corner of the building and glanced between Josiah and Patience. "Why don't you two start back without me?"

Josiah's eyes went wide, and Patience blinked as though similarly surprised at the opportunity William was offering.

William barely covered a laugh with a cough. "Hurry now, before you freeze or I change my mind."

Patience smiled her thanks to her brother, then tucked her hand around Josiah's arm. He would never tire of the thrill of her touch. Such a simple gesture, and yet it linked them together, and he relished her nearness. He would not waste this chance at precious time alone with her.

"To the Common as usual?" Josiah raised his brows at her as they set off. "Or is it too cold today?"

"Aye, let's. I don't mind the cold."

They walked in companionable conversation about the

week that had passed and quickly reached the Common. The street was empty, as was the land stretched out before it, the snow that covered the ground and blanketed the trees glistening in the midday sun.

He couldn't help admiring the way the reflection of the light off the snow shone in her eyes, though it brought to mind the tears he'd thought he had seen there during the service. He tucked her closer to his side and kept his voice gentle. "Did something in the sermon upset you?"

"Quite the opposite. I realized something today, from the passage the reverend read." She slowed her pace, and he matched his steps to hers. "When I left England, I thought that coming here would be the answer to all that had troubled me. That it would ease the grief of Mama's passing and offer a fresh start with my father. That somehow I would feel more settled and at peace." Her grip tightened around his arm. "But when everything was different than I expected, I felt foolish for hoping as I did."

"Hope is not a foolish thing."

"But it can be misplaced, and I have done so, for far too long. I have sought in my earthly father what can only be found in my Heavenly Father." She paused beneath a tree and turned to face him. "All this time, I have been striving to earn my father's love and acceptance, thinking it would bring me some sense of belonging, some peace to move on from the hurt of these past years. But I already had what I needed most, the love of my Heavenly Father. I don't have to bear the burden of striving with Him, for by His grace, He gives freely. His love is unconditional, not something I can earn nor lose, and in Him, I have true belonging."

Josiah's breath caught in his throat at her earnest words and the joy that radiated from her face. She stepped closer and reached for his hands, her slim fingers intertwining with his large ones. His whole body seemed to come alive at her touch.

"He has that love for you, too, Josiah." Her voice was soft but full of conviction. "With God, you are not an orphan because He is your Father. He has loved you every moment, even when you felt you were alone."

Josiah swallowed, his eyes burning with unshed tears. Her words fanned the flame of truth that had begun to burn in his soul over the past weeks. God had been near to him all these years. He was not alone. Not an orphan.

He traced his thumbs over her knuckles. "Not long ago, I would have struggled to believe that, but you have helped me remember God's love. I am not fatherless. I never have been."

She smiled up at him. A breeze stirred the branches above, sending a shower of snow upon her shoulders. A few flakes landed on her upturned face. Josiah reached out and brushed his thumb across her skin, wiping the melting flakes from her rosy cheeks. She sucked in a breath, and his gaze dropped to her lips for a split second before he pulled it away. They needed to keep moving before his self-control gave way and he pulled her into his arms to kiss her.

His attention caught on the frog pond just beyond her shoulder, and a grin tugged at the corners of his mouth. "I seem to remember a challenge you issued, the first time we walked this road together." He pointed to the shimmering ice. "Something about trying to skate again?"

She laughed, a sound more beautiful than a cardinal's song. "So I did."

He raised his brows in silent challenge, and she nodded, their laughter melding together as they cut a path through the snow to reach the frozen pond.

Without blades attached to their shoes, they could not move very fast. Instead, they shuffled their feet in a slow-motion sort of dance across the ice. He clasped both of her hands in his own, and together they slid and spun as though they were in the grandest of ballrooms. The wind was their music, the snow-covered trees and bright blue sky a more beautiful decoration than any house could contain.

"This is even better than I remembered." Patience's cloak swirled as she turned under his arm.

"That it is."

They slowed to a stop in the middle of the pond, and she looked up at him with an expression that set his heart pounding. He held her gaze, their breath coming in puffs of steam that mingled in the air between them.

He loved her. There was no doubt in his mind. No fear strong enough to hold him back. All the time they'd shared these past weeks, all the hours his mind dwelt on thoughts of her even when they were apart, all the hopes he'd allowed himself to hold, had grown into a love such as he had never known before. It did not matter what or who might stand between them—he would do everything in his strength to pursue her and share a life with her.

"Patience, you told me that I am not alone, that God is with me, and you are right." Finally, after so many years, his soul burned with a faith that could sustain him through whatever the future might hold, but he didn't want a future without her. "You must know that you, too, have made me feel as though I am no longer alone. Ever since that day we first met at the wharf."

She squeezed his hands as her gaze held his.

His heart beat harder than the sledge in his smithy. He stepped closer, his voice low and husky. "I know it will be difficult, with your father's loyalty and mine being at odds, but I care for you, Patience, more than words can say, and..."

His words trailed off as her smile grew until her eyes lit and the dimples appeared in her cheeks. "Aye, Josiah, I feel the same."

He could resist no longer. He closed the space between them and wrapped his arms around her. She nestled against his chest, slipping her arms around his waist. She fit perfectly against him, her head tucked just beneath his chin. He breathed her in, a mix of rosewater and cold winter air.

For the first time in years, he felt as if he belonged, truly belonged, with another person. He wasn't the orphan, the apprentice, or the man who came home to an empty house. With her in his arms, he was so much more.

What would she say if he asked her to share a life with him? To truly belong to each other?

He pressed a soft kiss on her head, barely brushing her dark hair beneath the hood of her cloak. No doubt, she would not even feel it, but the tiniest sigh escaped her lips, and she tilted her face to look up at him. His gaze fell to her mouth. Everything in him ached to close the inches between them, to feel her lips against his, but a stinging gust of wind brought him back to his senses.

"I must get you home." He wove his fingers through hers and led her off the ice. "I will talk to your father. I know it may be foolish to hope for his blessing, but—"

"Hope is not foolish." Her tempting lips tipped up in a grin. "Or so someone told me."

He couldn't help but smile, too, even as he braced himself for what lay ahead.

CHAPTER 29

*P*atience tightened her grasp on Josiah's arm as they approached her house, silently praying once more that Father would accept her choice. Was it possible he could understand what she felt? That she could love both her father and Josiah, despite their differences? For love was what she had come to realize she felt for Josiah.

She peeked up at him. His jaw was firmly set, his profile strong and resolute, but when he glanced down at her, his dark eyes softened.

If only they could have stayed out on the Common all day, a secret hideaway all to themselves, shining in icy brilliance under a bright winter sun. It didn't matter that it was the coldest of days—she'd hardly felt the chill as he held her hands and danced her across the ice. And when he'd kissed her atop the head, a thrill had ran all the way to her toes.

As sweet as it was to remember the tenderness of his touch, the words they'd spoken were even more precious. She clung to the hope they shared, both in God and for their future. She wanted to make a life with Josiah, even in the face of so much uncertainty. God would be with her, with both of them, but first, she must convince Father.

She paused before the front door and swallowed against the rush of nerves. Behind all her hopeful talk loomed the very real threat that Father would disapprove. That was why she had kept from speaking to him for so long.

She'd made excuses to put off the conversation... Father was often in pain and tired these past weeks, already out of sorts from the trouble with the tea. But those reasons fell short of the truth—that she was afraid of his reaction. Afraid he would forbid her to see Josiah again. That he would be disappointed in her for loving a Patriot and despise her if he realized she could sympathize with such views.

Afraid that, after years spent seeking his love and approval, she would lose it once and for all.

If it came to a choice between Josiah and her father, what would she do? Her heart ached just to think of being forced into such a position.

Josiah turned to face her, his hand finding hers and wrapping her cold fingers within his own. He searched her face and seemed to read there the trepidation that swelled in her heart. "No matter what happens, remember what you told me. God is your Father, and you have His love forever."

"Aye." She'd not forget that truth, whatever was to come.

Patience drew a fortifying breath and nodded decisively. She tucked her hand within the crook of Josiah's arm as they stepped forward together, but just before they reached the front door, it swung open and Mr. Cunningham strode out.

Patience smothered a gasp, and Josiah stiffened beside her. Mr. Cunningham's eyes widened. For a long, uncomfortable moment, they all stared at one another.

Then Mr. Cunningham squared his shoulders and composed himself into the polished visage he normally wore. "Miss Abbott,

I was just asking after you." His gaze flicked to Josiah and traveled down to the spot where her hand clasped his arm. His jaw clenched. "Your father said you were out with your brother."

"William had a business matter to take care of." She hesitated, glancing at Josiah. Good manners said she should properly introduce the two men, but good sense told her otherwise.

Mr. Cunningham, however, was not so easily satisfied. He looked Josiah over, a flash of disdain marring his features. "And you are?"

Josiah's arm tightened under her grasp, though his expression and stance did not falter. "Josiah Wagner."

"You look familiar for some reason, though I cannot imagine where our paths might have crossed." His words dripped with condescension.

Josiah made no reply, for which Patience was grateful, but she hated to see him treated as though he were a lesser man. She tugged her cloak tighter around her. "Please forgive us, Mr. Cunningham, but it is bitterly cold, and I must make my way inside."

"Of course. I wouldn't wish to detain you." His expression turned pleasant once more as he stepped out of the door, bringing him closer to her side. "I would stay if I could, but unfortunately, I am already promised elsewhere. I shall call upon you tomorrow afternoon."

He touched his hat, not waiting for a reply, and stalked away.

Patience exhaled a shaky breath. She could not let her resolve falter.

Josiah said nothing, but she did not mind, nor mistake his silence for weakness. She had come to greatly respect and admire his quiet strength, which spoke to his character more than any words he could say.

He offered a gentle smile and urged her into the house with a hand pressed to the small of her back. No voices greeted their entrance. Where might Mary and Libby be? It seemed Will had not yet returned either. Though she was thankful for the privacy this conversation required.

She fumbled with the tie on her cloak—fingers shaking from the cold or from nerves, she could not say. Josiah reached out and stilled her hand with his own, his dark eyes full of unspoken reassurance. He eased her cloak from her shoulders and hung it on an empty peg, then tugged off his hat, revealing his mussed and windblown hair. She smoothed her hands down the front of her gown to keep from reaching for one of the black locks that fell across his forehead.

With a final silent prayer for courage, Patience led Josiah into the parlor. Father sat in front of the fire, his back to them, cane propped against the side of the chair.

When he didn't turn at the sound of their footsteps, Patience cleared her throat. "Father?"

"You've just missed Cunningham." He spoke without moving, without looking in her direction. "Imagine my surprise when he mentioned that you were not in our family pew at Kings Chapel this morning."

Patience swallowed. This was not how she hoped to begin her conversation with him.

"He asked after you." He reached for his cane, his knuckles white as he grasped the top, but still he did not face her. "Thankfully, I was able to hide my surprise and spare myself looking the fool it seems both you and your brother are determined to make me out to be."

"That is not my intention at all." Patience clasped her chilled fingers together. This was going very poorly. "Please, if you will give me a chance to explain—"

"Indeed, you will explain. Immediately and without further deceit. Where is it you have..." He pushed off his chair and turned to face her, his words dying on his lips when he realized she was not alone. His eyes narrowed. "Who is this?"

"Josiah Wagner, sir." Josiah dipped his chin politely. "We met once before. I forged the hinges for your shop door."

Understanding dawned on Father's face. His mouth turned down in a harsh scowl as he swung his attention back to Patience. "This is where you've been? Is that why you've taken all those Sunday walks as well? Going behind my back to meet with a man you know I disapprove of?"

Josiah flinched, almost imperceptibly, but stood his ground beside her, silent in the face of Father's ire.

Patience squared her shoulders, drawing courage from Josiah's steady presence. "I have seen Mr. Wagner on my walks with Will, and this morning, we attended Old South alongside him. I told you, the night of Mr. Cunningham's dinner, where my affections lay. They have not changed. Mr. Wagner came home with me today so that we might speak to you and—"

"Now you wish to speak to me? Now, after expressly disobeying my wishes for a month, if not more?" Father's cane thumped against the floorboards as he strode toward them. Patience was tempted to duck her head under his harsh scrutiny, but she met his glare straight on. "You can have nothing to say to me that will change my mind. I told you to forget any foolish notions you might have toward this man." He pointed an accusing finger at Josiah, his eyes flashing with disdain as he spit out the words. "I'll not allow you to throw away your chance with a gentleman like Mr. Cunningham for a rebel blacksmith."

"Sir, if you might permit me—" Josiah's low, calm voice was cut off by a swipe of Father's hand through the air.

"I do not permit you. Not to speak to me. Not to pursue my daughter. Not to step foot in my house again." He slammed his cane against the floor. A vein bulged in his temple. "Leave. This instant. You are not welcome here."

Patience stumbled back at the rage and hatred emanating from her father. Tears welled in her eyes, both from the pain of realizing the depth of Father's refusal and from the hurtful words he'd flung at Josiah.

"Father, please." She reached out to touch his arm, hoping to break through his anger, but he stepped away from her grasp.

He shook his head, the look in his eyes shifting to one of utter disappointment. "I'll say no more. Do not press me further."

"I will go." Josiah spoke the words clearly, not with resignation but rather determination. "But know that I care for your daughter, and she for me. I pray you will reconsider for her sake, because she loves you."

A muscle jumped in Father's jaw. He stared at Josiah for so long that Patience dared hope his words had somehow softened Father's heart. But then his brows lowered and his teeth clenched. "Get out." He turned his back on them and stalked to the fire.

Tears spilled onto Patience's cheeks. She faced Josiah, longing to reach for him, to throw her arms around him, bury her face in his solid chest and feel the strength of his embrace around her. When his dark gaze met her own, the sorrow in his eyes made her heart ache even more.

"I am so sorry." She mouthed the words, hardly even a whisper.

He shook his head, dismissing her apology. She followed him to the door, despite her father's angry muttering from the parlor.

Josiah pulled the front door open, pausing to turn back to her. The sunlight reflecting off the snow cast him as a dark silhouette inside the wooden frame. His broad shoulders drooped. Was it sadness or defeat that weighed him down? Would he truly walk out of the door and out of her life all at once? This could not be their final goodbye. It could not be the end. She would not allow it.

She reached for him, grasping his hand as though she could anchor him to her forever. "Please, you cannot listen to what my father said in his anger. I will speak to him again. I cannot bear—"

"I am not giving up, but I would do anything to keep your heart from being wounded this way." He lifted her hand and dipped his head. His warm breath fanned over her knuckles, and her pulse stuttered. She held her breath as he pressed a soft kiss to her fingers, lingering for one blissful moment, a silent promise. Then he pulled away, squared his shoulders, turned resolutely, and strode out the door.

She watched him depart, her fingers tingling where his lips had touched. She swallowed against the tightness in her throat, blinking back another wave of tears. Father's disapproval was expected, but the strength of his anger and immediacy of his refusal to even listen to them pierced her heart like a thorn.

What hurt most of all, though, was that even the truth of Josiah's words did not sway him. Did Father not know how much she loved him? Did it truly make no difference to him how she felt? Could he not be moved by his own love for her? Or did he not love her as she had so long hoped?

She pressed a hand to her chest, but it could not quell the ache inside. Everything had gone wrong, but she would not give up. Just as she had kept her vigil at Mama's bedside, she would endure Father's wrath today and press on. Somehow or other, she must help him understand, must find a way.

But if she could not, would she dare to go against him?

CHAPTER 30

*P*atience clasped her mitted hands under her cloak as she strode through the quiet streets on Monday morning. It was bitterly cold again, all the more so without Josiah at her side. Her stomach clenched at the thought of Father's words from yesterday, of the anger and disappointment flashing in his eyes.

He'd not spoken to her the rest of the day. Instead, he'd holed himself up in his room, refusing to come down. When Will had returned, Father called him into the bedroom, and their angry shouts had been heard even downstairs in the kitchen as she and the other women prepared the evening meal. Patience flinched again just thinking of what Will had told her—Father forbid him to take her to Old South again and threatened to turn him out of the house should he do so.

Would things have been different if she'd told Father earlier? Once again, her name seemed to mock her, for it was her impatience to see Josiah, even without Father's blessing, that had caused such trouble. Or mayhap there was nothing she could have done to change Father's reaction. His mind was set the night of Mr. Cunningham's dinner and likely long before that.

Josiah was a good man, honorable and kind, gentle and hardworking. He could not provide the kind of life she would have should she marry Mr. Cunningham, but that was of no importance to her. Was there any way that Father would accept such reasoning?

She had stayed up long into the night, recounting everything that had happened to Libby's sympathetic ears, then praying silently for God to guide her. In the wee hours of morning, she had finally determined that she must first apologize to Father for not being forthright and seek his forgiveness. She prayed he was willing to make amends and allow her to speak from her heart. If not... well, she didn't wish to think of that outcome quite yet.

Light snow fell, driven by the wind to join the blanket of white that still covered the trees and rooftops from days past. Drifts of snow edged the road, and she picked her way along the trampled path in the middle, but when she rounded the corner onto Kings Street, she froze in her tracks.

Father's shop was in shambles.

She stumbled forward, half running, half slipping to the brick building. Red paint marred the white door, the word *Tory* in angry, dripping letters across the middle, splintered wood below as though someone had smashed it with a hammer or ax. Her fingers fumbled at the doorknob, but it was locked tight. Her cloak swirled in the wind, and swiped against the still-wet paint, leaving streaks of red against the black fabric. Whoever had done this had not been gone long.

"Father!" Panic choked her as she shouted for him.

No answer.

The windows were shattered, jagged edges of glass opening to darkness inside. Carefully picking her way around the shards that littered the snow, Patience peered in. Her breath left her in a rush, a cloud of steam fogging the sharp angles of glass.

The damage within was worse than outside. Torn fabric sprawled across the floor, beans and flour spilled from ripped sacks, broken jars littered the countertop and shelves.

Patience pressed a hand to her chest as she backed away from the wreckage. Her heart pounded beneath her fingers, and her breath came in short gasps.

"Father?" She called his name again but was met with silence as before.

A gust of wind flung snow into her face, blurring her vision. Or perhaps that was the tears burning in her eyes. Fear pierced her as sharp and cold as the icicles that hung from the roof. She must find help.

Josiah. His name was as clear in her mind as if it had been spoken aloud. He would know what to do. Spinning away from the destruction, she ran toward his smithy, pulled by the need for his comfort and steadiness. The wind whipped her hood from her head and yanked her hair from its pins. The snow was falling in earnest now. Head down, she pressed forward, slipping more than once on the slick cobblestones. The tears that escaped her eyes stung her skin as they froze on her cheeks.

Finally, she reached her destination. Soft light glowed from the windows and smoke curled from the chimney. She clasped the door handle, her fingers aching from the cold, and shoved the door open, stumbling in as the wind gusted behind her.

Josiah looked up from the glowing piece of iron upon his anvil. His arm paused in mid-air, holding the sledge aloft, and his eyes widened.

"Patience?" He blinked, as if uncertain whether she was real or an apparition. Resting his unfinished work against the stones of the forge, he strode toward her. "What is wrong?"

"My father...his shop..." Patience sucked in a breath, her

lips quivering. "I went to visit my father at his store, and when I arrived, nearly everything was destroyed."

He closed the distance between them, concern in his dark eyes, and wrapped her in his arms. She buried her face in his warm, broad chest.

"Is your father injured?" His voice rumbled low against her ear.

She pulled back just enough to look up at him. "I don't know. I could not find him. I did not see him inside when I looked through the window." She shuddered as thoughts of Father possibly wounded, or worse, invaded her mind. "I called for him but to no avail. I should have searched longer, but I came here as quickly as I could."

"You're frozen. Come. Stand by the fire."

He kept one arm around her as he steered her toward the glowing forge. She extended her hands toward the flames, desperate to ease the numbness of her fingers.

Josiah reached for her hands, engulfing them in his own. "Have you told anyone else about the damage to your father's shop?"

She shook her head.

"I will take you home, then go out and search. Stay a moment longer to get warm. I'll get my things."

He released her, and she immediately missed his steady comfort. He yanked on his coat and greatcoat as she silently prayed that Father was unharmed.

In moments, they were back outside. Josiah didn't offer his arm. Instead, he clasped her hand in his own. Strength and warmth radiated from his grip around her fingers.

"Tell me everything you saw."

She described how she had found Father's shop, the destruction wrought both inside and out.

Josiah's dark brows drew downward, his mouth a hard line. "I am sorry. I wish you need not see such violence."

"It's because he continued to sell tea, is it not? Will tried to warn him. He would not listen." She shivered as the wind howled through the street. "Oh Josiah, he was so angry yesterday, he wouldn't even speak to me after you left. What if something terrible has happened and I can never..." She couldn't finish her thought, for it was too painful to say aloud.

Josiah tucked her closer to his side, sheltering her from the storm that surrounded them and soothing the storm that buffeted her heart.

When they reached the house, Josiah held the door open for her, and she bustled inside. Snow tumbled from her cloak as swift footsteps sounded from the kitchen.

"Patience?" Mary hurried to the entryway. She clasped her hands to her chest, her shoulders visibly relaxing. "Thank the Lord you are safe."

"Patience! We were so worried." Libby scurried around her mother and tugged Patience into a crushing embrace.

"Has my father returned?" Her words tumbled out as messy as the melted show puddling at her feet. "His shop. The glass was broken. There was so much destruction. I looked through the windows, but I couldn't find him, and..."

Mary reached for her hands. "Slow down. What are you saying?"

Josiah stepped forward. "I beg your pardon, Mrs. Abbott, but I fear your husband's shop was vandalized. Is Mr. Abbott here?"

Mary's eyes widened as she shook her head. "We've not seen him since he left after the morning meal."

"What if he is still there?" Patience shuddered, squeezing her eyes shut against a fresh wave of panic. "I should have looked harder. If he is alone and injured and I left him..."

Josiah placed a hand on her shoulder. "You were right to seek help. I will go search."

He stepped back, and his hand fell away, leaving Patience shivering at the absence of his reassuring touch.

"Stay here. All of you. It is not worth the risk to go back out in the storm." Josiah reached for the door, and his dark eyes found hers once more. "I will return as soon as I have word of your father."

Silence filled the air in the wake of his departure. Patience stared at the closed wooden door for a long moment before turning to face Mary and Libby. Their matching blue eyes clouded with a mix of worry and confusion. Patience shivered, the cold of her damp clothes seeping through her as if it could reach her very bones.

"You must be frozen through." Mary eased the wet cloak off Patience's shoulders. "Elizabeth, take Patience upstairs to change, then come to the kitchen. Then we will talk."

Patience followed Libby upstairs. For once, the younger woman seemed speechless, her lack of conversation only adding to Patience's fears. She trudged up the wooden steps, silently praying that Father would be well, that yesterday's angry words to her would not be his last.

~

*J*osiah pressed forward through the driving blizzard, thoughts of Patience and the desperation on her face spurring him faster. A sickening thought lodged in his mind. Was this attack his fault? He had been the one to report Mr. Abbott. What if, in doing so, he'd made the man a target for violence?

He broke into a run as a desperate prayer escaped. "Oh Lord, forgive me if my actions have brought harm to Patience's father. Please, help me find him."

When he reached Abbott's shop, his footsteps faltered in the deepening snow. Even though Patience had described the scene, it was still jarring to witness the destruction. If the information he'd reported had inadvertently led to this... His stomach churned.

What would Patience think if she knew? He couldn't dwell on that now. He needed a clear mind to search, and if Mr. Abbott was somewhere in this storm, time was of the essence.

No footprints marked the ground around the front of the building, but the quickly falling snow would hide any recent steps. He ducked around the side of the building and saw the door torn from its hinges, the very ones he had made for Mr. Abbott in November. Josiah never could have guessed then how his life would be changed by Abbott's daughter.

Josiah rounded the back of the shop and drew to a halt. Mr. Abbott lay sprawled face down in the snow. His bad leg twisted at an unnatural angle, and his wig sat askew on his head where an angry red gash stood out against his pale skin. Josiah ran and knelt beside him, placing one hand on his back to see if the man was still breathing.

"Mr. Abbott. Can you hear me?" He spoke urgently, crouching to better see his face.

A shallow breath brushed Josiah's palm, and he let out his own sigh of relief. Patience's father was alive, but his condition was poor. Had he been attacked by the same mob who destroyed his shop? If so, he'd been lying unconscious in the snow for some time. Josiah needed to get him home where he could be warmed and receive the medical attention he needed, but could he possibly transport an unconscious man that far on his own?

"Please, Mr. Abbott, you must wake up. I need you to try." Josiah grasped Abbott's shoulder and shook it gently.

The man groaned and blinked slowly. He squinted at Josiah, his eyes unfocused. It was some progress, though he did not seem to recognize Josiah.

"Sir, you've been injured. I am going to get you home, but I need your help as much as you are able."

Abbott rolled onto his side, moaning as he did. "What... happened?"

"I had hoped you could tell me." Josiah clasped Abbott's forearm and steadied him as the man moved to sit up. "Your shop was vandalized. Were you attacked?"

Abbott pressed a hand to his head and grimaced. He pulled it away, eyes widening at the blood that covered his fingers.

"You've a bad wound on your head, and I'm afraid you may have injured your leg again."

The older man blinked once more, his gaze growing more focused as he examined his leg. He tried to move it and winced. "My leg. I remember."

Josiah waited for Abbott to explain, but instead, the man shifted as though attempting to stand.

"Wait, you'll need my help." Josiah pushed off the ground and came around Abbott's back, looping his arms beneath the man's own. "I'll lift while you stand. Try not to put any weight on your leg."

Abbott did as instructed, trying and failing to suppress another groan. Josiah braced himself, muscles straining as he raised the heavier man to his feet.

Once Abbott was standing, Josiah moved to his side and wrapped one arm around his waist. "Hold on about my shoulders. We'll go as slowly as you need."

Abbott twisted his head and stared at Josiah for a long moment. Then his eyes sparked with recognition. "It's you. The blacksmith that Patience..." His words trailed off as he furrowed his brow. "What are you doing here?"

"Patience came looking for you, and when she saw the damage, she sought my help."

"Is she well? Where is she?" Abbott's voice pinched with concern.

"She is safe at home, but terribly worried for you. We should get moving if you're able."

Abbott grunted but said nothing more. Thank goodness, the man did not argue against his help. Perhaps the pain was too great for him to expend any energy on anger against Josiah.

They shuffled around the side of the building at an excruciatingly slow pace. Abbott gritted his teeth as his gaze trailed over the destruction of his shop.

"I came too late." Abbott muttered the words. "It was already ruined when I arrived."

"No one was here?"

He shook his head. "I left immediately to report the damage to Lieutenant Croome. He told me to go home. I should have listened."

Josiah led them onto the road as he tried to piece together what had happened. "You must have been with the lieutenant when Patience came."

"Most likely. I returned, intent upon going inside, for I hadn't done so when I first discovered the destruction." He stumbled, and Josiah paused to steady him before they pushed on. "My bad leg. I slipped on the ice and fell. That's all I remember."

Josiah nodded. He must have hit his head in the fall. It was hard to say how long the older man had been out in the elements, but from the way he was shivering and from the damp seeping through Josiah's own overcoat, Abbott must be chilled through.

They limped on in silence. Josiah's back ached from hunching over to bear more and more of Abbott's weight the longer they traveled.

"I know who did this." Abbott glanced sideways at Josiah. "Men like you. Patriots, you call yourselves, righteously espousing liberty and freedom but denying me the freedom to run my shop as I wish."

Josiah pressed his lips together. Mr. Abbott's words stung as much as the wind that slapped against his face. There was truth to what he said. Much as Josiah still fully believed in the Patriots' cause, he had never wanted it to come to this.

"You'll not defend yourself?"

Josiah gritted his teeth. What could he say? Was there any defense that would speak to this man? Anything that might bridge the gaping divide between them?

Abbott was quiet except for his huffs of exertion and grunts of pain. When he finally spoke again, his voice was more subdued than Josiah had ever heard it. "I do not understand you. Why would you come to my aid after what I said yesterday? Why do you not speak up for yourself now? Press your advantage to try to change my mind?"

"Because I love your daughter." Josiah paused and looked the older man directly in the face. "I love Patience, sir, and I know how much she loves you. I came to help for her sake. I don't know that there is anything I can say to earn your approval, but I respect you enough not to use your time of weakness for my benefit. Mayhap you will respect me enough to allow me to speak to you again when you are well."

Abbott's eyes widened, and his mouth dropped open slightly. For a long moment, he simply stared at Josiah, then nodded once. No more words were spoken, but as they started walking again, Josiah tucked that tiny gesture in his heart, and hope flickered once more.

CHAPTER 31

*P*atience stared into the flames, but instead of their dancing light, all she saw was shards of glass, sacks of flour sliced open, the contents spilling out, and bolts of fabric ripped from the shelves and lying in crumpled heaps on the floor. Was Father there, beaten and broken as well?

She held her hands out to the fire. Her fingers shook. Even the dry clothing and hot drink Mary had offered could not rid her of the chill that had settled over her heart.

She peeked over her shoulder at Mary, who paced the kitchen, lips moving in whispered prayer. Seeing her stepmother's worry only compounded Patience's guilt.

Libby came to stand beside her, wrapping an arm around her waist. "Mr. Wagner will find him. All will be well."

"I hope you are right." Patience leaned against her stepsister.

They were quiet for a long moment, then Libby whispered, "He's a good man, Mr. Wagner. Mayhap some good will come of this if it gives your father a chance to see him that way."

Patience tried to smile at Libby's encouraging words, but the expression fell flat, for it seemed selfish to wish for such things now, not knowing where Father was or what had happened to him.

A knock at the door drew all of their attention, and they hurried out of the kitchen. Libby linked arms with Mary, who pressed her hands to her stomach, her face drawn as Patience reached for the door. She tugged it open, but it was not Josiah nor Father who stood there.

"Mr. Cunningham?" She raised her brows even as her stomach fell.

"I promised yesterday that I would call on you." His congenial smile dropped from his face as he surveyed the three of them. "Has something happened?"

Mary composed herself first, remembering the basic courtesies Patience had forgotten. "Please, come in out of the cold. I am afraid you've visited at a difficult moment."

Mr. Cunningham stepped into the already crowded entryway and shut the door behind him. He edged closer to Patience, eyes full of concern. "What is wrong?"

"My father's shop was vandalized, and as of yet, we do not know where Father is."

"I will seek help immediately." He reached for her hands and clasped them in his own. It was meant as a gesture of comfort, but Patience felt none. "Lieutenant Croome is still in town. I will enlist his aid."

"We appreciate your help," Mary said. "Mr. Wagner is looking for my husband as we speak."

"Mr. Wagner?" Mr. Cunningham's brow furrowed as he looked from Mary back to Patience. A hint of bitterness crept into his voice. "The man you were with yesterday?"

Patience nodded as she pulled her hands free from his grasp.

"Then I will join the search."

He turned to leave, but before he could do so, the front door swung open, and a gust of wind swept over them.

"Father!" Patience gasped.

His head was bent, one arm slung over Josiah's back, his bad leg dragging more than usual. Snow covered both men, and Father's hat was missing, his wig a disheveled mess. He looked up at her, eyes glassy with pain and complexion nearly as pale as the snow save for the bright red wound on his forehead.

"Patience, my dear girl." His voice was weak but full of tenderness that made her eyes prick with tears.

They all backed out of the way as Josiah edged into the house, his shoulders stooped to accommodate her father limping beside him.

"You must warm him and get him dry as quickly as possible." Josiah strained under the weight.

"Bring him to the kitchen." Mary strode ahead of them. "Libby, stoke the fire and fill a bowl of stew."

Mr. Cunningham stepped to Father's side, opposite Josiah, and helped ease him toward the kitchen. The two men did not acknowledge one another's presence.

"Thank you," Patience whispered to Josiah as he passed.

He met her gaze for the briefest moment, dark eyes full of compassion.

Mary turned to Patience. "Go upstairs and fetch the quilt from our bed, along with some dry clothing for your father."

Patience grasped her petticoats and dashed up the steps. She rummaged through Father's things to find dry garments, then tugged the quilt from the bed, wrapped it into a ball, and balanced the bundle in her arms.

She hurried downstairs and into the kitchen, where Father now slumped in a chair before the fire. His sopping-wet coat hung discarded over another chair, and Mary knelt beside him, gently easing the damp stockings from his feet.

Patience set Father's things on the table and joined Mary at his side, reaching for his hand. She shuddered at how cold his fingers felt. "Oh Father, what happened?"

"This leg of mine. I slipped and..." His voice faded into a cough. When the fit ended, he looked as though he were trying to smile at her, though it came out more as a grimace. He glanced over her shoulder to where Josiah stood, his hat in both hands. "Thank you for sending help."

She squeezed his fingers and looked at Josiah. His face was set in the serious expression he so often wore, but when his dark gaze met hers, his countenance softened. From the corner of her eye, she saw Mr. Cunningham scowl. He stood several feet away from Josiah, arms crossed over his chest.

Clearing his throat, Mr. Cunningham stepped closer. "Mr. Abbott, I will seek out Lieutenant Croome. He and I will ensure those responsible are met with justice."

"I already spoke with him." Father's voice came out rough and pained. "I appreciate your help as well, though I doubt we'll be able to determine who committed the destruction. We all know why it happened."

Mr. Cunningham nodded. "But Croome and I will do our best." He turned to Patience and lowered his voice. "I am sorry for what you had to endure today, Miss Abbott. Know that I am here to help you."

He turned and left, dipping his head in farewell to Mary and Libby but completely ignoring Josiah.

Mary draped Father's wet stockings over his coat on the back of the chair. "Girls, please wait in the parlor a moment. I will help your father into some dry clothing and fetch you when he is ready." She turned to face Mr. Wagner. "We cannot thank you enough for bringing him home safely to us."

Patience gave Father's hand one more squeeze before she released him. She and Libby left the room with Josiah following close behind. In the parlor, Libby glanced between

Patience and Josiah, then made herself busy tending the fire, even though it already blazed with a steady, warm flame.

Josiah paused at the doorway, and Patience turned to face him. She kept her voice low. "Where did you find him?"

"Just behind his shop. He wasn't there when you came, as he'd gone to see the lieutenant."

Patience sighed. At least she hadn't missed her father and left him exposed to the elements while she sought out Josiah. "So he wasn't attacked?"

"He fell. No one was there. He was unconscious when I arrived. From the gash on his head, I suspect he hit it when he fell. And I fear he might have reinjured his bad leg. He could not bear any weight on it when we walked home."

Patience pressed her lips together to quell the emotion rising in her chest. Father's condition was poor, but without Josiah, he could have been stuck in the storm for who knows how long. He might be in danger, even now, but at least he was home and could be cared for.

She reached for Josiah's hand and wove her fingers through his. "Thank you."

He dipped his head closer, so near she could see the drips of water clinging to his hair where the snow had melted. "What else can I do? I'll stay as long as you wish, or I can go find William and tell him what has happened."

"I didn't even think of Will. I was so caught up in my worry over Father. Can you tell him and send him home?"

"Of course." He traced his thumb over her hand before releasing her fingers and securing his hat atop his head. "I'll come back soon to see how your father fares."

The door closed behind him, and Patience sighed, missing the comfort of his presence already but thankful for his clear-minded thinking and decisive action. She turned to find Libby watching her with a knowing grin. Patience crossed the room to join her before the fire.

"I think that man is very much in love." Libby nudged her with an elbow.

Patience's cheeks heated, but she couldn't suppress a smile.

A groan from Father drifted out of the kitchen, shattering the brief moment of contentment. She squeezed her eyes shut and silently prayed that she would not lose another parent.

CHAPTER 32

*J*osiah rapped his knuckles on the door of Abbott's shop on Tuesday afternoon. The wood still bore the gashes from yesterday's attack, though the word *Tory* had been scrubbed clean.

William tugged the door open and greeted him with a somber nod. "Josiah, thank you for coming."

"I've the nails you requested." Josiah stepped in out of the cold and pulled a leather pouch from his pocket. "How is your father?"

"His leg is broken, the same one he injured in the shipwreck. The surgeon came yesterday evening and set the bone."

"And Patience?"

"Worried for him, of course, but caring for him well, just as she did for our mother." William crossed his arms over his chest with a frown. "I hate to see her endure this again."

Josiah scrubbed a hand over his jaw. He would give anything to ease her burden, but what could he do? He could not ensure that her father was healed and whole again, though he would continue to pray as he had often since the attack.

Guilt over his potential part in what had happened

continued to plague his thoughts. There was no guarantee that his report on Mr. Abbott had led to him being the target of this destruction, but neither was there any certainty that it hadn't. Josiah had said nothing to Patience, but he hated the thought of this secret lingering between them. What would she think if he told her? And if her father should worsen...

"Can you spare some time to help me?" William broke into his thoughts. "I need to board up these windows."

"Aye, I'll stay." He could not go back in time and erase the report he had shared, but he would do everything in his power to help now.

The shattered glass from the two front windows had been swept, but the gaping holes left the shop exposed to the elements. They made quick work of it, nailing wooden boards across the open space. It lessened the chill inside but also left the shop dimmer than before.

Josiah brushed his hands on his breeches as he surveyed the room. "You've made good progress."

"I came early this morning to start. I will salvage all I can, but the loss is significant." William leaned against the counter. "He and I have our differences, as you well know, but I wish it hadn't come to this."

"I am sorry." The weight of those words, the potential meaning behind it, was almost suffocating. "I cannot help but wonder if I might have prevented this if only—" Josiah halted at a knock at the door.

William furrowed his brow and crossed the room to open it. Josiah tensed at the sight of a red-coated soldier.

"I am Lieutenant Croome." The man greeted William with a clipped bob of the head. "Are you George Abbott's son?"

"Aye. William Abbott. How can I help you?"

"Edward Cunningham sent me to inspect the damage to your father's shop and gather any evidence that might help in our investigation. He is quite determined to bring the men responsible to justice." The lieutenant stepped into the shop, swept his hat from his head, and tucked it under his left arm.

Josiah held his place beside the counter and kept his expression neutral, but his stomach dropped as the soldier strode farther into the room. He recognized the lieutenant right away as the man he'd crossed paths with at the dock while delivering the padlock, the day after they threw the tea in the harbor. Hopefully, the lieutenant's memory of Josiah was not as clear. But when the soldier swung his gaze in Josiah's direction, his eyebrows rose in recognition, dashing Josiah's hopes.

"And you?" Lieutenant Croome approached Josiah, glancing at the handful of nails still sitting on the counter beside him. "Are you the blacksmith I heard about?"

Josiah straightened. What did the soldier mean? What had he heard? He shouldn't hesitate long in answering lest he rouse more suspicion, but his mind whirled with possibilities. Had Cunningham or George Abbott mentioned him? If so, in what light? Or did the soldier remember him from that day at the dock and seek to draw out more information?

"Cunningham mentioned a blacksmith who had come to Mr. Abbott's aid." The lieutenant picked up a nail and twirled it between two fingers. "A Mr. Wagner, I think he said. Might that be you?"

"Aye." Josiah clenched his jaw at the overly satisfied smirk that touched upon the soldier's face for the briefest of moments.

"I am glad to have found you here, then. I can accomplish two tasks at once." He dropped the nail, and it clattered onto the pile on the counter. "I'm curious to hear your account of how you discovered Mr. Abbott."

William strode forward, his brow pulled low. "Have you not heard it already? My sister informed me that you spoke with her and my father both yesterday afternoon."

Josiah couldn't suppress a frown. His stomach turned to

think of this man questioning Patience in the midst of her fears for her father's health.

"I did, but it is best to be thorough, and I prefer to hear from him directly." The man dismissed William as though he were a lesser-rank soldier on the battlefield and turned his attention back to Josiah. "It will be of great help to us if you state all you can remember."

The man's tone was congenial yet condescending, a sickening mix that made the skin on Josiah's neck prickle. He'd not be bullied, but he had nothing to hide in regards to Mr. Abbott. He recounted the events as succinctly as possible. Lieutenant Croome listened in silence, but the gleam in his eye suggested there was more going on in his thoughts.

When Josiah had finished, the soldier nodded. "This has been most informative." He paused and rubbed a hand over his cleft chin. "I cannot help but think we have spoken before. Have we met at some point?"

It was less a question, more a warning, and Josiah pressed his lips together, not wishing to answer. Thankfully, William stepped in and intervened.

"I am sorry to interrupt, but I have detained Mr. Wagner from his work long enough already. If you have finished your questions for him, I will show you around the shop." William gestured toward the newly boarded windows. "As you can see, I've repaired and cleaned much already, but I can explain how things were before I began."

The soldier scowled but quickly hid it behind a polite nod. "I saw the damage to the exterior before but was unable to inspect inside."

William led Lieutenant Croome to a pile of ripped fabrics that sat at the back of the shop, talking of how the colorful bolts of linen had been strewn across the floor. He glanced over his shoulder at Josiah and tipped his head ever so slightly toward the door.

Josiah nodded a silent thanks, slipped out of the store, and headed toward the livery. He must speak with John Ward and arrange a meeting as soon as possible.

A cold gust of wind swept over him, and he pressed his hat lower atop his head, but it was the lieutenant's words and suspicious gaze that chilled him to the bone.

CHAPTER 33

*P*ale morning light had just begun to thread its way through the clouds as Josiah approached the Liberty Tree the next morning. His coat hung heavy on his shoulders, pulled down by the pouches of musket balls hidden in both pockets. His thoughts weighed even heavier upon him.

John Ward and Alexander Stevens were already waiting for him. Josiah greeted both men as he joined them beneath the huge elm.

"What's the report?" John's breath clouded the cold air. "You seemed troubled yesterday."

"I did not want to tell you then, not knowing who else might be nearby to listen, but I had a conversation with a British soldier that has me concerned."

Alexander crossed his arms over his chest. "I don't like the sound of this."

Josiah recounted all that had happened, from the attack on Abbott's shop to the suspicious questions from Lieutenant Croome and the fact that he had seen the soldier before, the day after the destruction of the tea.

"It was clear he recognized me and meant to intimidate me."

"But even if he remembered you from that day at the wharf, what can he do?" Alexander shrugged. "Your presence at the harbor does not tie you to that night, and you had no part in the damage done to the shop."

Josiah glanced at John. "I fear that, inadvertently, I may hold some blame for what happened to Mr. Abbott."

John shook his head. "You may have been the one to report his loyalties, but that does not make you culpable for the actions of others."

"I cannot help but feel some responsibility. If I'd not informed upon him—"

"Someone else would have." John cut in. "You said yourself that he was outspoken and proud of continuing to sell imported tea. I am certain you were not the only one to notice."

"He's right," Alexander said. "His shop is on Kings Street, is it not?"

Josiah nodded. "Not far from where they burned the tea a sennight ago."

"It is much more likely the attack was related to the anger stirred up at that event than a result of the report you gave in November." John clapped Josiah's shoulder. "It is wise to be cautious, but we Sons hold our secrets close. That soldier cannot know of the role you play."

"I hope not, but I wanted you both to be on your guard, in case." Josiah reached into his pockets and held the bags out to Alexander. "And I wanted to give you these. If by chance that soldier seeks me out at the smithy, I'd rather not have something around that he could attempt to use as further evidence against me."

Alexander shoved the musket balls into his own coat. "I'll be sure they reach the right place."

"There is one more thing." Josiah shifted, scuffing the snow with his feet. "Abbott's daughter, Patience."

Alexander furrowed his brow. "What about her?"

"She and I are...well, we have been courting."

"A Tory's daughter?" Alexander's eyes widened.

"She knows where I stand, and that has not turned her away." But would her opinion change once he told her what he'd done? Josiah didn't give voice to that thought. "You met her brother, William, at the Green Dragon last month. His views are quite opposed to those of his father."

"I remember him." Alexander nodded. "So she is the reason you feel such guilt, I suppose."

"Aye, and I've determined to tell her the truth."

"Are you certain that's wise?" John stepped closer. "What if she were to share it with her father? He could very well report you to the lieutenant."

Josiah shook his head. "She would not betray my confidence."

"But you may lose her affection." Alexander peered at him, as though he could read Josiah's thoughts.

"A risk I must take, for I cannot ask her to share a life with me if this stands between us."

Alexander exhaled. "For the sake of your heart, I will pray she understands, but for the sake of our cause, I pray you are right to trust her as you do."

"My trust in her is well founded. I'll not put either of you in harm's way."

John placed a weathered hand on Josiah's shoulder. "If you do come to trouble, send word to the livery. I'll do whatever I can to help."

Josiah thanked him and bid both men farewell, then set off for the Abbotts' house. He would not put this off any longer.

≈

*P*atience scooped porridge into the bowl for Father. Another morning, another serving, even though the last one remained mostly untouched. But Mary insisted they keep trying to help him eat, and Patience was determined to do all she could to aid his healing. She added a dash of nutmeg and cinnamon, hoping the sweet and comforting smell might entice him to try more than a few bites.

A knock at the door pulled her attention from her task.

"It's rather early for a visitor." She glanced at Libby, who worked alongside her in the kitchen.

"Mr. Cunningham, perhaps?" Libby raised her brows.

"I hope not, though I'd rather him than that soldier again."

Lieutenant Croome had spoken with her at length on Monday afternoon about her father's shop and the attack there. His questions regarding Josiah in particular had left her uncomfortable.

Patience brushed her hands on her apron and strode to answer the door, steeling herself for who she may find there. When she opened it, her heart leapt. "Josiah, I'm so glad to see you. Come in."

A small smile greeted her, but his brow etched with concern. "How is your father?"

"He's still quite weak and has been in a good deal of pain, I'm afraid."

"And you?" He reached out and brushed his thumb over her cheek ever so softly.

She wished to lean into his touch, but his hand dropped to his side again. "I continue to pray and do the best I can to care for him."

"May I speak with you a moment? Alone?"

She nodded and ushered him into the kitchen.

Libby looked up from the table, the bowl of porridge cupped in her hands. "Good to see you, Mr. Wagner." She turned to Patience. "I will take this to your father and ask what else Mama needs my help with."

As Libby departed, Patience thanked her with a smile, but it fell from her lips when she saw the serious expression in Josiah's face.

"Patience, there's something important I must tell you."

She peered up at him, but he would not meet her eyes. Instead, he reached for her hands and kept his gaze locked on their intertwined fingers.

"You know that I stand on the side of the Patriots and that I was part of the destruction of the tea that night in December." His thumbs traced her knuckles. "But I've not shared all of my involvement with the Sons of Liberty."

She squeezed his fingers, encouraging him to go on, even as her heart began to beat faster.

"I joined the Sons nearly four years ago and found a bond of friendship there that helped, in some ways, to ease the loneliness I'd felt for so long. I believe in our cause, and serving it has given me purpose." Drawing a deep breath, as if to summon his courage, he raised his gaze to her own. "One of my tasks in recent months has been to report information regarding people who are loyal to the crown."

Patience's eyes widened. "Like a spy?"

"In a way."

Worry gnawed at her stomach. "To what purpose?"

"In part for our own safety, to know whom we can trust. And, at times, to identify those we do not wish to do business with."

"People like my father." The ache inside grew, and she tugged her hands free from Josiah's grasp. His own fell limp at his side.

"Aye."

"Are you saying..." She swallowed, unable to finish the thought aloud.

"In November, I reported your father's loyalty to the Sons. Our purpose was to boycott shops that continued to sell imported tea." His shoulders slumped. "I disdain violence. My hope was that peaceful measures such as boycotts would be effective. Now I fear my information could have made your father's shop a target for the rabble that thinks destruction the better course."

Patience stumbled back a step.

"I cannot change the actions I have taken for the Sons, nor do I regret being part of their cause, but I never wished for anything like this to happen."

"Do you...do you know the men who did this to Father's shop?" She clasped her hands together to keep them from trembling.

He shook his head. "Nor do I know if it truly was my information that led to the attack. But I wanted you to know. I refuse to have secrets between us."

Patience turned away and stared at the fire, the flames moving in a mesmerizing dance, even as they consumed the logs that fed them. Was that what would happen here in America? Would all the striving and purpose and right intentions still leave a path of destruction behind? Could good come out of it all?

"There is something more." Josiah stepped closer. "I have been helping to build the stockpile of munitions with musket balls from my smithy."

She spun to face him. "Musket balls? When you claim to abhor violence?"

"I hope it won't come to that, but our people must be able to defend themselves, if the need arises."

"I do not know what to say. This is...it is a great deal to take in...and my father..."

"I understand." He lifted a hand as if to reach for her but

then let it fall with a sigh. "I am sorry for the hurt this has caused you."

Patience swallowed, unable to gather her chaotic thoughts into words. Part of her longed to feel his strong arms wrapped around her, to press her face against his chest and let loose the tears that stung her eyes. The other part wished to flee from his confession and the confusion it brought.

Silence stretched long and uneasy between them. She stared at the ground, unable to look him in the eyes, though she felt his gaze steadily upon her.

When he finally spoke again, his voice was heavy with emotion. "I will leave you. I am sorry, Patience. You needed to know the truth...because I love you."

She sucked in a breath. Love? The word shot through her like lightning. He had never spoken so plainly before. It was a declaration she had longed to hear, yet now, on the heels of his confession, it left her thoughts and emotions even more in a tangle.

Blinking, she jerked her head up, desperate to see his face, even if she did not know how to respond. But he had already turned away. She watched through her tears as he strode to the door and out into the cold, never looking back.

CHAPTER 34

*P*atience rapped softly on the door of Will's bedroom, then clasped her arms around herself, shivering in the chill of the parlor. They'd not bothered to light a fire in the hearth there today since all of their time was spent between the kitchen and Father's bedside. Now that night had fallen, the cold darkness seemed well suited to her mood.

Her thoughts and emotions had been in a disarray ever since Josiah's confession yesterday morning. His words repeated over and over in her mind, relentless as the winter wind that buffeted the house. She'd spoken of it to no one yet but could not hold it inside any longer.

The door swung open, and Will peered at her, brow furrowed. "Patience? What is wrong? Has Father—"

She shook her head. "Nothing has happened with him, but I've something of importance to speak with you about."

"Of course, come in."

Will's room was much warmer, with a cheery fire blazing in the hearth. His coat and waistcoat had been discarded, draped over the edge of his bed, and a stack of newspapers covered the small writing desk along the wall. He grabbed the chair in front of it and set it by the fire, inviting her to sit, then perched on the edge of his bed beside her.

"I get the sense you've more on your mind than your worries for Father."

"It's Josiah. He revealed some things yesterday morning that...well, I don't rightly know what to think or how to feel."

Will listened intently while Patience recounted what Josiah had told her. When she finished, she slumped against the hard wooden slats of the chair. "I thought I'd come to know him well, but now I wonder. What if he isn't the man I believed him to be?"

"Or what if the fact that he was honest with you, even at risk to himself only further confirms his integrity?" Will propped his elbows on his knees and leaned closer, searching her face. "This does not change his character. It only reveals to you more of who he is. The deeper question you must ask yourself is, can you accept it?"

"I don't know," she whispered as she dropped her gaze to her lap. "To be honest, I had come to agree with his patriotic stance, or at least I thought I did. But now...this is different."

Will waited as she struggled to put her thoughts into words.

"It was one thing for him to be a Patriot, even for him to take part in destroying the tea. It is something more to know that he has been a spy who informed upon my own father. Does it not bother you?"

Will was quiet for a moment, then shook his head. "He did what he believed to be right in his duty to the Sons. I know it was not his intention to cause such harm as befell the shop, and I do not blame him for the actions of others."

She stared at her lap, rubbing her finger over a stubborn stain on her apron as Will continued.

"From what I've seen, Josiah is an honorable man, wholehearted in his dedication when he commits to something...or someone." He paused, waiting until she tipped her head up to look at him. "I trust he will be wholly devoted to you should you choose him, but that does not mean he will forgo his allegiance to the Patriot cause. You must consider if you are willing to stand beside him in the uncertain days to come."

"Even if I am prepared to side with the Patriots, what about Father? What if he..." She swallowed, unable to finish the thought aloud.

"You're afraid that Father may not recover," he said gently, "and that it could have been Josiah's information that brought all this upon him."

Tears pricked her eyes as she nodded.

"It is possible that Josiah's report led to the attack, but it is just as likely that it did not. Those men still might have destroyed Father's shop even if Josiah had never said a word." Will reached for her hand and clasped it in his own. "Can you live with never knowing for certain? Even if the worst should come?"

Tears spilled down her cheeks. Could she? Or would it forever mar the future she'd hoped for with Josiah?

"I would spare you all of this if I could. Father and the turmoil in this country..." He stood and pulled her to her feet, wrapping her in a tight hug. "Know that I will support you in whatever decision you make and pray that God gives you peace in your choice."

"Thank you, Will." Patience swiped at the tears on her cheeks. "I'd best be off to bed. I've much to think and pray on."

He bid her goodnight, but as she trudged up to her room, she knew sleep would be long in coming.

CHAPTER 35

*P*atience clasped her hands around the cup of tea, the heat seeping into her fingers as she carefully scaled the stairs the next morning. She paused outside Father's room, peering through the slightly open door. He slept propped against a pile of pillows, wrapped in layers of blankets. His eyes were closed, his mouth drooping open slightly. Mary bent over him, cleaning the wound on his forehead.

Patience stepped quietly into the room. Mary looked up, the dark shadows under her eyes evidence of a night as restless as Patience's own.

"How is he?" Patience set the cup on the bedside table.

"Not well, I am afraid." Mary smoothed the strong-smelling poultice over the cut on Father's head. It was stitched up but swollen and a dark color that turned Patience's stomach. "I do not like the look of this wound, and he is far too hot. I'll send Libby to Pierce's apothecary again. If he wakes, we must help him eat and drink."

If he wakes. Patience bit her lip at those words.

Mary straightened, wiping her hands on her apron. "You'll sit with him?"

"Of course."

As Mary slipped from the room, Patience settled into the chair that had been pulled up alongside the bed, her gaze fixed on Father's pallid face. His breathing was shallow, and sweat beaded along his forehead.

"Oh Father..." Her voice broke. "You must get well. Please."

She clasped her hands on her lap and bowed her head, quietly praying. His tea grew cold, but he did not stir. In the heavy stillness, her thoughts drifted back to Josiah. She'd lain awake long into the night, wrestling with her thoughts and emotions and crying out to God for wisdom. In the wee hours of the morning, she had come to a conclusion, and now was anxious to speak with Josiah again. But Father's care must come first.

"Patience?" A raspy voice followed by a low groan pulled her head up with a start. Father's face was contorted in pain as he tried to sit up in bed.

"I'm here." She reached for him, one arm steadying him while she rearranged the pillows to support him better. "You mustn't move too quickly."

"I have to tell you..." A hacking cough rattled his whole body and cut off his words.

Patience rubbed his back, willing the fit to pass. When it did, he sank back on the bed, eyes closed once more, his skin even paler than before. Sweat dripped down his temple, and she gently wiped it away with a handkerchief.

"Let me help you drink." She reached for the cup on the nightstand. The herbaceous smell of willow bark and chamomile tea drifted toward her as she lifted it to his lips.

He sipped gingerly, some of the liquid dribbling on his chin. She dabbed it away and tried hard to push back the memories of doing the same thing with Mama in her last days.

When she lifted the cup again, he shook his head slightly. "I must speak first." His voice was hardly more than a whisper.

Patience leaned closer.

"I am sorry, my dear girl." He turned his head to meet her gaze. "I was so angry with you when we spoke on Sunday, and—"

"You had a right to be." Patience frowned and ducked her head. "I was not forthright with you, and for that I must apologize and seek your forgiveness."

"You should not have deceived me as you did." He paused to cough once more. "But you have my forgiveness."

Patience clasped his clammy hand in her own and swallowed back her tears. "Thank you."

His eyes slid closed, and he was quiet for so long, she feared he had fallen asleep once more, but then he spoke again with visible effort. "I was angry, but I now believe I was wrong to dismiss your feelings so quickly. Mr. Wagner..." He smothered another cough. "If you had not sent him, I may have died alone in the snow. He helped me despite my treatment of him."

Father's grip around her hand tightened slightly, and Patience sank to the edge of the bed beside him. It was true— and one of the things she'd clung to in the midst of her confusion over Josiah's revelations about himself.

"He seems to genuinely care for you." Father's voice was strained but determined. "Can you forgive me for judging too swiftly?"

Patience's eyes widened. "Of course." She squeezed his fingers, her throat tight with emotion.

There was so much more she could say, but she would not press him further when it was evident their short conversation had drained him of energy. The forgiveness between them was a healing balm for her sore heart, and it would suffice for now. She helped him sip tea until he could not manage any more and slipped back to sleep.

Patience rose from her place at Father's side. Perhaps now would be a good time for a visit to the smithy. She collected the teacup from the bedside table and was about to make her way downstairs when the door creaked open.

Mary stepped in with a small smile that did not reach her eyes. "Mr. Cunningham is here to see you. He asked to speak with you."

Patience blinked. "Alone?"

Mary nodded. "Will you be uncomfortable with him on your own? Libby has yet to return from the apothecary. I thought it best to stay with your father, but if you wish me to—"

Patience shook her head. "I can manage. You should stay with him."

She brushed the wrinkles from her petticoat. Mayhap Mr. Cunningham was here simply to see how Father fared, or to discuss the attack on the shop again. She could only hope, though she suspected there was something more motivating his visit.

She stepped into the parlor where he stood waiting, looking polished as always. The blue waistcoat and trousers beneath a dark gray coat highlighted the color of his eyes as he smiled at her.

"Miss Abbott, I am glad to see you. How is your father today?"

"I fear he is not doing well. He sleeps much of the day, but we are doing our best to see to his needs and his comfort."

Mr. Cunningham stepped closer and rested his palm on her shoulder. "I am certain you are doing all you can. I will continue to pray for him. He has become a good friend to me these past two years, especially after I lost my own father."

Patience nodded, not trusting her voice.

"Please..." He dropped his hand from her shoulder to gesture toward the chairs by the fire. "Will you sit with me? I've a matter I'd like to speak with you about."

Dread coiled in her stomach as she took her seat and braced herself for the words she had no desire to hear.

"Miss Abbott, you must forgive me for being so forward, and at such a trying time, but I feel I cannot wait any longer." He perched on the edge of his chair and leaned closer. "I care for you, Miss Abbott. It can be of no surprise, for surely, I have not hidden my feelings."

Patience sucked in a breath and grasped her apron in her fists. Should she interrupt him now, before he could get much further? But Mr. Cunningham held her gaze, unwavering, and did not falter in his speech, pressing forward without hesitation.

"I would have held off in declaring myself, but after what has happened with your father, I know I've not the time to waste. He and I have spoken at length before, and I would like to seek his blessing again now while he is able to give it, should the worst happen."

Her stomach churned. *Declare himself. Should the worst happen.* Mr. Cunningham wanted to marry her and wanted to ask now, in case Father should die.

"Mr. Cunningham, I..." Her voice caught, but she cleared her throat and began again. "I do not think you should—"

He reached for her hands and stood abruptly, pulling her to her feet. His grip was tender but firm, and she had no choice but to stand, far closer to him than she wished.

"Please, allow me to continue. I know this is a trying time for you, but I hope to offer some comfort." His voice was low, almost hesitant, as he searched her face. "Ever since I met your father, he praised you so highly and talked of you so often that I felt I knew you, even before we met. I long anticipated your arrival and have enjoyed every moment in your presence since. Will you do me the honor of accepting my hand in marriage?"

She ducked her chin as she shook her head. "I am honored by your offer, but I...I am sorry, I cannot accept it."

Silence hovered between them for a long, uncomfortable

moment. He did not release her hands. Instead, his grasp on them tightened slightly.

"I understand your hesitation, given your concern for your father's health, but mayhap this news would be a boon to him. I know how much he has hoped for a match between us and believe it would do him good to see us happy." He peered intently into her face, his expression earnest. "We need not be in a hurry to wed, of course. Your loyalty to your father is admirable, and we would wait until things are settled."

The intensity of his stare made her heart race, but she squared her shoulders and gently pulled her hands free from his grasp. "Mr. Cunningham, I thank you for your understanding, but my answer remains the same. I cannot accept."

His brow furrowed. "I must admit, I did not expect this. I had every reason to believe you would welcome such an offer."

"I apologize if any of my actions have given the wrong impression." She had tried hard not to do anything to encourage his affections, but Father had given Mr. Cunningham much confidence in pressing forward with his offer. "I appreciate the kindness you have shown my family, and I know my father highly values your friendship."

He crossed his arms over his chest and stared at her, his jaw set in a way that transformed his expression from one of confusion to one of anger. "It's that Mr. Wagner, isn't it?"

Patience's eyes widened.

"I saw the way he looked at you, and you at him. I tried to convince myself it was nothing. But it appears I was mistaken." A muscle in his jaw twitched. "Would you truly choose a man like him over me? Your father would never approve. But then, if he were to die, he could not hold you to his will any longer. Seems rather convenient for your blacksmith." He spit the words. "It makes me wonder if he had a hand in the attack."

Her face flushed. "Josiah is the one who rescued Father and brought him safely home."

"Josiah, is it?" He scowled, his voice dripping with scorn. "I did not realize you were so taken in, so deceived by that man. Do you not find the timing of the event rather interesting? I saw him go into your house that Sunday. He came to speak to your father, didn't he? And he would have been denied, I've no doubt. So he sought to destroy your father's shop, mayhap even kill him so that—"

"Enough." Fury surged in her chest. "My father would be ashamed to hear you speak thus. How can you say such things that hold no merit?"

"No merit?" A humorless laugh escaped his lips as he bent so that his face was inches from hers, his voice low and menacing. "I have it on good authority that Josiah Wagner is a member of that rebel band that calls themselves the Sons of Liberty and that he took part in the treasonous destruction of tea the night of December the sixteenth."

Patience stumbled back a step, pressing her lips together to hide her shock. How could he know such a thing? Nearly two months had passed since that fateful night, and there could be no real evidence against Josiah. But what about the other things Josiah had been involved with? Could he be in danger for those as well?

She would not be the one to condemn him by revealing what she knew. She furrowed her brow as though utterly confused. "Where have you heard such things?"

"My friend, Lieutenant Croome, was the one who put the pieces together. I asked him to look into Mr. Wagner." Mr. Cunningham straightened, a look of triumph on his face. "The lieutenant recognized him immediately. We'd seen Wagner coming from the *Dartmouth* the day after those miscreants threw the tea in the harbor. Croome mistook him for a sailor, but upon further investigation with the captain of the ship discovered that he had just come from delivering a padlock he had repaired. A padlock that was damaged the night before."

Patience willed her racing heart to slow, even as her mind reeled with the implications of Mr. Cunningham's words. Was it possible Lieutenant Croome's suspicions were enough to arrest Josiah? To hold him prisoner in jail? To try him for treason?

Mr. Cunningham paced before the fire. "It is rather interesting how this has all come together. Croome wanted to arrest him that very day in December, after we spoke to the captain and learned the significance of the delivery. The lieutenant was certain it was evidence of Wagner's participation in the incident with the tea. Unfortunately, we had no way of finding him. The captain did not know his name. We could not track him. Until now." He paused and spun to face her, a sneer curling his lips. "Thanks to you and your involvement with him."

Fear clutched Patience's heart, but she refused to let it show. "I am sorry that my refusal has injured you, but I will not hear such conjectures born of jealousy and spite." Heat rose up her neck. She whirled away and stalked to the door. "I must ask you to leave, immediately."

His long stride ate up the distance between them, and she felt his tall presence beside her in a moment, though she did not turn to face him. He bent and spoke low, his breath hot against her ear. His voice was smooth and cultured once more, the voice of a gentleman used to being respected, a powerful man accustomed to getting his way. "I told Croome to hold off on arresting Mr. Wagner until I had spoken to you, but now that I have your answer, I will instruct him that he is free to proceed. Mark my words, you will soon regret this choice."

CHAPTER 36

*J*osiah tossed another log on the fire. He propped one arm against the rough-hewn mantel and rested his forehead in his palm as he watched the sparks scatter up the chimney. It was Friday afternoon, and he should still be at work in his smithy, but he'd not been able to focus all morning. He had finally given up after making an error that forced him to restart the piece he was forging. He'd sought the quiet of his house, hoping it would still his racing thoughts, but he was wrong. Instead, the empty space seemed to do just the opposite.

He did not regret telling Patience about his involvement with the Sons, but his heart ached at the way things stood between them. It had taken everything in his power to turn around and walk away after their conversation. To give her time and privacy to consider all he had revealed. Still, part of him had hoped she would call out, come after him, tell him all was forgiven. Especially after he'd confessed his love for her.

He hadn't planned to—not then, at least. But his declaration was the truth, and when he'd seen the hurt and confusion in her face, he couldn't help but make his feelings for her known. Now he could only pray that she could forgive him and that she felt the same.

He pushed off the hearth with a sigh.

Then there was the encounter with Lieutenant Croome. Josiah had not seen or heard from the man again since Tuesday, but the soldier's prodding words and assessing stare still lingered, putting him on edge.

A knock at the door interrupted his thoughts. He crossed the room and tugged it open, his eyes widening at the person who stood before him.

Patience stared up at him, one hand pressed to her chest as an expression of relief softened her features "Josiah, thank the Lord you are here. I went to the smithy, and when I could not find you, I feared he had already come, that I was too late."

"Too late? Who had come?"

"May I come in?" She glanced over her shoulder as though afraid someone had followed her. "I will tell you everything."

Josiah furrowed his brow but stepped aside to usher her in. Dark wisps of hair brushed her rosy cheeks, and concern filled her wide eyes. He crossed his arms over his chest to keep from reaching for her.

"Mr. Cunningham was just at our house. I came to warn you as soon as I could. You are in considerable danger."

"What do you mean?"

"Mr. Cunningham asked me to marry him."

A rush of heat surged through Josiah, enough to rival the flames of his forge leaping up the chimney.

"I turned him down, which angered him greatly. I'd never seen him that way before." She peered up at him through her dark lashes. "He realized you are the reason behind my refusal."

"I am?" Josiah exhaled, daring to hope again. He reached for her hands, clasping her cold fingers in his own. "You forgive me?"

"There is nothing to forgive." She squeezed his hands. "I have thought and prayed much these past days. I know the kind of man you are. Your actions with the Sons of Liberty do not change that. You did your duty to serve the cause you believe in. I do not hold you responsible for what happened to the shop, or to my father."

"Thank you." His words came out husky, and he swallowed against a lump of emotion as he pulled her into an embrace. "I never wanted this to happen to your father. I would never knowingly do anything to hurt you."

"I know. I trust you." Her arms wove around his waist, holding him as tightly as he held her.

He could have stayed that way forever, but she pulled back, her expression anxious.

"We don't have much time. Cunningham has set himself against you. He and Lieutenant Croome."

"What have they done?"

She told him everything Cunningham had said, from his attempt to place the blame on Josiah for the attack on Mr. Abbott's shop to the very real threat of the lieutenant's suspicions regarding the destruction of the tea. Every muscle in Josiah's body strained for release.

"You need to leave Boston." Patience's mouth was set in a determined line. "As soon as possible."

He dragged a hand down his face. "There must be another way. It seems cowardly to run."

"Not cowardly but wise. How could you stand against such accusations? I could not bear to see you arrested."

"I've nowhere to go. I cannot simply leave the smithy." He reached out and tucked a stray hair behind her ear, his fingers trailing over the smooth skin of her cheek. "And I will not leave you."

"But I will not stand by and watch you put on trial for treason." She squared her shoulders as she stared up at him. "Please, Josiah."

The weight of her words settled over him. She was right—he could have no defense should he be arrested, for while it would be difficult to link him to the report he'd given on Mr. Abbott's shop, it was not impossible. And the charges regarding the destruction of the tea were true. He had been there that night, had willingly committed treason against the Crown. Croome recognized him, placed him at the docks. With the collaboration of the captain, that seemed evidence enough to hold him in prison. If he were to go to trial and be found guilty...

He swallowed at the thought of a noose around his neck.

A heavy silence descended between them. He held her gaze a long moment before he allowed his gaze to drift around the familiar room.

For nearly ten years, he'd lived within these four walls, and he'd spent almost every day of the past fifteen years in the smithy just outside the door. Despite all the times he had longed for something more, this place was his. It belonged to him, something tangible to show for all the years of hard work. Boston had become his home. He had friends here, a cause worth fighting for, and now a woman he loved.

Could he truly just leave it all?

"We must hurry. I fear the lieutenant could come at any moment." Patience's words snapped him from his musings. "How can I help?"

She was right. He had to leave. He was not safe here. He ran a hand through his hair. He had to think. Clearly and quickly.

He crossed to the chest at the end of his bed and pried it open, lifting his knapsack from inside. He held it out to her. "Can you fill this?" He gestured haphazardly to the other contents of the trunk, suddenly conscious of what an intimate request it was for her to sort through his things. "My father's

Bible is on the nightstand, and I'll need clothing, as much as you can fit."

She nodded and immediately set to work.

"I'm going to gather some of my tools from the smithy."

"Be careful."

"Aye."

He eased the door open and scanned his surroundings. Seeing all was clear, he stepped out and strode to the smithy, entering through the side door. His thoughts crashed upon one another like waves on a rocky shore as he grabbed an empty crate and began to fill it with the most important tools of his trade. Each time he grasped one of the familiar tools, his mind began to settle, to focus on what he must do next. His rapid heartbeat slowed, and he breathed deeply of the familiar smell of smoke and iron.

He exhaled a prayer. "Lord, show me what to do."

Phineas Stearns. The name came to him as clearly as if it had been spoken aloud. The man he'd met that night in December aboard the *Eleanor*. Stearns had offered a place to Josiah if he were ever in need. He was certainly in need now.

He tugged his leather apron from the hook on the wall and stuffed it on top of the crate, hiding everything else stowed inside.

He would go to Watertown and seek out Stearns. Twenty miles should be far enough from Boston, and hopefully, the man could make good on his offer. Ward at the livery would be willing to help him get out of town. Nathaniel could find someone to watch over the smithy while he was gone and pass the information of his departure on to Alexander. There was still much uncertainty, but if he could make it out of Boston before Croome found him, he should be safe.

But before he left, there was something else of utmost importance that he must do.

⁓

*P*atience's fingers shook as she folded a pair of trousers and pressed them into the leather bag. Every creak of the house, every whistle of the wind, every pop of the fire made her catch her breath and glance over her shoulder. When would Josiah return? Surely, he had gathered all he needed in the smithy by now. Had the lieutenant already come and stormed into the shop to arrest him?

She worried her bottom lip as she rolled a pair of stockings and squeezed them into the final bit of space. How strange would it be for Josiah to leave home with nothing more than what he could carry? How difficult would it be for her to say goodbye?

She could not imagine her life without Josiah in it. She loved him wholeheartedly and wanted to spend the rest of her days by his side. But now she must watch him leave, for his own good. How long would it be until they could see each other again?

The door swung open, and she gasped as she spun around, bracing herself for the worst. When Josiah's gaze found hers, she sank onto the edge of the bed in relief.

A small smile lifted his lips. "All is well."

"Thank the Lord."

He balanced a crate in both arms as he shoved the door closed with his foot. He set the crate on the table, then crossed the room in several long strides and reached for her hands, pulling her to her feet.

"I have decided where to go, and I know someone who will assist me." His large, callused fingers tightened around her smaller ones as he relayed the plans he had made.

"What more can I do to help?"

"Do you remember where the print shop is? Where your brother works."

She nodded.

"Go there and inform Nathaniel of what has happened. Send him to the livery to talk to Mr. Ward and tell him I'll meet him there."

"Aye." She swallowed, holding his solemn gaze with her own. "I know I should leave right away, and yet I cannot bear to say farewell."

"Me neither." His thumbs traced soft circles over the back of her hands, and the touch sent shivers up her arms. "There is something else I must say first, before we part."

He stepped closer, so that mere inches separated them. His dark eyes traveled her face, as though trying to commit every feature to memory. Her breath caught in her throat at the intensity in his expression, a mix of determination and admiration that warmed her cheeks and caused her heart to trip faster.

"I don't know what is to come, if or when I can return to Boston. I cannot be sure what I will find in Watertown. I will have nothing to offer you. Not even the certainty of a roof above your head." His brow tugged low, but there was an ember of hope in his eyes that could not be extinguished. "But I know this—I love you. With all that I am, I love you, and I want nothing more than the honor of calling you my wife. Will you wait for me, Patience? As soon as I am able, I'll—"

"I love you too." The words poured out of Patience's mouth, edged in an exquisite mix of tears and laughter. "Aye, Josiah, I will be your wife."

His eyes widened, and for a moment, he seemed frozen in wonder, then he closed the small space between them and pulled her into his arms. She pressed her head to his chest, relishing the strength and warmth and closeness. His heart thudded against her cheek, a rhythm as fast as her own. His large hands on the small of her back anchored her against him as his lips brushed her head.

The tenderness in his touch stole her breath, and in those

precious seconds, she forgot the threats and danger and uncertainty and knew only the beautiful promise of their love. The knitting together of two hearts, of two lives that would—very soon, she hoped—become one.

Josiah smoothed one hand up her back, his fingers brushing the wisps of hair at the nape of her neck. He cupped her face in his large palm, his thumb brushing over her cheekbone, then tracing a path over her bottom lip as he gently tilted her chin up. Patience met his gaze, and the desire in his eyes made her cheeks heat. He dipped his head, and her eyes slid closed as his lips touched hers.

His kiss was soft and slow, as though to savor every touch. She wound her arms around his waist and leaned into his strength. Who could say how long it would be until she could see him again, but this was a farewell she would remember every moment until then.

He angled his head and claimed her mouth again, this time with purpose and passion that matched the longing she'd seen in his eyes. She pressed up on tiptoes, reaching her arms around his neck and burying her fingers in his hair. The world around them disappeared, and she could think of nothing but Josiah, his declaration of love, and the hope that echoed in every touch.

A rattling outside startled them apart. Patience froze as her gaze snapped to the door. They had lingered too long. Lieutenant Croome had come. Her heart seemed to stop, caught in her chest along with the breath she was holding. Josiah's eyes were wide, but his jaw was set in a firm, fearless expression. They stood in silence, waiting for a knock or a shout. For the soldier to burst through the door.

But nothing came.

"Wait here," Josiah whispered.

He crept to the door. Patience braced herself, clasping her hands together so tightly, her knuckles turned white. He slowly eased it open, and only the swirling snow greeted them. Her shoulders relaxed as he slid the door closed once more.

He returned to her with a sheepish smile. "Just the wind." But then his face grew serious. "Still, I should leave. Much as I wish I could stay, time is not in our favor."

She pressed her lips together and blinked. She would not send him away with tears. "Will you write to me when you arrive?"

He nodded, then pulled her into his arms and rested his forehead against hers. His breath fanned warm against her face, his voice husky. "And I will come back for you as soon as I am able."

She tipped her head to look up at him, a teasing grin chasing away the tears. "Until then, I suppose I must learn to be patient, after all."

CHAPTER 37

*T*wilight's silvery-blue light sank into the horizon as Josiah's horse trotted into Watertown. He'd not traveled this far outside Boston since he arrived five and ten years prior. He glanced over his shoulder, as though somehow he might still be able to see the town, though he knew he could not. Boston was miles away.

His chest tightened. Strange, that he should regret leaving after he had wished to do just that for so long. For years, he'd wanted to shed the confines of the city and own a little piece of land for himself. But he'd never imagined leaving like this—a covert escape, glancing over his shoulder until he had crossed over Boston Neck and put enough space between himself and the lieutenant to breathe deeply again.

And he could not have imagined leaving the woman he loved behind.

His arms ached to hold her. It wasn't what either of them wanted, this hurried goodbye with miles of distance and an unknown number of days apart stretching between, but the memories of kissing her and hearing her declaration of love blazed in his heart, warming him against the chill wind.

Josiah clucked to the horse to slow her as he took in the small town. John had been more than willing to loan him a horse from the livery, along with a pair of saddlebags for the few belongings he'd brought. It was the same mare he'd fashioned a shoe for that day in November when the *Dartmouth* first arrived. How much had changed in the months since then.

He scanned the houses and buildings, squinting in the growing darkness. When he spotted a brick building with a sign bearing an anvil hanging out front, he tugged gently on the reins. Leaning forward to pat the mare on the neck, he breathed a silent prayer that this was the right place, and that Stearns would be able to help him. A tidy saltbox house stood next to the smithy, smoke rising from the chimney in a warm, welcoming cloud. He dismounted, wincing at the tightness in his legs, unused to hours in the saddle. He looped the reins around a fencepost and strode to the front door, pausing to tug off his hat and run a hand over his wind-blown hair before knocking.

He waited a long, uncertain moment before the door swung open.

The man that answered furrowed his brow. "May I help you?"

Josiah breathed a sigh of relief. He had the right house. Now, to hope Stearns remembered him. "Mr. Stearns? I'm Josiah Wagner. You may not recognize me, but we met—"

"Aboard the *Eleanor*. I remember. What brings you this way?"

"Well, I had reason to leave Boston." He glanced over his shoulder, but the road behind him was empty. "I got word that some suspicion was placed upon me, some accusations about to be made regarding my participation that night."

Stearns nodded solemnly.

"I apologize for imposing like this, but I thought of your offer and wondered if I might take you up on it for a time."

"It's no imposition. You are welcome here." Stearns smiled, opening the door wider. "Please come in. Give me a moment to tell my wife, then we can get your horse settled in the barn and talk further."

Later that evening, after a long conversation over a warm meal at Stearns's table, Josiah stepped into the bedroom at the back of the house.

"It's not much." Stearns gestured at the small space. "But it is clean and warm and out of the way of prying Redcoats."

Josiah chuckled. "Just what I need. Thank you again for your generosity."

"Happy to help a friend in need, though don't think of it as charity since I'll be putting you to work tomorrow first thing."

"I'm glad of it."

"Until morning, then."

Josiah sank onto the edge of the narrow bed, the rope framing sagging under his weight. Exhaustion set in, the emotions of the day taking hold. As he riffled through his satchel for a night shirt, his mind strayed again to Patience. He thought of her placing these very items in his bag hours before, of the way she felt so soft and feminine pressed against his chest.

It was because of her that he was safe now. Her quick warning had given him time to escape. His throat tightened at the thought of where he might be now if not for her help. A tiny room behind the kitchen was significantly better than a jail cell with a trial for treason looming over him.

He dressed by candlelight, suppressing a yawn as he climbed under the coverlet. Tomorrow he would ask for paper and a quill so that he might write and inform her he was safe. How long would it be until he could see her again? He could not ask her to come here, not when her father was ill and he had no home to offer her. But he could not return to Boston until he was certain the threat of arrest had passed. Would that ever happen? Mayhap Croome would leave eventually, but would Cunningham ever release his grudge, or would he continue to seek vengeance as his jealousy festered?

Josiah rolled to his side and shoved an arm under the limp pillow. The old, familiar fear washed over him like a storm-driven wave, threatening to pull him under. Would he lose someone else he loved? Not to death but to distance and time? Was he destined to be alone again?

He gritted his teeth and pushed the thought away. God was with him. He was not alone, not now nor ever, no matter what happened. And Patience loved him in return and had accepted his proposal. He must hold onto the hope of their life together, even though that future was so unclear.

CHAPTER 38

She was running up the hill, the one near their home in Chatham, that looked over the ocean. If she could get to the top, she would see him. Father's ship would be there, on the horizon, and she could call to him, make him hurry, bring him home before Mama was gone. But her legs kept tangling in her petticoats, her feet kept tripping over stones. The hill seemed to grow before her, stretching higher and higher, never ending. She wouldn't be able to reach Father, and it would be too late...

Patience jerked awake, the Bible on her lap falling to the floor with a thud. Her heart pounded, and she drew a shaky breath as she blinked against the light streaming through the curtains.

Only a dream.

She stooped to pick up the Bible and placed it on the bedside table, her gaze falling on Father's wan face. How long had she been asleep in the chair beside his bed? It must be nearly noon, if the sun in the sky were any indication, and she'd been keeping vigil since dawn.

Father was failing. There was no way to deny what she saw

before her eyes. He had rarely woken since speaking to her on Friday, and it was Monday now. His breaths were shallow, his brow beaded with sweat, his pallor a grayish hue excepting the angry wound on his head that was swollen and darkening around the edges.

It's turning foul, the surgeon had said. Were it on an arm or leg, he'd have removed the limb, but there was little he could do for an injury on the head.

Patience's eyes burned from lack of sleep and unshed tears. She'd spent hours praying, both for her father and Josiah. The weight of uncertainty over both their fates pressed upon her, weariness taking root in her very bones. She had yet to hear from Josiah since his hasty departure, but neither had Mr. Cunningham made an appearance with news of his arrest, so she clung to the hope that he had escaped and found refuge in Watertown. Her hope for Father's recovery was less sure, and decreasing each day.

Carefully, she lowered herself to the edge of the bed, clasping one of his cool, clammy hands in her own. She had been reading to him from Psalms before she dozed off. Had he been able to hear her? If so, hopefully, the words had offered some comfort. Now, though, there were words of her own that must be said, lest she live with the regret of leaving them unspoken forever.

"Father?" Her voice was barely a whisper. He did not move. "For as long as I can remember, all I wanted was to know you loved me, to know I belonged with you. Ever since I was a child, I wished you would sail home to stay so that we might be together. And when you didn't return for Mama's sake..." Her voice faltered, and she paused to collect herself. "I confess, I never understood."

His face twitched, the slightest grimace tugging at his mouth, but whether it was in response to her words or an involuntary reaction to his pain she could not know.

She drew a breath and pressed on. "I came here hoping to start anew. I wanted your approval, but now I fear I cannot seek it for the decision that matters most in my future. I love Josiah, and I have agreed to marry him. I know it isn't what you wanted for me, but he is a good man, and he loves me, and I believe God brought us together. I wish I could have helped you see him as I do. I do not expect an easy life, but—"

Her words came to an abrupt halt when Father opened his eyes. Slowly and with effort, as though it took all his strength to do so, but open and looking at her. Their stormy blue color was clouded and glassy, but fixed upon her, nonetheless.

Patience's own eyes widened. "Father? Did you hear me?"

His throat moved, and he opened his mouth, but no sound came out.

"Let me get you a drink or a cool cloth or..." She started to stand, but his fingers tightened ever so slightly on her own, holding her in place.

"Patience." Her name rasped from his lips, followed by a strangled cough. "I am sorry. My... dear girl." He coughed, a wheezing sound that shook his frame and seemed to drain his last reserve of strength. His eyes slid closed, and he fell silent.

His words hung heavy in the air, the many things still unsaid even more so. He was sorry. For not coming to them in their time of need? For pushing her toward a man she did not care for while forbidding her to see the one she loved? For never showing her the love she so desperately desired?

Sorry could mean so much, but she could not ask him for clarity now, nor could he answer, even should he want to. Her heart ached. *My dear girl*, he had called her. Would that he had said he loved her, but it would have to be enough. At least he could know her heart. There was peace to be found in that.

"I love you, Father," Patience whispered. Hot tears spilled down her cheeks.

She pressed a kiss to his limp hand, then lay her head on

his chest. Her tears wet the blanket draped over him as the minutes passed. She knew not how many. It seemed time had stopped, just as it had when she lay beside Mama, holding her in her arms until she breathed her last.

The slightest rise and fall beneath her cheek was proof Father lived, but the stillness of his face seemed to say otherwise. His heart beat, but it was a faint sound, as though echoing from somewhere far away. He had no strength to lift his arms and hold her in return, and deep inside, she knew he would never hold her again.

The creak of the door drew her to her feet.

Libby stared at her wide-eyed. "Oh, Patience, has he...?"

"Not yet, but I do not think it will be much longer."

Libby crossed the room and placed the bowl that held a fresh poultice on the table, then pulled her into an embrace. "I am so sorry."

Patience clung to her stepsister, unable to reply but thankful for the comfort.

After a long moment, she stepped back, swiping the tears from her cheeks. "We should tell your mother."

Libby nodded. "I will."

"I'll do it." She needed an escape from this room, even if only for a moment. "Will you sit with him?"

"Aye."

Patience descended the stairs, the creaks of the steep staircase familiar now after months in this house. It still did not feel like home, but it was all she had.

What would happen when Father was gone?

Would Will still return to England as planned? Patience could not imagine being parted from him, especially now, but she couldn't go back with him and leave Josiah behind. Josiah would never wish to move to England himself, with his heart so committed to the Patriot cause. Yet she did not even know where he was, or how long it would be before she could see him again, let alone start their life together.

And what of Mary and Libby? Would they lose this house? Patience had come to love her stepsister and respect her stepmother. She swallowed, her chest tight at the uncertainty they would soon face as well.

She found Mary in the kitchen, and her face must have revealed her emotions, for her stepmother crossed the room quickly before Patience even said a word.

"I think my father's time is near." She pressed her lips together to hold back another round of tears. "I need a breath of fresh air for a moment."

Mary nodded and laid a tender hand on her shoulder. "Why don't you walk to the press and alert William? I will be at your father's side, so he will not be alone."

Patience thanked her, tugged her cloak on, and ducked outside. The chill air stole her breath as she started briskly down the street. She was desperate to distance herself from that house and what was soon to happen in the upstairs room, yet at the same time driven by urgency to find Will and return with him. She should be there at Father's side when he passed into eternity, just as she was for Mama, even though the thought of watching another parent's final gasps for air made her want to run away instead.

She paused beneath a tree and leaned back against the rough bark. Fresh tears welled in her eyes. She tilted her head up to stare at the sky through the bare branches, blinking the moisture away.

"Oh God, bring him peace." Her breath clouded the air. "Ease his suffering and draw him to Your side."

She fell silent, though her soul continued to cry out for her father and her own hurting heart. Patience was so lost in her prayer, she did not hear the approaching footsteps.

"Miss Abbott?" A gentleman's voice, full of concern, pulled her attention back. "What are you doing out here alone?"

She pushed off the tree. A rush of heat filled her face when she saw that it was Mr. Cunningham who stood before her, accompanied by Lieutenant Croome, no less. She clenched her teeth against the anger that churned in her belly, knowing what these two men had schemed to do to Josiah. The lieutenant wore a smug expression, but Mr. Cunningham's face was all kindness, almost tender, the same look he'd held toward her upon their every meeting until she'd rejected his proposal.

He stepped closer. "I had come to inquire after your father, but now that I see you, I fear I am too late."

She willed her voice to be steady. "He is still alive, though I doubt he has much longer on this earth."

"Were you going somewhere? Might I be able to accompany you?" Mr. Cunningham's brows dipped low in suspicion before he schooled his expression once more.

Did he think she was going to see Josiah and would fall for the trap of leading them directly to him? Disgust soured her stomach.

"I am going to fetch my brother."

"Will you allow me to escort you? It is difficult to be alone at such a time." He extended his arm.

Patience did not take it. "I prefer to go on my own, thank you."

His lips drew down in a barely suppressed scowl. "I spoke too harshly on our last meeting, hurt as I was by your rejection. I beg your forgiveness for such behavior and for the sake of your father and our friendship would ask—"

"It is for the sake of my father that I speak to you at all." The fierce anger that had been brewing spilled out. "You should be glad he does not know the way you threatened me, or you may have lost that friendship you speak of."

He stepped back as though she had dealt a physical blow.

Beside him, Lieutenant Croome smiled coldly, his gaze raking over her and holding on a spot at the hem of her cloak. "And you should be glad he does not know his own daughter's treachery."

Patience sucked in a sharp breath. "What do you mean?"

The soldier pointed to the swath of red on her cloak's dark fabric. "That stain. 'Tis a match for the paint that marked the door on your father's shop, is it not?"

With Father's health as it was, she had forgotten to clean the garment after the wind had swept her cape against the still-fresh paint. Was the lieutenant really implying what she thought? Did he truly imagine she could be so callous toward her own father as to take part in vandalizing his shop?

The soldier stepped closer, tipping his chin up so he stood even taller. "Rather convenient for you to have your father out of the way so you can run off with that rebel blacksmith."

Patience's mouth fell open at his accusation.

Mr. Cunningham cast a warning glance at the man beside him. "That is a step too far, Lieutenant."

"Is it?" Lieutenant Croome crossed his arms over his chest. "I've not been able to find Mr. Wagner these past few days. I wonder where he could have gone, and why he would have reason to leave?"

A chill ran down Patience's spine. With a confidence she did not feel, she met the man's suspicious gaze. "I have been at my father's side nearly every waking moment. I'll not stand by and listen to any more of these terrible accusations." She turned to face Mr. Cunningham. "My father valued your friendship, and for that I thank you, but now I must ask you to respect his final hours on this earth and leave me to grieve without any further harassment or unfounded claims against me."

Mr. Cunningham's eyes widened, and for a moment, she thought he might apologize, but instead, he clasped her wrist. "Your father valued my friendship...but also my wealth. He knew what he stood to gain if you and I wed. He was an ambitious man."

Patience cringed at his use of the word *was* to refer to her father, as though he were already dead and buried. She struggled to pull free, but Mr. Cunningham's grip only tightened.

"I, too, am ambitious. Your father's connections to the East India Trading Company and to the shipbuilders in Chatham could serve me well, and he was one of very few shopkeepers willing to continue selling the goods from England brought in by my ships."

Patience tore her arm from his grasp. Heat flared in her chest, and though inside she was quaking, her voice came out strong. "If my father is soon to die, then what good are these connections anymore? You have no reason to pursue me further."

He laughed, but there was no mirth in the sound. "Many would say the same and call me foolish for setting my mind on you when I could gain more elsewhere, especially now. But alas, you have captured my interest, and I'll not stand to see you with someone else. Please, reconsider my offer." His gaze slid to the soldier at his side. "I can protect you."

Lieutenant Croome glared at her, and Patience's heart seemed to freeze in her chest. Would the soldier truly try to accuse her of violence against her father's own property? Or would he attempt to threaten her further in hopes she betrayed Josiah and revealed where he had gone?

She backed up, the rough bark of the tree catching on her cloak as she pressed against it. She had to get away from these men, from their horrible accusations and schemes.

Pushing off the tree, she straightened her shoulders and stepped into the road where she would be better seen by other passersby. "I must find William and return to my father's side. I've lingered too long already."

She spun on her heel, not waiting for a response.

"I'll come to call again soon." Mr. Cunningham's voice followed her down the street, his tone congenial so that any stranger walking nearby would think nothing of it.

But she knew better. It was an ugly threat, wrapped in pretty speech.

She didn't slow her pace, nor glance back. By the time she turned onto Court Street, she was nearly running. She stormed up the steps of Edes and Gill's printing shop and burst through the door. Two men whirled from their posts to stare at her wide-eyed. She recognized one as Mr. Hadley and hurried to him.

"Mr. Hadley, I must find my brother. Is he here?"

"Aye, Miss Abbott. He's just in the other room." His brows drew low. "Are you well?"

She didn't have a chance to answer for Will strode out of the back room and was at her side in a heartbeat, palms pressed to her shoulders as his worried gaze met her own. "Patience, what happened?"

"Mr. Cunningham..."

"What did he do?" Anger flashed in his eyes.

"I'll tell you everything, but we must go home immediately. Father is dying."

CHAPTER 39

*P*atience curled on her side under the quilts and stared into the thick blackness of night. Father was gone. Just like Mama. Patience had kept watch at his bedside until he breathed his last, passing out of this world in the wee hours of the morning on the first of February.

The following three days had been a blur as arrangements were made, and today they had laid him to rest in the burying ground next to Kings Chapel. Patience had grieved his death once before, when they thought him shipwrecked and lost to the depths of the sea, only to discover that he still lived. But this time there was no mistake. Father was truly gone.

She tugged the quilt closer under her chin, burrowing deeper into its warmth, wishing for some comfort to the frozen parts inside her heart as much as for her chilled skin. The pain of losing Father was distinctly different than the grief she'd felt at Mama's death. When Mama passed, it had been a long, slow goodbye, and even in the sorrow, there was some joy in knowing that Mama's suffering was over. There'd been months to share words of love, reminisce together, and ensure nothing was left unspoken between them.

But there had been no time for such things with Father, and the silence of all that had never been said hung before Patience like a gaping cliff, leaving a gash of emptiness in its wake.

When Mama died, Patience had lost not only a mother but a friend. There was never a day in her life that she had been apart from Mama, so her absence felt as though a part of Patience herself was missing. And yet, there were years of memories and countless expressions of love for Patience to cling to. While at times those things caused the hurt to be even sharper, they also brought immense comfort. Mama would forever be a part of her, woven tightly into the fabric of Patience's life, and as time passed and the sharpness of the pain dulled, the joy of those memories grew and flourished.

But what would happen with Father? It would not, could not, be the same. There was still so much unsaid between them, so much misunderstood, so many years apart that could never be regained. Now the time she had hoped to share was cut off forever. In place of the deep, sharp wound left from Mama's death, his loss left her numb.

Patience slipped from the bed. She could not lay here any longer. The weight of her thoughts was too much to bear.

She fumbled to dress in the darkness, thankful her common gown laced in the front as she was certain to stab herself if she had to pin her bodice. She decided to forgo her cap, leaving her hair trailing down her back in its long, thick braid.

Easing the door open just wide enough to slip out, she crept downstairs and into the kitchen. The fire burned low and cast long, distorted shadows on the wall. She grabbed a candle from the table and lit it at the edge of the flames, then peered around the room. She needed to be busy. To find some work for her hands to distract her mind. But what should she do in the middle of the night?

A low, choked-off sob startled Patience, and she nearly

dropped the candle. The sound seemed to have come from the parlor. Was Mary awake and grieving her second widowhood? Her marriage to Father had been one of convenience and necessity, with respect and kindness between them but not love. Still, it was wrong to assume her stepmother felt no sorrow at his passing. Perhaps Father's death reminded Mary of the loss of her first husband or left her worried over what would happen to her and her daughter now. Had Father made any provisions for Mary and Libby? For herself?

Patience tiptoed to the parlor, her stocking feet silent on the cold floorboards. She did not know what she might say to her stepmother, but maybe they could ease each other's burden. She passed through the doorway and stopped short.

"Will?" Shock laced her voice, and her raised whisper seemed to echo in the room.

Her brother shot out of his chair, his eyes wide in the pale firelight. He swiped at his cheek with the back of his hand. "Patience? Why are you awake?"

"I suspect for the same reason as you." She spoke gently, crossing the room to stand before him. She peered up into his tear-streaked face, and her heart lurched. She'd not expected to see such emotion from him.

He swallowed and ran a hand through his tousled hair. He'd not bothered to tie it back. His coat and waistcoat were slung haphazardly over the back of the chair he'd been sitting in, and his stock dangled loosely around his neck. Had he never even tried to sleep?

Patience's gaze fell to the Bible on the small round table that sat between the two chairs by the hearth. It was open to one of the first pages, where years ago, a careful hand had written *Deaths* atop the blank white space. Patience bit her lip as she traced the newly added entry in Will's familiar script— *George William Abbott, 1 February, 1774.* She blinked back tears at Mama's name above it, also dutifully recorded by Will's hand.

He sank back into his chair, and Patience settled quietly in the one beside him.

"I was angry at him for so long." Will's voice was low and rough, as though his words were scraped over sharp stones. "I watched you, trying so hard to make up for the time you lost with him. I knew how much you wanted his affection, even though I didn't think he deserved your devotion, and I only grew angrier because I was certain he would let you down."

Patience sniffled as tears stung her eyes.

"And I was right." Will grimaced and pressed his hand into a tight fist atop the cushioned arm of the chair. "He did let you down, but not in the way I imagined." He looked at her, and the expression on his face broke her heart. "He left us again. Only, this time, we cannot follow."

He propped his elbows on his knees and bowed his head, silent for a long moment, then he reached into his pocket and pulled out a scrap of cloth. He held it out to Patience.

She took it, and her breath caught in her throat. "My sampler. He kept it all these years?"

The fabric was frayed at the edges and creased through the middle as though it had been folded and unfolded many times. She traced a finger over the uneven stitches and blinked to hold back the tears. Had he actually treasured her simple childhood gift?

"I found it in the pocket of his best coat," Will whispered. "He loved you, Patience. I know he wasn't the man you hoped him to be, but he did love you in his way."

Patience bowed her head and clutched the sampler to her chest as the tears flowed freely. How she had longed to hear those words from Father himself. Would it have assuaged the grief now if she had, or would it only change the pain she felt?

Will reached for her hand, holding it tight as sorrow and peace mingled in a strange and freeing way.

When her tears were spent, she pulled away to wipe her cheeks. "Thank you, Will."

He nodded, then leaned back in his chair and let his head fall against the upholstered back, staring up at the ceiling. When he spoke again, his voice was so low, she almost didn't hear it. "I am ashamed of myself."

He kept his gaze fixed above him, his face unreadable in the shadows as Patience waited for him to continue.

"Father made many mistakes, and there are some things he and I would never agree on, no matter how much time we spent together. And yet now, I am left forever with this bitterness between us. There is no chance to reconcile, to offer forgiveness, whether he would seek it or not. Or to ask for forgiveness where I was wrong." His voice cracked, and he scrubbed a hand over his eyes. "He did not understand me, but perhaps I did not fully understand him, either, even if I thought I did. There is no going back, and I wonder if my stubbornness is as much to blame as his pride and selfishness."

"You are right that we cannot go back, but you are wrong to think the bitterness must linger forever. There can be forgiveness still." Patience leaned closer. "Though you cannot reconcile with Father, you can forgive him in your own heart, so you might be able to move forward without that pain. And God will forgive you for any resentment or anger you harbored."

Will nodded once but did not speak. Patience silently prayed he would accept her words and see the truth in them.

"Will?" She waited until his weary eyes found hers. "I would say to you the same thing you said to me. Father loved you, in his own way. He wasn't the man either of us hoped him to be, but perhaps we were both seeking something from him that he could never give, even should he have tried."

He swallowed and ducked his head.

"I was so certain that coming here and being reunited with Father would fill that aching emptiness left behind by Mama's death. But he didn't. I don't think he ever could have, even if he had been every bit the father I desired."

She reached for the Bible, turning the delicate pages until the words of Ephesians lay open before her. This truth was what she had been so desperately seeking all along. Her conversation with Josiah had planted the seed, and her conviction had only grown more certain since that day, even in the midst of this sorrow.

This was the answer to her grief over Mama's death. This was how she moved forward from Father's passing, even with all the pieces left unfinished. This was the home she'd been searching for but never able to find, whether in the cottage of her birth or this house in a city filled with tension and upheaval.

She held her finger at chapter two, verse nineteen and read aloud, her voice steady and sure. "'Now therefore ye are no more strangers and foreigners, but fellow citizens with the saints, and of the household of God.'" Patience looked up at her brother. "We are part of God's household. He is our Father. He will never disappoint or fail me, nor you. All this time, I was looking for a place to belong, but it wasn't a place I needed. It was Him, my Heavenly Father."

Will searched her face for a long moment, then a small smile crept at the corners of his mouth. "The household of God. I like that. When did you come to this conclusion?"

Patience closed the Bible and placed it on the table again. "Josiah and I spoke of it, though I think it is something God has been working in my heart for quite some time now."

"You've not had a letter from Josiah yet, have you?"

Patience shook her head. It had been just over a sennight since he left Boston, and no word had come.

"I am certain he will write as soon as he is able."

"What if something happened to him? How can I know he is safe?"

"You cannot." Will held her gaze. "You must entrust his life to God, just as you have your own."

She sighed. "Yet another test of my patience."

A slight grin tipped Will's mouth as he nodded, though it didn't dispel the weariness in his eyes. "If Josiah continues in his dedication to the cause of the Patriots, I suspect you will need much patience and trust for whatever is to come."

She pressed her lips together at the truth of his words. The unknowns of Josiah's safety in this moment and the uncertainty of when they could be together again paled in comparison to what may come should they truly go to war with England. Was she prepared to go forward in faith, to cling to that which she had just spoken? Could she continue to find her strength and belonging in God, no matter what the future might bring?

"We must decide what to do about Cunningham." Will's voice, ragged on the edges, broke into her thoughts.

"What *can* we do?" She wrapped her arms around herself. Mr. Cunningham had not come to call on her yet, but he was present at Father's burial, and she'd felt his cold stare more than once. "Do you think he may have some sympathy for our loss and has decided not to pursue his proposal any longer?"

"I would like to think so, but I fear his pride has been so wounded that nothing will keep him from his goal now."

"But could the lieutenant actually bring charges against me? I've done nothing wrong."

"I suspect those threats hold little weight, but I would not be surprised if Cunningham sought to use them to his advantage in an attempt to coerce you into agreeing to his proposal. Nor would I be surprised if Croome hopes to use false accusations against you as a way to track down Josiah."

Patience shuddered. "If that is the case, then what about you? You are in danger as well, for what you did that night with the tea. If they suspected—"

Will shook his head. "Do not add to your worry. I was well

aware of the risk to myself when I chose to join the men aboard the ships, and I accepted it willingly. It is you I want to protect. And I will, even if it means we must leave Boston."

"Leave? Back to England?" Patience stood and clasped her hands in front of her. "I cannot."

Will stood to join her. "Nay, I wouldn't take you from Josiah, but I would take you to him."

"To Watertown? Even though we've heard nothing of his arrival?"

"It may be the best course of action. For now, I think it safe to wait a little longer." He failed to stifle a yawn. "I must get some sleep. Will you be well on your own?"

Patience nodded and bid him goodnight. As he closed the door to his bedroom, she silently prayed for comfort for her brother's hurting heart and for wisdom in what to do next.

CHAPTER 40

*T*he bed creaked under Josiah's weight as he settled onto the worn mattress. He'd stolen away for a few moments before the evening meal was served, anxious to read the letter that had arrived just as he and Stearns were closing the smithy for the day. He unfolded the page, and his pulse leapt at the greeting.

My dear Josiah.

It was the first letter he'd received from Patience since leaving Boston nearly three weeks ago. His own missive to her had been delayed by a bout of stormy weather, and he had begun to worry that it had never reached her at all.

He leaned closer to the window so the waning light could better illuminate Patience's neatly penned words.

I am so glad to know you are well. There is much to tell you.

His heart ached to read of her father's death. He felt her pain as if it were his own. How wrong it seemed for him not to be there to comfort her. But the strength of her faith inspired him, and he thanked God that she had come to a place of peace in regards to her relationship with her father.

He sucked in a breath at her next lines.

I do not think it safe for you to return to Boston as Mr. Cunningham and Lieutenant Croome continue to pose a very real threat.

Heat blazed in his belly as he read of the way Cunningham and Croome had accused her. He pushed off the bed to pace the worn floorboards. The walls of the small room seemed to hover closer around him, confining him. He needed to protect her, but how? After the risk she had taken to warn him and help him escape, could he go back to Boston and willingly endanger himself again?

Mayhap she could come here. He shook the thought away. It was too much to ask her to uproot from yet another home, to leave her brother and stepfamily behind, especially so soon after her father's death. Nor could he ask her to join him here when he was living in the back of another man's house.

And yet, he had spent so many years alone already. Now that he had someone to love, someone who loved him in return, every day apart seemed to stretch longer and more lonesome.

Josiah ran a hand through his hair, grimacing when his fingers snagged a knot. He read her final lines, words of affection, of how much she missed him and hoped for the day they could be together again. His thumb brushed over her name, signed *with all my love* at the edge of the parchment, and he could not help but wish to feel the soft skin of her hand beneath his own instead.

He sank back onto the bed. "What should I do, Lord?"

As with his time spent reading the Word, Josiah was growing more consistent in his prayers. God felt nearer now than He had in years, a comfort in the midst of so many unknowns. Still, he was out of practice in listening and waiting on God's direction. He longed for a clear answer, but none seemed to come.

A knock drew him to his feet. He tugged the door open to find a broad smile on Stearns's waiting face. The smile faded as he noted Josiah's expression.

"Bad news in that letter you received?"

"Some. Patience's father has died."

Stearns dipped his chin, his expression sober. "I am sorry for her loss and that you were unable to be with her."

"Aye." Josiah folded the letter and tucked it back into his pocket as he recounted the trouble that continued to exist with Cunningham. He had explained the situation to Stearns when he first arrived.

"I know you have a home and a smithy of your own in Boston, but if it is too dangerous for you to return, would you consider staying here?"

"I do not want to impose upon your generosity."

"Nonsense. I am glad for your help in the shop and would welcome your assistance for as long as you are able to give it. But I meant, would you think of settling here in Watertown instead?"

Josiah nodded. "The thought has crossed my mind. I had always hoped for a plot of land of my own. A place to grow things."

"To grow a family?" Stearns's eyes crinkled as he grinned.

"That too. But I promised Patience I'd return for her, and I've nothing here to offer her yet, nor do I know how long it would take for me to be able to do so."

Stearns rubbed a weathered hand over his chin. "I may be able to help."

Josiah's breath caught in his chest at the implication of Stearns's words.

"I heard yesterday of the passing of a widow that lived not far from here. The house isn't much and needs some work, but it sits on a nice piece of land. She had no remaining family to leave the property to, so it will likely go to auction."

Possibilities flared to life at the thought of a home of his own. A home to share with Patience. "Can you take me to see it?"

"Of course. Gladly."

The two men ventured out into the cold air, and Josiah followed Stearns as he led them down the snow-covered street. They walked for several minutes until Stearns came to a stop in front of a small house. Josiah halted beside him. The setting sun highlighted shingles and shutters in need of repair and a dilapidated fence stretching behind.

"As I said, it isn't much, but if you want to marry that young woman of yours, it's a start, at least." Stearns clapped him on the shoulder.

Josiah exhaled a cloud of steam as he stepped closer, observing the building in the fading light. Instead of seeing all the work that needed to be done, he imagined Patience's hand in his as he led her across the threshold of their own home.

If Stearns was right and the house went to auction, there was no guarantee he would win it. But he could certainly try.

Mayhap God had given him an answer, after all.

～

*P*atience wrung the water out of her shift into the large basin, then hung it to dry on the line strung from beam to beam across the kitchen ceiling.

"I much prefer doing laundry in the warmer weather." Libby scrubbed one of Will's shirts over the washboard. "Instead of hanging wet undergarments all over our kitchen."

"It is March now, so certainly, the weather will improve soon."

Libby raised her brows. "You have never experienced a Boston spring, or you might think differently."

"So much has happened since I arrived, it seems like the longest winter I can remember."

Libby met her gaze with a sympathetic smile. "And even longer now that you are separated from Mr. Wagner, I imagine."

"It has been nearly five weeks since he left and over a fortnight since his letter."

"Letters take time, especially with the storms we've had of late." Libby stood to drape the shirt over the line. "At least you know he is safe."

Patience nodded. "I'm thankful for that."

"Perhaps, in place of a letter, he will come back to Boston himself."

"Much as I wish to see him, I hope he does not. I still doubt his safety were he to return."

She'd not seen Mr. Cunningham since Father's burial, and Will had heard that Lieutenant Croome had returned to his station on Castle Island. Still, she could not forget their threats.

Mary stepped into the kitchen, a petticoat in need of mending slung over her arm. She took a seat at the table with a smile for both girls and set to work.

"Would you go to Watertown to be with him instead?" Libby plunged another garment into the water.

Patience nodded as she scrubbed a pair of stockings. It was a question she had asked herself many times these past weeks, especially after her conversation with Will. "If he asked, I am willing. But for now, he is staying with the Stearns, so we would have nowhere to live, even should he wish me to come."

"God will provide, in His time." Mary spoke quietly, but with conviction.

"But oh, if you should leave Boston, I would miss you dearly." Libby met Patience's gaze with a crestfallen expression, then shook it off and replaced it with a smile. "Let's think of happier things. Such as what you will wear for your wedding."

Patience laughed at her enthusiasm. "I don't know. I haven't allowed myself the luxury of such thoughts. It only seems to make our time apart stretch longer."

A knock at the door interrupted their musings. Mary stood to answer it. Patience's heart lurched at the familiar voice that rang out from the entryway. Mr. Cunningham.

"Good day, Mrs. Abbott. I have come to speak with Miss Abbott."

"I think you have said quite enough to Miss Abbott already." Mary's voice was sterner than Patience had ever heard.

Libby's eyes grew wide, and Patience was certain her expression looked much the same.

If Mr. Cunningham was taken aback by Mary's response, his congenial tone did not reveal it. "I understand your hesitation, but that is the very reason I wish to see her. I must apologize for my past behavior, and I have yet to offer my condolences for her loss."

Patience had no desire to see him, but neither did she want Mary to be placed in such an uncomfortable position. It was time to be rid of Mr. Cunningham for good. She wiped her damp hands on her apron, squared her shoulders, and strode to the door.

"Miss Abbott." His brows raised, then he bowed his head politely. "Might I have a moment of your time?"

"You may speak with me in the parlor."

"Are you certain?" Mary touched her arm, eyes assessing.

Patience nodded with more confidence than she felt and proceeded Mr. Cunningham into the room. She stopped a few steps in and spun to face him, not offering a seat nor any of the usual pleasantries. "What have you to say?"

An arrogant smile tipped his lips. "I see your hospitality has suffered in your father's absence."

She inwardly flinched at the insult but replied calmly. "I think it enough that I have granted you leave to speak at all, after the way you treated me the last two times we met."

"Things could have been very different between us, Miss Abbott. But if this is what you wish, then I will be straight to the point."

He stepped closer, towering over her, a coldness in his gaze as he stared down at her. Everything in her wanted to back away, but she held her ground.

"I will not renew my pursuit of you, which you have so heartily rejected, foolish as I think your decision to be." He clasped his hands behind his back and straightened. "I respected your father and truly mourn his loss, though for his sake, I am glad he is not here to witness the choices you have made. He would be outraged and disgusted to realize the people with whom you have aligned yourself."

Patience clenched her fists at her side but did not respond.

"It seems your blacksmith has left town like a coward and escaped punishment. For now." He sneered. "Whether or not you had some hand in that matters not to me, for I plan to sever all connections to you and your family. But know this, should Mr. Wagner ever return, I will ensure that he is arrested immediately."

He stalked to the door, then pivoted on his heel to face her again, his expression hard and haughty. "I expect we shall all soon know parliament's response to the treasonous acts of the sixteenth of December. I pray their retribution will put an end to the schemes of men like Mr. Wagner and his ilk. If I were you, I would reconsider whose side you are on."

He turned his back on her and departed, slamming the door behind him. Patience's shoulders sagged as her breath left her in a rush. Libby and Mary hurried in, their expressions full of concern.

"We heard everything." Libby pulled her into an embrace.

"I am sorry, Patience," Mary said. "I should not have even let him in the house."

"You needn't apologize. It was good that I let him speak, for now I know for certain that Josiah cannot come back to Boston."

Mary nodded, expression resolute. "Then you must go to him."

CHAPTER 41

*P*atience greeted Will at the door when he returned from work that evening. His gaze swept her face, brows pulling low as though he immediately realized something was amiss. "What has happened?"

"Mr. Cunningham was here."

"Did he threaten you again?" Anger flashed in his eyes. "I've a mind to go—"

She clasped his arm. "Nay, there's nothing to gain in you speaking to him."

"Speaking is not what I had in mind," Will muttered.

"Come." She tugged him toward the parlor. "Let me explain everything."

They sat together beside the fire as Patience recounted her conversation with Mr. Cunningham, as well as Mary's subsequent declaration.

"I am proud of you for facing him, though I still wish I had been here to defend you." His voice was low, his gaze serious. "And I agree with Mary. If you truly love Josiah and wish to share a life with him, then you must leave Boston, for as long as Cunningham remains, Josiah will not be safe here."

"I do." Warmth filled her chest and spilled onto her cheeks at the thought. "I'm willing to go where I need to so that we may be together."

"Good. Then I shall take you to Watertown tomorrow."

Patience stared at him. "What? But Josiah is not expecting me. He is staying with Mr. Stearns. We would have no place to live. Surely, I should write to him first."

"For once, it seems you are the patient one." Will chuckled, then sobered. "We can wait if you'd like, but every day that passes brings us closer to England's answer to our actions in December. I cannot say what the future holds, but there is much talk at Edes and Gill and around town. I fear there are hard days ahead." He reached for her hand. "You've lived through many difficulties already, and I am eager to see you experience joy."

"Thank you, Will." She squeezed his fingers as she blinked back tears.

"Think on it tonight, and in the morning, you can tell me what you've decided. Either way, you have my blessing."

∼

*P*atience carefully tucked the gown father had commissioned for her into her trunk, the last of her things. She'd lain awake long into the night, thinking and praying. Will was right—the journey of the past years had been long, with many uncertainties, sorrows, and changes. But God had sustained her each step of the way, and He would be with her now.

She did not want to put off her life with Josiah any longer. She'd gotten up at dawn, confident in her decision, and as soon as Will was awake, she'd told him she was ready. Now her heart leapt at the thought of seeing Josiah this very day.

"I wish you did not need to leave, and yet I am happy for

you that you will be with Mr. Wagner again." Libby perched on the edge of the bed, mouth turned down in a pout. "You must promise to write as often as you can."

"I will." Patience stood and brushed off her petticoat, then joined her on the bed. "Though mayhap I'll have to return, anyway, if we cannot manage to find a place to stay."

"I pray not, for your sake, much as I'd selfishly like more time with you."

Patience reached out and clasped Libby's hand. How strange, less than four months ago they were strangers, thrown together by Father's unexpected marriage. Now the young woman beside her felt like a dear friend and true sister.

"I will miss you," Patience said, and wholly meant it.

"And I you." Libby's eyes welled with tears, but a rap at the door set her quickly blinking them away.

"May I come in?" Will's voice called from the hall.

"Aye." Patience stood to greet him.

"I've made all the arrangements with Mr. Ward at the livery. We've a horse and cart waiting outside to transport us to Watertown. If we leave soon, we should arrive before dark."

Libby sniffled and pressed her lips into a wavering smile. "I will see how Mama is getting along with the basket of provisions for you."

As she slipped from the room, Will came closer, and Patience noticed for the first time that he carried a small bundle, wrapped in white cloth and tied with a light-blue ribbon.

He held it out to her. "Mama instructed me to hold onto this until you were to be married. Seeing as that day may come very soon, I thought I'd best give it to you now."

Patience took it from him, running her fingers over the silky ribbon. She swallowed against the lump in her throat. Mama had known her time would come before she had the opportunity to see her daughter wed. Even in the midst of her own suffering, she had prepared something for Patience, a gift of love to be shared after she had left this world.

She sank to the edge of the bed and clutched the package to her chest. It was the closest she could come to holding onto Mama again. A faint scent of lavender drifted upward. She lifted the bundle to her face and breathed deeply. Tears sprung to her eyes. "It smells like Mama."

Will's own eyes were damp as he nodded.

Reverently, Patience untied the ribbon and unfolded the delicate cloth. Inside lay a satchel of dried lavender with Patience's initials stitched on the small bag.

Mama had always tucked the little packets amongst her clothes. To keep away the pests, she said, and to remind her that spring was never too far off. Beside it lay a pinchbeck brooch in the shape of a flower with deep red and clear paste stones pretty enough to pass for garnet and diamonds.

She sucked in a breath. Mama had worn this brooch every Sunday, and though the stones themselves were of little value and the metal only made to look like gold, to Patience, it was priceless.

Will peered at the piece of jewelry in her palm. "You'll wear it for your wedding day, won't you?"

"Of course, and think of Mama as I do." As Patience lovingly traced the stones with her finger, her eye caught on a hint of lace peeking out of the fabric she'd first assumed to be simple cloth. "Look, Will, the wrapping of her package is a gift in itself. A new fichu. I thought Mama didn't have the strength to finish it."

She unfolded the delicate fabric to examine it further. Intricate white lace trimmed the edges all around. Mama had been working on it when she was confined to bed, but as her health continued to fail, Patience had assumed her mother had given up the tedious piecework. What an unexpected and precious surprise to know that Mama had pushed through her exhaustion and pain to finish one last gift for her daughter.

Patience lifted the fichu to her lips and pressed a soft kiss there with a whispered thanks for her mother and the love she had shown to the very end.

Will sat on the bed beside her with a sigh, rubbing a hand over the back of his neck. "I am happy for you, Patience, and I know Josiah will take good care of you. I could not entrust you to him if I didn't believe so. Still, I can hardly bear to think of leaving you behind."

His quiet confession pulled her back to the present. Will had determined that he would return to Boston as soon as she and Josiah were settled, and while he hadn't spoken much about England lately, she knew that the promise he'd made when they left still lingered in his heart.

"I cannot imagine saying goodbye to you either. Watertown is not so far from Boston, but England is an ocean away. Might you consider staying?" It seemed too large a request, but she could not help but ask.

"I've thought of it." His low voice brought her attention back to his face and the serious furrow in his brow. "But I promised Charlotte that I would return, and I'll not break that promise."

Charlotte Foster had been a neighbor and friend to both Patience and Will when they were children, though in the months before their departure, Patience had noticed a change in Will, an affection for Charlotte that seemed to go beyond friendship. He was a man of his word always, and if he had promised to come back to her, nothing would keep him from that. But a little part of her had hoped he would be able to stay.

"Might she be willing to come here instead?" She glanced at him a moment, then dropped her gaze to her lap. "Perhaps it is selfish of me to ask."

"I wondered the same thing, but I have yet to receive a reply to the first letter I wrote her upon our arrival. I am not certain it is wise to send another with such a request." He sighed and was quiet for a long moment. Then, shaking his head as if to put such thoughts behind him, he stood. "Either way, I'll not spoil your excitement with such talk. If your trunk is ready, I'll take it to the cart, and you can return to the other ladies. I'm certain they'd like a bit more time with you before we're off."

"I'll just add these." Gently, she placed the precious gifts from her mother atop her gown.

The sight of Mama's jewelry alongside the dress from Father made her chest tighten. So much in life was bittersweet. She was thankful for these tokens to cherish but would rather have Mama and Father by her side.

She traipsed downstairs ahead of Will and stepped into the kitchen, where Mary was packing a basket full of food. She glanced up from her task, smiling when her eyes met Patience's.

"'Tis nearly ready. It isn't much, but I wanted to send you off with something." Mary tucked a cloth over the food, then dusted her hands on her apron and stepped closer, eyes gentle to match her soft words. "I am thankful for these past months I've shared with you. I have watched you care for those you love and seen you press on through all the changes and challenges with grace and kindness. I hope you know that I am proud to call you my stepdaughter."

Patience blinked back tears as she stepped into Mary's outstretched arms. No one would ever replace Mama, but she was grateful for the care that Mary had so graciously extended.

Libby came next, her eyes bright with unshed tears. She held out a quilt, folded into a neat bundle, with initials stitched in one corner.

Patience traced her finger over the blue letters, a *J*, *P*, and *W*. Josiah and Patience Wagner.

She stared wide-eyed at Libby. "When did you manage this?"

"I started working on it the day after he proposed and have been hiding it from you ever since."

"It's beautiful. Thank you." Patience pulled her sister into a tight embrace.

Will returned from securing her trunk and tucked the basket and quilt under his arm. "Are you ready?"

Her voice caught in her throat. She swallowed. "I am."

Mary met her gaze with an encouraging smile. "We will be praying."

Libby grabbed her hands in one more tight squeeze. "Write as soon as you're able. You can even send a letter back with William."

He chuckled. "I'm happy to be a courier."

They said their final goodbyes and well wishes, and Patience followed Will outside. A thrill of anticipation filled her chest as he helped her into the cart and climbed up beside her.

"I wonder what Josiah will do when he sees you at the door this evening." He nudged her with his shoulder, a teasing grin on his face.

"I cannot wait to find out." She smiled back.

With a laugh, Will clicked to the horse, and they were on their way. The wind swept through her hair, pulling strands free from her cap. She brushed them back, and the smell of lavender that lingered on her hands filled the air. Patience closed her eyes and breathed it in. Whatever was to come, she would remember that spring was near and with it, fresh hope.

CHAPTER 42

osiah swept the hard-bristled broom across the worn floorboards of the kitchen in his house. He'd purchased the property in Watertown just over a sennight ago and had been hard at work readying it ever since. Under his care, it was becoming more of a home each day.

A home he prayed he would soon be able to share with Patience.

He'd written to her with the news and anxiously awaited her reply. Would she be content to leave Boston and start a new life here with him? He did not doubt her love, yet he prayed she'd not be disappointed in his choice to remain in Watertown.

He paused to swipe a hand over his brow, surveying the room. He'd cleaned out the fireplace, dusted the cobwebs from the rafters, and scrubbed the counter, table, and shelves. Stearns had waved him out of the smithy a bit early this evening so he could spend some extra time at the house before the sun set, but already the fading daylight cast the room in dim shadows.

He cracked open the back door and swept the dirt outside,

then set the broom in the corner. The place was sparse, for clearly, the widow had sold some of her possessions prior to her death. There was enough furniture and kitchen supplies to make do for now, but it could use a woman's touch. Would Patience be disappointed in the simple house, or would she be excited at the opportunity to make it her own?

A rap at the door interrupted his thoughts. He brushed his hands together as he strode to open it. A few neighbors had already stopped by to meet him. Perhaps another had seen the smoke curling from the chimney this evening and come for an introduction.

Josiah tugged the door open and froze. The person standing on his front step was the last person he expected and the one he longed most to see.

"Patience?" His voice came out edged in disbelief. Had he imagined her, or was she truly here?

A shy smile tipped her lips, then grew broader until her dimples appeared. "Hello, Josiah."

The sound of his name from her lips woke him from his trance, and a joyful laugh burst from his chest. Rules of propriety forgotten, he closed the space between them and wrapped her in an embrace, holding her tightly, as though he'd never let her go. She clung to him with equal fervor, face buried in his chest and hands pressed against his back. He breathed her in, rosewater and lavender and fresh air.

"What are you doing here? How did you—"

A throat cleared, halting his words. Josiah looked up to see William, waiting in the shadows behind his sister, an amused tilt to his brows. Josiah pulled back as heat crept up his neck, but he couldn't bear to release Patience completely, so he clasped her hand in his own.

She tilted her head to smile up at him. "Will brought me. I came to be with you. We went to the smithy first and found Mr. Stearns. He sent us here. To your...house?" The surprised lilt in her voice told him she'd not received his letter before departing. She met his gaze with a teasing grin. "Aren't you going to invite us in?"

"Of course. Both of you. I think we have much to tell each other."

The three of them settled around the worn wooden table in the middle of the kitchen as they shared stories of what had happened over the past weeks. Of Josiah's purchasing the land, sending word to Patience, and praying she'd be content with his plans. Of Patience standing up to Mr. Cunningham and making the choice to leave her family in Boston to come to him, even when she did not yet know he'd have a home for her to come to.

"Is the house nearly ready, then?" William crossed his arms over his chest, demeanor shifting to the protective older brother Josiah had seen so many times before.

"There is more to be done, especially outdoors as the weather improves. I am still living at the Stearns' but planned to move in soon."

"Good." William stood and clapped a hand on his shoulder. "Might I take a moment to look around?"

"Of course." Josiah nodded, thankful for a minute of privacy with Patience, even if William's expression warned he'd return soon.

The door closed behind William with a thud. Josiah stood, reached for Patience's hands, and gently pulled her to her feet. "I cannot believe you are here." He brushed his thumbs across her fingers as his gaze wandered the room. "I know it isn't fancy, but it is clean and—"

"It is perfect. More than I had hoped for." She squeezed his large hands with her smaller ones. "It is a home all our own."

"And I am ready to make it our own if you are."

"I am."

His heart swelled in his chest as all the years he'd spent

alone faded with her words. He dipped his head and captured her smile with a lingering kiss.

~

*P*atience stood outside the door of the smithy two days later, hand tucked into the crook of William's arm. They'd procured a marriage license yesterday and chosen the smithy as the place to exchange their vows. The air smelled damp and earthy, as though the world hovered between the remnants of winter and the promise of spring. She, too, waited on the threshold between the life she'd lived and the one she was about to begin.

She smoothed her hand down the flowered robe a l'anglaise from Father and readjusted the fichu from Mama.

"You look beautiful." Will nudged her with his shoulder.

When she saw the tenderness in his expression, she blinked back tears. "Thank you."

"I am sorry our parents cannot be here today to see you wed."

Patience touched her fingers to the brooch pinned at the neckline of her gown. "Aye, but I am so thankful for these gifts that make them feel a little closer."

Will nodded and covered her hand with his own.

Whether Father would have approved of her marriage or not, Patience still could not say, though she was certain Mama would have gladly celebrated this day at her side. There would still be bittersweet days, like this one, but God had granted her His peace, and she would not allow the grief of the past to shadow the joy of the present.

She peeked up at William. "I am glad to have you here."

"I would not miss it. Are you ready?"

"I am."

He rapped on the thick wooden door.

It swung open, and Mr. Stearns's smiling face greeted them. "Come in. The groom is waiting."

Will lead her inside, and Patience caught her breath when she saw Josiah. He stood beside the anvil, but this time, no tools were in his hand, no leather apron tied round his waist. Instead, he cut a handsome figure in a navy coat well fitted to his broad shoulders, with his black hair tamed in a neat queue. His dark eyes widened when he saw her, and her cheeks warmed at the look of admiration there.

When they reached Josiah's side, Will stopped and, with one last squeeze of her hand, released her before going to stand next to Mr. Stearns as a witness.

The reverend smiled at them both. "Shall we begin?"

She and Josiah both nodded their assent, and the simple wedding service began. Patience listened intently as the reverend spoke, her heart thumping in her chest. She glanced at Josiah, standing strong and serious beside her, and silently thanked God for the gift of this new life together.

The reverend turned to her. "Wilt though have this man to thy wedded husband, to live together after God's ordinance, in the holy estate of matrimony?"

"I will." She couldn't contain a smile.

Josiah held her gaze as he answered the same in turn, his dark eyes full of love and promise. The reverend instructed them to join hands, and they did so, their fingers twining together, a simple act made precious by the bond it represented, two lives becoming one.

"I now declare you man and wife." The reverend's voice echoed. "May this anvil before you serve as a symbol of your lasting union, forged this day, the sixth of March, 1774. What therefore God hath joined together, let not man put asunder."

Joy burst in Patience's heart, brighter than the sparks that usually sprang forth in this place. Josiah's broad grin and shining eyes radiated the same emotion. He dipped his head and brushed a chaste kiss upon her lips, though his expression told her he wished to linger longer. She would have welcomed it, would have wrapped her arms around him and relished his strength and closeness, but that would have to wait.

The ceremony complete, Mr. Stearns invited them back to his home for a delicious dinner his wife had prepared, complete with a bride's cake.

As daylight waned, she and Josiah thanked them for their kindness and generosity and prepared to leave. She turned to Will, who would stay with the Stearns tonight and planned to depart for Boston first thing in the morning.

She pressed her lips together, determined to put on a brave face, but her chin quivered. "I do not know how to say goodbye to you."

A muscle in his cheek twitched. "Nor I."

"You have my letter for Libby as promised?"

"I do. I'm certain you'll have one in return very soon, and I will write as well."

"And you'll come see me again before you go back to England?" Tears pricked her eyes, threatening to spill out.

He swallowed and nodded, his own eyes damp, then pulled her into a crushing embrace. "I am glad for you, Patience, and proud of the woman you have become. Never forget how much I love you."

"And I you," she whispered against his chest.

Both of their cheeks were wet when he stepped away. He cleared his throat and looked over her head to Josiah. "I entrust her to you now. I know you will care for her well."

"I promise. Always."

Then Josiah offered her his arm, brows raised as if to silently ask if she were ready. She reached for his hand instead. He grinned, and her pulse leapt.

They said their last farewells and made their way down the street, hand in hand, by the pale pink glow of sunset. When they reached their house, Josiah pulled her to a stop on the front step, then scooped her up in his arms. A tiny gasp escaped, followed by a giggle as she wound her arms around his neck.

He kissed her, long and slow, as though he'd been waiting all day to do so. Then he drew back, and his dark gaze met her own.

With Patience still firmly clasped in his arms, he swung open the door and stepped inside. "I love you, Mrs. Wagner. Welcome home."

EPILOGUE

*P*atience dug the trowel deep into the damp dirt. The earthy smell filled the air—and her heart—with promise. Late-April sunshine warmed her shoulders, and birds called to one another, as if they, too, were celebrating the joy of spring.

Patience turned over scoop after scoop of soil, not caring that moisture seeped through her petticoats where she knelt on the ground, nor minding the dirt that gathered beneath her fingernails. She tucked a row of seeds into the small furrow of freshly tilled earth, each one a promise of life to come and a pledge that she would be there to see the harvest.

She, too, was letting her own roots grow deep, grounding her to this place. This was home. This country that she had come to love, this plot of land with space to grow and build upon, and this man to share her life with.

Patience glanced at Josiah where he worked to repair the fence for the livestock they soon hoped to have. She leaned back on her heels, allowing herself a moment to admire her husband, with his coat long discarded, sleeves rolled to his elbows, and black hair escaping his queue.

In the weeks since their simple wedding, she had come to know him in a way she knew no one else in the world. His quiet strength bolstered her courage as they set out into this new future together. His tenderness toward her made her feel cherished and protected. Her own love for him seemed to grow every day.

Josiah swung the mallet over his head, driving the next fencepost into place. He shook the post, seemed satisfied that it was sturdy, then turned to meet her gaze. A slow smile spread across his face. He lowered the mallet to the ground, dusted his hands on his trousers, and strode toward her.

Patience stood, her heart fluttering in the way it always did when his dark eyes centered on hers and sparked with warmth. She wiped her hands on her apron and stepped forward to close the final distance between them.

He wrapped his arms around her waist. "Tired of planting already?" He raised his brows but couldn't hide the grin tugging at the corners of his lips.

She let her gaze rest on those lips a moment before tilting her chin up and smiling back at him. "Not at all. I just paused to admire the view."

He chuckled, but the sound lasted only a moment as he lowered his face to hers and captured her mouth with his. She lifted onto her toes and threaded her arms around his neck, relishing the strength of his shoulders beneath her fingers. She sighed against his lips and buried her fingers in his hair. His hands splayed across her back, pressing her even closer as he angled his head to deepen the kiss.

This was where she belonged. Here, in her husband's arms, on this little piece of earth they called their own.

He rested his forehead against hers. "Come, I want to show you something."

Patience could not resist the huskiness in his voice. She shifted to press another kiss to his lips before stepping back to take the hand he held out to her. Together they strolled toward the stretch of forest that ran along the back of their land. When they had first arrived, the trees had only been tipped in green, but now they were full of leaves and alive with the songs of birds and the chatter of squirrels.

Josiah pushed back a low-hanging branch and led her into the woods. The air was cool and clean, with a freshness born of the last spring rain and the spicy pines that rose tall and sturdy amidst oaks and maples. The ground was no longer bare but awash with color. Patience gasped. Bluebells, all in bloom, covered the forest floor, their green leaves and deep violet-blue flowers swaying in the gentle breeze. Dappled sunlight filtered through the branches above, and Patience turned in a slow circle to take it all in.

"It's so beautiful."

Josiah stooped to pick one of the blooms, twirling it between his thumb and forefinger. "They reminded me of the colors on your gown the day we wed."

He tucked the blossom behind her ear, then clasped her hand as they strolled through the sea of flowers. They stopped beside the brook that gurgled a soft melody as it tumbled over rocks and drifted deeper into the forest.

Patience rested her head against Josiah's shoulder. "I cannot believe this land is ours."

He slipped his arm around her waist and held her close. "And someday, Lord willing, we can walk with our children here and tell them the story of how Mama and Papa ran into each other at the harbor in Boston one day..."

His words dropped off as he placed a soft kiss to her forehead.

She tipped her head back to look at him, imagining what might someday be. "They'll gather a wildflower bouquet in their little fingers while I tell them how Mama was looking for someone, but even though I found him, life was not what I expected it to be."

Josiah's dark eyes searched hers, and for a long moment, they were quiet, lost in the memories of all that had led them to this place, the triumphs and hardships, joys and sorrows, good-byes and new beginnings.

"Then I'll hold them close"—she pressed a hand to his chest—"and tell them that I found so much more than I was looking for."

"What did you find?" He wrapped his arms around her, his voice low and thick with emotion.

"I found you. A love and devotion like no other. And God showed me that I will never be a stranger, for I belong to Him." Patience smiled as she leaned into her husband's strong embrace. "I found home. Home is with you. Whatever may come, wherever God leads us, my home will always be with you."

The End

Did you enjoy this book? We hope so!
Would you take a quick minute to leave a review where you purchased the book?
It doesn't have to be long. Just a sentence or two telling what you liked about the story!

Receive a FREE ebook and get updates when new Wild Heart books release: https://wildheartbooks.org/newsletter

AUTHOR'S NOTE

Dear Reader,

I hope you enjoyed Patience and Josiah's story. I had such fun weaving their fictional lives into the real historical events surrounding the Boston Tea Party. The Boston Tea Party is often called "the spark of the American Revolution," and rightly so, as it was a significant turning point in the path toward independence. It was the first organized protest of such magnitude against British rule, carefully planned by the Sons of Liberty and carried out with efficiency and order. The response of Britain and the consequences that followed would further push the American colonies toward separation from England.

We all recognize names like Samuel Adams and Paul Revere, but as I researched for this book, I loved learning the names and stories of so many others who played a role in the Boston Tea Party. Ordinary people who took part in an extraordinary event and kept their participation a closely held secret for years, some carrying it to the grave. However, others did share about their role later in life, and we now have over one hundred names documented. I found their stories fascinating and couldn't help but be inspired to model some of my characters after real men who were there that night in December.

Nathaniel Hadley was inspired by Nathaniel Willis who was, like my character, only eighteen years old at the time of the Tea Party. He was a publisher for the *Boston Independent Chronicle* and went on to serve in the military during the Revolutionary War. Later, he traveled west, settling in different cities and beginning a newspaper in each one. He was the grandfather of N.P. Willis, an author, poet, and editor who worked with writers like Edgard Allan Poe and Henry Wadsworth Longfellow.

Alexander Stevens was inspired by Ebenezer Stevens, who was a professional artillerist in Paddock's Artillery militia and took part in guarding the tea ships. He went on to fight in the Battle of Bunker Hill and was later promoted to the rank of lieutenant colonel. Following the war, he was a successful tradesman and the father of eleven children.

Finally, Phineas Stearns was an actual Tea Party participant. A farmer and blacksmith from Watertown, Massachusetts, he went on to fight at the battles of Lexington and Concord. In the book *Tea Leaves* by Francis Samuel Drake, Stearns is described as "distinguished for his benevolent and cheerful disposition, and for strong common sense and strict integrity." When I read that description, I couldn't resist writing him into Josiah and Patience's story.

I hope you'll join me for my next book, *Secrets of the Revolution,* which features Will's story amidst the aftermath of the Boston Tea Party through the battles of Lexington and Concord. I can't wait for you to meet Hannah and watch their love story unfold!

This journey of writing and publishing is such a dream come true, and I cannot end without thanking some of the special people who have come alongside me.

To the Christian Mommy Writers—what a precious gift it is to be part of such a beautiful community.

Jennifer, Heather, and Latisha—thank you for reading, brainstorming, encouraging, chatting, and staying up late for award ceremony moral support. I am so thankful for our friendship.

Tara and Tiffany—for our countless Marco Polos full of advice, encouragement, and laughter. I am so grateful for you both.

Lorri, Tammy, and Barbara—for reading these words one month at a time and helping make them shine.

Jamie and Stephen—the closeness, love, and friendship between Patience and Will is reminiscent of our own. I'm blessed to have you as my siblings and friends.

To my girls—thank you for cheering me on and celebrating this writing journey with me. I know I can call myself an author now, but being your mom will always be my favorite title.

Steve—you were there when these stories were born in the midst of some of the hardest challenges we've faced together. Thank you for your unwavering support as I pursue this dream. I couldn't do it without you.

My theme verse for this book was Ephesians 2:19, *Now therefore ye are no more strangers and foreigners, but fellow citizens with the saints, and of the household of God.* What an immeasurable gift it is to be part of God's household and to call Him Father. May my words always point back to the author of life and bring Him glory.

ABOUT THE AUTHOR

Megan Soja is a multi-award-winning author who writes stories with strong faith, rich history, and sweet romance. She lives in western NY with her husband and two daughters and loves having adventures, both big and small, with her family. When she's not writing, she enjoys reading, hiking, canoeing and kayaking, and playing French Horn.

SNEAK PEEK: SECRETS OF THE REVOLUTION

Don't miss the next book in the Harbor of Spies series!

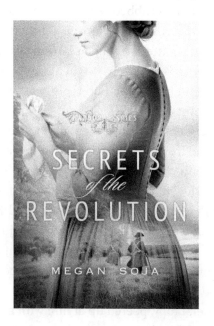

BOSTON
MAY, 1774

William Abbott had never broken a promise, but now he had no choice. Or rather, no reason left to keep it.

He sank to the edge of his bed and stared at the letter clasped in his hand, as though reading the words again could change what they said.

I am grateful for the closeness we shared as children, but we are not children now, and I confess, I did not imagine more than friendship between us. I never suspected your feelings had changed, and I must beg your forgiveness if any of my actions gave you reason to hope in such a way.

Will sighed and scrubbed a hand down his face. He had waited months for this letter from Charlotte Foster. He'd written her just days after arriving in Boston last December, but correspondence traveled slowly when there was an ocean between you. And now that her reply was here, he almost wished it had never come at all.

He dropped the letter onto the bed and stood to pace the small room. The fire in the hearth burned low and did little to stave off the damp chill that hung in the air. It was early May, but spring was slow in coming to Boston. The dark clouds that hovered over the harbor earlier in the day had blown inland. Now, rain pounded the roof, and lightning illuminated his bedroom with jagged flashes. A rumble of thunder echoed overhead, followed by a hesitant knock at the door. He strode to answer it.

His stepsister, Libby, peered up at him with a cautious smile and a plate full of food in her hands. Honey-blond curls framed her cheeks, made rosy by her work in the kitchen. "I brought you something to eat, since you did not join us for the evening meal."

"Thank you. Forgive me. It was inconsiderate not to come, though I would have been poor company."

"Mama understands. As do I."

He accepted the meal from her outstretched hands, the savory smell of fried sausage mixed with the sweet tang of stewed cabbage and apples making his stomach growl.

"I'll leave you alone." Libby ducked her head and backed away, then paused and met his gaze. "Unless you'd like some company. I know it isn't the same as having Patience here, but I am a good listener."

"Are you?" He offered a teasing grin, anxious to lighten the mood and divert the attention from himself. "I seem to recall that you are a good talker."

She giggled. "I am that too. But the offer remains."

Tempting as it was to hide in his room and nurse his self-pity, her offer was a kind one and reminded him of something his own sister, Patience, would do. He missed her, and the close bond they shared, but now Patience was married and living in Watertown, miles from Boston. Glad as he was for her happiness, he wished for her presence now. Talking with Libby would not be the same, and yet he felt a similar brotherly protectiveness for her. Even if she could not take Patience's place, perhaps he would welcome her companionship, after all.

He nodded toward the parlor behind her. "Well, then, I accept."

"You do?" Libby's blue eyes widened in surprise.

"Aye. Sit by the fire with me?"

She settled into one of the high-backed chairs in front of the brick hearth, and he took the other, balancing his plate on his lap. He sliced into the sausage and tasted it, humming appreciatively at the flavorful bite. For several minutes, they sat in silence as he ate, the crackling fire the only accompaniment to his overly loud thoughts.

At nine-and-ten years old, Libby was younger than Patience and different from her in many ways, yet the two had become dear friends in the months since being thrown together in a new family. The adjustment had been especially hard for his sister, whose high hopes for her reunion with their father were dashed by his unexpected remarriage to Libby's mother, Mary. Will, on the other hand, was used to being disappointed by Father and had come to expect little else.

But now their father was gone, leaving Will once more to

shoulder the responsibility of those left behind. Perhaps one good thing to come out of Charlotte's rejection was that it gave him the freedom to remain in Boston and see to the wellbeing of Libby and Mary, who was now a widow for the second time in less than a year.

Libby shifted in her seat and eyed him warily. "Are you testing me to see how long I will last without speaking?"

He chuckled. "Nay, simply gathering my thoughts while I fill my stomach."

"Patience told me you were like that."

"What? Always eager to eat?"

"Slow to speak. Thoughtful. That you like time to mull over things before sharing with others."

"She knows me well." He paused to spoon another bite into his mouth and chewed slowly. "But I'll not keep you in suspense any longer. Perhaps Patience also told you about Miss Charlotte Foster?"

Libby shook her head.

"She was our neighbor growing up. The three of us were good friends—Charlotte, Patience, and I. But over the past year, I had begun to think..." His voice trailed off on a sigh. Saying it aloud was harder than expected. "I came to feel—that is, I began to consider her in a different way."

He glanced at Libby, waiting for her reaction, but she proved true to her word as a good listener and waited quietly for him to continue.

"I told her as much before we left. I promised her I would return as soon as Patience was settled. But I received a letter from her today in which she expressed feelings quite the contrary to my own. In fact, she is to be wed—is likely married already."

"Married?" Libby gasped. "How could she? After what you told her?"

"She never promised me anything in return." Even now, despite how much Charlotte's reply hurt, he could not speak poorly of her. "The truth is, I should have known that day that she did not feel the same. She hardly gave a response to my declaration, but I convinced myself it was merely her surprise or some sorrow over our parting." He let out a scoffing laugh. "She did not have to wait for me. She did not tell me she would."

"I'm sorry, Will." Libby propped her elbow on the arm of the chair and rested her chin in her palm. "What will you do now?"

Will stared into the fire. What would he do, indeed? For years, the motivation for every decision he made had been the good of those he loved. First his mother, to provide for her needs through her illness and be by her side when she died. Then for Patience, to bring her safely to America. Keeping his promise to Charlotte had been the next foreseeable step...until today. He was not quite sure what to think or how to feel about the suddenly blank slate of his future.

"I suppose I will stay in Boston, for I've little reason now to leave."

"Patience will be glad of it," Libby said, "and you know you are welcome here with Mama and I as long as you wish."

"Thank you." Will scraped the final bits of food from his plate.

Despite the fact that his father had lived here for a time, Will considered it the Caldwells' home. Dr. Caldwell, Mary's first husband and Libby's father, had owned the house. Will's father only came to inherit it by marriage. In Will's eyes, it belonged to those two women, and he would not impose if they did not wish him to stay. But perhaps his presence could be of help to them. His work as a printer with Benjamin Edes and John Gill at the *Boston Gazette* could provide a comfortable living for the time being and keep his stepmother from needing to rush into another marriage.

He glanced at the door that led to his makeshift bedroom off the back of the house. It had previously served as an office for the late Dr. Caldwell. It wasn't much, but it gave him space of his own and afforded the ladies of the house more privacy. He could stay here. Keep working at the press. Remain near to Patience, who would indeed be very glad of that, though he knew she would sympathize with him at the same time. He could still care for those who needed him and could finally invest himself fully in the Patriot cause, without the thought of returning to England hovering over him.

Mayhap some good could come out of his disappointment.

Hannah Pierce blinked back the tears that threatened to blur her father's familiar scrawl. She traced a finger along the label on the blue-and-white delft jar—*Calendula officinalis*. Except that wasn't what the bottle contained. The buds were much too small, their color a faded yellow that edged toward tan. Dried calendula flowers were larger, with long, narrow petals and an orange hue.

She lifted the jar to her nose and breathed in the crisp, earthy scent. "*Matricaria chamomilla*. Chamomile," she said aloud in the empty apothecary shop, her voice wavering slightly. Even though there was no one to hear, she hated the pitiful tone. Shaking her head, she placed the jar on the counter.

Papa was making more mistakes lately. His once-sharp mind was not what it used to be. The change had begun two years ago, though it was only little things at first. A misplaced ingredient here, a forgotten order there. Then Mama died last October and his decline rapidly increased.

It had been six months since her mother's passing, and though her father was no longer lost in the throes of grief, his mental faculties had never recovered. Even this morning, when it was nearly time to open the apothecary for the day, he was still abed. In the past, he would have been behind the counter as soon as the sun rose.

Hannah spun to eye the jars lining the open shelves behind her. She stood on tiptoe to reach the jar of chamomile and pried off the lid. Sure enough, it was calendula inside instead. He'd switched the two. It was a simple thing to fix, and she set about doing so right away, but that did little to untangle the knot in her stomach.

How much longer could she keep her father's condition a secret? Their customers were used to seeing her around the shop. After all, their family home was right behind the apothecary and she'd grown up spending time there whenever she could. But what would they think if they knew how much she was doing in her father's place? They would take their business elsewhere, and be wholly justified in doing so.

She was no apothecary. It did not matter how much she had observed her father, how many questions she'd peppered him with around the family table, or how many Latin names she'd memorized until she knew the meaning of every single label in the shop. It did not matter that she could prescribe and prepare the right teas, tinctures, salves, and poultices to treat a multitude of conditions. She had not apprenticed and she was a woman. She would not claim a place that did not rightfully belong to her.

Still, she could not let Papa's reputation suffer, and who else was there to help? If only Andrew were to return home. She sighed and replaced the jars, now filled with the proper contents.

Her older brother had been the one to apprentice under their father. When he'd asked to travel to London two years prior for further training at St. Thomas's Hospital, Papa had readily agreed. But then Andrew had fallen in love with a young woman there and written to say they had married. Hannah knew he would have returned when Mama grew ill, but his wife was expecting their first child and could not manage the journey, nor would Andrew leave her alone. Hannah had written to him again, a month ago, to tell him of their father's condition, but had assured him she could manage. Perhaps she should not have been so confident of that in her letter.

For now, there was little else to do but continue her attempts to hide and correct her father's mistakes. It meant early mornings like this, perusing the shelves and deciphering Papa's scrawled notes in the large leather-bound book where he recorded every purchase, and late nights spent preparing all manner of treatments by flickering candlelight. But it was worth it if doing so could preserve his dignity while also ensuring the needs of their customers were met.

The door at the back of the apothecary creaked open, and Hannah turned as her father shuffled in. His wig was askew, his stock only half tied round his neck, but he greeted her with the same tender smile he had since she was a wee girl perched on his lap for prayers before bed.

"Good morning." She kept her voice bright as she crossed the room to meet him. Pressing a kiss to his cheek, she reached for his neckerchief. "Let me help."

"Thank you. I seem to have gotten myself all in a tangle." He tipped his chin up as she finished tying the cloth.

She tucked the ends into his waistcoat. "All better. I've some porridge warm by the fire. Will you join me before you open the shop?"

He glanced at the front door and furrowed his brow, as though her question had confused him, but then he looked back at her and nodded. "Porridge sounds good, and your company even better."

Hannah smiled, though her heart ached. He treasured her company now, but would there come a day when, like the chamomile and calendula, he did not know who she was?

If you love historical romance, check out the other Wild Heart books!

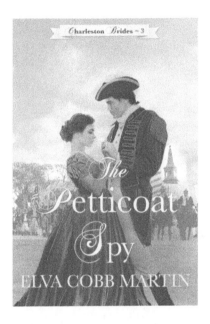

The Petticoat Spy by Elva Cobb Martin

A Southern belle turned spy and a dashing blockade runner fight a hopeless battle against the British.

When Anna Grace Laurens's parents are murdered by the British and her Charles Town plantation burned, she seizes her only option for escape—a desperate leap into the Cooper River. She'll do anything to survive...and get revenge.

John Cooper Vargas is used to danger as he sails his sloop upriver through war-torn colonies, but seeing a woman plunge into the river amidst Tory gunfire is something he wouldn't have thought possible. Until now.

Rescuing her draws him into a web of intrigue, but he can't let her fight the British on her own. As the American Revolution closes in around them, it may take a miracle for them—and their love—to survive.

～

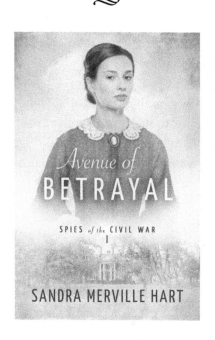

Avenue of Betrayal by Sandra Merville Hart

Betrayed by her brother and the man she loves...whom can she trust when tragedy strikes?

Soldiers are pouring into Washington City every day and have begun drilling in preparation for a battle with the Confederacy. Annie Swanson worries for her brother, whom she's just discovered is a Confederate officer in his new home state of North Carolina. Even as Annie battles feelings of betrayal toward the big brother she's always adored, her wealthy banker father swears her and her sister to secrecy about their brother's actions. How could he forsake their mother's abolitionist teachings?

Sergeant-Major John Finn camps within a mile of the Swansons' mansion where his West Point pal once lived. Sweet Annie captured his heart at Will's wedding last year and he looks forward to reestablishing their relationship—until he's asked to spy on her father.

To prove her father's loyalty to the Union, John agrees to spy on the Swanson family, though Annie must never know. Then the war strikes a blow that threatens to destroy them all—including the love that's grown between them against all odds.

~

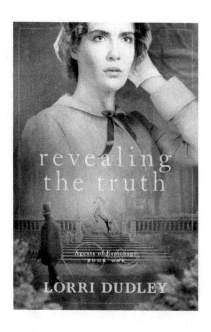

Revealing the Truth by Lorri Dudley

His suspect holds a secret, but can he uncover the truth before she steals his heart?

When Katherine Jenkins is rescued from the side of the road, half-frozen and left for dead, her only option is to stay silent about her identity or risk being shipped back to her ruthless guardian, who will kill to get his hands on her inheritance and the famous Jenkins Lipizzaner horses. But even under the pretense of amnesia, she cannot shake the memory of her sister and Katherine's need to reach her before their guardian, or his marauding bandits, finish her off. Will she be safe in the earl's manor, or will the assailant climbing through her window be the death of her?

British spy, Stephen Hartington's assignment to uncover an underground horse-thieving ring brings him home to his family's manor, and the last thing he expected was to be struck with a candlestick upon climbing through the guest chamber window. The manor's feisty and intriguing new house guest throws Stephen's best-laid plans into turmoil and raises questions about the timing of her appearance, the convenience of her memory loss, and her impeccable riding skills. Could he be housing the horse thief he'd been ordered to capture—or worse, falling in love with her?